The Island of
Labyrinths

STONES OF THE KINGDOM

Falcon Pass

Moonlady Falls

The Island of Labyrinths

The Island of Labyrinths

Stones of the Kingdom: Book Three

M. C. Foster

A Leaf It To Me Book

ISBN 978-0-9864581-3-2

Published by Leaf It To Me Publishing

This is a work of fiction. All characters, places and incidents in this book are a product of the author's imagination, and any resemblance to any real person, living or dead, is pure coincidence. No character or situation is intended as allegorical.

Cover design by Leaf It To Me.

CHAPTER ONE

Farren Blackarrow raised his sword to defend himself, the blade gleaming in the orange rays of the setting sun. He feinted and dodged, guarding against the cuts and thrusts of his opponent's blade. *She's quicker than I believed*, he thought as he sidestepped and shifted to and fro. A small bead of sweat began to form on his forehead and trickle irritatingly across his temple. He stepped backwards and yet another cloud of dust rose from the courtyard. A tuft of his red hair fell from his forelock and tickled his eyebrow. He raised one hand to rake it back. He blinked and felt a savage blow batter on his right shoulder, driving him back. His left arm was jarred again and again as he blocked blow after clattering blow that rained on him.

A rasp and clang of metal on metal, and he felt the sword twist and break his tight grasp on the hilt. Another blow to the blade and a jolt of pain shot through his fingers as the sword wrenched out of his hand and thudded to the ground. He leaped backwards to avoid the tall black-clad woman's backslash. He felt the firm stone of the wall against his back and the cold iron point of the woman's blade beneath his ear. *If that was to thrust in now, I'm dead.* His eyes met the stormy blue-grey eyes of his conqueror, and he saw them flash proudly as the metal trembled on his skin.

"Well done, Azariel!" he panted. "You've managed to disarm me at last."

The tip of her sword left his throat and she laughed. "It's taken me several years to do that."

He stepped away from the wall and stooped for his fallen blade. He straightened and brushed his sweat-damp hair off his forehead. "I'll come at you now," he said. "See if you can do it again."

He faced her in the middle of the barracks courtyard once more. She swept her long black hair behind her shoulders and flicked her cloak back. He watched her as she stretched her arms, sending points of light dancing off her elbow-length chainmail tunic and the heavy silver armbands that encircled her wrists. She rocked back and forwards on the heels of her boots and her eyes met his. He gripped his sword hilt and lunged forwards, stabbing and slashing. Her sword met his with a clash and drove his blade to the side. He whirled away and brought his left arm across in a backslash. Forwards and backwards they feinted and dodged, dancing to the near-rhythmic ringing of the steel blades.

The clamour of another ringing filled the cooling twilight air. *Chapel bell*, he thought. Azariel's eyes darted towards the spire where the bell swung. *Now's my chance.* He leaped within the circle of her sword before she could step back. Dropping his weapon, he grabbed her arms and pinned them to her sides. "I've got you now," he said.

The ringing died away, its last notes hanging in the evening air. Around them, they began to hear the footsteps and voices of people moving towards the chapel.

Azariel lowered her sword and slumped forwards into his arms, resting her head against the prickly woollen folds of his scarlet cloak. She felt his body heave and pant beneath her, keeping time with her own as she breathed in the sweetish salty smell of his sweat. She raised her head and shook the hair back from her eyes. He was smiling at her, red hair tousled and his angular face covered in dust. "That could have been fatal, looking away," he said.

"I know," she answered. "Curiosity could have killed the cat. Not that there was much to be curious about – I was expecting to hear the bell sooner or later. We'd better get ready for chapel. I need a drink before we go in."

"So do I. And I'd like to change out of this sweaty uniform, too." He lowered his head and kissed her quickly on the lips before he released her arms and stooped for his sword again.

She reached over for his hand and clasped it as they walked around and between the long grey stone barracks buildings. Her eyes skipped over the other soldiers strolling towards the chapel and looked ahead to the single thin tower jutting up from the line of whitewashed walls of the building reserved for the *minyasti*. There's our headquarters, she thought. They passed through the arched doorway into the corridor. She squeezed his hand before releasing it. "I'll pour you a cup of water and meet you in the common room when you're ready," she said.

"Thank you," he replied as he turned to the left towards his rooms.

She watched him as he walked briskly to the men's end of the corridor. Once his door had clicked closed, she strode into common room and stepped across the floorboards to the table where a ewer of water stood ready. She filled a cup to the brim and poured its cool wetness down her dry throat before filling another cup for Farren. The chapel bell rang a second time. She dragged a stool out from under the table and sat down to wait.

Before long, she heard his footsteps outside the door, and he walked in, adjusting the clasp of his thick belt around his narrow waist. "Here you are," she said, handing him the cup. "Better drink it quickly. Chapel will nearly have started."

He drained the cup, then set it back down on the table, wiping his mouth with the back of his other hand. "I'm coming. I was as quick as I could be about changing, but I couldn't have come over with my shirt sticking to my back." He slipped his hand into hers and they fell into step together as they quickly headed outside.

They followed the line of red cloaks and black leather uniforms of the other soldiers around the grey stone buildings to the courtyard. The long shadows of the walls fell across the pitted yellow-grey dust as the sun slowly sank lower, gilding a small wisp of white cloud that drifted across the clear sky.

Farren lengthened his stride to match her quick pace again. "You're galloping away," he said. "And speaking of galloping, when will you be free to come with me to take the horses out tomorrow?"

"I think I'll be free by mid-morning. I'm glad we're freer than the other soldiers to go and train up the horses, but I've got my responsibilities." She sighed. "I wish I could spend all the day with you, Princess and Storm – outside of the city again – but I've got to trail around with Janna Greyhawk as he teaches the acolytes. You're free, more or less, apart from that wretched research."

"Well, I'm not arch *minyaster* and you are. Anyway," he grinned, "training horses for the big race next week could be said to be lawful practice of my animal-taming Gift – not like your shapeshifting. I think I'll spend most of the morning with Storm and Princess, starting with the morning feed. I don't want the barracks grooms to fool with our horses before the competition."

He stepped back to allow her to pass through the gate that led from the barracks courtyard into the chapel gardens. The soft perfume of the cherry blossom wrapped around him, mixed with the tangier scent of hyacinth. "Yes," he said, drawing level with her once more. "Only a week to go until all the celebrations for the king's birthday, now. I guess you're invited to the banquet with your position."

"Yes, although General Alpherastin hasn't officially handed me my piece of vellum complete with red seals and ribbon, and probably won't until after the Sabbath, knowing him."

"Which gives you a mere three days to answer," he interrupted.

"And you will be there. It's not High Council, thankfully, so I'm allowed to bring my husband-to-be." She squeezed his hand. "But here we are at chapel, so we'd better shut up and go in."

He led her through the wide door into the incense-scented air of the chapel. In the wavering candlelight, he spied an empty place near the front. He strode towards it, careful not to let his footsteps clump too loudly on the stone floor. Most of the pews were filled with soldiers, but evensong had not yet started. He heard the soft thumps issuing from the doorway behind the altar and knew that whichever monk was officiating would soon step out and begin. The other three soldiers in the pew shifted backwards and he pressed past them, Azariel's hand still in his. He sat down, the carved designs of the wood behind him digging uncomfortably into his back.

He rose to his feet as one of the green-habited barefoot monks from the monastery of Saint Almach entered the front of the church. The gentle rise and fall of music began as the congregation sang the opening chant and the monk paced to where the yellow light of the altar candles lit up his young golden face and shaven tonsure. Brother Claran from the library, thought Farren. We'll have some good singing this evening, with him.

The chant ended and Brother Claran began to speak. Farren half closed his eyes and listened to the well-known words of the liturgy as the monk's melodious baritone voice rose and fell. Then as the singing began once more, he heard Azariel's soprano beside him soaring high and clear. His *minyastin's* heart lifted and he let himself fly free. The familiar quicksilver tingling of the Power coursed through his body, prickling briefly at his wrists, then fading.

In no time at all, evensong ended. He heard creaks, the rumour of footsteps and low voices behind him as the other soldiers left. Azariel rose from her seat, but he held her back by her black cloak. "I'd like to speak to Brother Claran," he whispered. She nodded and sat down again.

Brother Claran glanced towards them and walked over and sat down at the end of their pew. "I missed you today. Were you wanting to come to the library tomorrow?" he asked softly.

Farren nodded. "Well, yes. We've only got back one of the Stones and we need them all. And how many more old books have you got tucked away?"

"None," said Claran. "We have read through all the books in our library. I read the last one today. And there has been no other mention of any of the Stones in all of them except the Book of Lore that told how they were lost and that one that sent you off to Crajaval."

Azariel ran her hands through the length of her hair, then flicked it back behind her shoulders. "The end of the books at last!" she laughed. "But we'll have to search somewhere else – soon – to find out where the Stones are. Wayast won't hold back from us forever, and I don't want another war." She stared vacantly at the carved birds on the pew while her hand lightly touched her left collarbone and ran down her chest, stopping between her breasts.

"That is what I wanted to speak to you about," said Brother Claran, turning side-on to them and one hand twisting the knotted rope at his waist back and forth between his fingers. "I would have come to you, even if you had not waited for me. You two and Janna Greyhawk also. Do you remember – and you should – the verses from the Holy Book that I read tonight?'

"'If any among you lacks wisdom, let them ask the King of Heaven who gives to all generously and without upbraiding, and it will be given to them...'" quoted Farren quickly, grinning. "I wasn't asleep like some." He slid his hand onto Azariel's knee.

"I wasn't!" she protested, rapping his knuckles lightly with her forefinger. "But I understand." She turned back towards

Brother Claran, laughing quietly. "And there we've been bending our backs over dusty books all this time hunting for answers when all we had to do was ask!"

"Yes," said Brother Claran. "Mind you, I have a suspicion that if we'd asked for answers with the books in the library still unread, the answer would have been 'Go and read the books in the library.'" He looked down at his hands then back up at her and Farren again. "The words struck me as I read them before evensong. I had just come from the library and was wondering what to tell you about all that work for nothing."

"Not quite nothing," Farren put in. "We did get back one Stone."

"And Crajaval has gone," she said, twisting her opal ring around her finger. "No more phantoms in the northern mountains now."

Farren chuckled. "I wonder how many hunters have headed up the Illin-Ast now it's safe."

"You'll be up there as soon as we're on leave," she said, running her hand up his arm. "But for now, we've still got three Stones missing and we have to ask the King of Heaven where they are. Let's start." Her thick straight hair fell across her face, cutting off her view of the others as she bowed her head.

She waited, keeping the stray thoughts that wandered through her mind out of the centre of silence and listened for the soft, compelling voice of the Power. *Speak, Master; your servant listens*, she repeated. Her heartbeats and breath played in her ears and strange lights crawled across the darkness as she closed her eyes.

A hundred slow heartbeats later, she brushed the hair back from her face and looked at the others. "Did either of you hear an answer?" she asked.

The men shook their heads. "Give Him time," said Brother Claran. "You know Him. You'll get an answer before long."

Azariel stood to go. "Thank you very much for all your help in the library," she said to the monk. "If there's anything we can do for you…"

"Oh, you've done plenty for all us monks at Saint Almach by keeping the Wayasti and their gods out of the Kingdom. Don't mention the small bit of help I've given you. I spend most of my time in the library anyway, and it's been a pleasure working with you."

She followed Farren out of the chapel. Outside, the sun had set, leaving a pale rose backdrop for the silhouettes of the cherry trees in the garden. Azariel breathed in the scent of the blossoms as she and Farren strolled past them. Mixed with this smoky city air, but still lovely. Then the savoury smell of the cookhouse blended with the scent of the blossoms, and she felt pangs of hunger gnaw at her stomach. "I wonder what the cooks are sending over to the *minyasti* tables tonight," she said. "I hope it's as good as what I can smell from the mess-hall."

"Let's hurry and find out," replied Farren. "But I'd like to see to the horses' fodder before I see to my own. Come on."

Azariel smiled and walked beside him past the *minyasti* quarters and on to the stables. Lamplight shone through the doorway, outlining the figures of the grooms as they moved from loosebox to loosebox with buckets and haynets in their hands. One of them was whistling shrilly as he worked. Her nose twitched with the dusty tang of hay and horses that filled the air as she and Farren entered the stables. She followed Farren to the large double loosebox where her black gelding, Storm, was stabled along with Farren's mare, Princess.

Storm whinnied a greeting at their approach, then he and Princess pushed against the lower door to nuzzle and whicker at Farren. She patted Storm's thick neck and scratched the fuzzy back of his ears. The gelding turned his head to her, bumping her shoulder with his chin as he swung around. "Good to see you again, Storm, old fellow," she murmured. "And I can see that they're feeding you plenty of that oats we bought for you. You had better be ready to run, my fine warhorse, and win one of those contests if you can."

She watched while Farren finished petting and murmuring to his chestnut mare, and both horses began to feed. He brushed the horsehair from his hands and drew her arm through his as they left the stables. The deep sapphire sky that showed above the wall between the black squares and triangles of buildings was sprinkled with a few spring stars, and the lights that flickered through the windows guided her and Farren back to their quarters. The smell of stewed beef and the sound of voices greeted them as they walked inside. She almost ran to the women's washroom to clean her hands from the stable grime, then back down the corridor to the common room.

She opened the common room door and saw a white-haired man seated in a padded chair with a carved staff across his knees. Beside him, a thin blond lad sat at the small round table playing cards with Farren and a long-legged girl with nut-brown hair. *Trust Farren to start playing cards with the acolytes. Where's Taramaritan Redstone?* She looked around and noticed the other woman standing by the dining table with a jug and beaker in her hands, lamplight shining off her straight golden hair. "Hello everybody," Azariel said. "Sorry I'm a little late, Janna," she added to the older man.

"Now we can start our meal," Janna said. "And why apologise to me? You're the arch *minyaster* now." The old man leaned on his staff and walked to the table.

After the meal and more card-playing, when the candles had burned down several inches and the acolytes had gone, Farren yawned. "I'm off to bed," he said. "I want to be up early to work with the horses, so I need my sleep." He stretched his arms and got up from the card table, dropping his hand of cards. "Sorry to break up the game."

"Good, good," Janna said. "I was thinking of leaving, too."

"I'm not surprised," Taramaritan chuckled. She twirled the large ruby ring on her right hand around her finger twice. "You've fallen asleep twice during this game already."

"At my age, I have some excuse, young lady," said Janna. "Could you lend me your arm, Farren?"

For goodness sake, Janna, you're not that old! Azariel folded her card hand together, then scooped the deck together into a neat pile. Once Farren and Janna had moved away from the table, she pushed her wooden stool back and got to her feet, a yawn welling up in her throat and ears. "Are you going to sleep as well, Taramaritan?" she asked.

"Not me," the other woman answered. "I want to do a little stargazing tonight. It's a clear night and I should have been up the tower a few hours ago."

"Goodnight to all, then," Azariel said. She walked out the door to leave, but Farren touched her softly on her arm from behind. She turned to him, seeing his brown eyes sparkling and a smile on his face. "I can't let you go without giving you this," he whispered before he kissed her gently.

"Thank you," she said. She touched his cheek lightly, feeling the short growth of stubble that was starting to creep through his skin. His teeth flashed white in the candlelight as his smile widened. "Goodnight, beloved." She turned and walked away down the corridor.

She shut her door behind her. *I won't bother lighting a candle, she thought. I can get undressed in the moonlight.* Her fingers fumbled as she unlaced the high neck of her chainmail tunic, and she dragged it over her head. She threw it over the back of a chair, following it with her black leather uniform and white cotton underclothing. A small ache nagged at the top of her right shoulder. She stretched, relishing the ease of movement without the metal weighing her arms down. *It won't be long till I'm asleep.* She turned back the covers on her bed and lay down. *I wonder what we'll be doing tomorrow after we've taken the horses out now that there are no more books in the library.* She rolled over, ideas crawling through her mind. *I can think about that in the morning, though.* She pulled the blankets around her chin and drifted into sleep.

She was flying, seeing the plains of the Kingdom spread beneath her like a map. Her path took her up the Illin-Ast River, speeding towards the northern mountains. Up and up she soared, above the jagged snow-capped mountain peaks, above where the great-eagles wheeled. Below, she saw all the lands: the Kingdom, Wayast, Helmn and even Elend. Then she flew over a narrow strip of land that lay between the northern mountains and the sea.

It looked like a wild country, even from the great height at which she flew, speeding northwards. Not a city, not a farm, not a road nor even one sign of human presence. Only forests and sand dunes topped with coarse grass. Below her now lay water, water to all horizons, rippling and heaving with flecks of white foam bursting up from time to time.

She felt herself falling down to where black and white birds skimmed and swooped to ride the winds, wailing as they flew. Now she sped low, almost near enough to touch the heaving green water. A cloudy, hazy mass on the horizon darkened and slowly revealed itself as an island, a dark hill rising out of the ocean. The turbulence of the sea below her increased and the water stood in steep mountains and valleys. The mountain of water nearest her reared up, a grey-green horse with a snow-white mane. With a roar, it crashed down, smashing itself into a running river of foam that streamed up onto the land. Sand crunched beneath her feet as she landed, the wave ebbing away around her ankles. She stepped forwards, another wash of water pouring around her boots.

Ahead, she saw a bright green glow against a dark wall of vegetation. Stumbling on the sand, she walked towards it. The glow brightened and came into focus. An emerald-like globe wrapped in silver pulsed with light. Around it, dark shapes like smoke wreathed and twisted. Azariel reached forwards to touch the green globe. Her hand was silhouetted against the brightness. Soon, she would feel the smooth touch of stone beneath her fingers...

Farren's grasp closed on the empty air. For a few seconds, he lay blinking at his hand folded into a loose fist beside him on the pillow. He pushed the covers off himself and sat up, feeling the chilly spring air embrace his body. He shivered as he looked out the window at the pale blue sky. A few birds were singing outside and he could hear the daytime rumblings of the city. *I nearly had one of the Stones in my grasp*, he thought as he dressed and shaved. *Finding it in a dream is one thing, but how will we find it in truth?* He pulled his riding boots out from under his bed. *Time for me to get busy. I still have to break my fast and take some exercise myself before I can spend good time with the horses. Dawn's broken already.*

He ate quickly and hurried out of the *minyasti* headquarters to the stables where Storm and Princess were waiting for him.

CHAPTER TWO

Azariel woke at dawn on the day of Caph Domastin's birthday celebrations. *These last seven days have flown by,* she thought as she looked out of the window at the first rays of sunshine gilding the vivid green young leaves on the trees outside. A cock crowed somewhere nearby. *There's the banquet to get ready to go to first – and I'd better start doing that soon – then the riding contests!* Her heart thumped and she felt her pulse quickening in anticipation.

She threw back the covers and rolled out of bed before beginning to search for her dress uniform. *I should have laid t out last night.* She rummaged through the oak chest to the right of her bed and fished the uniform out. *Good. It's nct too rumpled and rusted from disuse.* She laid the chainmail and belt out on the bed then pulled the tunic and trousers on to pad down the corridor to the women's washroom. She washed quickly then returned to her room, warm and slightly damp. Sitting on the lid of the trunk, she began to brush her long blue-black hair, singing softly to herself as she stroked the bristles along each strand of hair. When her hair had been freed from tangles at last, she reached for a small glass bottle on her dresser and opened it. The bitter herbal scent of rosemary wafted up as she tipped a little oil onto the brush. She carefully re-corked the bottle and brushed her hair again until she could see it glisten with the early morning light in the mirror opposite the window. Satisfied, she braided a single lock of hair beside her face with a silver thread.

As she pulled her uniform on properly, she wondered what Farren was doing. In her mind's eye, she saw him meticulously at work with razor and pumice stone. *He does like to keep himself tidy. Even more than I do. He'll be extra picky today for that banquet.* She eased her left boot over her foot and above her ankle and glanced down at her hands and the two silver rings. *My rings need polishing again.* She found the soft leather cloth she kept for her *minyaster's* rings and stood by the window so that the sunlight fell full on the gemstones. She removed the lapis lazuli ring from her left hand and quickly burnished the bright blue stone and the white metal, rubbing out the black flecks of tarnish. *It's getting badly chipped. I hope that won't affect its strength for when I need it in battle. I should ask Taramaritan – the Ringsmith ought to know.*

She slipped the ring back onto her left hand and took off her most powerful ring from the long fourth finger of her right hand. The opal ring flashed in the sunlight as she twisted it to and fro, watching the threads and sparkles of colour swirl through the milkiness before she carefully rubbed around the network of silver threads that bound it. With both rings gleaming in the sunlight, she turned her attention to the jewelled armbands of protection that circled her forearms. *No need to do those. They're only a month old.* She flexed and stretched her arms in the square of sunlight falling through the window, letting the light catch the diamonds and emeralds set in the damasked silver. *And they're much more beautiful than the old garnet ones that got shattered when I fought Crajaval.* Finally, she threaded her betrothal earring out from her left ear and burnished the cluster of diamond and onyx to a blaze as well.

She was gazing at the white fire of the diamond when she heard a knock on the door. "Come in," she said, sliding her earring into place and turning towards the entrance. The handle creaked and Farren walked in, face flushed and shiny, and his hair damp from washing. *He's done himself proud,* she thought. *Even though he's handsome enough without that.* She ran her eyes over him from his water-smoothed hair to where his scarlet cloak brushed the backs of his knees. The silver lieutenant's star winked on his shoulder in the folds of red wool. *How did such a good-looking man like him choose me? And he's got the heart to match his looks.* "Good morning, sweetheart," he said. "I'm glad to see you."

She stood up and tilted her head back as he pressed a kiss onto her mouth. The skin on his cheeks felt smooth and water-soft, the sweet aromatic tang of bay and walnut leaves clinging to him. His brown eyes flicked up and down her as his fingers stroked through her hair. "You are so beautiful," he whispered, then grinned and tugged lightly on her braid.

"Thank you," she answered. She pressed closer to the warmth of his body so their armour grated together as she nuzzled his throat. "And you look as handsome as ever."

He smiled and drew back from her slightly, hand resting on her forearms. "Do I have any horsehair on me anywhere?" he asked. "I've been up before dawn so as to see to them for a final inspection and I feel as if I've hurried washing."

Her eyes swept up and down his body, over the tight neat contours in the black leather and the waterfall of his cloak. "Not one," she said. "I take it you mean you were up at dawn to see to the horses, not the horsehair. But even so, I'd be surprised to ever find any dirt on you at all – except after a fight."

"Or during one, probably, not to mention blood," he laughed. "But come along to the common room for a little breakfast. The feast isn't until mid-morning, and we have to collect the Guild's gift to Caph Domastin before then."

"Is the book finished?" she asked. "I haven't seen it since I finished embroidering the covers and bookmark."

"I finished the illuminations yesterday while you were with Janna and the acolytes. Taramaritan took it after that, so I hope she's finished gilding the pages by now."

She walked before him into the common room. Two uncut loaves of bread, a full jug of milk and several platters of jam and honey stood on the table. *None of the others have eaten yet.* She sat down on the end of one of the benches and slid along slightly as Farren picked up a serrated knife and sawed one of the loaves into slices. She took a thick slice, buttered it and smothered it in honey. Her mouth watered at the sweet smell. "Going to leave some honey for Janna and Taramaritan?" he chuckled. She looked indignantly up at him, one finger catching a sticky cascade of honey that poured off her bread as she chewed her first bite.

The door creaked open, followed by the soft padding of footsteps. She turned her head and saw Taramaritan, red-eyed and her hair dishevelled. The blonde held the ornamental book the guild of *minyasti* had made for the king. "I've been up all night finishing it," she yawned. With a wry grin, she added, "I don't have to worry too much about my looks, though. I'm not attending Caph Domastin's birthday feast. I'm going to catch up on some sleep before I come and watch you two in the jumping and racing and whatever else you're doing."

Azariel stood to take the book from Taramaritan. She eased it open and ran her eyes over the rich reds, greens, golds and blacks of the writing and illuminations, breathing in the sharp smells of fresh ink. "You certainly can write a beautiful flowing hand," she said, raising her gaze to look at Farren. "This is as good as anything else the king would have in his library."

"It's not all my handiwork," he said. "Some of it's Janna's. The pictures are all mine, though."

***

Thank goodness that's over, Farren thought as he walked out of the palace banqueting hall into a corridor after the feast, the taste of red wine lingering on his palate. *I'm always afraid that I'll drop something or do the wrong thing when I'm around the king.* "Now for the contest," he said softly to Azariel.

She flashed a smile at him, her eyes gazing keenly into his. "You're relieved to be out of there, aren't you?" she said.

"Yes." He stepped to one side to allow one of the Kingdom nobles to pass him. "You seemed calm enough among all the dukes and duchesses and so forth."

"I'm a bit more used to them, as I have to turn up for High Council. You ought to talk to General Alpherastin about it – he doesn't care for formality. You've seen him at it."

He laughed. "He can get away with it, being the General. But never mind. You did well with your little speech and presentation of the book. We're out of the palace now, so let's go and find our horses."

They walked across the central square of the city towards the barracks, disturbing the grey and white pigeons by the fountain and sending them clattering their wings into the sky. Back behind the iron gates, they threaded through the buildings to the stables, where their horses waited. Farren's fingers nimbly tightened and checked the newly polished tack on both Storm and Princess. The horses' coats, black and chestnut, gleamed where the sun fell on them, matching the gloss of the leather. He led his mare out to the yards and mounted. His heart was thumping in anticipation and he felt Princess shifting restlessly beneath him as he rode her slowly out of the city to the open grasslands, where a collection of tents and wagons had gathered around a fenced-off area.

He looked out of the city gates at the open plains that spread out north and west towards the mountains that stood purple-grey and hazy in the midday sunlight. The light wind billowed the new spring grass in waves by the side of the cobbled highway and ruffled his hair. He breathed it in, catching a sharp green tang of juicy crushed grass. Princess tossed her head and snorted, ears pricked. "Easy, my lady," he said. "I know you're eager to be galloping again."

He let the mare walk briskly as he and Azariel headed towards the tents and the crowds of people. A buzz of voices mixed with the beckoning cries of stallholders describing the amusements and refreshments they had on offer. A smell of horse dung, hay, spiced ale and hot sausages filled the air. He sniffed. *That always takes me back to the fairs Father used to sell horses at.* He scanned the perimeter of the fenced-off ring and spotted an area free from sideshows and hot sausage stalls but full of horses. "This way," he said, gently nudging Princess towards it.

Other horses and riders drifted along with him, hundreds of hooves rumbling on the grass. Around the edge of the fenced ring, knots of people had gathered; standing, sitting and lying on the grass on coloured rugs. Storm's nose butted against his leg and he turned to look at Azariel. "Here's hoping we don't make fools of ourselves in front of this crowd."

"You're the least likely person to do that," she replied. "Do you know what order the contests are held in?"

"I guess it will be like the horse fairs: fancy stepping first, then racing and jumping last of all."

"Let me guess – you're entering Princess in all three?"

"I might." Another horse swerved in front of them, and Princess pulled up. "Watch out," Farren said, glancing up. A spotted stallion swung his powerful hindquarters two paces in front of them, making Princess raise her head awkwardly. The rider wore the long hair and beard of an Elendi. "The race hasn't started yet, stranger."

The Elendi rider half turned in his seat and looked back at them. "I'm helping you get used to the sight of my horse's rump," he said, Elendi accent sharpening some of his vowels. "It's all you're going to see during the race."

Farren chuckled. "He's a good beast, certainly. What's his name?"

"Dolphin." The Elendi rider patted the spotted stallion's shoulder.

"Dolphin?" asked Farren. "Strange sounding name."

The Elendi man chuckled. "I suppose it would sound odd to a Kingdom man like you who's never seen the sea. A dolphin is... it's like a fish but it's not a true fish but a beast. It has the body of a fish, a head like a pig and long snout a bit like a fox's. They're great leapers, which is why my horse has this name. He'll out-jump and outrun any horse alive."

Farren smiled. "Pity you didn't have him in the Kingdom last time my mare was in season."

"Hunt me out next time," the Elendi rider said. He nudged his stallion with his heels and edged him away from Storm and Princess.

Azariel looked at Farren and saw him gazing after the spotted stallion. She smiled and glanced away. A small canvas awning caught her eye and she squinted in the bright sunlight to make out the roughly-painted lettering on the sign hanging in front of it. Dust filled the air and blew into her mouth and nose, carrying a stable-smell from the crowd of horses around them. *Entries*, she read silently. "This way, beloved," she said. She nudged her black gelding to the queue in front of the tent and waited, her leg squeezed in between Storm and Princess. The air quivered with voices, snorts, stamps and shouts. Storm tossed his head restlessly and she felt excitement prickle in her wrists.

A rather flushed and sweating steward passed a grubby scrap of paper up to her. "You can enter one event, two or three," the steward said in a bored voice. "Team entries are permitted."

She nudged Farren with her elbow and held the paper up to him. "So what happens with team entries?" she asked.

"If it's the two of you, you divide the three events between you. Your points are added up for the final total, like they are for an individual rider. If you both ride in the same event, the average of your two scores counts toward the total. You get told the total at the end." The steward produced a rather chewed-looking charcoal pencil from somewhere on him and prodded it towards her. "Write your names on the paper and what you want to go in for."

She raised her eyebrows and glanced at Farren before passing him the paper and the pencil. He nodded to her and wrote quickly on it. "There you go," he said, handing both back to the steward. "Thank you."

"What did you enter us for?" she asked as they headed their horses away from the queue. "Let me guess... You're in for the fancy stepping; Storm's in the race and the jumping."

"Almost right," he said, smiling. "We're both in the jumping."

She halted Storm beside the fence and dismounted. A fresh breeze was blowing from the northeast, brisk and cool, bursting with the scent of apple blossoms from a nearby orchard. An eddy of wind blew a white flower past her face, snatched from one of the trees. She caught the flower and handed it to Farren. "All the best for your ride," she said softly. "I'll wait for you here."

"Thank you." He leaned forward and tucked the white flower into Princess's bridle before turning her towards the gap in the fence where the other riders were waiting to compete.

She watched the horses and riders come into the ring one by one to perform. Idly, she scratched along the crest of Storm's mane. At length, Farren and Princess entered the ring. Her heart kicked in her chest as she watched him, poised in perfect control astride the dainty chestnut mare. Princess stepped delicately around the ring, hooves lifted high in a springy trot, then moving into long, flowing strides that made her look as if she was floating in the air. He made the mare perform a series of complicated steps. At the end of the sequence, Princess reared, forelegs neatly curved, then leaped and kicked out behind her. She landed, mane and tail swirling around her with the wind. Farren saluted the crowd with his sword drawn before leaving the ring.

Azariel craned her head forwards and around to watch him as he merged into the crowd of horses. Princess's chestnut rump was swallowed up in the mêlée of bay, black and grey backs, and she relaxed. *He'll be around here soon.* She closed her eyes and leaned on the narrow wooden rail at the top of the fence, listening to the sound of hoofbeats and feeling the sun on her back.

"Falling asleep, sweetheart?" Farren's voice behind her made her open her eyes and turn around to see him dismounting beside her. Storm inched over to one side as Princess pushed forwards.

"You did well, you and Princess," she said, straightening up and kissing him on the cheek.

"Not too badly," he said lightly. "My lady did everything I asked her to." He ran his hand down the chestnut mare's neck and withers. "Yes, you did. I don't know what I'd do without you, my lady. You're a good horse."

She circled her arms around Farren's waist from behind, pressing her face into the soft wool bunched on his shoulder, as he continued crooning to the mare. "It's nearly time for my race, beloved," she whispered.

He turned around and embraced her, sliding his fingers through her hair. "Then good luck. I'll ride over to the track to watch you."

The racetrack had been marked off half a bowshot from the ring. A red and black pennant carrying the Kingdom arms and surrounded by tiered seating marked the end of the track. She ran her eyes over the long straight stretch of turf. *About a mile long.* "Are you ready, old fellow?" she asked Storm, patting his neck. She turned the gelding away from it towards the other end and took her place at the start line with about thirty other horses. A small vein was throbbing in the gelding's thick glossy neck. She sat poised and tense on Storm's back, her heart hammering and her mouth dry.

The stewards marshalling the race bustled around, directing horses and riders backwards and forwards into a straight line. Then they drew back. She ran her tongue around the inside of her mouth. One of the stewards brought out a long silver trumpet. He raised it to his lips and blew. She punched her heels into Storm's sides and let him leap forwards into a gallop. A roar rose from the crowd, almost drowned by the thunder of hooves.

Azariel looked around and saw a tight knot of a dozen horses around and in front of her, leading the race. *Storm, , that spotted stallion, the General's white horse and some others. We can do this.* "Come on, Storm. Keep it up, old fellow," she urged. The black gelding shook his mane as he galloped, sending a wave of horse-sweat scent up to her. From the corner of her eye, she saw a sorrel horse dropping back behind her on one side and a steel grey a little behind the sorrel.

She rocked and swayed with the big black gelding's gallop, peering through his pricked ears. Dolphin, the spotted stallion, pushed in front of her, blocking her view ahead. A light touch on the reins and Storm veered slightly to one side, ready to overtake. Clumps of dirt flew up from the soil and flicked back from the stallion into her face and over her arms. She blinked and bent her head to her arm, brushing the cold grit out of her eyes. The stallion had inched ahead and Storm had fallen behind General Alpherastin's horse. She punched her heels into him again and stood in the stirrups to lean forward. Wind stung her eyes, ripping tears from them with the speed, so she narrowed them to look ahead.

Dolphin had shifted a little to one side and taken the lead by two lengths. The Kingdom flag at the end of the track billowed in the wind, making the silver stars and crown sparkle in the sunlight. Shouts rose from the group of spectators, faint at first above the hoofbeats, the snorts and the squeak of tack, but growing louder. She gritted her teeth and spurred Storm on. Storm burst ahead for a few heartbeats, passing General Alpherastin and leaving the steel grey behind on his flank. A bowshot remained between the horses and the finish line. A thin red ribbon stretched across the width of the track, ready for the winner.

Dolphin surged a full five lengths ahead of the other horses and snapped the red tape. A roar went up from the crowd, but the cheering was swallowed up in the thunder of hooves as the other horses swept in behind him, manes and tails tossing, nostrils flared. Azariel saw General Alpherastin beside her, sweat dripping off his flushed face. His eyes met hers and his teeth flashed in a grin as his white horse inched a neck ahead of Storm. The shouts of the crowd rang in her ears as the shadow of the Kingdom banner passed over her, the General still ahead as they crossed the line. She reined Storm in to a halt and patted his neck.

"The two soldiers were in next," called a voice somewhere to her right. She turned her head and saw another steward standing underneath the tiered seats. A collection of well-dressed lords and ladies were leaning over towards the steward and she made out Caph Domastin in the centre of them. "The white horse finished second; the black came third."

She swung Storm off the track and into the shadow of the nobles' seats. General Alpherastin stood in front of her beside his horse, patting and stroking it. "Congratulations, sir," she said to him.

"Thank you, Azariel." He wiped a thick clump of sweaty foam off the white horse and shook it onto the ground. "You didn't do too badly yourself." He turned away as his horse bent its head to the grass and began grazing, then he looked up at her again. "By the way," he said, "I've been wanting to talk to you all day. I didn't get the chance to over lunch – you were at the wrong part of the table. But I didn't expect to see you like this!"

"What is it?" She shifted in the saddle and twisted her rings straight around her fingers. *He wouldn't want to talk to me except about something tactically important.*

"Well, I won't tell you here. I've got to get my Starlight here seen to." He patted the horse's withers again. "And I'll need to tell that man of yours as well. Or rather, I won't tell you. The messenger who brought the news can tell you. Are you or Farren riding in the jumping?"

She nodded. "Both of us." Storm tugged the reins from her hands and put his head down to crop the grass.

"Good. I'll see both of you in the beer tent over there afterwards, then." He pointed to a large green canvas marquee. A snatch of lively music drifted over from it. "Good luck for the rest of the contest. Wish I had someone to ride in a team with."

Storm wove through the crowds of horses and people, jerking his head up as he bumped into one or two. Farren was waiting for her half a bowshot away from the stewards' tent. "Where were you, sweetheart?" he asked, nudging Princess towards her and leaning over to brush his hand lightly down her arm. "I waited for you after the race."

"Sorry," she replied, taking hold of his hand and squeezing it. The point of his emerald ring dug into the fleshy part of her fingers. "I met General Alpherastin. I could hardly help it, seeing as he was only a neck ahead of me at the finish. He's got a message for us and he wants to meet us in the big beer tent by the racetrack after the jumps."

His face creased into a grimace. "That doesn't sound good. I hope it's nothing to do with Yellow Claws." His frown smoothed into a smile. "But I can – we can – worry about that later. They're just setting the jumps up now for our competition."

"How high are they?" She touched Storm's black flanks lightly with her heels and made him walk on a few steps closer to the entrance to the jumping ring.

"Not too high. Higher than the ponies' jumps, but lower than the ones for those who aren't part of the team contest." He swung Princess in beside Storm. "How's Storm after the race? Not too tired to jump?"

"What do you think?" She stroked the gelding's shoulders. "He's not even sweating."

"If the General's message does mean we're riding out, that will be just as well."

The grass near the entrance to the ring had become heavily pitted and pocked with hoofprints and dung. She slackened the reins slightly and let Storm slump his head forward while a steward briskly ordered her and Farren into a line waiting to jump. She scratched the gelding's neck idly and closed her eyes, breathing in the smell of crushed grass and mud and listening to the thud and thunder of hooves. She opened them again to watch another horse, Dolphin, soar over one jump and clatter a second down.

At last, her turn came. She spurred Storm into the ring and guided him over the obstacles. He cleared the first three, but the fourth, a wall made of crates painted to look like stones, crumpled as the gelding hit it. *Don't get nervous on me now, Storm.* She finished the round with Storm hitting two more fences but without baulking. "Good on you, old fellow," she said, patting his neck. "Now we can get that saddle off you and you can rest." *At least for now. After we've talked with the General, who knows?*

She dismounted and began to unbuckle Storm's tack. The leather was soaked with sweat and the hairs underneath the saddle were rubbed against the natural growth, clearly marking the shape of the saddle-skirts and girth. She led him beyond the crowd and let him roll in the grass. He snorted and thrashed his hooves in the air for a moment. She stood back as he got up and began to graze. She kneaded at the gelding's muscles, wiping off sweat and horsehair from his sleek coat.

Vaguely, she glanced up at the other horses hurdling the obstacles. A swirl of red caught her eye and she looked up to see Farren and Princess in the ring, lightly bounding over fence after fence. The mare's ears pricked forwards as she cantered towards another, the treble hedge where all the other riders and horses had balked, fallen or knocked down rails. Azariel drew her breath, hearing an echoing gasp from the watchers near the rails around her. Her heart thudded loudly as Princess bunched herself and sprang. A solid wooden clunk sounded across the hushed audience as a gaudily striped red and white pole bounced backwards from the mare's hoof. Azariel let her breath out. *Bad luck, Farren. That's a hard fence.*

His eyes met hers as he left the ring with two jumps knocked down, and turned the mare towards her. She let go of Storm's bridle as he dismounted and landed with a thud in the grass. She wrapped her arms around him and kissed him on the cheek, tasting the salt of his sweat. "How do you think we did?" she said, drawing back from him slightly.

"We'll find out before long. I think there's only five more of the team competitors left to take their turn – but I'm not sure."

After a short wait, they clustered around the ring with the other horses and riders as four of the stewards, by now looking very sweaty and red-faced in their black fur-trimmed uniforms, carried a little collapsible table and several large bags to the middle of the ring. The largest, fattest and sweatiest of the stewards bawled out the names of the winners. Azariel squeezed Farren's arm as she heard their names called out in third place. Her hand linked with his, she walked with him to the stewards' desk and collected the large leather bag that clinked and rattled.

"The beer tent for us, I think," Farren said. "We'll have a look at what we've won in there while we wait for General Alpherastin."

"And I think I saw a water trough near a tether-line outside it, so the horses can have a drink as well."

"Lead the way, my lady," he said as he loosened the girths on Princess's saddle.

"I don't think she knows the way."

"Art thou not my lady, fair maid?" he asked, dark eyes sparkling.

"The bards are in the tent," she replied. "Save the poetry for in there if they decide to pass the harp to the audience."

They found a small table with three stools beneath it in a corner of the large green canvas marquee near the makeshift stage where a group of four minstrels were playing. The air was laden with the sweet yeasty scent of beer and the camp-smell of canvas and grass. "Can you see the General in here yet?" he asked her.

She ran her eyes across the bevy of people inside and shook her head. "Right. I'll get a drink for both of us and we'll take a look." She sat down at the table, one arm resting on the leather bag and watched him saunter to the barkeeper and the tall stack of barrels. The minstrels stopped playing and she applauded with the few others paying attention. Farren returned with two battered pewter pint tankards of foaming beer and hooked a second stool out from the table with his foot before he sat down. "Let's see what we've got."

She loosened the leather cords tying bag shut and pulled out three smaller canvas bags. With her dagger, she cut the tightly knotted binding on the first bag and emptied it out onto the tabletop, revealing a number of small jewels and some silver coins. "That's nice," she said, picking up one of the gems, a lapis lazuli bead, and holding it up to a crack of light to admire the vivid blue colour. "We'll have to think about what we're going to do with these – and what we'll use the money for." She scooped the money and stones into the bag again and pulled the bindings tight as best she could. The next bag held a hock of bacon and a thin tapering dagger with a green stone in its hilt. She drew the dagger from the tough leather sheath that encased it and looked at the damasking on the blue steel blade. "That's for you," she said, carefully handing it to him hilt first.

"It's almost a twin to yours," he said, testing the edge with his thumb and turning the thin blade to and fro. "Probably came from the same maker." He slid it back into the sheath. "I'll put that on my belt later. What's in the third?"

She shook the last bag and heard it jingle. "More money, I'd wager. We're going to have to find a banker – or buy a lockable chest." She untied the strings and glanced inside. A small cascade of gold and silver coins poured out over the table and she began to separate them into piles.

"Count them later." He leaned back from the table and took a mouthful of beer from the tankard. "I still can't see the General."

"Getting the messenger who brought him the news we need to hear, I suppose." She sipped at her beer and let the bittersweet taste roll around her mouth.

The air filled with the low babble of voices, mixed with some applause, as the musicians brought their set of reels to a halt. "Now," the harpist announced. "It's time for me to follow tradition and circulate my friend here," he paused and waved the wooden harp, "around the room – or tent – and let you have a go. Who's first? You, sir, in the green?"

The companions of the man chosen by the harpist roared encouragement as he got up from his stool, somewhat unsteadily, and took the harp. He twanged a few of the strings and began to pick out the tune of a popular song. After a few bars, he began to bawl out the lyrics, accompanied loudly by his companions.

Azariel leaned closer to Farren and took his hand. "I'm glad he doesn't know the version of this song that I heard when I was in my cadet unit. All those with delicate ears would bolt."

The song finished and the man in green sat down, his companions clapping him hard on the shoulder. The harpist came back from the far end of the tent and took the harp again. "Now, who's going to follow that? One of the ladies? How about you, the dark-haired lady all in black? You look at least partly Zenifi – give us one of the old songs."

Azariel straightened and saw the harpist looking directly at her, a snaggle-toothed smile on his weather-beaten face. "I haven't touched a harp for years," she said.

"Go on, Stormwolf," urged Farren. "Time to try again."

"All right." She took the harp and sat down on a stool near the middle of the tent, experimentally plucking at the strings in a scale. *Why is it at moments like these that all I can think of are bawdy ballads?* She forced her mind away from the songs at the top of her mind and searched around for one of the ballads her mother had taught her. "The lady, she went down to the woods," she began singing, twisting the ankle of her free leg around the one that bore the harp as she saw the eyes of the audience fix her.

> *Briar-rose, celandine, sweet columbine.*
> *Down to the woods in the sweet autumn-time.*
> *Down to the woods, ripe berries for to find.*
> *The lady she went down to the woods…*

She turned her eyes away from the audience and watched the harpist slip out of the marquee.

At last, she brought the song to a close. As if he had been listening, the harpist reappeared through a small flap in the back of the marquee near the beer barrels. He paused to hold it open and the heavy shape of General Alpherastin followed him in. The two men walked almost in a procession towards her. "Thank you, lady," the harpist said, taking the harp from her before turning and coaxing more of the watchers to play.

General Alpherastin leaned on the table with both hands. "Right, you two, come over to my office and we'll talk."

"Can't we talk here, sir?" Farren asked. "There's room for you at this table."

"We can't." The General straightened up and stared around the marquee. "Tell me... how many Nightravens can you see in here?"

"The only ones I know are that woman Stessa and The Hawk," Farren said. "I don't see them here."

"Exactly. You don't know how many there are because you don't know who they are. There's three in here – the harpist is one of them." He winked at them. "Now tell me how many of the Wayasti Harriers are in here."

Azariel took a long pull at her beer and felt the dryness at the back of her throat vanish. "Good point," she said. "We don't want to be overheard."

"You're not stupid." General Alpherastin put his hands on each of their shoulders. "Finish your beer and come over – and don't stop to stable your horses, either." He turned and walked between the tables and out of the tent.

This does not sound like good news. She stared into the amber depths of her beer and swirled what remained of the foam on top. *King of Heaven, what now?*

CHAPTER THREE

Farren's boots echoed on the stone steps as he and Azariel climbed the stairs to General Alpherastin's office. "I wonder where he went to," he thought out loud as they reached the top of the stairs and began to walk along the whitewashed corridor to the General's office. "Did you see him after the stables?"

"I think he is here." Azariel tossed her hair back from her face. "I just saw his horse in the stables being rubbed down and generally being made a fuss over by the grooms. After all, that white stallion has just proved itself to be the fastest horse in the Kingdom."

"The fastest? But he only came... Oh, I see. The winner was that Elendi horse." He squeezed her hand. "And who came next?" His free hand reached over and playfully tugged a strand of her hair.

She bent her head slightly and smiled up at him. Then she drew herself up proudly. Her hair cascaded down her squared shoulders in a river of rosemary-scented blue-black and her eyes flashed triumphantly. *My sweetheart, my Stormwolf. So beautiful and so proud,* he thought, a strong desire to crush her to himself and kiss her passionately sweeping through him. He tore his gaze away and knocked on the General's door.

"Enter," said the General's deep voice crisply. She opened the door and he followed her into the small office. General Alpherastin's reddened face smiled at them over a paper-strewn desk. Farren's hand went to his right hip for his sword, ready to salute. "Don't bother," said the old soldier. "It's just the four of us."

Four? He heard a rustle in the corner and turned. A woman sat draped on a small wooden chair, looking up at him with wide sky-blue eyes. He took in her sleek, bobbed golden hair, her full smiling lips and voluptuous figure, and recognition plunged a knife of ice into his stomach. *Stessa of the Nightravens,* he thought. *Not her again!* A memory stirred in the back of his mind; the memory of Stessa, ample breasts bared and hands clawing at the lacings of his trousers as she tried to seduce him. *Get out of here!* he thought, shaking his head to clear it. He looked at Azariel. She had stepped back towards the wall, staring at the floorboards with her shoulders slumped. He stepped back beside her and felt for her hand. Her fingers curled fiercely around his. *Sweetheart, it's all right. You don't have to worry about that blonde hussy.* He looked at General Alpherastin, hoping the swirl of emotions stayed hidden.

Azariel's stormy grey eyes narrowed and hardened and her expression seemed to freeze into a smooth wall. "So what is the news, General?" she asked, voice level and expressionless.

"Stessa will tell you. Farren, you've worked with her, I know. Have you met her, Azariel?"

General, you probably don't realise how tactless this meeting is. Farren shot a glance at Azariel. *Azariel's been afraid that that woman's going to steal my affections for a long time.* He squeezed her hand gently and felt her nails bite into the back of his hand. *No chance. But I wish I could make both of them realise that.*

"We met about three years ago in an operation against the Claws before Farren and I were posted to the Watchtower of the West." Azariel's voice still sounded expressionless, though with a brittle edge to it.

"I shared a tent with you, Stormwolf, if I remember rightly," came Stessa's honey-smooth voice. "That was when I met Farren, too. I remember that time well enough."

Stessa's blue eyes raked him up and down, and he frowned at her. "And what's your news, Stessa?" he asked.

Stessa leant forwards with her elbows on her knees, allowing her low neckline to loosen and sag still lower. Her flower-shaped pendant dangled above her abundant cleavage, pointed tips of the petals almost brushing her skin. He gritted his teeth and looked up at Azariel's profile, fidgeting uncomfortably.

"The Yellow Claws are on the move again," Stessa said. "One of the other Nightravens and me shadowed a band of twenty from Lebhern-y-Hyalda to the Wayasti border. We saw a Wayasti cross the border and meet them in a valley on the eastern slopes of Seranya-y-Doma. A novice sorcerer, I found later." Stessa's perfect teeth flashed in a wide smile and she caressed the hilt of her dagger. "He was quite talkative with a few strong drinks in him, and he talked in his sleep as well."

"What happened?" asked Azariel and Farren together.

"The Yellow Claws began to move from then on. They moved southwards down the river and the day before yesterday I found where they were headed." She paused and toyed with her pendant. "They're going to the Watchtower of the South, and I think that there's only one reason for their going there. That novice sorcerer didn't have much to say, but he knew enough to let me know that the Stone of Water is in danger."

"Where and when did you leave the Claw unit to come here?" Azariel lifted her head and looked the other woman directly in the eye.

"Yesterday, as soon as I clearly saw where they were headed." Stessa turned and gazed out of the window. "I left them a little south of Tapatarman and came here." She grinned. "I'd already sent my last messenger pigeon back earlier."

"Yesterday..." said Farren. "That will mean that they will arrive at the Watchtower of the South tomorrow, if they aren't there already."

"Don't be too worried," said the General. "The Watchtower is well guarded. Colonel Annan and his nine men are there. And isn't…"

Azariel felt a knot tie itself tighter in her stomach, and her head and shoulders sagged limply. "Taramaritan ought to be there, too, General," she said quietly. She shuffled her feet and twisted a lock of her hair, staring at the smudges of ink and sealing wax on his desk. "I brought her back here because of the King's birthday and the book we were making." She clenched her fists, driving the tips of her nails into her palms. *Why did I do that? I should have sent somebody out there in her place.*

"The Claws will travel slowly and stealthily," said Stessa. "It's mostly farmland that the unit has to make its way over, so they'll mostly travel at night. But I think you'd better be at the Watchtower. There may be a sorcerer with the Claws, although I don't know for sure. I didn't get that close to the whole lot of them."

Azariel turned to Farren, mind buzzing with a hive of questions. *How much do they know about the Stone? What do they want with it? How much do they know about it?* She drew a deep breath, then exhaled slowly, releasing the thoughts. "We had better get ready to leave at once."

"How soon can you start for the Watchtower of the South?" asked General Alpherastin.

"We should be able to start by tonight," Farren replied. "Storm and Princess need to rest after the contest. And I mean start, not get there. They can't go all night."

She tossed the hair back from her eyes. *Why did I call Taramaritan back?* She ran her hand through its whole length and viciously yanked a tangle loose. *I shouldn't have sent her. Why didn't I think?* She let go of Farren's hand and paced over to the narrow window. She stood staring out over the tops of the other barracks buildings and over the walls to the city. Stessa's gaze caught hers in the reflection on the glass and the blonde woman smiled at her. "Don't worry too much, Stormwolf," she said.

"I'm not. Just angry at myself." Azariel laid her hand on her sword hilt, then smiled and twisted the lapis lazuli ring on her left hand. "At least you've dealt with one sorcerer with the pack. There are soldiers at the Watchtower. Even if we don't get there before the Claws, we might come in time to stop them getting away with the Stone."

She heard footsteps then felt Farren's hand reaching for hers, warm and reassuring. Her fingers closed around his and their rings grated together lightly. "That's right," he said. "But we can't press the horses too hard. If we are too late, we can't chase them back to Wayast with jaded horses. General," he said, turning away from her, "may we leave at nightfall?"

The General stood up. "Don't ask me. The Stones of Protection are more the business of you *minyasti*. It's certainly your job to protect them. It should be Azariel you ask, not me. But by all means, go as soon as possible." He took a scrap of paper from the desk and screwed it up.

Azariel turned from the window and walked to the door. "Will you be coming with us, Stessa?" she asked. *She is such a good fighter. We could do with her if there's going to be a fight coming up. I'm useless compared with her.* She nibbled at her lower lip. *But in spite of that, in spite of the fact that I shouldn't mix personal things with my work, I don't like to see her near Farren more than she has to be.*

Stessa laughed. "Are you asking a Nightraven what her plans are? I might be – or I might not."

Azariel drew her sword, and she and Farren both saluted General Alpherastin. She strode out of the door, letting her cloak sweep behind her as she left and almost ran down the stairs and across to the *minyasti* headquarters.

The common room door closed behind them and she felt his arms wrap around her, pulling her close. "All quiet, sweetheart?" he asked. "You're not still fretting about Stessa's fancy for me, are you? You know I love you and there's no other woman who comes close to you."

She buried her face in the thick red wool of his cloak, breathing in the scent of horses, woodsmoke and lavender soap that hung about it. "I don't know why you chose me instead of her. She's excellent at what she does; they call her the Weapons Mistress because she's so skilled; she's priceless to the Kingdom and heads turn when she enters a room. They never turn for me."

"Oh, yes, they do. I know mine always does." His fingers slid through her hair and caressed her scalp. "And she's a mistress of deceit and mistress to a few too many people. Anyway, she can't hold a candle to you." He ran one hand down her cheek and stroked his thumb across her lips lightly. "Why wouldn't I choose you over her?" Cupping his hands around her face, he kissed her softly. "I love you," he whispered. She looked into his brown eyes and saw the pupils dilated to pools of black. "But we can't linger here for long," he sighed. "We've got to pack and leave for the Watchtower of the South."

***

They left at nightfall. As they passed through the cobbled streets, hoofbeats ringing loudly on the rough stones, she gazed at the lighted windows and the soft white plumes of smoke rising from chimneys and hazing the first few spring stars. Woodsmoke and the savoury aromas of cooking filled the air. *Soon we'll be out of here and into the free countryside,* she thought. She looked ahead at the massive city gates. A few soldiers were patrolling the walls beside it, their shapes standing sharp and black against the pink and cobalt western sky. One of the guards turned his head towards them, then jogged down the small flight of stone steps beside the gates and creaked one of them open far enough for a horse to fit through.

She followed Farren through the gap and saw his cloak rise and fall as the northeast wind that rushed freely outside the walled city swept it up. Her own cloak tugged at her shoulders and her hair blew across her face. She shook it back and enjoyed the gentle tug and tickle of hair billowing and streaming in the wind. The Seranyai-y-Taranar stood in flat black jagged shapes against the dying light in the west, and the silhouette of a tall pine dominated the skyline. She headed Storm around to the left, turning southwards so that the brisk wind pushed her cloak against and around her body. Behind them, the gate squeaked shut and she caught the rasp of a catch sliding home to lock the gate. She shivered a little in the cold night air.

"Better ride along the side of the road to ease their hooves," he said. "And don't go too fast. They've had a hard day today." The light clopping of Princess's hooves on stone changed to a gentle thumping on the earth and grass.

She nudged Storm onto the grass level with Princess. She gently rose and fell with his quiet trot. "How long shall we travel for tonight?"

He turned his head to look at her then away at the sky. The angular lines of his nose and chin were outlined against the bleached dregs of the sunset. "The horses are good for another few hours, I think," he said. "We'll ride until..."

"Moonrise," she broke in. "That's a few hours off yet, as the moon's on the wane."

"That sounds reasonable. Keep looking eastwards and we'll find a place to sleep then."

"At an inn?" She slowed Storm to a walk. The two horses plodded side by side, almost catching her leg between the two big warm bodies.

"If one's around. If not, we can sleep rough by the horses. It's not the first time we've had to do that, and it probably won't be the last time, either."

She rubbed her hands together and blew on her chilled knuckles. Her lips and the tip of her nose felt like ice in the night air. "I hope it won't freeze overnight, for your sake. I can always change into wolf-form to sleep outdoors, but you can't." She flicked a strand of her hair from her right shoulder to around her left and let the tips waver like waterweed in the wind.

"I don't expect a frost with this northerly wind, especially this far into spring. And if you do decide to shapeshift, then you can take your cloak off and give it me before it changes with you."

She laughed, then they rode on in silence. The sky continued to darken and the stars stood out, points of white and off-white fire against deepest indigo. *Patterns I know well,* she thought, craning her neck back so the links of her chainmail dug into the back of her head. An owl called somewhere in the distance and she faintly caught a dog's bark blown on the wind. *There are the four stars of the Cross and the Guides beside the zenith.* She scanned the sky from side to side. *And that's the lights of the sorcerers' Scorpion to the west. Our Hunter and the Hound are still hidden. I wonder if we'll see them rising before the moon does.*

She continued to gaze at the stars, head flung back, until her neck ached. Fruitlessly, she shrugged her shoulders and tried to knead the muscles in her neck through the double thickness of her chainmail. Her fingers slipped into the gap at the top of her armour and she shuddered as a ripple of cold swept down her back at her own touch. *I had no idea that my hand was so cold and numb. I should have brought gloves.* She pulled the hood of her cloak over her head against the cold night air and buried her fingertips deep into Storm's mane. The warmth of the horse's neck flooded into her fingers and she could feel the rough hairs of his mane over her hands and the still-icy metal of her rings. She heard Farren yawning from beside her and looked around at his shadowy form in the darkness. His eyes glittered bright white and light glinted from his armour. She glanced away from him to the east.

"Moonrise," said Farren, leaning over almost in front of her and pointing. The pale half-disk of light climbed above the horizon, scattering shadows from clouds, trees and bushes around them. Another light burned to the east of them, a point of yellow light amidst the silvery-blue and black. *Is that an inn? No – it's too far from the main road to make that likely.*

"And we're sleeping out of doors," she said. "Time to look for a good place."

She headed Storm around Princess to the right-hand side of the road. His hooves echoed as he crossed the cobbles. *Should I change shape and look for a place? I'd certainly see better.* Her eyes flicked in and around the clumps and tufts of grass, the boulders and the trees, looking for shelter.

"Over there," Farren said. He put Princess to a trot and headed towards a spinney of silver poplar trees, where the white undersides of the young leaves flickered in the moonlight. A few scattered bushes under the poplars cut the keen wind off from the space shaded by the branches. "Perfect," she said. She slithered off Storm's back and began stripping the tack off him.

They turned the horses loose to graze and fished around inside the saddlebags for the blankets they had brought. "Will you be staying in your normal shape?" Farren asked. He shook out the folds of one of the blankets and looked up at her. The shadow of a branch fell across his face, hiding it momentarily as a gust of wind stirred the trees.

"I think I will," she said. "It's not that cold and I know shifting shape unsettles Storm. I don't want to be kicked while I sleep. So you do have to share the blankets after all." She knelt down and patted the grass, feeling for rocks, roots and hidden branches. The ground seemed reasonably smooth, and she spread her two blankets out flat.

"Stormwolf, sweetheart, I wish I could share them with you." He drew his sword and lightly laid it down in the grass beside the saddles between them. "One more year to wait."

Kneeling up, she drew her own sword and placed it beside his with a small chink of metal against metal. She tilted her head back as he bent down towards her, and kissed him on the mouth. "Goodnight, beloved," she said, squeezing his hand. "Hope the ground doesn't grow rocks underneath you as you sleep."

"Or underneath you, sweetheart. Sleep well."

She rolled herself up in her cloak and blankets and settled down with her head on a saddlebag. *This one must have that bacon I won in the race in it,* she thought, scenting the smoky tang rising and mingling with the smell of leather. She heard Farren moving around behind her, then the soft rustle of blankets and grass. Lying awake, she listened to the night sounds around her: the hissing of the wind through the grass, the fluttering of the new leaves, the rhythmic sound of the horses cropping grass nearby and, very faintly, Farren's slow breathing. *One more year to wait,* she thought, wriggling around to avoid the hilt of her dagger digging into her. *One more year until I can sleep in the circle of your arms and feel your warmth around me.* She stared up at the stars overhead as the branches swayed and shifted with the wind. Drowsy warmth crept up from the cloak and blankets and engulfed her completely.

***

Farren awoke before dawn the next morning, cold and muscles aching. He rolled over and felt the grass damp beside him. Inhaling, he caught the clean smell of grass mingled with the sweet-sharp scent of spring flowers. Overhead, a bird chuckled. He sat up, pushing the dewy blankets off himself, and looked around for the horses. The skin on his cheeks and chin itched, and he raked at it with his fingernails. *No chance of a shave before we reach the*

Watchtower, he thought. *I wish I had some water with me. And not just for shaving with, either.*

He stood up, rubbing warmth into his chilled arms, then whistled for the horses. Princess whinnied from somewhere to his right. He waited, idly folding his blankets into neat rolls and stuffing them into the saddlebags. Princess and Storm trotted around the trunks of the silver poplar trees. "Good lass," he said to his mare, patting her neck as she nuzzled at him, warm breath huffing over his face. "Are you ready to keep going?"

He turned away from Princess and reached for his sword. After wiping the dew off it with the saddlebags, he slid it into the sheath on his right hip. Azariel lay like a shadow in the grass, her long figure wrapped in dark grey blankets and her face veiled by her black hair. Crouching by her side, he gently shook her shoulder until he saw the glint of her eyes opening behind her hair. "Stormwolf, wake up. Time to eat and get on the road again," he said gently.

She smiled and sat up, shaking the tangled locks back from her face so that they hung down on one side of her head, cascading over her shoulder like a horse's mane. Digging her knuckles into the dark circles beneath her eyes she yawned. "Good morning, beloved," she said. She shrugged and twisted her shoulders, grimacing a little. "Bacon is very lumpy to try and sleep on, and so are stones. I thought I'd avoided them all last night." She rolled onto her hands and knees and looked down at the flattened grass where she had lain. "I should have left the bacon behind."

A pang of hunger shot through his stomach and his mouth filled with water. "Bacon is always better inside than out. Shall we cook some up?"

She rolled her blankets roughly around each other then reached for her sword. "Have we got time for a fire? We've got to beat the Claws to the Watchtower. We might be too late already."

"Don't panic, but you're right." He strode over to the saddles and opened Princess's saddlebags. "We'll make do with bread and cheese for now. A pity – I would have liked some of that bacon." He fished out a loaf of bread and a small wax-coated round of cheese. "We'll get something decent to eat at the Watchtower with Colonel Annan and his company."

He hacked off a rough chunk of the bread with the dagger Azariel had given him and tossed it to her. Then he cut another for himself before paring the wax off half the cheese and slashing the cheese into slices. His stomach growled eagerly as he bit into the springy bread. He munched at the slab of bread and cheese, strapping the saddlebag back up as he ate. "Can you hand me the waterskin?" he asked. "I think it's with that one you were sleeping on."

She passed the leather bag to him and he threw his head back and drank from it before he handed it back to her. With the dry crumbs from his mouth washed away, he got to his feet and whistled the horses back. He picked up Princess's tack, and gently slung the saddle across the chestnut mare's back. From behind him came the jingle and squeak of Azariel working with Storm. Before he mounted, he checked the arrows in the quiver at his left hip and settled his bow back into its grip on the saddle. He paused for a moment, running his hand over the bow's curves and recurves. Then he put his toe in the stirrup and swung himself onto Princess's back.

He lightly tapped the mare's sides with his heels and she moved off. Soon they were travelling at a brisk canter alongside the cobbled road. He rocked gently with the fluid motion of the mare, feeling her tug very lightly at the reins. The fresh morning breeze ruffled his hair, and his left cheek felt colder than his right. *Northeast wind still, but it's cooler than yesterday.* He glanced over at Azariel. A few wisps of her hair blew across her face towards him. He smiled, then let his eyes travel across the expanse above him. *Will it rain today?* Long fingers of cloud reached across the sky, white except where they were tinged with the flush of early morning sunlight. *Good. We won't get wet. I hate riding in drizzle.*

He checked Princess to a walk and heard Storm's hoofbeats slowing in unison on his left. An indistinct shape had appeared on the highway and was approaching. He watched the other traveller draw closer and heard the rumble of iron-bound cartwheels and the clop of donkey's hooves. A woman was driving a donkey-cart loaded with spring vegetables towards the city. "All the traders going to market in the capital," he said to Azariel.

"She'll hear you," she answered. "And she's the first in a long line of traders. Look further and you'll see them coming."

He watched the procession of people coming the other way, returning the greetings the traders called out to him and Azariel as they passed. Some rode in carts or on horseback; others trudged on foot. One after another they came: a donkey so laden with vegetables that all he could see was its fuzzy grey ears, muzzle and feet protruding from the bunches of spring onions and young carrots; a litter of piglets scurrying over the road and squeaking to each other like giant pink mice; a plump woman carrying large baskets of eggs and butter that nearly overbalanced as she stumped puffing along the road. He noticed a few Elendi traders among the Kingdom folk: fishmongers and sellers of metal goods, and even a huge wain that carted tree trunks, drawn by gigantic horses and driven by burly, bearded men. He closed his eyes and breathed deeply as the clean, sharp aroma of pine wafted from the passing timber wain, letting it block out the stench of manure the piglets had left.

By mid-morning, the flood of traders had dwindled. The great expanse of Lake Tapatdehi lay to the south, mirroring the sky. "We're nearly there," he said to her, pointing. "Hope we get there in time."

They rode for another hour before he spotted the tall grey Watchtower. Slowly, it grew in front of them. "Have the Claws come yet?" he asked her. "You're the tracker of us two. Can you see anything?"

She glanced from side to side. "We're in time," she said, looking back up at him. "There are only a few hoofprints and tracks, and no signs of a fight."

"Good," he said. "We can ease up a little." He slowed Princess back to a walk and let her plod along, head slumped down, as they rode into the shadow of the tower. Under the stone walls, he dismounted and began to unsaddle his mare as she grazed. Azariel banged on the Watchtower door. "Who's that?" called a voice from the top of the tower.

"Azariel Stormwolf and Farren Blackarrow, *minyasti* of the Kingdom. We're here on an urgent message," she called back up to the sentry.

The Watchtower door flew open suddenly and a barrel-chested man with close-cropped brown hair strode out. "Blackarrow!" the man shouted, and slapped Farren on the shoulder, making him gasp and drop Princess's bridle. "Ouch! Missed your cloak and got your armour."

"Good to see you again, Annan," panted Farren, shaking the other man's hand. "And that blow hurt me just as much as it hurt you. You certainly haven't got soft living on Taramaritan's cooking."

Annan laughed, then greeted Azariel with a bear hug. "Good to see you both here again. Now, why are you here and what's this urgent errand of yours? Don't tell me the Wayasti have invaded again."

"Not quite as bad as that." Farren picked up the bridle. "The Yellow Claws are on the move and heading here to try to take that Stone of yours, if the Nightraven report is true."

"Hellfire!" The other man's face changed from a grin to a grimace. "That pack of rebels again. I thought we had wiped them

44

out in the war last year. Obviously not. Just as well you came. By why you and not some other messenger come to tell us?"

"Stessa... the Nightravens report that there may be a sorcerer with them, although they're not sure," said Azariel.

"Oh, so golden girl Stessa's been trailing them, has she? Always thought she was a Nightraven. She isn't coming too, is she?" He gave a low whistle and rolled his eyes before laughing loudly. "The lads would like that. It might stop them pulling my leg for a few minutes." Then he frowned. "But, now, a sorcerer. That's no good. Come inside and we'll talk plans."

"I'd better take the horses down to the lake first." Farren looked over at Princess. She was rolling on her back beside a green tangle of blackberry and gorse, snorting and churning up the lush grass. Her hoof caught in the shrubs, and she jerked and twisted it free.

"Don't trouble yourself, Blackarrow. One of my lads can do it." He turned away from the door towards the inside of the tower. "Hey, Varro! Take the *minyasti's* horses down to the lake for a drink and a feed, will you? Thanks!"

Farren reached for Azariel's hand and threaded his fingers through hers as he stepped over the threshold behind Colonel Annan. He ran his eyes over the familiar objects on the ground floor of the tower: the dark, dusty stables; the sandbarrel for cleaning chainmail; the bales of hay piled in a heap and the strings of onions against one wall. "Just like being back at the Watchtower of the West," he whispered in her ear. He dropped back behind her, still clasping her hand as they reached the circular steps and followed Annan up to the hatch and pulley that led to the round common room at the top.

The gurgle of pouring liquid came through the square opening. He scrambled up into the room and Annan handed him a mug. "A bit of your favourite cider," the Colonel said. "A drink to whet your appetite before lunch. Well timed, you two."

One by one, the soldiers drifted in and ate. Farren sipped at the cider as he leaned back on his stool against the wall. Azariel took a long draught from her mug, then walked to the window. "I'm sorry I ordered Taramaritan back to the capital and left you here on your own," she said.

"What are you talking about?" Colonel Annan's face flushed and he swung around to look Farren in the eyes. "What have you been telling her about me and Taramaritan?"

"Nothing at all," he replied, almost biting his tongue with trying not to laugh. "You're telling her yourself."

"What I meant was I'm sorry I left you here with no *minyast* to guard the Stone. I should have sent in a replacement. We needed her to do some work in the capital." She turned away from the window and raised her mug to her lips. Her eyes flashed sapphire at the Colonel. "But I doubt that you'd find anyone to replace her, from your point of view."

"You're as bad as my lads! Enough of that and onto the Claws. I'll have to make use of the two of you strategically, just in case there is a sorcerer or two with them. I saw a bow on your saddle, Blackarrow. Any good with it?"

"Why do you think I took the name Blackarrow?" He threw back his head and drained the last mouthful of the cider, rolling the sweet fire around his mouth. "I've taken a good hunting trophy with it, and killed a few Claws. Does that pass as good enough?"

"Good enough in my books. And what's your weapon, Azariel? You don't have any of those Nightraven tricks about you, do you?"

The flash in her eyes died and she looked at the floor, letting her hair fall forwards around her face. "Plain swordswoman," she replied. "And I can handle a spear."

"Great! And you're both fighting *minyasti*. Now I'll have to think over what to do next." Colonel Annan picked up the bottle of cider from the table and splashed out a stream of pale gold into his mug. "Have another drink, either of you?"

The Colonel sat silently all through the midday meal of oatcakes, cheese and salad. The other soldiers chattered among themselves and asked for gossip and news from the capital. After lunch was over, Farren climbed to the fighting top of the tower and sat down with his back to the wall. He leaned against the warm stone and closed his eyes. Through the rough floorboards beneath him, he heard Annan's voice rising and falling, interrupted from time to time by other voices. *I really ought to go and get the horses inside the building,* he thought. He shrugged and eased a cramped muscle in his shoulder. *But not yet. They need to be able to graze for a bit longer. They've had it hard with the journey almost straight after the racing and jumping.* He stretched out his legs and relished the warmth of the sunlight on them. A slight giddiness wrapped around him. *I shouldn't have had that second mug of cider on a practically empty stomach.* He yawned and shook his head, trying to clear it. A bumblebee lazily droned past and landed on the crenulations, creeping slowly over the chipped edges of the stone. His eyelids felt heavy and soon he let his head drop. Warmth and light-headedness overtook him and swallowed him.

A cold shadow fell over him, cutting off the sunlight. He jolted awake, a sudden icy thrill shooting through him. Azariel was standing over him, the yellow light of afternoon striking a gleam off her hair and high cheekbones. "Have you slept well?" she asked.

"Too well," he said, stretching life back into his limbs. "Where are the horses? I was going to bring them in before the Claws came."

"I stabled them earlier before I went on watch up here earlier this afternoon. You've been asleep for quite a while." She held out her arm and tugged him to his feet. "You were good to look at, sleeping there. Even better than the springtime scenery in the sunshine." She slid a hand through his hair and tilted her head up to kiss him on the cheek.

He rested his hands on the thick folds of the black cloak on her shoulders. "I'm sorry. I should have been awake to help get ready for the attack. I heard Colonel Annan talking to the men before I dozed off." His grip tightened on her shoulders as a pang of anger flooded through him, then relaxed. "What am I going to do now?"

"You're on first watch tonight," she laughed. "You've made ready for that at least. You'll be up here keeping watch while the rest are sleeping. So don't fret about time lost, beloved. Sleeping only volunteered you for night duty."

He turned away from her and leaned on the wall, looking out to the northwest where the mountains stood faint and purple against the yellow sky. Piles and plumes of dark cloud hung behind the mountains, whipped by the wind. A pair of geese flew overhead towards the lake, calling out to one another. His gaze flicked after them, then back to the tree-studded plains. The wind hissed around the tower, carrying the high bleating of lambs. "I'm surprised the Claws haven't reached here already," he said. "They can travel fast when they have to."

He felt her ease in beside him, her hair tickling his cheek. "I don't think you'll have to wait much longer," she said softly. "Look over there."

He looked where her long white finger was pointing. Three or four bowshots away from the tower to the west, he spotted a haze of dust thrown against the sunlight from behind a line of poplars. Several starlings swooped and darted up from the trees, shrilling in alarm. Straining his eyes, he picked out a few dark shapes moving among the trunks of the poplars beneath the trees. A few heartbeats later, he recognised them as a party of people on horseback. Something flashed on the foremost rider. *Sunlight on armour.* "It's them," he said aloud. "We'd better sound the alarm."

CHAPTER FOUR

Azariel swung down the ladder into the common room. "They're here," she said over her shoulder to the other soldiers before racing down the steps. With one hand on the cold stone wall to keep her balance, she hurtled down the circular stairs. She leaped over the last few steps to the floor. The landing jolted her hard, but she collected herself and ran over to the door. Looking around for the heavy beam that pinned the door closed, she saw it leaning against the doorsill. She grabbed the beam and heaved it into its place, the rough wood jabbing splinters into her fingers. With satisfaction, she heard it thud into place. *Now for the windows,* she thought. *It's good there's not many in the lowest level.*

She pulled herself up onto a haybale to reach the first shutter to seal off the main windows. The dust lay thickly on the wooden slats and blackened her hands as she tugged the shutters shut with a squeak. She dusted her hands off on her thigh and vaulted backwards off the haybale. Half-running, she went into the privy to close the second window of the ground floor. She wrinkled her nose at the stench in the small room. *They need some more camphor in here, or aromatic resin,* she thought. Fiercely biting her breath back, she quickly closed the shutters. *But better a stink inside than an enemy. But they really ought to do something about that.*

She stood by the door, her rapid breath drawing in the earthy smell of the stables. Dust motes danced in the slim beam of evening light that filtered through the shutters. She pressed her ear to the door and tried to ignore the sounds of the other soldiers arming and preparing, and listened intently for the sound of the Claws' approach. *I'd hear better in wolf form, but I need to stay in my usual shape for this.* She listened to the alarm calls of birds, shrill, clear and close. Then she caught the sound of horses whinnying, stamping and snorting. Then silence. She drew her sword from its sheath, its rasp loud in the alert hush. She pressed herself against the stone by the door and raised her sword ready to meet any Claw that breached the door.

She heard footsteps to her right and turned her head to see Colonel Annan leading four other soldiers down the stairs. They arranged themselves in a semicircle around the door and stood with their naked swords ready. *I'm glad they're here,* she thought. *The door is the weakest part of the door and there's no way I can hold it alone.*

Farren crouched by the stone battlements at the top of the Watchtower, eyes darting to and fro over the flat grassland beneath him. Around him, five other soldiers positioned themselves about the circular fighting top. His hand tightened around his bow. *Nice of them to bring it up for me.* He felt for the arrows in his quiver. One by one, he clicked them out of their clips and rested them against the wall, ready to use. Still looking over the battlements, he took one arrow and fitted it to his bowstring. Again, he glanced around, looking at the Watchtower's chief archer. All the other men were crouching like he was, looking like bowmen lurking beside the castellations of the battlements. A golden ray of sunlight shone over the walls and lit up the brilliant scarlet of a soldier's cloak. Beneath him, he noticed another light starting to glow in the twilight, a faint blue sheen from the stones of the wall. *The light of the Stone,* he thought. *When the sun sets, it should blaze in a fountain of blue until morning, as long as the Stone stays in its place.*

He glanced over the battlements once more. The Claws had ridden within a bowshot of the tower. The riders had dismounted and huddled together. He waited, heart drumming in his ears. The cluster of Claws broke up and moved towards the Watchtower on foot. *When are we going to counterattack?* he wondered, flicking his eyes over to the chief archer. In the half light, he saw the commander's hand curling around the bowstring. *Now.* Farren felt himself tensing, sinews taut along his arms, legs and back; he forced himself to relax. *You don't want shaky hands, Blackarrow,* he told himself. He took a few deep breaths to calm the tension and gathered himself to spring up and draw. *Where shall I shoot first?* He glanced over at the Claws again and picked out one of the dark shapes as a target. The sinew of the bowstring bit the inside of his fingers as he drew his bow, cutting into the ridges of hardened skin.

From his left, he saw the chief archer move, and he sprang to his feet. His right arm held the bow rigid before him as his left glided backwards. He let the string loose and felt the feathers and string sting his forearm as the arrow hissed down. It plummeted and buried its head in the ground by the heel of the man he had aimed at. *Damn! One arrow wasted.* He stooped to fit another arrow to the string. He looked for a target and chose a bulky axeman. He shot again, but as he loosed, he heard answering shots hissing upwards from the Claws, soft deadly whispers beneath the voices of the Claws. He ducked behind the battlements as they flew past. Pressing close to the gently glowing stonework, he peered over the battlements again to look at the Claws, trying to pick out one of the archers among them as his next target. *I can't waste a single arrow.*

The Claws, lit up by the soft blue stonelight, approached the tower in groups of three: one archer, one axeman and one carrying a huge rectangular shield in each group. The shield bearer he was watching swung the shield over his head, tilted slightly towards the battlements. Farren trained his bow at the trio of men, hunting heart and lungs to aim at. Three pairs of legs marched under the shield, looking like an oversized insect. *Cunning,* he thought. *Very clever of them.* He smiled and twisted the ring on his left hand. *That shield can keep arrows off. Can it keep off fire?* He laid his bow down and tightened his fists. *King of Heaven, give me the fire I need.* The metal of his rings heated and a wash of fire spread out from them through his veins, prickling and tingling at his wrists and shoulders. He ran his tongue around the inside of his lips and drew a deep breath.

Catlike, he bounded onto the walls in one smooth movement. *"Zyrasti, virgasai!"* he shouted, lifting his arms, palms out and fingers splayed. The last hairline of burning gold vanished below the horizon to the west and the Watchtower spouted and blazed cobalt light in answer. Fountains and lightnings of blue burned around him, eye-searingly bright. He struck fire blindly down towards the Claws, orange after-images crawling in front of his eyes. Frightened yells and shouts of *"Minyastin!"* came from the foot of the tower.

He reached one hand to the block of stone beside him to steady himself while his eyes cleared. *They think I caused the Watchtower to blaze. And it was only the Power's perfect timing!* Energy built up and burned behind his fingertips and he flashed it down in emerald green fire. One of the shield bearers crumpled up, collapsing under the length of the shield. Several bows swung towards him, arrows glittering in the blue light. He dropped down backwards behind the stone balustrade, hearing the hiss and whine of arrows overhead. The crash of an axe striking hollow wood reached his ears. *They've reached the door! King of Heaven, keep Azariel safe!*

The axe thundered again and again, followed by the tearing sound of wood splintering and breaking as the door began to give way.

Azariel saw the tip of an axe slice through the ash-wood planks of the door. Her heartbeat drummed almost as loud as the axeblows in her ears. Her hand tightened around the hilt of her sword, digging the metal of her rings into the callused pads on her palms. *It won't be long now until they're through.* The muscles in her legs felt as poised and triggered as mousetraps, ready to leap. She bared her teeth, watching the door shudder at each blow. Through the small gap torn by the axe, she glimpsed a flash of green flame cutting through the wash of blue light. *Farren's at work.*

Footsteps shuffled beside her and she heard breathing as a hand touched her arm. Colonel Annan leaned close to her. "Don't use your sword," he whispered. "Use your fire."

"Not mine – the Power's," she replied almost automatically. Annan had silently walked back to his place, blue light gleaming off his naked sword. *Never mind,* she thought. *This is no time for lessons.*

She checked her rings and twisted the lapis lazuli on her left hand so that it sat straight. She steeled herself and waited for the touch of the Power. A quicksilver burning began at the top of her head and flooded down her spine and arms, leaving her rings hot and her fingers tingling. Excitement and eagerness dried the inside of her mouth. The door shuddered again as an axehead smashed through, widening the gap. The axe wavered backwards and forwards, squeaking as it was pulled loose. *A few more blows and they'll be through.* She tossed her head, flicking back the strands of hair from her face and pulled herself up to her full height. *I'm ready for them. Let them come!*

Farren heard the boom of the axe on the door and felt his stomach knot. *Azariel, Azariel, I hope you'll be safe down there,* he thought, fighting a momentary impulse to race down the tower to fight beside her. He looked back down at the Claws and saw them circling the door. One man's shield had fallen. Again, he stood on the wall and felt the white-hot blaze of flame burst from his hands towards them. One Claw dropped beneath the fire. Three archers broke off from the group and swung their bows up towards him. Instantly, he ducked back behind the shelter of the stones as the arrows sliced through the air.

He heard the soft, deadly sound of an arrow striking flesh beside him. The archer beside him threw back his head and howled, letting his bow drop. The man pitched forwards, half draped over the wall. *Hellfire! He's been hit by the arrows meant for me.* Farren bit his lip and glanced back over the battlements. The Claw archers were fitting arrows to their strings again. *I don't know how badly they hurt that fellow the first time, but this time they'll finish him off. I've got to pull him down now.* He stood up and gently hauled the wounded soldier up by his shoulders. He pulled him away, then dropped down below the level of the wall. One of the Claw arrows struck stone and splintered with a sharp crack, but the others hissed overhead. The wounded man sagged to his knees. One arrow jutted out from his shoulder, trapped by bone and armour, and a second transfixed his thigh. *Thank the Power! He'll live, if his greater veins are untouched.*

Farren dragged the man to the centre of the tower, keeping low. "I'll see what I can do for you," he said softly.

"Don't touch me; it hurts!" The man's face contorted. "Just leave me. I'm going to die! It's gone too deep into my thigh and chest to do anything."

"Rubbish," Farren answered. "Haven't you ever taken that bow of yours hunting? If they had got your lungs, you'd be spitting blood by now, and the other one's on the outside of your thigh, not the inside." He reached for his dagger. "I'm a minor healer. Keep still and I'll get that one out of your thigh and cut the other down to size so you can go down and rest up."

Farren bent over the other man. "Grit your teeth," he said. He began to whittle at the tough wooden shaft of the arrow through the man's thigh, ready to snap it. From below came the splintering and crashing of axes on the doors, followed by fierce, eager shouts from the Claws. *They're through the door! What do we do now from up here?*

Azariel saw the axes rip the door to pieces and the jagged hole filling up with the dark shape of the axeman who lunged through, swinging his weapon at the soldier nearest the door. Her palms and fingertips prickled as she raised them. Dark blue fire crackled out of her ring and the axeman fell. Several of the figures halfway through the door hesitated. Trembling fire built up in her hands and arms again, and she rocked to and fro on her heels, waiting. Behind her, Colonel Annan bellowed, "Get the archers down here! We need all the men we can get!"

Footsteps rang on the steps and faded away as the doorway filled with Claws. She threw scarlet and black fire at them, feeling it break shimmering white-hot from her hand as it flew towards the Claws. One Claw dropped his axe and crumpled to the floor. Another axeman leaped over the bodies and threw his axe at Colonel Annan, ripping his sword out in the same movement.

She dodged to one side as the axe chopped through the air. More Claws filled the doorway, ripping it wider. *How many are there out there? Are five of us enough to stand in this gap?* She punched a bolt of multicoloured flame towards them from her opal ring and smelt a tinge of smoke in the air. *Oh, no! Don't tell me I've set the door on fire!* She scanned the wood and picked out a small patch of charring in the grain.

A snarl sounded close to her, then a heavy blow cracked onto her collarbone and she staggered backwards. A man was towering over her, sword whistling at her in a backslash. *Why did I look away?* Her hand flashed her blade out and up in defence. Sword met sword in a bone-jarring shock as she countered her attacker's stroke. Other shouts and clashes of more metal on metal rang in her ears as she shifted and dodged, looking for a chance to stab at the Claw. Tense and swift, she drove the man's sword back as it slashed at her, stepping further and further back from the door. *I'll finish against the wall, and then I can't run anywhere else.* She felt her sword skewer the man's arm and wrenched it free as his blade hacked down at her undefended body. *But I won't finish there if I can get my left hand up.*

She bared her teeth in a snarl as she felt his blow strike her chest, knocking the breath out of her as the links of chainmail drove into her. Fighting for breath, she lunged at her attacker, making him step back a pace to counter the thrust of her sword. She threw a punch with her left at him, fire burning down her hands and blazing in silver lightning out of her lapis lazuli. The metal of her ring pulsed with heat as the fire took the man in the chest, felling him.

She staggered forwards, sheathing her sword. Her mouth had become as dry as parchment and her heart was thundering in her ears. *Life's good; stay alive,* it throbbed in the veins in her throat. The ground floor swarmed with Yellow Claws and a chorus of alarmed and angry neighing came from the stabled horses. She flung bolt after bolt of lightning into the Claws, aiming for the axemen. More bodies dropped, but the Claws surged in further. Footsteps pounded on stone behind her, growing louder. *Farren and the others are down. Now we'll drive them off.*

Farren's shoulder pushed into hers and she caught the familiar outdoor smells that clung to his cloak. "My fault," he whispered. "I left off to help someone who got hit."

"Not your fault." Her hand sought his. "Now, let's fight together."

She felt his fingers twine through hers and she smiled. *Two are better than one...* she quoted mentally. Tossing her hair back from her shoulders, she braced herself. "Kingdom soldiers, fall back!" she ordered. Heat quivered in the palm of her right hand, then leaped out at the Claws, scarlet at first, then turning blackish-purple in the blue light. Fire flashed from Farren, catching the corner of her eye. Behind her, she heard the shuffles of the Kingdom soldiers, followed by cheering as bolt after bolt of flame sprayed the inside of the tower and dropped Claw after Claw.

The cobalt blue light in the walls flickered and vanished. She strained her eyes through the darkness as the whoops and yells of the remaining Claws made the air ring as the Kingdom soldiers fell suddenly silent. Shapes filled the gap in the door, blotting out the starlight that faintly shone through, pale after the brilliant blue. "They've got it somehow," she hissed at Farren. "Come on." She let go of his hand and turned to race up the stairs to the common room where the Stone was kept.

She pushed through the hatchway into the room. Footsteps thudded on the wooden roof above. "He hasn't got away yet," she whispered. "We could still stop him." She winced as she stumbled and clattered into a chair in the dark. *That's put him on the alert.* She heard Farren fumbling in a corner, and edged her way over to join him by the ladder.

"Hellfire, how many times do I have to kill you?" snarled a voice on the roof. Then scuffling, a whimper and the sound of something heavy falling.

Farren quietly eased himself through the trapdoor onto the roof. He saw the blue glow of the Stone, masked in places by the raider's hand, shining onto the wounded archer who sprawled with his back to the battlements. Farren stepped forwards, his footsteps booming on the floorboards. The raider launched himself backwards over the stone wall and the blue light of the Stone vanished.

Farren rushed to where he had seen the raider disappear. Azariel ran beside him, feet pounding the floorboards in rhythm with his. He groped at the stone wall and felt a rope knotted around a castellation. Azariel's hand brushed over his. "Cut it," she said.

"No," he replied. "Then one of the other Claws will just grab the Stone and we'll have a mad midnight chase. I've got another idea. Grab this and pull for all your worth!" He put her hands around the rope and felt her knuckles tighten around it. Leaning over the battlements, he found more of the rough prickly cord. He seized the rope and heaved, twisting it around his hands to stop it sliding free. One of his boots slipped on the smooth wooden boards beneath him. He braced himself and tugged at the tightly coiled hemp again, feeling the raider's weight resisting him.

Snarls and curses filled the night air from below and he laughed. "He can't stop us pulling him up without breaking his own neck," he chuckled to her. "And listen to him curse! Or, on second thoughts, don't listen. He's got a disgusting vocabulary."

He continued to haul the raider up. The rough hemp bit and burned his hands as he pulled, hand over hand. His muscles ached with the slow effort and dampness broke out on his forehead. The rope jerked wildly in his hands. "He's kicking like a hooked fish," Azariel panted. "The sooner we land him, the better."

The rope thrashed more convulsively and he felt it flaying the skin off the side of his thumb. He bit his lip, ignoring the stinging pain and continued to pull. Then the blue light of the Stone rose over the battlements, shining off the red and yellow insignia of the Yellow Claws. Farren lurched backwards as the Claw lunged towards him from the wall, suddenly slackening the rope. He heard the rasp of Azariel's sword being drawn and reached for his own.

She stepped into the ring of light cast by the Stone, the cobalt glow flashing from her blade, her eyes and her bared teeth. Her sword clanged against the raider's. She slashed and cut the man back, quick and smooth as a cat. The blue stone-light flickered off the steel blades as they whirled and jabbed. Farren darted from side to side, looking for a chance to thrust in at the Claw. Another clash, then the Stone flew from the raider's hand, light flaring around the top of the tower. The Claw screamed and doubled over, clutching at his upper thigh. Azariel's sword flashed in the blue glow again, ripping at the throat. The Claw dropped.

They stood over the fallen man, both breathing hard. The blue light shone onto Azariel's stained sword and the body of the Claw, the yellow insignia on his chest dyed with blood. From below, the shouts and the hoofbeats of the last Claws leaving rose to the top of the tower.

Azariel knelt beside the body and covered the man's face and wounded throat with his cloak. The stink of fresh blood and filth struck up at her and she grimaced. *At least it's not my blood, or Farren's.* She reached for the Stone. Her fingers closed around the warm globe and glowed purple against the light behind. She quickly wiped and sheathed her sword, then cupped both hands gently round the Stone. "It's safe," she said. "Let's get it down into the alcove where it belongs."

"You take it," said Farren. "I want to see if there's anything I can do to help that archer." He pointed to the wounded man lying against the wall behind them. "If he hadn't been here, then the Claw would have got to the bottom before we could get to him. You heard the scuffle – he must have tried to stop the Claw getting away, in spite of having a couple of arrows through him." He rested one hand on his sword hilt and ran the other through his hair. "I hope he's not dead."

She nodded and walked to the ladder. Cradling the Stone in one hand, she cautiously backed downwards, feet feeling for the rungs. She stretched for the next narrow bar and her feet touched the smooth wooden floor. She stepped down and turned towards the alcove in the southern wall of the Watchtower. The Stone's light fell on the small pillar in the alcove. She settled the Stone into its place, screwing her eyes shut tightly as it flared. The smooth surface between the silver filigree cooled slightly. She opened her eyes; the stones of the wall crawled and flickered with blue light.

She drew a deep breath and let it out slowly. The pulsing excitement in her arms and spine faded, leaving her drained and a little dizzy. *A good night's work,* she thought, straightening one of the chairs near the table. *I can't hear any more fighting going on downstairs, so the Claws must have left.* She shrugged her cloak back into place and winced as her armour pushed into the bruises on her shoulder and chest. *Thank the Power that's all that's wrong with me.* She returned to the ladder and began to climb back up to Farren and the other archer.

CHAPTER FIVE

Farren crawled into a hammock slung on the wall of a room halfway up the tower and tugged the rough wool of the blankets under his chin, tired from keeping watch after the skirmish with the Claws. He stretched and yawned, relaxing himself for sleep. The man in the bed on the other side of the room breathed heavily and deeply. Farren closed his eyes to block out the blue glow in the walls. *Azariel must be more comfortable than me down there in the stables.* He shifted and inched forwards slightly, trying to get his head higher than his heels. Smiling, he remembered the lengthy debate between her and Colonel Annan when the Colonel had offered to give up his bedroom to her while he slept in the stable straw. *I could have told him he was wasting his time. My Azariel's stubborn as steel and she never lets anyone, even me, treat her as if she's delicate. Even when she really needs it.*

He rolled onto his side, feeling the swaying of the hammock beneath him. The blankets smelt faintly of lavender and soap. *Well, nothing much happened while I was on duty, but everything's easier now that the raid's been and gone – and we won. Hope that wounded man's comfortable enough. He did well, keeping that raider busy while we came.* He concentrated on his heartbeat and tried to slow it and his breathing. His head became heavy and unmovable, and he drifted into sleep.

***

He was standing up to his waist in water. Waves heaved and crashed around him, foaming green, brown and white. Ahead, he saw the grey-gold shore and the trees of an island. He stepped forwards, obeying the push of the surf that roared about him. Seabirds wheeled above him and he heard them calling to each other. The wind carried the wild tang of salt. Another rush of water foamed about his knees and raced ahead of him, strong as a river. Beneath his feet, the sand slipped away as the wave receded. Five more steps and he stood on damp ground, hearing the sand crunch and grind beneath his water-heavy boots.

Ahead stood a dark tangle of trees that grew close to the coarse grass and sand of the beach. The trees stood utterly silent; not even a whisper of wind stirred them. Darkness and silence permeated the woods, and a cold black mist crept between the tree trunks. His vision seemed to sharpen as he stepped forwards and he perceived a green glow within the woods. A path opened between the trees and glowed with emerald light. He began to tread the path, his footfalls sounding dead and muffled although he walked on stone.

Ahead, he saw a globe of light burning through the darkness that surrounded him. Black forms writhed around it like mist and a stench of rottenness filled his nostrils. His stomach churned. He came closer to the globe of light, which revealed itself as a green Stone, wrapped with silver. A little further forwards and he would be able to grasp it.

Then suddenly, he was flying above the island, looking down on the blackness and on a clearing in the middle. Higher and higher he rose until the air grew cold around him and the island seemed no more than a black speck in the midst of green water that deepened in colour as it spread out from the land. He saw the northern mountains of the mainland, their peaks shining with snow and sunlight. Beneath him lay grasslands, the small southward arm of the mountains, winding rivers shining like threads of light and a green lake, all made tiny by distance. He recognized the landmarks of the Kingdom and looked down from his airy pinnacle to see the Watchtower of the West.

He was falling, falling, falling. Down he rushed at terrible speed, the wind shrieking in his ears and ripping tears from his eyes. Blood hammered through his head and his heart pounded. The ground approached quickly. Soon, he would strike it and be killed.

***

Azariel woke with a start, fingers clutching at the straw about her as she tried to check her fall. She sat up, breathing hard. Horses were shifting and stamping in their stalls and a few footsteps tapped on the wooden floorboards above her. She looked around, heart still racing from her nightmare. *I hope that fall never comes true.* She drew a deep breath, inhaling the oaty tang of the straw, then exhaling the last traces of fear as she shook her hair back from her eyes. *But that's the second dream I've had about the Stone and that island to the north across all that water. I wonder if that's the signal that we've been praying for.* She slid her hands through her hair and scraped out a handful of dried stalks. *I must look like a straw-stuffed scarecrow at the moment. I had better get myself presentable.*

She tossed the frayed blue horseblanket off her legs and carefully wriggled off the straw pile. Groping under a pile of fallen straw, she felt the smooth soft leather of her riding boots. A gust of wind swept around the walls of the Watchtower, followed by the patter of raindrops on the shutters. She shivered. *A rainy day for going back to the capital. I had better make sure our saddlebags are watertight.* She finished shaking straws out from her boots and pulled them on.

She quickly brushed the rest of the tickly straw out of her hair with her fingers and threw her black mane back from her face. One of the horses in the stables nearest her snorted loudly, making her start. She picked up her chainmail, shaking it until it jingled to loosen the stray straws before she pulled it on over her head. The armour settled awkwardly on her shoulders and she yanked and tugged the cold metal links into place before lacing up the high neck and tossing on her cloak. As she buckled her swordbelt around her, she heard footsteps and looked up. Colonel Annan stood at the foot of the stairs. "There you are, lady," he said. "Good morning. It's time for breakfast."

Once upstairs, she sat close to Farren as they ate large steaming bowls of porridge and honey. She added an extra spoonful of honey onto her porridge and stirred it into the gooey mass. *That will help keep us warm as we ride.*

He finished eating and rested his hand softly on hers. "Time to go, Stormwolf," he said. "We've done all we need to do here."

She followed him out of the common room and back down to the stables. Farren unbolted the loosebox where Princess and Storm were crammed. She carefully rolled her gear into the saddlebags and strapped them very tightly shut. "We never ate that bacon," she said, heaving the unopened bag over to the door and catching a trace of the aroma.

"All the more for the two of us back home." He put his two bags down beside hers. "I'm looking forward to having a good hot bath back at headquarters," he said, shrugging and twisting his neck to and fro. "That hammock's left me with my shoulders all wrenched into knots."

She sidled up to him and elbowed him lightly. "I see you've shaved this morning, anyway."

"Of course I have! Having to leave it for one day was bad enough."

She ran a hand over the smooth skin of his cheeks, feeling the hard, sharp line of his jaw. "As smooth as a swordblade," she murmured. His brown eyes looked into hers and she felt her breath and heartbeat quicken as her fingertips tingled. He kissed her, lips velvety and crisp against hers for a brief second. She drew closer to him and pressed her cheek against his.

Storm butted her in the back with his muzzle. She squeezed Farren's bare forearms once, then turned away. They finished packing the gear and saddling Storm and Princess, then led the horses outside.

A gust of wind and drizzle sprinkled across her face as she took her black gelding out and swung herself into the saddle. To her left, she heard the scrape and gentle squeak of Farren doing the same. A pale sheen of rain hid the lake to the south, leaving only bushes, clumps of grass and a few dark trees visible. "What a foul day to be riding in," he said.

"Some people, unlike you, don't mind drizzle." She turned her head to look at him. A fine mist of water droplets had caught in his hair and on the shoulder of his cloak, covering it with little silver beads.

"It gets into everything," he grumbled, drawing the hood of his cloak over his head so that his red hair was hidden by brilliant scarlet. "I wish it would rain decently or not at all. And we've got to take things slowly after all the horses have been doing. We're going to be riding nearly all day!"

"As long as I don't end up covered in mud, I can tolerate it." She gathered up the reins and hauled Storm's head up from the fresh grass. "Let's go."

She eased into the rhythm of riding, swaying with Storm's easy canter. The drizzle fell, plastering her hair damp and lank onto her cheek. A thin cold trickle of moisture worked its way down the back of her neck. She reached behind her head and pulled the hood of her cloak up. She rode in silence, hearing only the squeak of the leather tack, the thudding and squelching of eight hooves in soft mud and the gentle tapping of light rain on her hood.

"What will we do once we get back to headquarters?" he said, voice muffled by the thick woollen hood.

"Get cleaned up and rest from the ride, I suppose. The horses, especially, will need a long rest." She reined Storm in to an easy walk and shook the hood back from her head slightly to look at Farren.

"I didn't mean that; I'm talking about after that. What work will we be doing?"

She recalled her two dreams of the island and the Stone, images of black smoke and foaming water flooding through her mind. "I think I know," she said. "I've had dreams..."

He turned his head, brown eyes keen and intense. "You too? What were yours?" The two horses inched closer together so her knee almost knocked into his.

"The Stone of Earth – the green one – and seeing it in a dark place on an island in the middle of a great expanse of water to the north."

"My dream exactly. And I had it twice."

"Last night?" She saw the quick flash in his eyes as he nodded. "I think this is the answer to our prayers about where to search next."

He ran one hand across his forehead, sweeping off the rainwater and shaking the drops off his hand. "North through the mountains again. At least it will be easier this time, as it's spring now. The phantoms won't be there to bother us either if we have to travel up the Illin-Ast. But we'd still better let the horses rest for a few days before we set off anywhere."

"And let the drizzle clear so we don't have to ride in it, too, I suppose," she laughed. "How very convenient!"

They bandied plans around as they rode on through the rain. By the time they reached the capital, her legs felt stiff and numb from riding and her cloak had become heavy with water. Hunger pangs gnawed at her stomach and the acrid smell of wet wool dominated the air around her. *Not much longer now, not much longer now. Then we can get dry, warm and fed.* Firelight and candlelight shone warmly from the houses surrounding the main street as she and Farren entered the city.

Once they had stabled their horses, she staggered into the welcoming warmth of the *minyasti* headquarters. A hot bath, dry clothes and a warm meal, then she tumbled into her bed and slept.

Farren woke late the next morning to the sound of rain beating on the roof. *I'm glad we're going to be here inside today,* he thought, slipping his hands behind his head and gazing around the room as he lay in bed. A spider's web shimmered between two tines on the trophy elk's head hanging on his wall. *When did that get there? I haven't been away that long!* He pushed the covers back and shivered in the chilly air. Quickly, he pulled a dry uniform out of the wooden chest beside the bed and pulled it on. *The gear I was wearing yesterday won't be dry yet. At least it'll have a good chance to dry out thoroughly while we talk plans and let the horses rest.* He finished lacing up the neck of his black leather tunic and pulled his boots on before heading to the men's washroom to shave.

When he came into the common room, Janna Greyhawk was sitting at the table with a crumb-covered plate in front of him and a cup of something steaming in his hand. "Good morning, good morning," the older man said as Farren rummaged in the cupboards near the table for a plate and knife. "I didn't see you coming back last night. Did – did everything go all right?"

"The Stone's safe, but they almost got it. But would we be back if it was stolen?" Farren sat down and sawed off some slices of bread and cheese. "And we've got something else to tell you about the Stones and what we'll be doing next, but I'll wait until Azariel and Taramaritan come. It'll sound better coming from the arch *minyaster.*"

"Taramaritan won't be here." Janna reached for his staff and stood up. "She left for Illinlebh-Yan yesterday to buy from the jewel merchants. Apparently her Ringsmith's supplies are running low, especially in rubies. She heard that a group of traders had come up the river from Elend with a good supply from the mines."

Farren laughed. "Who's paying for that?"

"The same person that pays your wages, Farren." Janna stopped walking across the room and swung towards him, blue eyes flashing. "It's part of her job. After that, I think she's going back south again."

"Azariel will be sure to send her there. That leaves only me, you and Azariel in the capital at the moment. Telling you what we're up to won't take long."

Janna strolled across the room and lowered himself into one of the armchairs. "Not quite, not quite. Marian Greenleaf and her husband Verrin Snowcloud arrived from the southeast yesterday. They've already been in for breakfast – you and Azariel are running late today."

"As we spent half the night before last fighting, and travelling the night before that, I'm not surprised."

The door creaked behind him and he turned. Azariel glided in and sat down beside him. He felt her hand searching for his and he reached for her. Her skin felt damp and warm from washing and a scent of rosemary hung about her. He finished eating and carefully cleaned the last few crumbs off his fingers before leaning his elbows onto the table. *I wonder when the other two will come back into the common room. It's a cold day and there's a fire burning here, so it shouldn't be long.* He watched Azariel eating, studying the curve of her lips and glimpsing a flash of her strong white teeth. "Where are the acolytes today?" he asked after a while. "It's quieter than normal in here."

"Off with Marian at the market buying healers' herbs and powders. Both of them have got a trace of healing gift in them, and Marian's making sure she trains it thoroughly." Janna looked up from his armchair, firelight playing softly on his silver hair. "They won't be back until noon."

"We don't need to talk it over now," she said with her mouth half-empty. "We'll head to the study and look at the map before we tell you our plans."

"Well, well," said Janna. "It all sounds interesting. Tell me later and have fun with your maps."

Azariel tore into her bread and cheese and gulped the end of it down. He slid his arm around her waist as she got to her feet and they walked upstairs to the study. Two pigeons huddled on the windowsill, hiding from the rain. They fidgeted as Farren closed the door and one of them purred musically to the other. A balding man in the green robes of a healer, who was sitting at one of the desks with a quill pen in his hand, looked up at them. "Good morning, you two," he said. "Bet you'd rather be here than outside."

"Good morning, Verrin," Azariel replied. "Hope we won't disturb you too much."

"You can't be possibly be noisier than the acolytes are. I'm glad my wife's taken them off for the morning, leaving me in peace to write up all of her new cures into the books." He tapped an inkwell with the end of his quill pen and grinned, exposing the yellow flash of a gold tooth.

Azariel strolled over to a large desk under the window and hooked one of the high-backed chairs out from underneath it with her foot. "We won't take your light if we use this desk, will we, Verrin?"

"Not at all." He bent back over his writing and dipped the pen into the inkwell.

Farren felt a flush of warm blood flooding his face. "Do we have to sit at that desk, Stormwolf?" He shuffled his feet. *Does she have to remind me that I fancied Corinna Sunfire when I was an acolyte? I wish I'd never scribbled her portrait on the desk!*

Her eyes sparkled mischievously at him. "It's got the best light, Farren," she teased.

"I'm finding that map straight away and I hope it's large enough to cover that wretched doodle over. I wish I'd never done it!" He turned to the shelves and flicked his eyes over the two rows of scrolls and books. *It will be a scroll instead of a book, and it will be reasonably well used.* He spotted a tight roll of vellum free from dust and dog-eared at the corners. He reached for it and unrolled it a little way. A blue line ran across the scroll, passing down from a cluster of roughly drawn black triangles, intercepted by a straight line and two castles with curved runes beside them. He smiled. *That's the Illin-Ast running from the mountains to Illinlebh-Yan and 'Zan. This is what we need.* He tucked it under his arm and carried it to the desk by the window. His shoulder still ached from the strain of hauling up the Claw two nights before. He unrolled the map in front of Azariel, wincing as he saw the faded blue picture of a curly-haired woman on the smooth close-grained wood. He pulled the map over the scribble and sat down on the chair Azariel had placed for him.

He ran his eyes over the map, taking in the lines and letters. Rain danced on the roofs of the buildings outside and spattered through the open shutters onto the wooden floor. A few droplets struck the back if his neck. A gust of wind howled around the building, making the windowpanes rattle. The pigeons shifted and fluffed up their feathers. "Well," he said, "where is this island likely to be?"

"Somewhere to the north," she said. "Do you remember the dream, flying over the mountains?" She closed her eyes. "I did that once." Her voice became soft and dreamy. "When I rode the northwest wind to come and rescue you from Crajaval." She sighed.

"Yes. And I remember the dream. I hope we're not going to be flying in reality. That fall in the second dream was terrible." He gently laid his hand on top of hers. "You didn't see an island when you were up riding the wind?"

"I can't remember; I wasn't taking much notice," she laughed. "At least that dream told us enough to know where the Stone is, more or less. What else it meant, we'll find out later."

"When we get there." He squeezed her hand then released it. "We need to know which way to go through the mountains first."

"Does this map show an island to the north? It's not an old map – it's newer than the one over at the library – and may have something on it that others don't. You know what the Elendi sailors are supposed to be like for exploring things."

"I don't see what the age of the map has to do with it, but let's see." He bent over the map and traced a finger lightly across the top of the vellum, making it rustle slightly. He studied the fine drawings of the mountains that ran across the northern frontiers of Wayast, the Kingdom and Helmn. Beyond them, the coast was inked in, but not much more. *A sailor's map,* he thought. *It only shows the coastline of the north and has some strange marks – I think – near those cities on the coasts of the other countries.* He looked further to the north of the map to where the ocean spread to the red margins. At the very edge of the map, a small speck of land had been drawn. "There," he said, pointing to the spot. "And it's the only one. Just to the northeast of the Kingdom and three miles or so out to sea." He raked his hand through his hair. "I'm glad it is shown, even though it isn't named at all. Nobody lives north of the mountains that I know of."

"A map for the use of fishermen." She leaned in front of him so that her long hair hid the map. "It lies due north of the Illin-Ast," she said. "That's good. We could travel up river again. At least we know the way to the source of the river."

"And the trip would be easier than before. But after Moonlady Falls... It's a pity that nobody lives north of the mountains. There's no passes marked and the mountains are only sketched in." He rested on one elbow and stared out the window as he fidgeted with his betrothal earring. "We can navigate by the sun and stars easily enough," he said after a pause. "We'll have to take our chances with the passes and so forth."

"We'll find a way," she said, raising her head to look at him. Her hand slid around his waist and pressed the links of his armour into his stomach. "The Power will help up do it."

He leaned over her so that his cheek touched her soft hair. "You're right," he said, voice just above a whisper. "I haven't forgotten that."

She shoved her chair back from the table. "Well, we've found it. We know how we're going to go through the mountains. Let's tell the others what we're doing."

"Later." He got to his feet and pulled her up by the hand. "We've got until noon before we'll see them all. Let's find somewhere reasonably dry for sword drill."

***

Farren pushed back his chair after the midday meal and looked around at the other *minyasti*. Janna and the acolytes were sitting opposite him, Marian and Verrin to his left and Azariel beside him, arm coiled around his waist. She shifted and sat up straighter as she cleared her throat. "Well, seeing as we're all here, we had better tell you our plans," she said. "You can tell the rest of the Guild at the next council if we're not back by then."

"Good, good," said Janna, tapping his fingertips lightly on the table. "You've been hinting thing since breakfast."

"This is to do with the Stones of Protection, isn't it?" Verrin glanced from him to Azariel and back again. "You two are always doing something about them. I'm sure I overheard you talking about them. Turned up another clue or two?"

"Yes," Farren said. "We've been shown in a dream where they are."

"A dream?" Marian banged her cup down onto the table, spilling several drops of liquid. "I hope you two youngsters haven't been led astray. Dreams are, well, dreams and not always reliable." She turned to Janna. "You need to stop these two youngsters gallivanting off on a hunt for the wind."

"I'm not arch *minyastin*; it's not my responsibility anymore," replied Janna. The acolytes looked at each other and giggled.

Azariel's face and voice hardened slightly. "When you pray for a sign and two people have identical dreams twice each, then you have some idea that a dream is a message and not a whim. I've received Vision several times before and I'm not arch *minyaster* for nothing, even if I am younger than you – and gave you the slip so I could go and fight last year." She shook her hair back from her face. "Anyway, we're off north again. To the north coast to seek an island about three miles off from the shore."

Janna nodded his head. "Good, good. And who will be your deputy while you're gone. If you're not here for *minyasti* council, who will head it? And if you don't return…"

She ran her fingers through her hair and played with the end of a strand. Farren felt her hand tighten around his waist, and he reached out to stroke the black wool of her cloak. "Arruran Silverhand," she said at last. "I would name you, Janna, but if war should come…"

"I'm an oldish fellow with a bad back," completed Janna. "And so I can't ride in the wars any longer. Good choice, good choice. It's such a pity that there are so few fighter *minyasti* now in the whole Guild."

"And you need every one of the healers if war does come!" Marian stood up and put her hands on her hips. Her gold-and-silver hair lashed around her face as she spun towards Janna. "Don't you take us lightly! Who patches you up if you get hurt? Who had to stitch up Azariel when she got that nasty slash from her fight with that Wayasti sorcerer? Not you fighters!"

"Calm down, Marian, dear," said Verrin. "They're not stupid."

Farren picked up the crumbs that had fallen from his plate with the tip of one finger. "You make it sound as though we're all barbarians who couldn't even find our ma—middles with a map. How many pure fighters are there, anyway? And how many pure healers?"

"Well, I do have some fighting talent, seeing as you mention it, but nothing worth talking about." Marian fixed him with her sharp brown-eyed glare. "And, young man, I'm grateful that you didn't say what I thought you were about to say."

He grinned and felt Azariel dig him in the rib. "I wouldn't think a healer would be offended by any body parts that exist." He glanced away from the older woman and at the acolytes. *They're another story, though. I don't want to offend them, especially little Kiihaon.* Kiihaon fixed him with her ice-blue eyes and held his gaze. He blinked and looked away, rubbing his eyes. The acolyte burst into giggles. "Uncle Farren! That's a good one! Couldn't find his manh…"

"Go and wash your mouth out, Kiihaon!" barked Marian.

"Time for me to step in and change the topic." Azariel stood up. "I won't use my position to interfere in the old arguments between the fighters and the healers. Even though I'm pure fighter myself."

"And off we go again," chuckled Janna. "Kiihaon, what have I told you about using your truthreading Gift discreetly?"

"Sorry, Janna Greyhawk," the girl said. "I just wanted to know what he was going to say and it was so funny!"

Farren stared down at the feathery walnut wood grain in the table. He slid his arm around Azariel and pulled her closer to him so her head rested heavily on his shoulder. Her soft hair brushed his cheek and he breathed the scent of rosemary in before kissing the crown of her head. *No need to tell the company that I learned the phrase "couldn't find his manhood with a map" from my Stormwolf. I don't want to shatter the ice maiden front she puts on to the council.* He rubbed his face on her hair as a rush of warmth filled him. *But I know that underneath that – well! I've got something to look forward to when we're married.*

The conversation bounced back and forth between Marian and Janna. "Looks like we've finished discussing our plans," Farren whispered in Azariel's ear. "Now all we've got left to do is let the horses rest a day or so more before we can go."

"And wait until the drizzle lets up," she said. "How convenient."

CHAPTER SIX

The drizzle cleared after a few days, leaving a pale blue sky streaked with gentle white clouds. The cool morning breeze ruffled Farren's hair as they rode out through the city gates. He breathed deeply and savoured the scents of grass and spring flowers. He turned Princess north into the wind along a rough cart-track and nudged her to an easy canter. A short line of poplars ran near the road, bare branches reaching skywards, tipped here and there by the first few bronze leaves. The mountains spread along the horizon in front of them, their snow-tipped peaks gilded by the rays of the sun and standing bright and clear against the sky. A flock of birds swept and scurried across the sky, calling to each other as they flew. A small shiver of pleasure rippled down his back. He looked over at Azariel on his left. Her hair was flowing behind her in the wind, a river of glossy black. Her eyes were shining and her lips were parted. He smiled. *She's enjoying this. So am I.*

She turned towards him, a tendril of hair wandering across her face. "How long shall we follow this road for?"

He ran a hand back through his hair and tried to remember the details on the map. "Well, we could continue to the Watchtower of the North and then go east under the foothills."

"Won't that be a slow way to travel? We'd have to stop at the Watchtower for a courtesy call to whoever's there – Arruran Silverhand, probably – and we wouldn't get to the Illin-Ast gorge until after nightfall."

"The other thing we could do is go cross-country to the Illin-Ast. The sky's clear, so we won't miss our way to the gorge."

"What about farmland?" She shrugged her cloak back into place, the links in her chainmail glittering and sparkling as the sunlight caught them. "We're in the middle of calving and lambing season, and we don't want to upset the farmers. They pay the taxes that feed us, you know."

He saw a flock of sheep grazing by the side of the road and watched them amble away from the cart-track as he passed them. A lamb that had been lying on its side enjoying the sunshine scrambled to its feet and galloped, tail whirling behind it, after its mother. "There's cart-tracks and cattle-tracks criss-crossing the plains to all the little hamlets and villages. We can take them."

"So when do we stop heading due north?"

He screwed up his eyes and looked around for the sun, then down to the break in the mountains. "We'll ride for about another half hour, then we'll turn off at the next crossroads we find after that."

"Good idea. Come on." Her fingers plucked at the bridle and Storm's head lifted, ears pricked. The black gelding snorted as she thumped his flanks, and he lengthened his stride into a gallop.

He slackened the reins and let Princess chase after the other horse. Azariel turned her head and looked back, her hair masking most of her face as she rode. She laughed at him over her shoulder through the flying black strands. "I'll catch you yet," he called after her, urging Princess on.

Princess levelled with Storm, and Farren edged her across the path of the gelding. Azariel lurched forwards as her horse slowed abruptly from a gallop to a trot. He put out his arm to steady her shoulder. "Careful," he said.

"I can keep my balance," she said, raising one hand to stroke his. "And I like you coming close to me like this."

He guided Princess so close to Storm that his leg was pinched between the hot sides of the horses. Bending over, he kissed Azariel on the cheek. Then her arms tightened around him and he found himself losing his balance as she heaved him from his saddle. He relaxed his rider's grip on Princess and slipped his feet from the stirrups so that he lay on his side across Storm's shoulders, with the saddlehorn and saddlebags digging into his stomach. He laughed and gripped her tightly. Then he felt Storm's stride change from the gentle rock of a walk to a canter that shook him wildly. "Slow down!" he shouted, twisting and trying to right himself. "I'll be off if you're not careful!"

He felt himself sliding downwards. He clutched at her to check his fall. To his horror, he saw her lunge sideways as well. *We're both off!* he thought as his weight toppled over backwards. His back slammed into the ground, then something caught him on the side of the head, making his vision spin and explode in coloured lights. The world was filled with nothing but hard ground beneath him, pain lancing through his skull and hot, heavy weight pinning him down. Then the pain cleared and the pressure lifted.

He opened his eyes to see Azariel on her hands and knees above him. "This is the moment people come along and find two *minyasti* rolling in the grass together," she said. "Are you all right?"

He felt for the aching place on his head. His fingers found a tender swelling and he winced as he probed at it. His hands, when he brought them down to look at them, were covered in dust. *Good, there's no blood.* His back screamed at him as he tried to sit up and his spine dug into a rock. "I've got a good whack on the head and some bad bruises on my back, I think." He looked at her and saw blood trickling from a graze just below her elbow. "And it looks like you didn't get off unscathed either. What did you do that for?"

"I'm sorry." She reached for him and helped him to his feet. "I've always wanted to try and sweep you away. The ballads, you know. They often sing of the hero sweeping his lady from the saddle and riding off with her, and I wanted to try it the other way around. It's not as easy as the ballads make out."

He wrapped his arms around her and pulled her close so that her chin dug the links of his chainmail into his collarbone. "It's all right," he said softly. "Next time, I'll do it to you. You're lighter than me and I won't drop you." He rested his head against hers, relishing the soft silk and faint rosemary scent in her hair. "We'd better be on our way, though. Make the most of the sunny weather." He ran his hands through a lock of blue-black at her neck and kissed her before he caught Princess and remounted.

They rode on in silence, hearing nothing except the squeak and jingle of the tack and the drumming of hooves, mixed with the distant bleating of lambs from the surrounding farmland. The mountains grew larger as they rode northwards, edges standing sharp and clear against the sky. The sun rose higher, swinging from east to north as the day warmed.

Azariel looked ahead and saw a thin strip of golden brown dirt cutting across the green of the grasslands and intersecting with the cart road. "There," she said, pointing. "We've ridden for an hour and there's a road running almost northeast. Let's turn off."

Farren crinkled his eyes up and looked ahead. "Yes," he said. "But it's running more east than northeast, so we'd better keep using the mountains to steer by."

"So we head for..." She ran her gaze across the sweep of the mountains from the almost-black slopes covered by the Ulfskin-Aza forest to the golds and browns of the Illin-Ast gorge.

"The gorge, of course."

She nodded, glancing up at the gap where the foothills parted to reveal hazy blue peaks beyond them. With a light touch on the reins, she headed Storm off the cart road onto the thinner track. The track was knobbed and etched with deep ruts, mostly filled with water left by the rain. Patches of thick mud lay in places along the road, pugged and pitted by hooves, and smelling strongly of dung. Storm stumbled a little as he walked, noisily tugging a hoof free from the muck. "We'd better not ruin this road any further," she said.

"Ride by me up here." Farren was steering Princess smoothly along the dandelion-spangled grass. "It's a lot better."

She lost count of how many intersecting tracks they zigzagged along, always heading for the gap in the mountains. The sun rose higher, beating down on her from above instead of shining on her face. A brisk northeast breeze blew, blissfully refreshing in the heat, and she caught the smell of Storm's sweat mingling with her own. Her armour and uniform felt as hot and heavy as a moving oven and a small patch of sticky perspiration stuck her shirt to her back between her shoulderblades. *Sometimes I wish our uniform was any colour other than black,* she thought. *To say nothing of my arch* minyaster's *cloak.* Storm's neck was flecked here and there by little streaks of white foam and the reins had grown slippery. *He's hot too.*

She glanced down at a track that met the one they were riding along, and picked out a cluster of houses among some tall oaks and silver poplars. A stream, still brown and swollen from the rain, ran alongside the new track. "There's a village down there," she said, pointing. "Time for a rest and meal. Storm's getting all sweaty."

"I was looking out for a place to halt, too." He headed Princess down the track that bordered the creek. "We'll see if we can buy some fresh food to eat here and we can save all the dried goods. Do you have much money on you?"

She unlaced the pouch belted to her side. "A fair amount," she replied. "I've got some of my winnings from that race with me."

They unsaddled the horses in the cool shade of a blossoming crab apple tree growing beside the stream at a place where the water flowed through a terracotta pipe under an earthen bridge. Storm got down onto his knees before he rolled, kicking up grass and small clods of mud, while Princess bent her head to the stream to drink. A duck trailing a milling cluster of ducklings waddled away from the horses, quacking indignantly. Azariel watched them go, then turned away, one hand on Farren's arm, towards the houses.

After buying a lettuce and a long loaf of fresh bread, they returned to the crab apple tree. She leaned her back against the gnarled trunk and stretched her legs out in the shade while she ate, feeling her knee stiff and aching from her fall. She unbuckled her cloak and let it drop, then unlaced the neck of her chainmail tunic. The cool spring air breathed over her skin and sent a shiver of relief down her spine. She closed her eyes and rested her head against the knobbly bark of the tree behind her. The warm smell of sunwarmed spring grass and flowers wafted around her.

A few light footsteps pattered nearby and she opened her eyes. A small circle of children had gathered around to watch her and Farren. She smiled at them. *Just like me at that age, staring at every soldier that came through my little mountain village.*

One of the children stepped forwards out of the group, a shy grin on his face. He cleared his throat, then burst into nervous giggles. "Go on," said one of the others.

"We won't hurt you, youngster," said Farren. "You can talk to us if you like."

"Are... are you two both soldiers?" asked the boy.

"Yes," she said. She sat up straight and raised her right hand to show her opal ring. "And we're both *minyasti* too."

The boy's eyes opened wide and he stepped backwards. "What are your horses called?" he asked after a pause.

Farren got to his feet and whistled. The two horses lifted their heads from the grass and strolled slowly over to him. "This one's mine," he said, patting his mare's chestnut neck as she nuzzled him. "She's called Princess. The black one's called Storm. You can pat them if you want to."

The group of children clustered around the horses and began stroking and talking to them. One of the older boys turned to Azariel. "Can we see your swords?"

She stood up and drew her sword, letting the sunlight play and dance off the polished blade. She saw an answering flash from Farren's sword and a glint of challenge in his brown eyes. "A duel?" he said. "Let's give them a demonstration."

"Are you going to have a fight?" asked one child.

"Will there be any blood?" said the boy who had asked to see their swords.

"I hope not," said Farren. He sheathed his sword again. "But you can all sit up here out of the way." He picked up the children one by one and seated them on the bare backs of the horses, three on Princess and four squeezed onto Storm. Azariel kept her eyes fixed on him as she waited, sword poised in her hand as she flexed and readied her muscles for the fight. *I hope my knee's not too stiff for this after that fall.*

"What about your *minyasti* stuff?" asked a girl from the group on Princess's back. "Will you do any of that? I'd love to see that."

"And she wants to do it herself when she's older, don't you, Ronallin?" put in another girl.

"We won't use our fire," Azariel said slowly. She picked out the girl who had spoken first. *Maybe she will. But she's too young to show any signs of quickening yet.* "But I'll show you something I can do afterwards."

Farren unsheathed his sword and held it up and ready in his left hand. Her eyes met his and she fixed his gaze for a few heartbeats, a line of fire flashing in her mind's eye between them.

For one pulse, her heart flared with love and longing for him, before it was swallowed up by the thrill of challenge burning in her. "Ready?" she asked.

"Ready," he answered.

She surged forwards, her blade whirling in the sunshine. With a clash and a jolt, the two swords met. She whipped her sword away for the backslash and again the ring of steel on steel filled her ears as her blade blocked his. She shifted and feinted, dancing in and out of reach, ignoring the dull throbbing pain in her knee. Then she leaped forwards, dealing a flurry of blows at him. She retreated a few paces and gripped her hilt more firmly. She looked into his eyes as he edged nearer, seeing them sparkling and inviting her closer. *He's good,* she thought. *Very good indeed.*

He came at her before she could sidestep out of reach. Raising her sword to block his blows, she stepped backwards. *I'm on the defensive now, and he knows it.* She leaped back and dodged from side to side, trying to avoid the rain of blows on her sword. *I've got to make him work to get at me instead of him making me work.* Again she countered his sword-stroke, driving his blade aside. She heard the rasp of metal sliding over metal, then felt his sword sear into the back of her wrist. *Don't stop to look at it!* Biting her lip to block out the pain, she scythed her sword in a wide semicircle that was checked by his chainmail. A small trickle of blood was running down her wrist and she heard it dripping onto her boots. His eyes darted down. *Now!* She lunged forwards. Stroke after stroke, she drove him backwards.

He stepped out of the shadow of the tree into the sunlight. His eyes screwed up tightly as he stepped into the glare and she thrust her sword forward with a strange, twisting blow that struck onto his, driving the blade down and out of his hand. It fell into the grass with a soft thud. *Done. Now to show them what else I can do.*

She dropped her own sword and stooped towards it. Still crouching, she closed her eyes for half a heartbeat and concentrated on the shape of her body. *I hope this won't terrify them all.* She felt her body shape changing and her head began to spin with a storm of new sensations, smells and instincts. "Wolf! Werewolf!" gasped childish voices.

Head still whirling, she lunged at Farren, jaws open wide. Her front paws scrabbled at the chainmail on his front and one found a hold in the folds of his cloak at his shoulder. The sweet-salt smell of his sweat flooded strong and exciting into her nose. "Steady on," he said, voice tinged with laughter as he held her around the ribcage.

She lolled her tongue out and swiped it over his chin. Then she concentrated again and returned to her own shape. "There," she said, turning to the children. "That's something that I can do. And you got your blood after all." She looked down at the stinging cut on her wrist.

"What's it like being a wolf?" asked the eldest of the boys.

"A lot of fun, but I can't talk and I can't see colours. I hope I didn't scare you too much."

"I've heard my big sister tell some scary stories about werewolves," said another child.

Azariel smiled wryly. "Most people have." She bent for her fallen weapon and slid it into the sheath. "And they're not true, on the whole."

"I'm sorry I cut you." Farren sheathed his sword and stepped closer to touch her wounded arm. He cupped his hands gently around her wrist then tightened over the thin cut. His eyes burned at her, then he bent his head to kiss her fingers. "I didn't mean to do that. But well done, Stormwolf. That's the second time you've disarmed me in two weeks. You really are improving. And I thought I had you beaten, too."

"It's all right," she said, clamping her left hand over his hands. Their rings clicked together. "It's only a shallow cut and it'll

stop bleeding soon. But we had better get on the road again soon –
if the horses are rested enough." She turned to the children. "I
hope you all enjoyed watching that."

"Thank you!" the children said. They slid and wriggled off
the horses and wandered back towards the houses while she and
Farren re-saddled the horses and prepared to ride again.

***

The shadows lengthened and began to creep eastwards.
Farren reined in Princess and looked backwards over his shoulder
down the hillside. To his left, he saw the Illin-Ast shining golden in
the light of the evening sun. The shadows of the mountains fell
long and purple across the hillside and sloped away down to the
plains of the Kingdom. The northeast wind hissed through the
grass, carrying the smell of earth and pine past him. A white ship of
cloud sailed overhead, its shadow streaking across the grasslands.
"There it is," he said softly. "Our home country. Look well,
because this will be the last we see of it for a while."

He dropped the reins onto Princess's neck and let her graze
the soft grasses between the coarser tussocks. The mare snorted and
tore at the tufts of green. He glanced over at Azariel. She was
illuminated by a ray of sunlight that stole around the purple bulk of
the mountain to the northwest of them, gleaming golden on her
smooth high cheekbones and red lips. Her face was turned towards
the Kingdom and her hair streamed around her in the wind as if it
was trying to tug her back to the plains. Almost involuntarily, he
leaned closer to her, a slight catch in his breath. *She's so beautiful,* he
thought. *My sweetheart.*

He dismounted and walked over to where she sat on Storm.
Sunlight caught the diamond in her betrothal earring in a sudden
flash of white fire. He rested his head against her knee and felt her
hand sliding over his scalp. Her fingers ran through his hair, gentle
and caressing. "Shall we travel any further tonight, or shall we stop
here?" she asked.

"Not here, Stormwolf," he murmured in reply. "We're too exposed to the wind up here on the hilltop. I can't shift shape like you to stay warm. Let's go down into the valley. You know the good campsite down there." He turned to look down at the dark northern slope of the hill below and sniffed the scent of the pinewoods. The wind hissed and roared through the trees. *I wonder if the scars and burns from our fight against the phantoms are still there. At least the phantoms themselves aren't!*

Suddenly, her hand clutched his hair firmly. He looked up as soon as she had freed him to see her straining forward, knuckles white as she gripped Storm's bridle, eyes fixed on the plains below. "What's up?" he asked.

"There are some people moving across the plains down there," she hissed. "And it makes me feel uneasy for some reason. I didn't think anyone came up here."

"People?" he replied. "Farmers, hunters..."

"In armour? Look!" She pointed and he saw some mounted figures shining orange in the setting sun. "They've got dogs with them, too."

He spun away from her and scrambled onto Princess's back. "They won't be from the capital or we'd have seen them preparing to ride this morning. They aren't too far away, so if there were any others coming up here and they packed last night, we'd have been travelling with them all the way. They can't be Helmni. We're not that close to the border. The Helmni wouldn't come in arms to the Kingdom in peacetime."

"People from a guardpost?"

"Maybe." He followed the figures with his eyes. The leader of the group swung towards the hills, and as the rider turned, a flash of light flickered from beneath the horse's hooves, the reflection off a sharp-shod hoof. The hair on the back of Farren's neck prickled. "Did you see that?" His hands tightened around

Princess's bridle. "The horses are sharp-shod. No Kingdom horse has that. They're Claws or Wayasti, and they're heading our way."

"They can't possibly know what we're up here for or even who we are," she said, dark eyebrows creasing into a frown. "They might not be coming after us. They might not even know we're here."

"They will if we don't get off the hilltop and into the valley."

The party of riders turned sharply at the foot of the hill. The leader's horse, a big bay, began bounding up the slope.

"They know we're here. They either spotted us a while back or they've got a sorcerer who's seen us with a scrying mirror." She shook her hair back and turned Storm towards the northward face of the hill.

"Come on, Azariel!" He punched Princess's flanks with his heels and headed her down the slope into the pinewoods. "If they've got dogs and they are after us, we can't lose them in the woods," he said over his shoulder. "But if we can get as far ahead as possible, then we can think of some way to shake them off."

"The river?" she asked as Storm drew alongside Princess. "They'll lose the scent if we cross water, and we can cross here."

"The gorge in the next valley is too narrow to hide in," he shouted. "And they'd see us on the other bank. They saw us on the hilltop; we stood there for too long."

He ducked as Princess plunged into the forest at a canter. The larger branches skimmed over his head and the needles whipped across his face, filling his lungs with their resinous green aroma. The mare dodged around tree trunks, leaping fallen ones, snapping dead twigs off as she passed. A broken branch grazed his arm as he leaned to one side to avoid an overhanging bough on the other side of him. He strained his ears to catch any sound from behind, but all he heard was the roar of the wind in the pines and the drumming of the horse hooves.

Before long, he felt Princess slowing to a walk as she climbed the slope on the other side of the valley. Still zigzagging around trees, they scrambled up the steep hillside. He checked Princess at the crest of the small rise, wiping a line of sweat off her neck as he looked back. "Can you see anything?" he asked. "You've got better eyesight than I have."

She craned her neck to one side to peer around a tree. "I can see... yes! They're just descending the slope on the other side, I think. The light's almost too dim to see anything far off. What now? Along the edge of the gorge like last time?"

"No," he replied. "Stay hidden in the trees."

They kept riding at a brisk walk through the forest. The ground seemed flatter here, and the horses moved more easily. Now and again, Princess broke into a trot, but he reined her back. *You can see I want to move fast, don't you my lady? But I don't want to ride you to death.* The trees pressed in close around them, cutting off the view. To his right, he heard the rush and roar of the river. *That's the gorge over there, and where we want to stay away from for now.* He smelt the tang of the pines fading and being replaced by the earthier smells of the dead leaves and humus. *Out of the pinewoods and into the denser stuff. I wish our horses didn't make so much noise.*

Princess snorted. *She's tired. We really need to rest, but if we stop for long, we'll be in for a fight. Against the dogs, too.* He halted the mare for a moment and heard Storm's hooves stop as well. Leaves rustled around him in the twilight air. In the distance, he heard a long, wild howl. "Dogs?" he asked.

"A wolf calling." Her voice sounded breathless and tired.

From behind them came an answering bay and a volley of barks. "That's them – and they're not far behind, either!" he said. "Come on!"

CHAPTER SEVEN

Azariel heard the dogs' baying renewed behind her and punched Storm's flanks with her heels again. *Why? Why are they chasing us?* She heard him snorting and panting, and felt his sweat damp on her hands. "I hope the Claw horses are as jaded as ours," she hissed to Farren. "I don't think Storm will be able to keep up this pace much longer."

"Neither can Princess," came his voice from a little way ahead in the gloom. "But I've got an idea."

She checked Storm's canter to a trot, then a walk. A branch brushed through her hair and she reached up to push it away. A spattering of dew fell in her face. "So what shall we do to escape the dogs?"

"They're tracking by scent, aren't they? That means all we have to do is to confuse our tracks somehow."

"We're a long way above the river; there's no way we can cross water and lose them that way." She listened intently, expecting to hear the drumbeat of hooves behind her.

"That's not what I'm thinking, Stormwolf. They're not tracking our scent but Storm and Princess's. So if we let them run loose for a little, we can hide. Then when the Claws catch the horses, they haven't caught us."

"What about the horses, though? What will happen to them? I don't want Storm being killed by them." She ran her hands through her gelding's sweaty mane. *You're a good horse, Storm. I don't want to lose you.*

"No." He sighed. "But I don't think they'd kill a pair of good warhorses that came into their possession. The Claws raid studs for mounts frequently. Just ask my father! They'll keep them, especially a mare of breeding age. Or they may just strip them of their gear and let them go."

"And us? What do we do then without horses or gear?"

"We'll work something out later, Azariel. For the moment, we've got to act or they'll catch us. We've had a long day and we're outnumbered if it comes to a fight." Princess's hooves slowed, then stopped. Azariel reined Storm in behind the mare. Farren twisted in the saddle towards her, angular face pale bluish-grey in the twilight. "We might even be able to steal them back tonight. But I'll go up this tree with a saddlebag of gear. You go up another one somewhere else. We don't want to be too close together and let the dogs catch a concentrated scent of humans."

Humans? She smiled to herself. If that's the problem, then I'll foil them and be able to keep a watch on them, too. "I'll run as a wolf," she said aloud. "You hide up your tree and I'll hunt our hunters."

She heard the jangle and squeak of him unbuckling a saddlebag, then the clap of hands around a branch. A rustle of leaves and a few groans of effort, then silence. "Kiss me before you change shape," he said softly from the branches.

She edged Storm beneath the tree where his voice came from. Princess sidled out of the way and walked off. "Off you go, my lady," he whispered to the horse. Azariel felt his hand brushing her cheek and she raised her face to him. His warm soft lips pressed firmly onto hers for the space of a heartbeat and she smelt the sweetish-salty masculine smell of his sweat. Then he pulled away and she heard a rustle climbing higher. "I love you," she whispered after him. "May the King of Heaven keep you safe."

She rode a few paces on into the woods and slid her feet from the stirrups. After a deep breath, she slipped off Storm's back, concentrating and changing shape as she landed. Her limbs contracted and her face lengthened as they realigned themselves. The world changed around her and she looked about on the blacks, greys and whites of the forest undergrowth, lit by the starlight that pierced the canopy. Indescribably vivid scents of leaves, old and new, spring flowers, wood and beasts filled her nostrils and the thousand small sounds of the forest magnified. She landed on her shewolf's paws in the leaf mould. For a few heartbeats, her mind rolled and boiled in a cauldron of instincts and emotions. Then her human will and intellect came to the forefront and ruled. *That's better*, she thought. *Now, how close are those hunting dogs?*

She pricked her ears and listened behind her, just catching the faint rumour of hoofbeats approaching. *Not too far behind, but not far enough.* She trotted to the side and began to double back along the way they had come. In the distance, the other wolf called again. The urge to answer the howl welled up inside her as she heard the dogs baying nearby in reply. Stifling the impulse, she crept through the undergrowth to where the dogs ran.

The sounds intensified and mingled with the smells. The ground beneath her paws trembled. She raised her head and saw the men, all wearing the Yellow Claw insignia, armed and mounted on sharp-shod horses. She ran her eyes over them and counted fifteen men following three tall hunting dogs, which were broad-shouldered, heavy-jawed beasts with smooth coats. *Mastiffs,* she thought. *To hold us if they caught us. I hope they don't harm Storm and Princess. And I hope they can't scent Farren up his tree.* She paced closer to the trio of dogs and ran beside the leader, hidden from them by the tangle of bushes. *They'll hear me here, but they seem too bent on their quarry to attend to me. They're well trained!*

The leading dog snuffed the air and bayed. *He's found a more intense scent*, she thought as she sniffed. Her wolf's nose caught the prickly scent of Storm, and Princess's smoother note mixed with the heart-tugging musky traces of Farren. *If they find him, I'll tear their throats out!* Involuntarily, she half-turned towards the dogs, hackles rising and lips already writhing back from her fangs.

The dogs led the men towards the elm tree where Farren waited. She padded along to the tree itself and looked up. His shape was outlined against the stars as he pressed close to the trunk and clung to the branches, the gear bag balanced across his thighs. She heard his breathing, coming light and quick. *Not silent enough to escape dog or wolf ears, but silent enough for a human to miss.* She slunk behind the trunk of the elm and watched.

The dogs paused beneath the elm tree. One of them snuffled the ground, then the air. The dog paced forwards, following the trail left by Princess, then turned his head, sniffing the air again. "What's up?" one of the Claws asked the dog. "What have you found?"

The dog whined, sniffed the ground and looked up at the tree. Azariel's hackles rose again. *Oh no! They can scent Farren up there! But I'll try to fool the Claws, at least.* She stepped out from behind the thick trunk of the elm, hackles raised, tail down and teeth bared. She snarled at the dogs, then glanced up at the men. Ears laid back, she wheeled around and scampered back into the undergrowth. *I hope that looked realistic enough.* She stopped running and padded softly back to the men and dogs.

"Just a scared shewolf, eh?" said one of the Claws. "Get on, Fang. Follow those horses. Chase yourself a lady friend some other time."

She heard the words and felt sick. *At least the dogs have gone and Farren's safe.* She waited until the last of the Claw horses had passed, then she returned to the elm tree and curled up to rest in a shelter formed by two huge roots that jutted out from the trunk.

***

Farren listened to the hunters talking beneath him. He held his breath and froze rigid as the dogs halted beneath his tree. *What do I do now? They can still smell me up here, even though the horses have moved on.* He gripped the rough branch of the elm tighter, trying not to rustle. *Or can they sense my animal taming Gift?* He willed the dogs to go away, not quite using his Gift. Then he heard the men mention the shewolf and saw a lean grey shape dart away. *Good on you, Azariel.* The hoofbeats began again and the party moved off into the darkness with a swish of branches. Finally, the sounds were swallowed up by the rustles and creaks of the forest, and he breathed freely again.

He swung his legs around so that he straddled the branch he sat on and leant back against the trunk of the elm. The hard bark dug into the bruises on his spine, making him wince, but moss was cushioning the back of his head damply. *Shall I go down or shall I wait up here? I can't risk falling asleep up here where I could fall.*

He waited for a few minutes up the tree until his limbs grew numb with the cold and damp. *At least it's not winter, but that northeast wind is chilly.* He stretched and tensed his arms and legs, and raised a hand to try to massage his aching neck through his chainmail before easing his cloak out from underneath him. He curled the warm wool around himself. A light spattering of dewdrops fell to the ground and the tree rustled with his movements. He looked up and saw the frilled and ruched seed-heads at the tips of the otherwise bare twigs outlined against the indigo sky. A sheen of dew glinted pale silver. *The moon has risen.* He looked down to the foot of the tree. *Where's Azariel?*

He wedged the gearbag into a fork of the elm and swung himself down to the lower branches, making them rustle and creak as he descended. *I hope the Claws are too far off to hear me. I can't hear them.* He balanced on the lowest bough and looked around at the moonlit forest floor. Beneath him, he spied a coiled silver shape. *That's her.* "Azariel?" he said softly.

The shewolf pricked her ears and looked up at him. She stretched her long, slim legs and scrambled to her feet, shaking her fur free of dead leaves and dirt. Then she reared herself up so that her forepaws rested on the tree trunk beside him. Balancing precariously, he reached down and felt for her furry ears. He caressed her lightly, running his fingers over the velvety grey fur. "Don't change back yet," he said, seeing her stare deeply at him, her eyes changing from lupine to human. The shewolf blinked and luminous wolf eyes gazed at him once more. "Where are the Claws?" he asked. "Can you find if they've found Storm and Princess yet?"

The shewolf rubbed her head against his hand before loping off into the undergrowth. He heard her crackle through a patch of bracken, then nothing. *I had better find a place to sleep. But not here where the Claws could come.* He climbed back to where the gearbag was wedged and strapped it around his neck. Working from tree to tree, he moved away from the Claw's track. *I should be far enough away for them to miss me now. It's risky, but I need to sleep.* He clambered down and let himself into the leaf mould, landing neatly on his feet. Drawing his sword, he sat down with his back against the smooth trunk of an ash. *It's good to feel the ground beneath me instead of narrow branches,* he thought, feeling the cold earth beneath his hands and legs. He shivered and felt inside the gearbag. *What's in here?* His fingers found the prickly-soft wool of a blanket. He tugged it out and wrapped its comforting warmth around himself along with his cloak.

An owl called somewhere in the branches above him and he looked up. *Will Azariel be able to find me when she comes back? Her sense of smell is good, but is it good enough?* He glanced back towards the tall elm he had started from. *I should be able to see her around the tree.* He chuckled and eased the blanket higher onto his shoulders. *My animal taming Gift won't compel her if she's in her wolf shape. I've tried that before.* He crossed one leg over the other and waited, remembering how her mind had felt when he had tried reaching her with his Gift, warm and welcoming but vast and overwhelming. He smiled drowsily.

***

Azariel pushed her way through the bracken and continued to pad along the track of the fifteen mounted men and the dogs. *This is the easiest trail I've followed! I'd be able to track them without taking my wolf-shape; they've broken so many branches and so forth as they've passed.* She sprang over a rotten log and startled a rabbit that was crouched on the other side. It darted away from her in a scurry of paws. Instinct leaped inside her, triggered by hunger. Her mouth flooded with saliva as the wolfish longing to hunt and feel the satisfying warmth of meat and fresh blood surged. *Not now!* She turned her head back to the trail and continued to jog-trot along.

A volley of sharp, yodelling barks broke from the dogs. *That's a bailing bark. They've reached the horses.* She galloped towards the sound, ears pricked. "We've got them!" a voice called.

She rounded a clump of elderberry trees and halted. The Claws burst into a clearing where Storm and Princess were grazing. Storm raised his head and snorted at the dogs as one danced back and forth in front of him. The Claw leader reined his horse in and swore loudly. Azariel lowered her ears as his voice boomed, muffling the sound. "Where the **** are they?" he demanded after his first outburst of obscenity. *Closer than you know,* she thought, her tail waving like an exultant banner behind her. *What are you going to do now?*

"How did they get off the horses without leaving a scent?"

"I'm damned if I know. But take the horses." The Claw seized Storm's bridle. The black gelding tossed his head and snorted. Another man grabbed Princess and the mare shied away, ears laid flat. "What now?" the second man asked.

"Keep the horses," said the leader, running his hand up and down Storm's neck. The gelding bent his head and scratched his face against the Claw's armour. Azariel lowered her tail slightly. *You traitor, Storm! But I suppose you were a Claw horse once.* "Those two *minyasti* won't travel far without their horses or gear and we

94

can catch them tomorrow by daylight. These horses are a good bonus. That mare – look. She's got the Illin-Ast stud brand on her."

Princess lunged at the man who held her, ears back and teeth bared. She nipped the man's forearm, catching a patch of bare skin rather than armour. "Bitch!" he swore, cuffing her with his free hand, then rubbing his arm. *Good on you, Princess! Do it again.*

"So how are we going to find the *minyasti*? Have we got the scrying mirror?"

"Jaster Mhir has it back at Ulfskin-Aza and is probably laughing at us while he watches us and them. He ought to be here, and I wish he had come himself instead of sending us out to deal with two *minyasti* alone."

A sorcerer with a scrying mirror, she thought. *So that's how they knew we were around here. I should have known! Surely they don't know what we're trying to do, though. But I'd better get back to Farren before they turn around and find him. We need to make ourselves very scarce.* She turned and loped back along her trail.

She stopped beneath the old elm where she had left Farren. Raising her head, she scanned the branches. Moonlight and starlight gleamed silver off the dewy twigs and the seed-heads. Farren had gone. *He's found somewhere to sleep. I'll have to track him.* She snuffed the air, searching for his scent. Faintly, she detected the sweet, musky trace. Breathing deeply, she followed his trail.

He was dozing with his drawn sword across his knees when she found him. Her ears caught the soft sound of his deep, slow sleeping breaths. *I had better wake him.* She closed her eyes and concentrated for a moment, feeling her body change once more. For a few heartbeats, she strained to see through the darkness of the moonlit forest. *I keep forgetting how hard it is to see in the dark after I've changed back.* Listening carefully, she heard his breath once more and looked towards the sound to where he slept.

As her vision adjusted, she gazed down on him in the moonlight, seeing the soft silver make the sharp lines of his nose and chin stand out as if chiselled in stone. His lips were slightly parted and his breath stirred the tips of the hair that lay over his forehead. She smiled and stroked his hair. *He's very handsome.* His skin flinched under her light touch. "Wake up," she whispered, running her hands softly across his face. She heard a catch in his breathing and saw him twitch. "They might come back soon." She tugged the blanket back from him as her fingers met the prickle of stubble on his chin. The blanket came away, revealing his mail- and leather-clad body and a warm knot of desire tied and untied itself inside her. *Better stop there,* she thought, lifting her fingers away from the top row of links in his armour, heart hammering inside her chest. *Oh, but I'm aching to let my hands wander further down and further in. One more year left to wait. Who made the stupid rule that* minyasti *betrothals had to be so long?*

"Wake up, Farren," she said, a little louder, resting one hand on the shoulder of his cloak. She bent down and kissed his lips hard as she shook him.

He opened his eyes and smiled at her. "What news?" he mumbled sleepily.

"Plenty, but let's not stay here. Let's move further into the woods and I'll tell you. Two people should be able to elude fifteen horsemen and three dogs – and two extra horses – easily enough. You move through the branches and I'll run in wolf-form." She helped him to his feet, then dropped down into wolf shape.

She led the way into the forest. After about half an hour of climbing a steep bush-clad slope, she spotted a large hollowed-out poplar tree and re-transformed. "This will be good enough to sleep in," she said, picking herself up from her hands and knees. "I'll keep first watch for tonight. Tomorrow we'll think of some way of getting Storm and Princess back."

"I hope I get my bow back, too. I should have taken it instead of the gearbag. But good night, sweetheart." He circled his arm around her shoulders and kissed her softly on the mouth before stepping into the hollow poplar.

She heard him rustling around inside the old shell of a tree. A few paces off, she leaned against the trunk of another tree, gazing up at the canopy and listening to the rustles and strange birdcalls of the forest at night. A ratbird bustled and waddled across the leaves, prodding and snuffling at the leaf mould with its long beak. A light breeze rustled the branches and she shivered. *It's cold and he's got the only blanket. I'll keep watch and sleep in my furs and he can have my cloak.* She unbuckled the shield-shaped clasp at the neck and tiptoed softly back to the hollowed-out poplar. He had already fallen asleep, curled under the blanket in a pile of dead leaves. Leaning over, she tucked the black wool around him, then slipped into wolf shape. She laid her head down on her crossed paws and listened until it was time to wake him for his watch.

***

At dawn next morning, Farren watched Azariel glide off into the bushes in wolf-form to track the Claws. *She's lucky,* he thought. *She'll be able to find something decent to eat as a wolf.* He ran his eyes up and down the trees nearest him. *A pity the gearbag contained nothing except ropes and a blanket. I should have picked one that had food in it. Even if Azariel catches something, I can't eat raw meat and I shouldn't light a fire either if we're trying to stay hidden. And no berries or nuts available at this time of the year. At least it's not winter so there are young leaves about.*

He searched around the clearing and found a tangle of blackberry beneath a cluster of birch trees. The soft young leaves proved easy to chew, although they left a slightly bitter aftertaste in his mouth. He ate a couple of handfuls, then drank as best he could, draining dew out of moss and large leaves. *I'm glad Azariel's not here at the moment,* he thought as he pressed his face into a thick clump of moss on the bark of the hollowed-out poplar he had slept in. *It must look like I'm passionately embracing a tree.* He drew back, wiping the scraps of wet moss off his face. *My old trainer told us how to find water in the forests if you're stuck and can't find a stream. He never said how much of an idiot you'd feel like, licking moss.* He laughed and sat down, leaning back against the old poplar and scratching at the bristle on his chin. *It's almost wet enough to shave.* Thoughts began to play around his head. *Now, how are we going to get Princess and Storm back?* He stared up at the patches of blue sky that dappled the leaves overhead and listened to the clear, cool liquid song of a bellbird. Ideas flashed through his mind and he closed his eyes in concentration.

Something warm, heavy and soft leaned suddenly on his legs. He opened his eyes to see the silver and dark grey head of a shewolf lying across him, green-gold eyes staring and a small blot of blood smeared over her muzzle. "Glad to see you've managed to have something decent to eat," he said, caressing her ears. "Did you find the Claws?"

The shewolf nodded and her eyes changed from golden to dark smoky sapphire ringed with white. A thin line of silver light flashed down her body and he smiled as she returned to human form. "Sweetheart, it's good to see you again," he murmured as she sat up and nestled between his arm and side. He pulled her closer to himself and dropped a kiss onto the top of her head. "I've got an idea for getting the horses back," he said.

Quickly, he outlined his plan to her. "Good," she said. She brushed her hair back from her face and turned slightly towards him. "It should work. When do you want me to change shape again?"

"When we're close to their camp. I want to walk with you. Let's go."

She clambered to her feet and threaded her fingers through his. He walked softly behind her as she glided almost silently through the trees. His eyes roved to and fro over the ground, scanning for twigs that might snap as he listened for the sounds of the Yellow Claw encampment and concentrated on the heightened sensitivity of his soles. His heart began to beat slightly faster and all his senses seemed to double. *Just like hunting,* he thought. *Only this time, like that time back in the war, I'll lose my life, not my quarry if I'm heard or scented. Or I'll lose my Azariel.* A knot tied itself in his stomach, and the hairs on the back of his neck prickled.

They rounded another tree and she slipped her fingers out of his and slowed her walk. *We must be getting nearer.* He licked his finger to test the wind for its direction. *Those dogs had better not be able to smell us.* The left side of his finger chilled a little. *Northerly wind from off the hills. I hope the Claws aren't that way.* "Are we downwind or upwind of them?" he whispered.

She turned to face him, holding her hand up for him to halt. "Downwind," she mouthed, then put her finger to her lips. He crept to her side. "How close?" he breathed into her ear.

He felt her mouth trembling on his ear in turn and heard her answer. "Half a bowshot. I'll change here and go on as planned." Her lips left his ear and travelled softly across his cheek. Then the thin band of light passed down her body again and she vanished in wolf-form into the undergrowth. *Now to see what I can do to get near to the horses and take them while she draws the others off.* He looked around and saw a tall birch tree growing nearby. He walked to it and jumped to reach the branch that stretched above his head. His hands met the smooth bark and for a few heartbeats he hung with his feet off the ground. Then he swung and arched himself upwards to that he could clamber onto the branch, kicking against the trunk to push himself up.

He climbed higher and peered out through the leaves. Ahead of him, he saw a place where the trees thinned out to a clearing where smoke curled. *That's where they are.* He crawled along to where the birch's branches were interlaced with those of another tree. *Now to play at being a tree-cat while she's a wolf.* He began to manoeuvre from branch to branch, tree to tree. *I haven't done this sort of thing since I was a boy playing tag with my brother or sneaking out from my bedroom after lights out,* he thought. *But I've grown since then, so I'd better not try some of the branches that could carry me back then.*

He worked his way to the edge of the clearing. Using the leaves around him as a screen, he looked down. The Claws were gathered idly around a small fire, eating and lounging. The sound of voices drifted on the air to him, blown with the smoke that stung his nose and eyes. The dogs lay tethered by the campfire and every now and then, the Claws tossed them scraps of food. Then he spotted the horses, hobbled in a group at the edge of the clearing near a bundle of gear. *A pity they're tied,* he thought. *One whistle or a touch on their minds and Princess and Storm would come running to me.* He crouched on the branch and waited.

CHAPTER EIGHT

Azariel watched Farren haul himself up into the tree, the sinews of his forearm standing out hard and clear. She followed him with her eyes as he clambered away through the leaves and branches to lose himself in the foliage. His scent lingered in the air, tracing where he had gone to her wolf senses. *Look at how he moves. Muscles, strong arms, lithe lean body – very nice!* She turned her gaze away from where he had vanished into the trees and softly padded towards the Claws' clearing. *I've got to draw the dogs and the Claws off so the Farren can step in and take Storm and Princess back. Now, how shall I do that?* She paused at the edge of the clearing and looked around. The men were grouped around their campfire, eating and laughing. *Careless! If we were hunting them, we wouldn't proclaim our whereabouts like that.* She glanced past them to the dogs, the horses and the bundles of gear. *The gearbags. Time for a little raiding.*

She slunk over to the gearbags and looked at the men. They seemed intent on each other and the dogs, and unaware of her. She sniffed at the bags and scented the aroma of dried meat in the nearest one to her. Using her teeth, she worried at the leather thongs that bound the bag closed. They tore and she slid her muzzle into the dark, aromatic inside. Probing with her nose, she found food and reached further in to seize it. *I'll take it back to Farren,* she thought as her jaws closed over a hunk of barley bread. *He'll be glad of something more filling than leaves and shoots for breakfast.*

She slid the loaf out of the bag and then plunged her head in for more. *The more I take, the less food they'll have while they're hunting us.* Nosing inside again, she found some dried fruits and carefully drew them out, the sugars almost tasteless to her wolf's tongue. Then she heard a heavy footstep nearby through the leather and something hard struck her side painfully. "Get out of there!" yelled a man's voice. She yelped, only half acting, and struggled to pull her head out of the bag. Her muzzle broke free and she looked up at a tall man standing above her, waving a short stick. *So far, so good.*

She curled her lips back from her teeth. Snarling, she surged forward at the man, her jaws snapping just short of his leg. The stick battered her about the ears, dizzying her for a moment, and the man gave a panicky yell. She turned her head and clamped her fangs over the stick. She bit hard and felt it splinter in her mouth before she leaped at the man again.

"Get the dogs!" he yelled. "The bitch is after me!" The man stepped backwards towards his companions, his hand reaching for his sword. *You're a slow draw,* she thought. *Even I'm quicker with my blade than that.* She saw the morning sunshine flash on the blade and she sprang clear of its glittering arc as it swung down towards her, singing with vibration in the air.

She heard the other Claws bustling, then snuffling growls and yaps from the dogs. "Kill!" one of the Claws ordered, unleashing the dogs and pointing at her. She snarled at the dogs, stooped and seized the barley loaf and turned to run into the woods. *That's right, start a wolf-hunt to catch that starving animal that's after your food.* She hurdled a fallen log and surged to a full gallop, heading away from where the horses were tethered.

She cocked her ears back to listen for sounds of pursuit. The barks and bays of the dogs sounded loud and clear, and she heard their paws drumming on the ground a couple of bowshots behind. She plunged through a clump of bracken and its rustling drowned all other sounds for a heartbeat. After turning and twisting around a few more trees, she began to double back on her track.

"Don't send all the dogs, you fool!" roared one of the Claws in the clearing. "We need one to track those *minyasti*. What if that wolf kills them all? Hey, Goldie! Come!"

Foiled! She turned back into the woods once more. *They're only sending two of them after me. And now what do I do?* She plunged through a cluster of gorse bushes and felt a jab of pain in the pad of her left forepaw. Involuntarily, she yelped, losing the loaf. *That'll lame me eventually if I don't take it out soon.* She ran on, feeling the thorn drive deeper into her paw. Behind her, she heard the dogs' bays sounding from behind a nearby thicket. *They're gaining on me,* she thought, front foot pulsing and throbbing around the splinter. *Time to turn and fight.*

She doubled around the thick black trunk of an old mountain beech and charged the mastiffs. Both dogs slid to a halt, paws scraping up dirt, leaves and sticks. She rammed the first one, a brindle, sending it sprawling, then reared up over the second, lips writhing back from her teeth. Her teeth closed on its throat and crunched down hard. A rush of salty warmth filled her mouth and she felt the dog slump heavily in her jaws, breath bubbling and harsh. She dropped him to the ground as the brindle tore painfully at her shoulder.

The brindle's deep growl burbled between its long fangs, drowning the dying rasps of the other mastiff. She twisted and thrashed, wresting herself free from the brindle before its jaws locked. Dark blood from the dead dog stained the forest floor and tainted the air. She stood poised, ready to charge again.

***

Farren crouched on a hick branch, gripping the one above him for balance. The grey wolf-shadow slipped into the Claws' camp and soon, one of the Claws came after her. *Azariel, stay safe,* he thought, heart hammering and mouth dry. *May the Power protect you.* The man struck her around the ears with a stick. Farren's fists tightened and his breath hissed short and fast through his clenched teeth. *I'd like to leap down and challenge you to a fight right here and now, Yellow Claw,* he fumed. Then he smiled as Azariel charged the man, her long white fangs flashing in the sunlight. He bit his lip as the Claw drew his sword, but heard the others calling for and unleashing the dogs. *Good,* he thought.

Tearing his eyes away from following her as she ran from the dogs, he crept closer to the edge of the clearing. The branch trembled beneath him as he looked down at Storm and Princess. He leaned over, gripping the branches around him more tightly. He ran his gaze over the horses, checking how they were tethered. Ropes were knotted around their forelegs to hobble them. *One quick slash of the dagger and our horses are free.* He prepared to swing down from the branches.

He heard one of the Claws calling one of the dogs back from the hunt. Turning his head, he saw one of the men walking towards the gearbags. The rest were still gathered around the campfire, one or two on their feet, but most of them still sitting down. *I'm a fool!* he thought, resisting the urge to smash his fist into the branch nearest him in frustration. *Of course they're not going to risk all their dogs on a raiding wild wolf, and I'm a fool to think that they would. Now we're no closer to getting Princess and Storm back and she's fleeting for her life from those dogs.*

He watched the Claw busy himself with a gearbag, then glided away through the trees. *I hope he was too busy to hear the branches rustling.* He pushed his way through the intertwined branches and swung himself from one tree to another, startling a bird that flew shrieking through the green canopy of the forest. *I hope that doesn't get them suspicious.* He heard a wolf's howling yell to his right, followed by a series of snarls and growls. *They've found her! I'm not waiting up here any longer!* He climbed down to a lower branch and leaped to the ground with a sharp jolt that spread from his heels up his shins. After collecting himself after the jarring landing, he ran towards the sound, thrusting and crashing through the undergrowth. Thorns tore at his cloak and slashed scratches across his arms and face. *I don't care if I'm caught here; I've got to help her.*

He yanked his cloak free from around a branch, hearing the cloth tearing free, and ran on. With the snarls a little way ahead of him, he strained to see through the undergrowth. *Sweetheart, sweetheart, I hope I'm in time to help you.* He caught his feet on a tree root and fell sprawling on the ground. As he picked himself up, he saw the brindle hindquarters of a mastiff emerging from behind a tree. He drew his sword and lunged forwards.

The mastiff backed into him with a yelp of surprise and he drove the point of the sword deep down into its back. A gurgling howl broke from the dog and it sank down, the life sighing out of it. Farren wrenched his sword free from the dog's body and knelt to put his arm around the shewolf's shoulder. She flinched as his fingers touched the matted pelt. The smooth silver fur felt sticky with saliva and the skin beneath was swollen and oozing blood. "Are you all right? How badly hurt are you?"

The fur beneath his hands changed to the hard, cold metal of chainmail and he felt smooth hair brushing his cheek. "Yes," she panted. "I'm all right. I was about to change back when you came. I've got a thorn in my paw – my hand, I mean – that was holding me up."

She held her left hand out to him with the dark needle embedded deep in her palm. He cupped her hand softly and held it in his own. "Let me get it," he said. He gently squeezed the tip of the thorn above the surface of her skin, pinched the thorn between his fingernails and drew it out. "That was a long one. I can imagine how that would hurt you when you had to run on it." He bent his head and pressed a kiss into her palm. "But what about your shoulder?"

"You saw what happened to my shoulder. I'll have some bad bruises there." Her hand lingered on his cheek a moment before she slid it slowly away. "I'll bathe it in water and whatever herbs you suggest and can find later. But not now. You'd better get back up your tree, because I heard someone coming from over there." She pointed towards the clearing where the Claws camped.

He nodded and stood up. "What about you?" he asked.

"I'll manage." She leaned over towards him and her lips brushed his. "You had better go. I'll come back with something for you," she whispered in his ear.

He scrambled up the nearest tree and climbed until the branches grew too slender to carry him. Balanced on one branch and grasping another beside him, he looked down to where Azariel stood, already in wolf-form beneath him.

She bent over the dead mastiff. *I had better make this look like my work before I leave.* She tore at the stab wound on the dog's back and left it jagged before worrying and tearing at the mastiff's thick neck. She left the ripped carcass and bounded over to where she had dropped the barley loaf. Quickly, she paused to lick the blood from her muzzle, then wiped her head against a clump of moss to clean himself. *Farren won't want dog's blood on his bread. He's not that hungry – yet.* She gently picked it up in her jaws and turned back towards Farren's tree. The soft rustle and pad of a footstep sounded a little way behind her and a voice whispered, "Now I've got you, shewolf."

She glanced into the undergrowth and saw a man crouching and fitting an arrow to a polished walnut recurve bow. *He's not very well hidden. But he thinks he's after a wild wolf glutted and drowsy after eating or wounded after a fight.* She dropped the loaf and braced herself ready to spring away, keeping one eye on the archer. A sharp shock of familiarity jerked her head back towards him. *That's Farren's bow! If I can kill him, we've got it back!*

The Claw's right arm hauled on the string and she leaped aside as the first arrow sang through the air. The arrow punched into the dirt beside her with a solid, deadly smack. She galloped towards the archer. "Damn you!" the man yelled, fitting a second arrow to the string. She reared herself up on her hind legs and changed shape. The man's eyes and mouth dropped open in shock. The arrow clattered off the rest and tumbled down to the forest floor. She whirled her sword from its sheath and up at the Claw in one long smooth move. The soft resistance of flesh met the point, then it plunged on into the man's thigh as he screamed. She tugged her sword out, trailing streamers of bright blood, and slashed it across his throat.

She wiped her blade clean on the fallen leaves and sheathed it. The hot stink of blood assaulted her nose and she felt streaks and drops of gore drying on her face. She looked down at the dead archer, a shudder passing down her spine. *There's no chance that those slashes will pass as anything but sword cuts. I'll have to make this look like wolf's work as well.* Her stomach crawled as she dropped down into wolf's shape. She forced herself to tear and tug at the wounds with her teeth, disguising the straight slashes left by the sword.

Returning to her woman's shape, she reeled away and vomited in the undergrowth. She spat the taste of blood and bile from her mouth in disgust, then buried her face in her hands. *What foul work, having to dishonour the dead. King of Heaven, forgive me! But I only did it to save myself from being caught – and Farren. I've got to remember that.* She opened her eyes. The bow was lying beside the body. She picked it up, then turned away from the dead man.

She rummaged around in the bushes and found the barley loaf. Leaf mould and bits of twig clung to the dark crust, so she wiped it clean on her cloak as she walked back to Farren's tree and stowed the bread in her hood. She slung the bow over her shoulder and began to climb. Balancing carefully, she handed the bow to him.

"Well done!" he said as he took it from her and ran his hands over the polished curves of the wood. "And thank you. Now we'd better get out of here so we're not found when the others come searching. You're all in black, but I've got this wretched red cloak on."

They found a cherry laurel tree growing a short walk from where the archer and the dogs had been killed. Glossy foliage clung to the branches sweeping down almost to the forest floor in a wall of dark green. "Perfect," she said. "Even your cloak will be hard to see in here." She twitched her cloak back behind her shoulders and scrambled up the branches that jutted out almost at right angles from the twisting trunk. *The last time I climbed a tree was last autumn when I was gathering walnuts in the Ulfskin-Aza.* Memory flooded back through her as she pulled herself up to the next branch, smooth bark comfortable under her hands. *I thought he was dead back then.* She paused and turned her head. Farren, the bow across his shoulder pinning his cloak around him awkwardly, swarmed up the tree and passed her. He stopped a bodylength above her and eased himself around to sit on an almost horizontal limb of the tree, resting his feet on a lower branch. He twitched his bow off and looked down at her as he hung it on a thick twig. His dark eyes shone, his lips were parted smile and his rumpled chestnut hair fell across his forehead. A wave of grateful longing swept through her. She climbed to where he sat and flung herself sideways in his lap. Her arms circled his neck and she kissed his open mouth fiercely. *Oh, Farren, I'm so glad you are alive and here with me.*

He drew his head back from her. "Steady, Stormwolf," he laughed huskily. The black centres of his eyes had widened and the links of his chainmail rose and fell over his chest as he breathed hard. "We can't spend the rest of the day kissing in the trees."

She eased herself off his lap and onto the branch beside him. "So what now? We still haven't got the horses back."

"I'll think of something if you give me time," he said. "But we'll wait until nightfall. Darkness will be better for a raid." He glanced away from her toward the clearing. "It's a pity we can't see what they're doing. After your morning's work, they may move on, or they may guard the horses more closely."

"I hope I haven't made so many kills that they start to get suspicious." She grinned. "At least one of them may have heard some nasty werewolf legends and realize that a normal wolf isn't quite that rapacious."

"If they find the kills, you may have started another story off." He chuckled quietly. "Let me see... 'Once upon a time, in the haunted hills beyond the Illin-Ast, there lived a savage she-werewolf...'"

"Stop it, Farren," she laughed. "I hate gruesome werewolf stories." She ran a hand through a strand of her hair and gently tugged a tangle loose, then reached back and fumbled in her hood for the loaf. "Spoils from a raid," she said as she handed the bread to him. "You must be starving. Eat up then you can put your mind to plans, not horror stories."

"Sorry, Stormwolf. I can't resist teasing you." His hand brushed over the back of her arm as he reached for the loaf. "And thank you."

***

The sun fell golden on the brilliant green of the leaves around them at the end of the day before the light was swallowed up by the long purple shadow of the mountains. A soft twilight lingered, filled with the belling of thousands of birds. Farren stretched his legs and fidgeted to ease the cramped muscles in his buttocks. His head pulsed with thirst and his stomach growled at him. "Almost time to strike and I won't be sorry to get out of the trees, even though they've given us the cover we've needed."

"Yes. Just as well those Claws kept looking down on the ground for a wolf, not up for people." She yawned. "I'm stiff and my shoulder's throbbing. Best to limber up for some action. I hope they've fed Princess and Storm for us."

He blew on his hands to warm them in the rapidly chilling air. "Don't talk about eating – or drinking! We've had next to nothing all day."

"Well, if you fancy eating raw dog meat, there's plenty there for the taking."

"Not after it's been lying in the warmth all day." He shifted slightly on the branch, felt for a lower one and stood up. A faint smell of smoke drifted over from the Claws' clearing. "Well, they're eating," he said. "But I don't really want to invite myself to dinner."

"It's nearly nightfall." She leaned over on her branch, her hair hanging down in curtains along the sides of her face. "Do you want me to raid the gearbags again for you?"

"We'll wait until it's really dark."

"What are we going to do? You still haven't told me the plans."

He leaned his head against the trunk of the cherry laurel tree. The moss clinging to the bark felt soft and soothing against his pulsing temples. *Don't worry about food! I'm so thirsty!* "This time, I'll go in and draw them off while you free Princess and Storm. They'll chase me more readily than they'll chase a wolf. I've got my bow now, thanks to you, and while I'm in darkness and they're lit by the fire, I can strike and not be seen while you slip into the camp in whatever shape works best."

She bumped him lightly with one hip as she scrambled to stand beside him. "Not so fast," he said. "It's not even twilight yet."

"I'm not moving in now. I'm going to see how the camp lies."

She slithered down the tree and changed shape. Then her grey form vanished into the undergrowth. He waited, watching the patchwork of leaves and sky change from glossy green on blue to black on white and finally to black on starlit indigo. His legs grew tired of standing and he turned around and sat back down on the branch. *How much longer do I have to sit on hard knobbly branches? Where is she?* He looked towards the red-orange glow coming through the trees from the clearing. Something rustled at the foot of the tree. He looked down and saw a dim wolf-shape rearing up against the trunk. "Azariel?" he whispered. "How does the land lie?"

He clambered down a few branches, then dropped to the ground, landing with a thud. He brushed the dirt and dust off his leather-clad legs and hands. Azariel stood beside him, a woman once more. She pressed close to him. "They've lit a ring of fire around the horses," she whispered, lips tickling his ear. "The last of the dogs is in there. I think they're afraid of the wolves – or at least one wolf! The men are about ten or fifteen paces away from them around another fire. I was listening to them. They're going to camp here and wait until their sorcerer comes to help them with his scrying mirror. They don't know where we are. If we don't regain the horses tonight, we are in a deep, mud-filled hole of trouble."

"Can you leap the ring of fire?"

"Easily, as a wolf," she answered. "It's about knee high in places, from what I can tell. Can Storm and Princess clear it from a standstill?"

"They should be able to. I'll whistle to them once I've drawn the men away." He checked the arrows in the quiver at his belt, feeling a shaft sitting snugly in each metal clip. "May the King of Heaven go with you."

"And the Power protect you, Farren, my love. You've got the dangerous part to play."

He reached for her in the darkness and drew her close to him. Her lips searched for his and he bent his head to kiss her. "Be careful too, sweetheart," he said. "You have a dog to fight." Reluctantly, he let her go and turned to climb back up into the trees.

He groped his way from branch to branch, tree to tree. The early starlight shone faintly through the gaps in the canopy. *Enough to see by, but my hands and feet are more my eyes at the moment,* he thought as he reached for a foothold. He stepped onto a nearby limb and felt it buckle beneath him as he leaned his weight onto it. Instinctively, his hands gripped the other branches and his other foot began to search for a hold. The dead branch snapped and he hauled himself back up, rough bark scraping at his palms. *That'll put them on guard if they're listening.* He moved on and saw the dark lines of the tree trunks thin out against the fireglow.

He braced himself between the trunk of one tree and a twisted branch. *That's safe enough for me to use my hands. Where are the men?* He peered between the leaves. Ahead, he saw the silhouettes of men grouped around one fire and a ring of firelight to the right flickering on a patchwork of manes, heads and tails mingled with shadows. He felt for the quiver at his belt and unclipped an arrow. *Just one. I don't want to waste any.*

He fitted the arrow to the string and drew his bow. The group of men clustered around the fire, black shapes on golden-orange. *Do I shoot to kill or only to wound and alarm? One Claw killed is one Claw less to hunt us. But I don't like striking to kill out of the darkness without warning.* His muscles relaxed and he let the bow ease off slightly. Then he drew it back fully again. *No. They hunted us with dogs and took our horses when we had done nothing to them. I'll have to shoot to kill.* His eyes narrowed as he picked out one of the dark shapes and trained the head of the arrow on it. *This shot's almost as far as my bow can range accurately. Even if I don't quite kill, I'll alert them and that's what's needed.* The string slid from his left hand and the arrow hissed into the darkness.

One of the Claws yelled and leaped to his feet, clutching at his side. *Arm or body? I can't see from here.* The others gathered around the wounded man and stood around gesturing and pointing. Firelight glittered on metal as they fumbled around for their weapons. *They've seen the Kingdom colours in the fletchings. Time to move.* He slung his bow over his shoulder and began to grope and work through the trees around and away from the clearing.

Crouched in the darkness, Azariel saw the Claws as they found their weapons and plunged into the forest. Their feet thudded out of the clearing. One man, the wounded one, stayed by the campfire. *Never mind him.* She slipped into the clearing and ran towards the ring of fire. The flames were burning as high as her wolf's shoulder and the smoke stung and choked her. She sped towards the wall of flame, gathered herself and launched herself over, feeling the hairs of her belly fur singeing as she cleared them.

She crashed into the mastiff with a snarl, fangs exposed and ready. The heavy-set dog yelped and leaped backwards. She darted in and closed her fangs over its throat. Her teeth clamped down and she shook the mastiff as she ripped his life out of him. Then she whirled around to find Storm and Princess, changing shape as she moved.

She slid through the snorting, frightened horses to find her gelding. "Storm, Storm," she whispered, then heard his answering nicker of welcome. The other horses shifted and tossed their heads. *Poor things. What a way to tether them! What would have happened if I were a real wolf intent on killing them? They can't escape or even defend themselves.* She jerked her foot out of the way as one of the Claw horses' sharp-shod hooves came down. *Perhaps it's just as well.* She reached out and felt for Storm. "I'm glad your bridle's on," she crooned to him, caressing his neck and muzzle. "But where's your saddle? No time to put it on. Let's get you untied. Steady now." She drew her dagger and stooped to cut his hobbles.

***

Farren saw the men crashing through the trees beneath him. *I'm not far enough away yet,* he thought, freezing in place. *They'll find me before too long.* He inched backwards on his branch until he felt the trunk firm behind him. Then he took an arrow and aimed at the party of men again.

He heard a sharp cry that trailed off weakly into a whimper. *I've killed one. Now, I've got to call the horses back before the rest of them find me.* He saw the Claws swarming through the trees and looking around in his direction. His heart kicked in his chest like a wild horse and his breath came short and fast. *Do I call the horses now, or should I wait? There's a risk either way.* He forced his breathing to slow and calm, then put his fingers to his lips to whistle shrilly. *No escape for me now that they've heard that. God Incarnate help me fight for my life!* His arms and hands tingled in response to his prayer and the metal of his rings grew hot. The emerald glittered, a point of green flame in the darkness. *Thank you.* He looked down at the approaching Claws, shouldered his bow and tensed himself, ready to spring or to fight.

Fire burst from his fingers in streams of lightning and two Claws dropped at the foot of the tree. The others halted then turned, like iron drawn to a lodestone, towards the elm where he waited. He glanced around at the other trees nearby. *Can I get to another branch and away from here?* All of the sturdy branches nearby seemed tantalizingly close but just beyond his range.

"Over here – this one!" shouted one of the Claws, pointing towards him. Quickly, they ringed the tree below him, pale, starlit faces turned up towards him.

"We've got you now, *minyastin*," one said, stepping closer to the trunk.

"You'll have to come up and take me. Do you think I'm fool enough to come down and take you all on at once in the dark?" His fists tightened and both rings glowed as energy prickled in his fingers.

Starlight glittered on a ring of swords around the base of the tree. "You'll have to come down some time, you know."

"Don't wager on that." His hand trembled as he raised it, then he let fire fly from his onyx ring. The deep green lightning crackled over the heads of the men and struck the undergrowth beyond. *The longer I can taunt them and hold their attention, the more time Azariel will have to get the horses free and come here.*

One of them took three paces back and threw his sword up at him. The blade whirled awkwardly through the air several feet above him and clanged into the trunk. It clattered down a few feet before the hilt snagged on a gnarl. He reached down for it. "My drill sergeant would have beaten me with the flat for throwing away my weapon like that. Not that I mind you being an idiot," he said, deliberately keeping his voice calm but hearing a rough edge creep in. *I can't do that icy voice as well as Azariel can. I hope she comes soon.*

***

Azariel stood up from cutting Princess's hobbles, Farren's whistle reaching her ears. She felt for Storm's bridle and scrambled onto his back as she saw Princess leap the ring of fire. She nudged Storm with her heels and felt him rear up and surge forwards. A wall of smoke stung her eyes, then Storm was galloping along Princess's trail. Ahead, she heard voices and a clatter of metal. She ducked under a branch as Storm smashed into the bushes. *They've found him!*

CHAPTER NINE

From his perch in the tree, Farren looked down at the circle of Claws. Dimly, he heard the rumble of hoofbeats over the taunts of the Claws. *I'm going to have to drop so that Princess can find me. I can't expect Azariel and the horses to fight through to me here. I've got to go to them.* He drove the sword the Claw had thrown at him into the trunk, then tensed. His breath raced and he fought to slow it. One of the Claws had inched closer to the trunk. Farren carefully gauged the distance between himself and the Claw, then leaped down, fire flashing from his hands. His heels thudded into the head of Claw nearest the tree and felled him.

Quickly, before the other Claws could draw back in after evading his fire, he drew his sword and backed up firmly against the tree. *Hellfire! I've jumped too soon.* The Claws swarmed in at him, shouting, and he drove them back with blade and fire. Two of them swung their swords at him at once and collided with each other awkwardly. Seizing the chance, he hacked at the arm of one, feeling the blade bite, then knocked the weapon from the other with the backstroke. Then he leaped back to where the tree guarded his back as another of them surged forward.

Farren kept stabbing and slashing at the Claws nearest him with his left hand and letting lightning fly from his right. His rings turned to burning circles around his fingers, ready to flare into fresh fire. Blows caught his shoulders and hips, bruising but turned aside by his chainmail. His ears rang with the din of metal on metal, and the battle-yells of the Claws. *How far away is she?* Sweat trickled down his face and the back of his neck, and down his arms, flowing into a fresh gash on his arm and stinging. He swept his sword around and forwards, driving a Claw sword back and felt it land heavily on the man in front of him. Another blow fell on his shoulder, knocking him slightly off balance.

He whirled his right arm in front of his chest, summoning up a shield. Another Claw lunged at him and was thrown back by the invisible wall of energy. Panting, head throbbing and muscles aching, he watched the Claws circle him, battering at the shield. *I'll hold it until Azariel and the horses come. It's going to tire me out, but the shield will keep them off me. Eight to one! I'm lucky I survived this long.* He leaned against the trunk of the tree. His sweat started to itch and sting as it wormed into a nick on his chin, and he longed to wipe it away. *I can't move – not until I want the shield to drop.*

Princess's fighting neigh rang out she crashed through the undergrowth, hooves flailing at the Yellow Claws. "Yes!" he shouted exultantly as he saw a man dropping stunned beneath her hooves and teeth. The mare squealed in pain and tossed her head. *She's got no armour and she can't fight through to me.* He released the shield and lunged forwards, thrusting the Claw ahead of him backwards. *I've got to get to her!*

Azariel's wild wolf-like yell shattered the air. She broke onto the Claws like a black wave, sword drawn and red fire flashing from her hands. He smashed his sword hilt backwards into the Claw nearest him and ran to Princess. Azariel reached him, her sword slicing the air like lightning and fire flying from her opal ring. From the corner of his eye, he saw the Claws drawing away as he took Princess's bridle and vaulted onto her bare back. "Come on!" he shouted and he turned Princess and spurred her away from the battle. Hoofbeats drummed behind him, almost drowned by the shouts of the Claws. His head spun from the effort of holding the shield. He clung to Princess's back and bent low over her neck, forehead almost touching her mane.

The shouts of the Yellow Claws faded away into the distance, muffled by Storm and Princess's hoofbeats and the crash and swish of the undergrowth as they thundered deep into the woods.

Azariel sheathed her sword and guided Storm so close to Princess that she could almost have reached out and seized the mare's tail. The gearbag strapped to her back under her cloak had twisted around under her arm and she pushed it back. "Are you all right?" she said. The two horses trotted along a narrow deer trail between dense bushes that rubbed her leg.

"More or less," he panted. "That shield's taken it out of me, though. And I've got a nasty cut on my left arm."

"It's not too bad, is it?" Storm drew level with Princess and she saw Farren lit by the patchy starlight through the trees.

"I'll need to bind it up so it stops bleeding. I'm bruised all over." He yawned.

"You need some rest," she said. "Where are we heading?"

"You lead," he said. "I'm too weary to think of a good plan. But act fast; they'll be on their horses before long."

"They've got no dogs now, so we should be able to lose them in the dark. Let's head for the treeline. Which way's that?"

In the half-dark, she saw him point to the right a little. "That's the way the slope goes," he said.

"Up we go, then."

She turned Storm uphill and rode on until the trees grew thinner and the air cooler. The moon rose, bathing the forest in silver light. The wind hissed off the slopes, driving away the heavy, damp smell of the forest with the dry tang of wild thyme. The wind caught her hair and blew it over her left shoulder, and she felt it tug her cloak. Moonlight shone off the tussock and mountainthorns. "We're out of the trees," she said over her shoulder.

"Anywhere good to camp that you can see?"

She ran her eyes over the hillside, taking in the silver and shadow shapes. Ahead of her, the slop rose gently to a ridge that stretched from one side of the skyline to the other. *West to east as far as I can judge from the stars,* she thought, flicking her gaze up to check the constellations she knew. "That'll do," she said, catching sight of a cluster of rocks on the top of the ridge. "Good shelter from the wind and unfriendly eyes up there, and plenty of grazing. There should be some rabbits, too."

"Good," he yawned. "Let's go. I'm tired and thirsty."

***

Farren woke, feeling a cool wind stroking through his hair. The scent of wild thyme and tussock filled his nostrils and he breathed the aroma in. Distantly, he heard the clear call of a hunting falcon somewhere in the hills. Keeping the blankets firmly pulled around his shoulder, he rolled over, stretching the sleep out of his legs. Opening his eyes, he saw the sunlight shining on the top of the wind-worn rock above him and beyond that, the snow-caps of the mountains. He inched himself up onto one elbow and saw Azariel sitting with her back against the rock, the toe of her boots resting beside their swords in the grass. Her eyes were closed and a strand of hair was meandering across her face. *Asleep? She should have woken me so that I could keep watch for a bit.* "Azariel?" he said aloud.

She smiled and he saw her blue-grey eyes gleam in the morning sunshine. "Yes?" she said.

"Oh, you are awake. You should have let me take watch." He pushed back the blankets and looked down at his wounded arm. *Good. It's closed over slightly.*

She drew her knees up and hugged them to her chest. "No need to worry," she said. "I've been keeping an eye on the Claws."

"Are they that close?" His heart began to pound and he rolled the blankets into tight, neat folds. "Where are the horses? We'd better leave soon."

"I said not to worry. I can see their smoke in the trees a good way down if I peer around the rock. We've probably got a decent time before they come. I've never seen such careless hunters in my life. They don't seem to know the meaning of stealth."

He scratched the bristle on his chin. *I wish I could get to some water. I need a shave and I really need a drink.* He looked around the rock towards the dark tangle of trees. Scanning to and fro, he saw a white curl of smoke reaching and writhing into the sky, ascending from a short distance below the treeline. "They're cautious enough when they want to be. But they know we're aware of them now. Eight – ten – however many there are of them – can't hide from two as easily as the two can hide from the ten. But they'll trail us until they've caught us. It's us who need to hide. However, it certainly isn't the way I'd hunt them if the boot was on the other foot."

"Are they signalling to their sorcerer ally?" She spoke near his ear and her hand brushed his arm, just short of the wound. He flinched slightly.

"Might be. But you said you heard he had a scrying mirror, so he won't need a signal. Probably just cooking breakfast." His stomach gnawed at him and his mouth moistened slightly at the idea of eating. "I wish we could have ours. I'm starving."

"I'm sure you are – and thirsty."

He listened for the sound of the river. From far off, he heard the rush of water above the hissing of the wind in the tussock. *Where are we?* he thought, looking between the rocks at the tangle of forest. *I'm going to have a look around.* Scrambling for a toehold and clutching at tussocks and mountainthorns, he pulled himself to the top of the rock. *I'd better not stand up and let myself be seen.* Lying on the gnarled surface of the rock, he raised his head and looked around.

The rock stood in a cluster of boulders on the crest of a ridge that swept down from the peak behind him. To his left, another mountain jutted upwards, standing bright and defiant with the morning sunlight gleaming on its head of snow. A light collar of cloud wrapped around it, silver against the golden tussock. To his right, the land sloped gently downwards, mostly covered by the forest. He watched the trees closely for a few moments. *No Claws coming out yet, but their fire isn't too far off. If any of them goes far enough away from their camp, they could see me.* He looked ahead of him and saw the ridge running down and abruptly ending in a ravine. *That's the river gorge, so that must be east. A northeasterly wind today. Now, where are Princess and Storm?*

He glanced to the right again and saw nothing except tussock and thorns between him and the forest edge. Looking down the other way, he saw a small tussocky valley between the mountain and the ridge where he was lying. Rabbits were nibbling at the coarse grasses that grew around the wild thyme. *That's a meal.* Sharply aware of his hunger again, he stood up and looked around for his bow. He stopped and grinned as he saw a long grey canine shape working through the short spiky mountain plants. *There she goes.* Beyond the rabbits, a stream flowed down the valley. He followed it with his eyes down to where it opened out to a broader, flatter valley where it met the river. The horses were grazing by the stream, morning sunlight gleaming off their coats. He took a deep breath and whistled for them.

Princess raised her head from the stream and looked up towards him. He saw her toss her mane and knew that she was neighing to him, though the wind was blowing any sound away. She and Storm began to canter up the slope towards him. He looked back to where Azariel was stalking the rabbits and saw her, in human shape once more, holding something in one hand. Sunlight gleamed from metal in the other hand. *That's her dagger; she's skinning a rabbit.* With his gaze fixed on her, and the approaching horses, he slid down off the rock. He picked up the horses' bridles from the ground and stowed the blankets back into the gearbag. Shouldering bridles, the bag and his bow, he walked down the slope to meet her.

She sat on a stone, her cloak pushed back from her shoulders, bent over the rabbit draped over her knee. He saw the gleam of the dagger as it cut slits in the skin of the rabbit. She tugged at the pelt and stripped it free from the carcass. She gave a little groan of effort as she hacked off the rabbit's head and paws. She stood up, carcass dangling from one hand, and flung the pelt away. The bloody skin flew towards him and he stepped out of its path. "I'm not that hungry!" he called.

She turned to him, her eyes bright with laughter. "Sorry," she said. "I didn't hear you coming."

"It missed me." He drew her close and kissed her smiling mouth.

"And I missed you. What did you see?"

"Just the river and the landscape. I think we'd be best to follow that stream down to the main river and continue up the Illin-Ast." He braced himself as the horses swarmed up to him and nearly knocked him over as they nuzzled and nudged at him. "Steady there," he said, running one hand down Princess's neck.

"How about something to eat?" she asked from the other side of Storm. "We should be able to light a fire somewhere hidden enough to roast this?"

"What about the smoke?" He scratched around the base of Princess's ears as the mare rubbed her head on his shoulder.

"I'll use plenty of dry fuel and keep the flames roaring. That won't smoke much."

"Let's go. Whatever you do with that rabbit, I'm having a drink."

He trudged down the slope through the tussocks. The clear liquid music of the stream rose to meet him, blurred slightly by the wind. He almost ran to the edge of the water. The sunlight played on and in it, picking out white and speckled stones on the stream bed and glinting brilliantly off each ripple and rapid. He lay down on his front, ignoring the stones and sword hilt that dug into his stomach. *At last. A good drink. I had better be careful I don't drink too much at once.* He buried his mouth in the water and drank, taking it in little sips. A shudder of pleasure glided down his spine and he sighed with relief as he raised his head from the water. Bunching himself up to kneel over the stream, he scooped some up in his hands and splashed liquid over his face. He wiped the water away from his eyes, tiredness falling away from him with the droplets. Azariel knelt beside him, the ends of her long black hair dripping and her lips wet. He dashed another handful of water over his face and felt the hard bristle on his chin. "When you've finished drinking," he said, "I'll tidy myself up a bit."

He stooped over the stream and fished around in his belt-pouch for his shaving gear. He listened to the trickling and laughing of the stream as he stropped the razor and lathered his face with the lavender-scented soap. Azariel's footsteps padded to and fro behind him, and he heard her humming. A faint tang of smoke drifted on the air. *Good. I'm starving.*

"Get the horses!" she shouted. He whirled around to see her stamping on the fire.

"What's up?" he asked, reaching for Princess's bridle and plunging his shaving kit loosely into his pouch.

"Claws," she said as she bridled Storm and scrambled onto his bare back, the gearbag hanging clumsily around her neck.

He turned his head as he grabbed his bow and the other bridle to see a lone horseman on the crest of the ridge. He sprang onto Princess and urged her to a canter. "To those rocks and the mountainthorns over there," he said in a low voice to Azariel.

Storm drew level with Princess and began to climb up the mountainside, his legs powerfully propelling him up the slope. Farren leaned forwards as Princess began to climb. "Come on, my lady," he whispered to her.

He gripped her mane to prevent himself from slipping down her back. *How did they find us? The smoke? Surely not – we didn't have it going long enough. They must have seen me on the rock. Blackarrow, you idiot!* Ahead, Azariel crashed into the thick mountainthorns, her cloak catching on the clutching twigs. Two strides and Princess was pushing between the bushes as well, following Storm's stamping. Thorns ripped at his own cloak and grazed his hands. The rustling and snapping ahead of him moved from one side to the other, then stopped. He checked over his shoulder. The tough mountainthorns had closed behind them. *Good; they can't trace us easily.* Princess pulled up suddenly. He jerked his head around and saw Azariel dismounted and standing by Storm immediately in front of him. "Get down," she whispered. "Your head's above the thorns."

"Sorry," he said. He slid off the mare's back and landed hard on a rock among the thorns. "It was my fault they found us in the first place. I can't have been careful enough on the rock."

"Too late to worry now about whose fault it was. We've got to find out if they're still following us."

"You look," he said. "Your cloak's black while mine's scarlet. I'll take Storm and keep moving up the slope."

"I wonder who chose that colour for the army," she said as she unbuckled her own cloak and tossed it over to him. He shook the folds of wool out and put her cloak on over his own as she kept talking. "Bright red is beautiful and bold, but useless for any stealthy work. The Nightravens are lucky, wearing blacks and greens. But better still, grey fur." As soon as he had buckled on her cloak, she handed him the gearbag.

He took the bag as she changed shape and dropped to the ground on her four paws. "Won't they get suspicious if they see a wolf around again?" he whispered. The shewolf looked back at him over her shoulder and rolled her yellow eyes. He grinned as he recognized the grimace of exasperation in a wolf's face. Then she turned away from him and pushed her way through the mountainthorns.

She thrust her muzzle out from under the thorn bush where she crouched. The bushes squeaked and rustled in the northeast wind. She wormed her way forwards and peered down into the little tussocky valley. Men on horses were pouring down the slope of the valley on the other side of the stream, black, white and grey shapes hung with brilliant armour. The men reached the stream and crossed it, the sound of splashing hooves just audible to her sharpened hearing. The smoke of the fire was still curling upwards, black against the patched white of the sky. A gust of wind wafted the smoky breeze towards her.

The Claws crossed the stream and began to climb the slope beneath her. *They're headed towards the wrong part of the thorns.* Her tail twitched happily, rustling the thorns. *We'll be able to lose them easily. Nine, ten. I think that's all of them, and all going to the wrong place. We'll head up the hill.* She looked back to the stream and up the hill. *Any sign of their sorcerer friend yet?*

Another gust of wind billowed the smoke towards her and she stifled a cough. *So much smoke for such a little fire.* She looked again, then gasped as she saw a red line of fire on the other side of the stream. *Tussock fire! And the wind's blowing it this way. The stream won't make much of a firebreak.* She spun around and galloped through the bushes back along her trail, the smell of smoke almost drowning the scent of horses.

She tracked him up the hill and changed shape while still running as she reached him. She staggered forwards, finding her two feet. His arms checked her and held her up. "Are they coming here?" he asked. She heard the soft clink of metal, then felt her cloak drape around her shoulders. "Have this back. It's warm wearing two." She raised her head and let him fasten the clasp at her throat.

She looked into his brown eyes and leant against him briefly while she caught her breath. "They're going the wrong way," she panted. She rested her head on the wool of his cloak. "But the tussock's afire. I didn't stamp the fire out enough."

His clasp tightened around her. "Get on Storm and ride down out of here," he said. "We've got to get out of the reach of the fire."

"No. Not down." She gripped his arms, feeling the hard metal beneath her hands and the tautness of the muscles beneath. "The Claws are down there. Go up. But let's get out of these thorns. They'll burn like fury once the fire reaches them."

She scrambled onto Storm's back. The gelding's nostrils flared wide and she caught the traces of smoke in the air. She pulled her foot clear of a tangle of thorns and thumped his sides with her heels. The black horse sprang through the thick thorns as he climbed uphill. Another gust of wind swirled past her, heavy with smoke.

Another thorn branch tore at her hands and arms, and she broke through the mountainthorns to tussock. Wind blew her hair around her face from behind, smoky and cold. She turned and looked back down the slope. Farren was emerging from the thorns, a small trickle of blood staining one cheek. "Your poor face," she said. He raised a hand to touch the scratch. She laughed in spite of her racing heartbeat and tension as she saw one of his cheeks smooth and the other still covered with chestnut bristle. "We were in a hurry to leave, weren't we?" she laughed. "At least your interrupted business was less serious than mine. I've set the hill afire."

"It's still uncomfortable," he grumbled, scratching the bristles.

"Not as uncomfortable as being roasted." She looked down the valley and saw the fire raging up the slope towards them. "The fire's crossed the stream."

"It's going to follow us. Where can we run to?"

She turned her head and scanned the hills and mountains above them. The peak of the nearest mountain was covered in spring snow, but below that, runners and rags of scree reached into the tussocks. *Scree doesn't burn, but can we climb there faster than the fire?* Her eyes ran down the slopes to a saddle to the west. Hummocks and crags of naked rock jutted out from the ridge leading to the saddle, which broke here and there into small cliff faces. "There," she said, pointing. "Make for that ridge. Those crags will make a natural firebreak." She gathered up Storm's reins and prepared to turn him.

"Look down there," Farren said. She spun around. Smoke billowed in her face and she bundled up the edge of her cloak and held it to her face to breathe. A thin black band surrounded the stream in the valley and saffron flames leaped and ate at the tussock between her and the water. Iron grey smoke wreathed upwards, clouding the sky. Through the heat haze cast by the flames, she saw men riding down the valley away from the thorns where they hid and towards the river. "Claws," she said through the cloak, then let it fall. "We've lost them now. But enough time wasted. Go to the ridge." She turned Storm's head and urged him uphill again.

She let the gelding have his head as he cantered up the slope out of the valley, zigzagging slightly. A crackling roar rose from behind her, blown with the smoke on the wind. *It's reached the thorns. Hopefully we can make it to the ridge in time.* The wind doubled in intensity as they neared the saddle, and her eyes started to smart and water. Storm panted and she felt his flanks heaving beneath her. She struggled to keep on his smooth back and clutched his mane to help balance her. Wind whistled loudly in her ears, but she heard the brittle sound of hooves striking stones. The black gelding stumbled and she looked down. A strip of loose stones dotted here and there with short, spiky plants ran down a bowshot from the ridge. She swung off Storm's back and landed slipping on the scree. "Thank the Power," she breathed. "There's more of a firebreak than I thought, at least here."

"I'd like to get further into it before we stop," he said. "I'm going to the ridge and the top of the crags."

Beneath them, the hillside flared in black and orange-red. Birds flew from the mountainthorns as the flame devoured the bushes, shrill cries carrying on the wind. An eagle hovered above the leading crest of the fire, stooping now and then on the small animals fleeing from the flames. The air shimmered and danced in the heat, and the roar and crackle of the burning rose to the top of the ridge.

Farren watched as a larger shape burst bellowing from the flames. An alphurrhn, a winged bear of the mountains, flew upwards. He took his bow from his shoulder and felt in his quiver for an arrow. *I'd better be ready in case it attacks, but I think it's escaping rather than hunting.* He watched it climb into the smoky sky and fly away towards the river. *I hope it finds the Claws and has one of their horses for supper.* Beneath it, the fire climbed higher, spreading south and west with the wind behind it, and came to the end of the mountainthorns. He gazed at the tussocks burning through stinging and watering eyes, and a cold knot tied itself in his stomach. "I hope these rocks really will act as a firebreak and the fire won't spread down into the next valley. Otherwise, we'll be trapped here," he said, coming over to her and curling his arms around her. "It's going to take too long for that to die down." He coughed as a gust of rolling white smoke hit him. "I'd rather not spend the night on this windy ridge. There's not much shelter and it's too cold."

She laughed. "Too hot or too cold? But we could always go down the other side of the ridge now."

He shifted around on the gravel, feeling it slide under his feet. He tightened his grip around her to steady himself. "That would really put the Claws off our trail, too. Do you think the fire will follow us, though?"

She ran a hand through her hair and looked down the slope, then into his eyes again. "Probably not. Fire burns upwards, not down. But we need to make sure that it won't."

"I can't see what we can do to stop it spreading." He flicked his eyes back down to the line of flame that climbed up the mountainside, more slowly now, but still steadily. "We haven't got anything to make a controlled fire with to create a firebreak, and we don't have enough water to damp it off – we don't have any water. To burn this ridge off like that, you'd need a lot more people than just the two of us."

She smiled at him, sapphire eyes sparkling in her pale face, and her hands wandered up the back of his head through his hair. "Is a steady northeast rain enough water?"

"What? Oh – you're going to invoke the windspirits, aren't you, Stormwolf? Good idea. What's the northeast's guardian? The Cat, isn't it?"

She shook her head, her hair tugging loose from where it had coiled beneath his chin. "The Falcon," she said. "Let me go and I'll call her." She pulled out of his arms and scrambled onto one of the tall rocks on the ridge.

CHAPTER TEN

She scrambled onto the top of one of the rocks. The wind caught her cloak as she stood up and she felt it pulling her lightly. Choking smoke billowed in her eyes. She blinked and rubbed away the tears, then looked around. The fire was ravening at the slope and had almost reached the gravel at the foot of the scree. A few stinging smuts and sparks blew onto her arms. To her left, the mountain towered to the blue vault of the sky, the smoke tinting her view of the white peak. She glanced behind her down the other side of the ridge. It wound away in twists and wrinkles, golden with tussocks and dotted with broom, gorse and mountainthorn. A gust of wind buffeted her and she planted her feet wide to steady herself on the rock.

"Do you want me to do anything?" Farren looked up at her, both horses' bridles in his hands.

She shook her head. "Get under cover; the rain could be heavy. There's a rock over on the north side that could be big enough."

He nodded and led the horses over the edge of the ridge. A long flat rock jutted out from the mountainside and he guided Princess and Storm under it. "I can't see what's going on from under here," he said.

"Do you want to get soaked?"

"No; I'll leave that to you," he replied, chuckling. He retreated under the rock.

She breathed deeply and thought. *What shall I say to summon the Falcon? Or shall I just command rain?* Smoke stung the back of her throat and she coughed as she searched in her mind for the words in the Old Tongue she needed. Below her, the fire spread, a line of orange at the edge of a blanket of black. *I can't command her. In the order of Heaven, she probably well outranks me. King of Heaven, give me the words and let the Falcon answer me.* She clenched her fists, raised both arms and threw back her head. *"Ker lypatho Domastin y Nataral, rhuakaso an Tyrrkhaier Magnan ilnasa van shirrasa ma serach."*

She waited, her hair billowing out behind her. The wind grew stronger, screaming in her ears and tearing at her cloak. The smoke thickened, heavy with the tang of resin and a faint crackling reached her ears. *By the smell of that, it's not just grass burning but trees. If the King of Heaven and the Falcon don't answer soon, even rain will struggle to put it out, unless we get enough of a deluge to put the Illin-Ast in flood.*

She called a second time. This time, the sky darkened with clouds above the smoke and she felt a few cold wet drops spatter onto her upraised hands. *Thank the King of Heaven; it's raining,* she thought as drops flicked and splashed onto her face. The wind increased its ferocity, heavy with smoke, cold and biting. Her skin tightened into little bumps along her arms. She looked down and saw the fire touching the edge of the scree and licking along the border as if trying to find its way around. The sky grey darker and she heard thunder rolling in the mountains beyond the river. A shiver of mixed cold and excitement travelled down her spine.

A spear of lightning cleft the thick masses of dark blue-grey cloud overhead, leaping to the peak of the mountain. Thunder roared, then a second bolt of lightning flickered and flared. Again the thunder spoke. Then, amidst a wreath of purple-magenta lightning, a great grey and black falcon appeared. The raptor screamed twice and circled above Azariel before plummeting down. She pulled up and hovered for a heartbeat over her head, the wind of her wings stirring Azariel's hair. A sharp clean smell, almost the scent of pine and lavender mixed, filled the air.

The Falcon turned and flew to the clouds again. She soared in circles, sweeping the lower clouds and the bands of rain into a tight knot. A nimbus of turquoise lightning flickered around the trim shape of her wings and body, defining him briefly against the swirls of cloud. Thunder boomed again, echoing off the sides of the valley and almost making the ground shake. The Falcon screamed in answer and stooped, wings tucked tight to her body, almost as swift as lightning herself. She levelled her flight above the course of the Illin-Ast, flew southwards for a few heartbeats, then spiralled up again, wings threshing the air. The clouds swallowed her up and she vanished. Rain poured down in a heavy curtain, lashing at her. On the southern slope, the line of red leading the fire dulled to black as billows and plumes of white smoke rose to meet the rain.

Farren heard the thunder and the bird's calls die away and stepped out from under the rocky overhang. Rain fell onto his face and he pulled his hood over his head. He looked up and saw Azariel standing with her hands on her hips, facing down the southern slope away from him. The soaked cotton of her trousers clung to the contours of her legs. "Stormwolf?" he said softly. "Did the Falcon come? I missed her."

She turned to him, hair plastered in stripes across her pale face by the wind and rain. "She came and the fire's out, as far as I can see. It can't spread much further. Let's get on. It's getting cold up here."

He stooped to pick up the gearbag and led the horses out from under the overhang. Storm shook his mane as the rain fell on him. Azariel scrambled from the rock onto the gelding's back and Farren tossed the reins back over Storm's head to her, followed by the bag, before he swung himself onto Princess. Leaning backwards, they rode down the northern slope of the saddle. The tang of smoke and wet earth hung in the air and his stomach gnawed at him with hunger again. Princess paused in her slow, steady walk to tear a mouthful of grass from between the tussocks. "Wish I could eat that," he said to the mare, pulling her head up and nudging her on. "You've already had something to eat this morning."

"It's a shame I couldn't get those rabbits into the gearbag in time. We'd better stop and find something to keep us going," Azariel said. "We also need to work out where we're heading. Look ahead. This valley doesn't run straight north-south; it twists and turns like one of Shadira's corkscrew curls."

He laughed, remembering the brunette guard back at the Watchtower of the West. "Would Shadira thank you for saying that? But I'm all for halting and eating – if there is anything to eat up here out of the forest."

He looked ahead where Azariel had indicated. Scrubby, brushy plants dotted the tussocks here and there as the valley wound its way down from the saddle, skirting the mountains. *No streams in this valley. But I'm not as thirsty as I was.* Almost without thinking, he brushed the rainwater clinging to the unshaven half of his face down and drank a few drops of it. The water tasted odd, a mixture of salt and soap mixed. A scrap of sunlight crawled down the valley towards them and he looked up. Here and there among the thick, soft grey clouds, patches of blue and white showed. The dapple of sunlight reached them and glinted off some young green spikes of spring growth and a handful of yellow flowers nearby. "This will do for a small lunch," he said, reining Princess in and dismounting.

He brushed what he could of the rainwater off the grass and sat down as she slid off Storm's back. "Thank the King of Heaven," she said as she nestled in beside him. Her hair still dripped, and her cloak clung to her shoulders as if still heavy with water. He carefully tore the long leaves off the flowering dandelions and handed her half. "Fresh green salads again today." He bit off a mouthful of the bitter leaves and chewed them. *Wish we still had some cheese to go with this, but all our food's sitting in the Claw's gearbag.* He looked again at the young plants and smiled. "And there's more. I thought this tall thing was mullein at first glance but it's not; it's borage. Eat it while the bristles are tender."

He munched his way through the tender leaves and looked down the valley. The rain eased gradually but the air remained cool and the northeast wind blew keenly. "Stormwolf," he said, swallowing. "I think we ought to leave this valley and go back to the river. I don't fancy getting lost in the hills and not knowing where we are until we get to the Ulfskin-Aza forest, if that's where we end up. This cloud's covering the sun and it'll definitely cover the stars, so we won't be able to use them to find our way."

"What about the Claws?"

"We'll have lost them for a while, at least until their sorcerer comes with his mirror. But we need sleep, decent and shelter tonight if we're going to be any good for a fight if – or when – they come back. The gorge is more likely to have a rainshadow in it."

She clambered to her feet. "Let's go, then. We'll have to cross over the hills again."

They swung to the right and threaded their way through the broom and gorse. The ground swelled into steep curves beneath them, dotted with rocks as it rose to the top of the mountain. He gripped Princess's mane as she climbed, stopping himself from slipping backwards on her damp back. He shook his hood off his head and looked up at the ridge above them. Spiky silhouettes of the scrubby bushes stood sentinel along it. Suddenly, he tensed. One of the shapes moved and vanished into another. *What was that? Claws? Surely not!*

He reached for his bow, tension prickling the back of his neck. "Wait a moment," he said softly to Azariel. "There's something up there on the ridge."

"Do you want me to shift shape and scout it out?" She reined Storm in beside him.

Two shapes appeared on the ridge and a third below it: a thin white animal. "Goats!" he said. His hand tightened around his bow. "Looks like we might get a hot meal of meat after all today."

"Do you want me to go and get it?"

"I don't think you'll need to. These goats won't have seen many humans before and you know how inquisitive they are. Wolves, however..."

"They know to be the enemy and will run like the wind," she finished for him. "Good. I like watching you hunt."

He unclipped an arrow from the quiver and fitted it to his bow as he rode along. The goats still stood on the ridge, watching. *Not close enough yet; not for an uphill shot into the wind.* The cool northeasterly breeze hissed through the tussocks into his face. Faintly, carried on the wind, the cry of a young kid drifted down. *I had forgotten that.* His eyes flicked to and fro over the shapes on the ridge. *I had better make sure I don't shoot a doe goat with a kid at foot.* Princess raised her head and scrambled up another ten paces of the hillside, bringing him within fifty paces of the ridge. The watching goats turned and darted over to the other side.

He swung off Princess's back, arrow sliding off the rest but still remaining nocked in place. "Wait here," he whispered, to Azariel. "Or if you want to watch, leave the horses and creep up to the ridge with me – in your own shape." His left hand found the bowstring and his three middle fingers hooked around the tough sinew. He reached the top of the ridge and knelt behind a broom bush, turning his head to peer around the broom down the slope.

A black and white goat, a young male with horns less than a foot long, nibbled at the bright green leaves and shoots of wild roses further down the slope. Cautiously, Farren twisted round, grip of the recurve bow settling into the palm of his right hand. The piebald buck turned to one side, then bent its forelegs so that it knelt to crop the lower branches of the rose. Farren fixed his eyes on the little hollow behind the foreleg and drew the bow, the sinew of the string biting into his fingers. *Downhill, into the wind. Tricky.* His eyes measured the distance between him and the buck, then he trained one of the bronze sighting lines set into the wood of the bow onto the hollow behind the goat's leg. The bow reached full draw; his shoulder and chest strained to hold it steady, then he let the string free.

The arrow whistled down through the grass and buried itself in a clump of tussock two paces short of the buck. The goat raised its head and stared at the three red feathers near it, scrambling to its feet. It sniffed at the arrow, nibbled the fletchings then turned back to the rosebush.

Swiftly, he fitted a second arrow to the string, drew and aimed. He let the arrow fly, bowstring catching his bare right forearm with a slash like a whip. The point took the buck behind the shoulder and passed through, leaving a bright stain of scarlet on a white patch of hair. The buck raised its head from the roses and bleated, a high, almost childlike cry that twisted Farren's stomach, almost killing the flush of satisfaction surging through him. The buck staggered a few paces along the hillside, walking dizzily, then lay down under a bush, head low.

"Good shot!" Azariel darted from behind him down to the goat. Shouldering his bow, he marched down the hillside towards his arrows. He pulled the first free from the tussocks, then searched around on the other side of the rosebush for the second. The shaft was covered in bright frothy blood. He wiped it, then his fingers clean on the wet grass and leaves before clipping it back into place. "Don't skin the goat yet," he said to Azariel, who was leaning over the carcass. "Just gut it. We'd better find some shelter for the night first and we've got to carry that on horseback."

She stood up and wiped her dagger on the grass. A strong, organic smell rose from the dead goat, mixing with the sharp scent of blood. She bent down, taking the buck by the hind legs. "Wait," he said. "I'll call the horses and we'll sling the meat over them. Don't carry it on your shoulders and get bloodier than you have to." He put his fingers to his lips and whistled.

The horses came cantering down the hill, slipping slightly on the wet grass. He slung the goat across Princess's withers before shouldering the gearbag and mounting. They rode slowly downhill. The roar of the river rose from the valley and as he looked ahead, he saw it brown and swollen. The northeast wind blew chilly in his face and thin grey clouds spun across the sky, cutting off the afternoon sunlight. He shivered and drew his cloak around himself.

Halfway down the slope, Princess and Storm pulled up. A cliff face fell in front of them down to the bottom of the gorge where the muddy river swirled and foamed. "We can't get to the river valley tonight," he said, looking back over his shoulder at her. Her cloak still clung damply to the outline of her torso and arms. "We'll have to find somewhere up here on the hillside." He shivered as another gust of wind swept around them. "Damn. We should have stayed back in the other valley."

"Too late to go back there now." Her voice sounded toneless and tired. "Try the pine wood over there." She pointed with one pale hand to the north. A dark green clump of trees clung to the slopes, a patch in the golds and grey-brown of the tussock. He pulled Princess's head up from the grass and nudged her towards the spinney.

The northeast wind hissed and roared in the pines, echoing the note of the swollen river. Princess picked her way slowly and steadily along the slope, head hung low. Farren buried his cold fingers into the wiry warmth of her mane as she stepped around a tumbled heap of boulders at the foot of a small landslide. On his left, between the pile of rocks and the stand of pines, the hillside gave way to a rock face. In the middle of the bare rock, a wide black gap opened. He drew Princess to a halt and looked back at Azariel. "A cave," he said. "Perfect. I only hope that no Claws, alphurrhns or other beasts are in there first."

He guided Princess around the rocks and into the cave. Her hooves echoed faintly off the stone walls. He shook the hood back from his head and looked around at the dim, dry interior of the cave, glad to be out of the bone-chilling northeast wind. He waited until his eyes adjusted to the gloom and scanned the gnarled grey walls and roof. "It's dry enough in here, and seems more than big enough for us and the horses," he called back over his shoulder.

He dismounted and bent over the patch of sandy dirt by the mouth of the cave, gearbag swinging clumsily across his shoulder. He tossed the bag into the dark mouth of the cave. In the fading afternoon light, he saw the marks of claws scored on an old tree stump. *Alphurrhn, common bear, lion or dragon?* He glanced around for more marks and saw a cloverleaf-like print in the mud, a large pad surrounded by four smaller pads. "Cave-lion," he said aloud.

"What?" He felt her hand on his shoulder and her wet hair brushing his cheek as she bent over him. "Found some tracks? Fresh ones, it looks like."

He straightened up and told her. A look of worry flashed over her face, but soon faded as her eyes took on their fighting flicker. "If we can build a fire, it will leave us alone," she said, slurring some of her words slightly. "If it doesn't, then we can fight it off. You fought all those men single-handedly last night; you can fight a lion with me beside you and the horses."

He winked at her. "I know," he said. "But let's get a fire built. There should be plenty of wood over in the pines so we should be able to spark up a blaze. I'm freezing."

"Are you?" She yawned. "I'm not that cold, even though I'm shivering. Look at me." She held out one arm and he watched as it quivered like a trapped bird.

He ran his fingers over her icy hand, then touched her cheek. A sick, cold anxiety grew in the pit of his stomach as he felt the chill of her skin and saw the pale blue of her lips. Her clothes were drenched and her whole body trembled. "You're very pale. Oh Stormwolf. Oh, hellfire! You're wet through, aren't you – wet, cold, pale and shivering. And you stood on that hilltop in the wind and heavy rain." He unclasped her wet cloak and began feeling for the laces at the neck of her armour. "You're dangerously chilled."

"What are you doing?" she said sharply, pushing his hands away.

"I've got to warm you before you start to die of cold. Get into the cave."

He half dragged her into the cave, fumbling with the laces at her neck as he hauled her along. *How on earth do I peel the armour off someone else?* Thoughts whirled in his brain, the instructions given by a trainer in cadets about exposure. A sharp arrow of desire pulsed through him. *Strip the victim off completely and use body heat to warm them skin to skin. The lads used to laugh about getting to rescue one of the pretty girls and now it's happened to me. But I can't do that; not unless I have no other choice. I don't trust myself.* He tugged at the metal around her hips and she unbuckled her sword belt as he pulled the chainmail up. "I'm going to get some wood for a fire," he said. He drew a deep breath and swallowed, mouth dry. "Take the rest of your wet things off and lie down on Storm's back with a blanket over you." He felt a warm flush of blood in his face and fidgeted with his betrothal earring. "But I am coming back and I need to take care of you, so… Stormwolf, I don't want to spoil things by seeing all of you just yet."

She laughed weakly through chattering teeth. "Don't worry about me. I'm not going to seduce you. I'm an ice maiden now."

"I'm not." He chirruped to the horses and called them into the cave. *Mine isn't the only warm body handy. Perhaps theirs will be warmer.* Taking Storm's bridle, he led the gelding to one side of the cave near the back, stooping for the leather bag of gear as he passed it. "Down, Storm," he murmured. "Your mistress needs you." He ran his hands over the horse's withers and pushed down firmly. Storm's legs buckled and he sank down to the floor of the cave. "There," Farren said, turning to Azariel and feeling inside the bag for the blanket. "Lie down on him with this over you while I go and make a fire." He handed the oblong of grey wool to her and left the cave.

Azariel listened to his footsteps die away before peeling her leather gear off. Her woollen underclothes clung to her shoulders and hips, translucent with rainwater. *I'm going to leave that on. Wool stays warm.* Her thoughts crawled slowly through her mind. She draped herself over Storm's back and pulled the blanket around her body. The rough blanket and the horsehair prickled her bare legs and the gentle warmth of the gelding's body crept up into her limbs. Bit by bit, she felt the blood flowing freely in her shins and elbows. *And I never even noticed myself getting over-cold.*

Footsteps crunched on the gravel and entered the cave. She turned to see Farren standing at the back over a pile of small logs and pinecones brushing needles out of his cloak. He rustled around with the sticks and logs, then a flare of yellow firelight played on the walls and the smell of smoke and pine resin filled the air. She yawned and laid her head down on Storm's neck. The gelding snorted and tossed his head beneath her. "Don't move, old fellow," she mumbled.

She heard the chink of armour falling to the ground to one side of her, followed by a few footsteps grinding on the gravelly floor. The warmth of Farren's leather-clad arms wrapped around her shoulders and she felt the crisp prickle of his cheek brushing hers. "Come on, Stormwolf," he murmured in her ear. "Over to the fire and let it warm you. Your uniform will be dry by morning so just use the blankets for now. I'll get that goat roasting as soon as some good coals have formed."

She slithered off Storm's back, clutching at the blanket. He lifted it around her shoulders, then guided her over to the fire beside Princess. The warmth of the flames stabbed into her as she sat down. His arms wrapped around her waist and pulled her backward so that her head rested on the slightly damp leather of his tunic. She felt his chest rise and fall beneath her and heard the gentle beating of his heart. "My sweetheart," he crooned. "I should have seen it happening to you sooner. You're that much slighter than me and you were wetter, too." He nuzzled her cheek, his chin warm and prickly.

She leaned back on him with her eyes closed and her muscles limp. His head pressed close against hers so that his breath hissed into her ear and the tip of his chin nudged the back of her scalp. The pine logs in the fire crackled and she opened one eye to see it spitting sparks. She sat up straighter and drew her knees up to her chest. "Sorry," she said, tilting her head back to look at him. "It's getting too hot on my bare skin."

His eyes flicked away from hers to her legs, then back again with a catch in his breath. "Don't worry," he said. "I've got to stoke the fire anyway. And there's the goat to roast." He shifted behind her and she wriggled forwards as he stood up. "Excuse me while I go and get it. Do you want the skin to sit on?"

"May as well," she chuckled. "Even green with all the fat and blood still on it." She leaned back against Princess and watched him as he went to the side of the cave where he had dumped the goat carcass, then bent over it with his knife. The smell of blood mixed with the slight tang of smoke in the cave. After a while, he stood up again, the black and white pelt dangling form one hand. "This knife you gave me isn't too bad," he said, wiping the blade on a patch of the pelt. "It isn't quite the perfect shape for a skinning knife, but it does what I need it to." He spread the skin on the floor of the cave, then turned back to the carcass. "Now, I'll get some strips off this, and then I'm going to cook a meal for you."

She clasped the blanket across her chest and drew her legs underneath herself, ready to rise. "I'll do it," she said.

"No, you won't. You lie there and let me look after you. I don't get much of an excuse to pamper you, so I'm going to take it now." His brown eyes danced in the firelight as he came back to the fire carrying several strips of meat.

"I don't need pampering." She tossed her hair back from her face.

"Yes, you do. You don't get the treatment you deserve, arch *minyaster*. Anyway, you're the one who went halfway down the road to freezing to death." He reached for his belt pouch and opened it. "And I'm the one with the herbs for the cooking." He reached inside the pouch and drew out a handful of crushed sprigs.

She sniffed. "Rosemary," she said, catching the faint trace of bitter green scent. "When did you pick that?"

"The day before yesterday. I smelt it and thought of you," he said, smiling. He cut dozens of tiny slits in the meat and worked the herb into them, pushing the sprigs down under the thin white outer layer of fat. He skewered the steaks with a strong stick and placed it over the glowing red coals before easing in behind her. "Lean back on me again, Stormwolf." His right arm tightened around her stomach, fingers gently kneading into the soft skin while his left hand stroked her hair. "I can't smell the rosemary in your hair any more now," he whispered. "Just grass and smoke."

She rubbed her cheek against the smooth damp leather on his chest and inhaled. "Do you want to know what you smell like, beloved?" she said dreamily.

"Not horrible, I hope," he chuckled. He stretched one arm past her and turned the meat. Fat sputtered into the fire and a sharp, acrid smoke rose, followed by a mouth-watering scent of roasting meat. "This is going to take a long time to cook,

Stormwolf," he said. "Lie back on me and try to warm up some more while it cooks."

She snuggled against him and pulled the blanket tighter around her. "My mother used to sing as a way of timing meat cooking," she murmured. "A ballad for the bacon, two for a steak and a whole grand epic for a roast, she told me."

"Will you sing to me now?" His hands rubbed over her forehead and she felt her hair catch in his ring.

"All right." She stared into the fire, softly and tentatively at first but then more strongly, singing the ballad she had sung when the bard in the ale tent had passed the harp around. Beneath her, his chest hummed and vibrated as he sang with her down the octave. She glanced back at him and smiled. "Don't you dear join in with the next song if you want me to get through it without laughing."

"Why? Is it bawdy?"

"Yes. Most ballads are."

"Better not, then. Try something else. Or rather, don't. These steaks are thin and they look done." He reached forwards and lifted the spit with the meat off the embers. "Thank the King of Heaven for something hot," he said, brushing the rocky floor clear of gravel and sand before laying the meat down. "Try not to burn your fingers."

She wriggled away from him, clutching the blanket tightly around her hips and shoulders. *I hope my clothes dry before tomorrow. This is awkward.* She pulled her share of the steaks off the sticks, the hot fat and juices scalding the tips of her fingers. Her mouth watered and her stomach growled. She sucked a finger to cool it and caught the savoury taste of just-done meat and rosemary. Hungrily, she tore at the thin steak, licking around her lips to catch the juices.

He looked over at her and smiled. "What shape do you think you're in at the moment?" he teased.

"Human," she replied. "As a wolf, I'd think this was unbearably hot, dry and overdone. But right now, I think it's delicious." She attacked another slice with her teeth.

They ate in silence until a third of the cooked meat was gone. She breathed out a sigh of content that turned into a yawn. Farren carefully wiped the tip of one finger around his mouth, licked it clean and yawned in reply. "I'm tired and so are you. You go to sleep and I'll keep watch."

"Today, I'm not going to argue about that with you."

She nodded and leaned back on his chest, nestling close to him and relishing the warmth of his body. She stared drowsily into the flames. *Even if I was in wolf shape, I couldn't ask for a better mixture of smells than what's here. Roasting meat, woodsmoke, horses, grass, pine and him.* She swallowed down the moisture that rose in her mouth to meet the scents. Her eyelids fell closed and she drifted off to sleep, lulled by the deep steady rhythm of his heartbeat and the crackling of the flames.

Her head and torso were jerked suddenly, and she woke, hearing the rasping of a sword drawn from the sheath and the horses snorting. She opened her eyes and looked behind her across Princess's back. Farren stood by the mouth of the cave looking out with his sword drawn, the red light of the firecoals catching a russet sheen off his black leather uniform. She coiled the blanket tightly round her and got to her feet. Drawing her own sword from the pile made up of belt, cloak and armour, she walked over to him. Firelight reflected palely back from two points of glassy yellow-green. A growl rose out of the darkness. "The cave's owner has come to evict us," said Farren. "The cave-lion has returned."

Another growl, then the eyes turned away and vanished into the darkness. Briefly, she saw the tawny hindquarters of the big cat lit up by the flame, then nothing. The wind hissed and roared through the pines nearby. Farren yawned. "Afraid of the fire," he said. "I'm glad to see you well rested. How are you?" He reached for her sword arm with his right hand. "You're nicely warm again."

"Thanks to you, beloved," she said and smiled at him.

She sat down on the hard floor of the cave with her back to the opening. The fire had shrunk to a circle of red embers and charred logs in the middle of a nest of ashes. She laid her sword down beside her and stared into it. She rested her sword down beside her and stared into the fire. Farren laid his sword down beside hers with a soft ring of metal on metal and his shoulder pressed against hers. "Can I sleep now?" he said.

"Of course you can." She arched her back and tried to strain the cramped knot out of her neck..

He nodded. "You'll need more firewood. That lot I fetched earlier has all gone."

She pulled the blanket back up across her chest, covering where the neckline of her woollen underclothes fell to the scar between her breasts. "Do you know if my clothes are dry yet? If they are, then you can have the blanket."

"I don't know. I haven't looked. And I haven't looked, if you know what I mean. At you while you were asleep." He yawned again and shrugged his cloak forwards across his shoulders and began wrapping himself up in it. "Not much, anyway."

She shot him a sharp glance, then turned away. *I trust him to control himself. I only hope this blanket stayed over me enough while I was sleeping to keep me decent.* She clambered to her feet and walked to where her black leather uniform was spread out on the rocks. The leather was dry and stiff to the touch, although the seams and folds of material were still cold and wet. "It's dry enough," she said, half to herself. "Don't look round," she called. He grunted in reply. She shook out the trousers and tunic then glanced behind her. Farren's head was turned away, staring towards the fire.

Quickly, she pulled her clothes on and laced them up. "Have the blanket," she said, kneeling beside him and draping it over his back. "And sleep well."

"Thank you," he said drowsily. He turned his head towards her.

She bent and kissed him on the lips. "Good night."

She strolled out of the cave and walked to the pines. The wind had torn a gap in the gap in the clouds and the hard stars shone in the indigo sky. She pushed into the thick prickly needles of the copse of pines and felt around on the ground and lower branches around the trunks for dry dead wood. The trees groaned and muttered in the darkness above and around her, and the air was heavy with the green-earthy scent of the old needles. Twice, she heard a faint rustling and the padding of animal feet a little way off, but saw nothing in the gloom when she turned to look. *The lion's still around. I wish I hadn't left my sword behind.* She collected a large armload of logs and cones, and returned to the cave.

Farren was dozing, wrapped in cloak and blankets, his red hair reflecting the sheen of the fire. *You are a good-looking man, Farren Blackarrow,* she thought as she smiled down at him. *And not just handsome to look at, either.* She stooped to let the wood tumble onto the floor of the cave then stacked some onto the fire. *He could have gaped and pawed at me if he had been another sort of man. I'm lucky to have him.* She sat down beside him and gently laid her arm across his chest. He stirred and grasped her arm, his hands warm, firm and golden. Her heart beat faster and she felt drawn to him like iron to a lodestone. *Careful,* she thought. *I shouldn't paw at him, either.* She sighed and ran her free hand through his hair, then around his shoulder as he fell asleep again, still holding her hand. *I'd love to hold him all night, every night, closer than this and closer still. But the time isn't right for that yet. Later. Just one more year left to wait.* She stared into the fire and snickered with laughter. *I must be cured of the cold now if I'm thinking like this.*

After several hours, the darkness began to lift. Farren had rolled to one side, freeing her. She stood up and stretched her cramped muscles, stumbling as her numb leg flared to life in a million needles. The scrap of sky at the cave mouth turned from deep indigo to cobalt, to pale gold and finally to light blue. The wind rustled and stirred in the pines and grass outside, almost drowning the morning shrilling and liquid belling of the birds. She gently shook Farren awake. "Time to move on again," she said. They ate the rest of the cold meat, stowed the blanket into the bag and led the horses out of the cave.

They rode beneath the cliff until it dwindled to a small scrubby fall of rocks. Sunlight glittered off the rain-beaded grass and tussocks, and the rush of the swollen river rose from the valley. A long spur led off from the hillside down to the valley, and they headed the horses along it. To the north, the gorge widened into river flats. A hare leaped from behind a broom bush and darted downhill, a golden spray of rainwater flying around and behind it as it ran. The hare vanished into a clump of mountainthorn.

Farren reined Princess in on the crest of the spur. "Time to look back," he said. "We had better see whether those Claws are still around."

"Perhaps they think we were caught in the fire," she said as she turned Storm so that she could look back down the gorge. "But you're right. We'd better look."

The valley lay empty. She watched the rocks and trees closely for signs of movement. Shapes moved through the brush near the river's edge and she stiffened, then relaxed as a small herd of deer glided down to the water to drink. She scanned the air above the trees and scrub, watching for the flight of startled birds. *Nothing there, either, but what's that bird?* A distant black winged shape flew from the south towards them. *Eagle? No, it's too big for that, unless it's a great-eagle. It must be an alphurrhn hunting.* She watched it approach, the shape and colour growing clearer and more detailed as it came. "Orange is an odd colour for a bird or an alphurrhn," she said aloud. "Do you know what it is, Farren?"

"Can't tell, but look: it's beginning to circle. Don't worry about it." He pulled Princess's head up from the grass. "Let's go down to the river and drink. There aren't any Claws there."

She pulled Storm's head up and tightened her fingers around the reins. Before she nudged him down the northern slope, she glanced backwards at the winged shape once more. It began to turn in the sky above the spur covered in thick bush. It stretched out a horse-like head with horns and crest, and a long snaking neck that flowed into a slender lizard's body and tail. Between its outspread red wings sat a dark human shape. A cold line shot down the length of her back. "A dragon-rider," she said between clenched teeth.

"What?" Farren spun around. "That's their sorcerer or I'm a mountain goat." He thumped Princess's sides with his heels and headed her down the slope. "Let's get as far away from them as we can."

She spurred Storm down the slope into the broad river flat where the Illin-Ast flowed, sparkling in the sunlight. Ahead, the cuplike cluster of peaks descended into the white shining line of Moonlady Falls as they fell to the river.

"Should we go to the Falls themselves and hide in the corridors and stairs in the rock behind it?" he asked. "I never thought I'd willingly go back into that dungeon – once was enough – but it will be a good place to hide. The stairs will give us a fighting advantage."

She looked back over her shoulder, half expecting to see the dragon in the air once more. The sky was empty apart from a flock of herons rising croaking from the river flats. "No good," she said. "We can't hide from a scrying mirror. They'll find us wherever we go. And what about the dragon? A good stream of fire from that, if it's trained well enough, and…"

"Can't you block dragonfire?" He reined the mare in on the level ground.

"Someone in the histories has, I think. But I'm not sure. But you've got to remember that it'll take more than five months to rid that place of Crajaval's influence. All the strength the Power can give us will be blunted. You should know that better than most."

His eyes closed and he shuddered, pain twisting his face before he mastered himself. "So what will we do? Sit and wait for them to find us?"

"They'll find us whether we wait or not," she said, shaking the hair out of her eyes. Sunlight gleamed off the water dazzling her eyes and she blinked. "Why don't we choose our place for a face-to-face combat rather than let them choose it for us?"

"Good idea – but we're still going to have a drink at the river first." He turned his head to look up and down the river. "Where's that bridge that was here last time?"

She scanned the river flats ahead of them. *It shouldn't be far.* "Closer to the Falls, beyond the crabapple trees. Is that where you want to fight them?"

"Well, they can only come a few at a time on the bridge," he said. "And if we get on the other side of it, we might be able to cut the chains on it – it was almost falling apart when we were here before – and give them all a bath in the Illin-Ast. It's deep, too."

She looked along the golden line of the shining river. "Well, there's the Falls ahead of us. Let's go."

She put heels to Storm again and cantered to the riverbank. The big gelding splashed into the shallows at the edge, churning silt and gravel into the clear water. He bent his head and drank while she slipped off his back, landing with a small splash. She crouched a pace upstream from the horse and scooped handful after handful of water up to her mouth. More hooves squelched and crunched into the shallows beside her. She dashed a last handful over her face, blinking and gasping with the cold shock. Wiping the droplets off her face, she re-mounted while Farren drank. Then they rode along the broad curve of riverbank, past a stand of flowering crabapple trees to a place where the banks became steep and sheer, dropping twice a person's height before reaching the surface of the river.

A swing bridge attached to two carven pillars of granite at each end hung high above the Illin-Ast. *Still as ugly as ever, though not as ominous,* she thought as she ran her eyes over the figures of moons, mazes, humans and animals carved in the stone. She dismounted and led Storm across, feeling the bridge sway and teeter beneath her feet. The gelding balked, tossing his head and slanting his ears back, but she tugged him on. "You've crossed it before, Storm. Twice, including once at a full gallop with hellhounds behind you. You can do it again." The river swirled and lapped below them. She eyes the old wooden planks and the gaps between them uneasily. *I hope this will hold us still.* She peered down and glimpsed the sand and rock of the riverbed, blued by the distance underneath the crystal-clear water. The soles of her feet felt suddenly cold and an answering chill tingled in her spine. *So deep and so clear.* The chains creaked and screamed as the bridge quivered and swayed. At last, she stepped onto firm, steady ground on the northern bank.

She re-mounted and turned Storm around as Farren led Princess across the bridge. The mare kept her ears pricked forwards and she walked swiftly until she had reached Azariel and Storm. Azariel reached for her sword hilt but then released it. "We won't be using swords this time," she said, seeing Farren drawing his.

He smiled at her and turned the emerald ring on his right hand straight while his sword lay balanced across Princess's withers. "I will. But here we go again, fighting at Moonlady Falls. I should have picked some of that crabapple blossom for you as a token."

"Get it later – after we get through this."

"I hope we do. I'm not looking forward to that dragon."

She nudged the lapis lazuli ring straight on her left hand, then stared at the flecks of blue, red and green in the opal on her right before raising her head and looking southwards again. The sky was empty, apart from a distant hawk circling above the golden flanks of the nearest mountain. She bared her teeth and tossed her hair back. "We can face it," she said. "It's only a beast, after all. And it could be a cold-drake."

The sun crawled across the streaky blue above them while they waited and watched the sky above the hill. Then the batlike shape of the dragon cut across the white clouds. It spiralled upwards, threshing the air with its wide leathery wings, then turned towards them. In the shadow beneath it, riders galloped over the tussock and gravel. She breathed deeply and quickly, feeling the blood course ready and eager through her veins. She leaned over to Farren and kissed his cheek. "Ready?" she said.

"Yes. In the name of God Incarnate, yes!"

CHAPTER ELEVEN

Farren ran his eyes over the line of horsemen before glancing up to the dragon flying above them. *We can manage the horsemen easily enough,* he thought, flexing his fingers around his sword hilt. *But the sorcerer and the dragon are more dangerous.* He looked down at the emerald ring on his right hand. The leaf-green jewel pulsed and sparkled with inner lightning, and the silver circle, along with the onyx on his left hand, heated to a fiery band around his fingers. He fixed his gaze on the approaching Claws. *Those horsemen have to come at me one at a time over half a bowshot of rickety bridge. They're all going to have a swim.* He limbered his muscles ready to fight as his heart hammered against his ribs. Light flashed from the Claws' swords and armour, and flickered from the sharpened horseshoes on the hooves of the dun and piebald horses. The sound of drumming hooves mixed with the rushing of the river and the hiss of wind through the grass. *One bowshot away from me; half a bowshot from the bridge. Time to act.* "Shield me from the dragon and the sorcerer, Stormwolf," he ordered. "I'll cut the chains of the bridge."

"Don't do that! We've got to get back somehow."

He scratched his chin. *I still haven't shaved properly. I'll be growing a ridiculous-looking beard and I can't do a thing about it now.* "Ah… yes," he said aloud. "I forgot about that. I'll have to hold the bridge alone. Defend me from the dragon."

"I intend to."

He nudged Princess onto the bridge, hearing the rusty chains groan and creak as she stepped onto it. The line of planks swayed like the water beneath it. *No good.* He swung off the mare and coaxed her to step backwards. *I'll have to fight unmounted. Two horses rearing and stamping on the bridge could easily send us all into the river and bring the bridge down. It'll be easier to keep my balance unmounted on the unstable ground.* He twitched his bow off his shoulder and tossed it onto the ground beside the horse. *I won't use that, either. I don't want to waste my last few arrows.*

He strode onto the bridge, sword drawn, and clenched his teeth. The bridge swayed and bucked as the first of the Claw men rode up, sunlight gleaming from his sword and the sharp-shod hooves of his dun stallion. Farren rocked and pivoted, keeping level and poised, ready to fight. A cold shadow passed over his head with a flurry of wings. The dragon roared and he heard a frightened neigh from the horses behind, followed by the crackle of lightning, but he kept his eyes fixed on the Claw as the span of planks between them lessened.

He raised his right fist to the level of his shoulder, swaying to keep level. The dun stallion's flanks were stained dark with sweat, flecked in places with white foam, and its wild, white-rimmed eyes betrayed its fear. Farren opened his fist and threw fire at the big horse's chest, feeling the flare and prickle of lightning bursting from his fingertips. The blue flame struck the horse in the centre of the neck and it reared, squealing. Its legs buckled beneath it and it fell heavily, making the bridge jump and twitch like a whiplash. The rider toppled into the chains holding the bridge with a clatter and ring of metal on metal.

The Claw sprang up from the wreck of the horse, swinging his sword up and out to the guard stance. Farren inched forwards and sliced at the man's neck. The swords met with a jarring blow that stung his hands and he brought his blade down and back, narrowly missing the man's thigh. The Claw lurched forwards, the steel edge whistling through the air an inch from Farren's face. Farren drove it back, his arms feeling as heavy and clumsy as windmill blades. Another quick backslash and he caught the Claw on the wrist. *You're not used to left-handed sword fighters, are you?* He tried to swallow the sticky saliva out of his mouth, then battered at the Claw's defences. The Claw's sword flew from his hand over the edge of the bridge. The man looked at him, tongue running around his lips, eyes darting to and fro.

"Do you want your sword back?" asked Farren, stepping closer to the man and lowering his sword. The Claw's face paled and he shrank back beside the body of the horse. Farren stood over the other man, groping for the Claw's belt. His hand closed over the leather as he pulled the man close. Fists pounded him on the back and he swivelled his hips sharply to one side as the other man's knee crunched up and hit him on the thigh. "Go and fetch it, then!" He jerked the man forwards, tripping him and heaving the man over the side of the bridge.

The Claw yelled and clutched at the edge of the planks as he fell, making the bridge dance and lurch. The chains creaked. "Kingdom scum," the man snarled through gritted teeth. Farren struck the whitened knuckles of the man with the flat of his sword. The man splashed into the river and was swept away by the swift water.

The dun stallion lay dead in the centre of the bridge. *That'll make it hard for any of the others to come across mounted – except the sorcerer.* Farren glanced at the sky to see where the dragon had gone.

The dragon wheeled and plunged down a second time towards the two *minyasti*. Its huge leathery wings beat the air, propelling it down, a red-orange lightning bolt. It stretched out its long neck and roared as it plummeted from the sky.

Azariel watched the dragon as it came, keeping her eyes fixed on the figure of the sorcerer that sat astride the base of its neck. She shuffled into a firmer position on Storm's bare back and raised her arms in front of her chest, ready to attack. Her rings pointed outwards and her armbands of protection guarded her heart. *At least this is a cold-drake, not a fire-breathing dragon. Will it attack me again or Farren this time?* The dragon's legs were tucked up beneath its body as it stooped, streamlining it. The wind from the dragon's wings stirred her hair and blew it back from her face as the dragon passed over the bridge.

The sorcerer pointed his fist towards Farren as he stood facing the Claws. "Duck!" she shouted as white fire blazed from the sorcerer's hand. She bit her lip, mouth dry with alarm as Farren dropped to his knees, the bolt searing the air above his head. Breathing hard, she raised her own ring and let green fire fly hot, sparkling and tingling from her hand at the sorcerer.

The bolt of green lightning flew wide of the sorcerer but smashed into the outspread wing of the dragon. It roared again, arching its neck up and threshing its tail in coils and spirals as it soared up towards the grey clouds that were massing in the blue. Faintly, she heard the voice of the sorcerer shouting at the dragon but she did not catch the words. *That's where you're vulnerable,* she thought. *I'll shoot your steed next time, not you.*

The sorcerer aimed his fist at her and a flood of cobalt blue flame burned down, cutting him off from her sight. She whirled her left arm up, blocking the blast with her silver armband of protection. The blue energy shuddered into her arm, and the emeralds and diamonds in her armband flared bright and fierce as they absorbed the light. She tossed her head, flicking her hair back from her eyes, and pulsed red light from her opal ring in return.

The dragon wheeled away from the scarlet flame, its shadow racing across the windblown grass as the beast fled away, then vanishing as the clouds cut off the sun. Then it turned once more and began to dive, ready for another attack.

Farren stepped backwards as two Claws leaped at him from the top of the dead stallion's body. He staggered, shaken by the impetus of the two men behind their swords. He regained his balance, lashing out wildly with his sword. Collecting himself, he raised his blade in front of himself to block the next stroke, the impact ringing in his ears and jarring his arm. He danced to and fro on the bucking bridge, fighting the two men back with blow after blow. "Come on," he growled, baring his teeth. "I'll fill the bridge with a wall of your bodies."

The head and shoulders of a third Claw appeared on top of the dead horse behind the other two. Farren's heart and stomach lurched inside him and he raised his right hand, fist clenched and ring out, as he blocked first one sword then the second with the sword in his left. A bolt of turquoise fire spurted from the emerald ring and took one of the Claws in the chest. The man dropped like a sack of sand and Farren jumped back as the third Claw leaped from the back of the horse onto the bridge. The other Claw's sword slashed across his left arm and he howled as he felt the white-hot line of pain sear across the muscle and skin. He brought his sword up to catch the backslash, twisting to one side as the newcomer stabbed at him. One of the men crashed into him, knocking him back. He swayed for balance as he battered the swords of the two men away.

The bridge swayed and bucked with their movement and he lost his footing. *Shield me!* he thought as he fell. He dropped his sword and raised both arms, summoning up a wall of invisible energy between himself and the Claws. The air shimmered around and above him as he lay, chest heaving for breath, on the splintering wooden planks. Blood flowed from the cut on his arm and dripped down into the river. *That will stop them for a while.* The swords of the two Claws struck on the glassy barrier and their faces contorted in surprise and anger. He reached to the side, extremely, careful not to move so much that he broke the shield, and picked his sword up. One end of the hilt had caught in a crack, holding the sword in place. *I'm lucky that didn't fall through the gaps into the river. I'm glad of the chance to catch my breath, but I'd better drop this shield before it takes too much out of me.* He stared into the eyes of one of the Claws and raised his right hand, letting the shield dissipate as he scrambled to his feet. "No!" the Claw shouted as Farren pulsed red light towards him. The man reeled backwards, scarlet light engulfing him.

A fourth Claw ran onto the bridge and hesitated by the only one of the trio left, standing out of the reach of Farren's sword. Farren looked from one man to the other. "Who's next?" he asked, the well-worn grip of the hilt rubbing the calluses on his left hand beneath his onyx ring. "Who'll try to cross the bridge?"

He watched and waited as the Claws scanned the grey sky for the sorcerer. *I wonder where he's gone,* he thought, keeping his eyes fixed on the other men.

Azariel saw the dragon dive down from the sky for a fourth time. Storm shifted uneasily beneath her and tossed his head. *I had better finish the sorcerer soon,* she thought. *Oh, Farren, don't get yourself killed!* The dragon plummeted down, tail streaming behind it and wings streamlined against its body as it dived. She punched both hands towards the dragon as it plunged, aiming both rings at its pale wings and belly.

Emerald and peacock blue light streamed out from her rings like a river, scorching her with their intensity. The flood of flame drowned the red-orange of the dragon and she heard it roar and scream. The acrid smell of burnt scales and sinew drifted on the wind. Then the dragon fell from the air, burnt and buckled wings fluttering weakly. She dropped her hands to her sides, head spinning and strength drained by the ferocity that had burned through her. She heard the sorcerer screaming, then a loud thud as the dragon struck the ground on the far side of the river. She threw back her head and gave a wild yell of triumph, making Storm start.

A mutter rose from the five Claws on the opposite bank. Then with a clatter of weapons and horsehooves, they turned and fled downriver. Farren sheathed his sword and clambered over the back of the dead horse and slid down the other side. A flash of white light flared through the air from his hand and one of the riderless horses buckled and collapsed. The other free horses scattered and bolted away from the main party of Claws.

Thank the Power for that! She raised her hands and dropped the reins, letting Storm wander to join Princess grazing. Her fingers were reddened as if sunburned on the lowest knuckle. She blew on them, soothing the slightly painful heat. *They must have carried a greater current of fire than usual. No wonder I feel so drained.* She stretched her arms and slid her feet from the stirrups to stretch her ankles, and felt the weariness melt. The wind blew cool around her and a very faint drop of moisture splashed her bare forearm.

Farren walked back to her, bow slung over his shoulder and his arm scarlet with blood. His hand tightened over her left knee and squeezed. "Well done!" he said, eyes flashing. "They've gone, and I hope they've gone for good."

"Yes." She smiled and rested her hand over his. Another drop of rain fell onto her arm and another onto her cheek. "I'm surprised they all turned tail like that, though."

"Well, what could they have done? No dogs, no dragon, no scrying mirror, no leader. Only the five of them against two *minyasti* on an unstable bridge. They wouldn't have lasted very long."

She dismounted and embraced him, smelling the sharp stink of blood and sweat on his skin. He dropped his head on her shoulder with a groan. His hair was matted in places with gore and she felt a warm trickle of liquid on his arm. "My beloved, you're wounded," she said. Lightly, she wiped the mixture of blood and raindrops from his face with the tip of her fingers. "How badly?"

"I haven't looked," he said, raising his head to look into her face. "It's my sword-arm, too." He turned his arm towards her. She winced as she saw the long gash along the back of his forearm dripping dark blood and exposing sinews here and there. She shuddered and clamped both hands down hard over the wound. "Beloved, that must hurt. I'll stitch it up as soon as I've stopped the bleeding." She tightened her other hand over the warm, sticky bleeding.

He shook his head. "No need for that. Not here. We're right beside Moonlady Falls and the healing waters below the waterfall. I'll wash it better. The horses will be all right grazing here."

She kept her hand clamped over his arm as they walked to the foaming pool at the base of the waterfall. Haze blew up from the water, mixing with the rain, and she caught a quick glimpse of a gemstone in the blue depths. Her boots crunched over the stones, which were still blackened from the fire where they had burned Crajaval's hellhounds and belongings. *Are we the first people to come back here since we killed her?* She shook her head back and wiped the moisture off her face with one hand. "I'm unhurt, so I'll wait for you in the caves." She nodded towards the cave mouth beside the falls that led into the heart of the mountain.

Farren stood still and stared at the dark opening and stared as if the cave lay at the horizon rather than half a bowshot away. His hands shook and his breathing came fast and noisy. She paused and studied him. "You'd better bathe it quickly. It must be a worse slash than you've had before, beloved."

His mouth was pulled into a hard line and the colour had drained from his face. His gaze was fixed on the cave mouth and he seemed unaware of her. "King of Heaven, it hurts so much," he muttered. "I can't take it much longer."

She bit her lip. *He's reliving his time there. I've been fool enough to remind him, as if there weren't enough reminders out here already. Being hurt and tired won't help him either.* "Farren?" she said softly, still keeping her hand clamped tightly on his wounded arm.

He started and almost jerked his arm out of her hand. She tightened her grip. *Dakhryan Blackhound, the mind-healer, told me what to do if the memories overpowered him.* "Farren," she repeated, "take a deep breath right now and tell me where Princess is."

Farren froze but she felt his muscles quivering and his chest heaved as if he were running hard. Swiftly, she let go of his arm, bent to scoop a handful of cold water from the pool beneath the waterfall, then splashed it onto his face. "Farren, come back to today," she said firmly. "You've got to tend to your wounded arm now. Drink from that pool and wash your arm in it, or I'll push you in."

He shook his head and blinked, then looked at her. "I'm sorry. I..."

"If you want to talk about it, you can talk about it while you bathe your arm in the healing spring." Gently, she pushed him towards the water. "If anybody should be apologizing, it should be me for even suggesting that you should go in there. Don't go in if you don't want to. It only looks like a light shower that will pass soon."

He knelt beside the foaming pool and plunged his wounded arm into the clear water. "I'll be all right. I should have been prepared for a reaction like that. Dakhryan Blackhound warned me. I still get nightmares about it, you know." The half-dried blood staining his arm washed off and vanished. The ugly purple-red slash closed, covering the white glimpse of sinew. He gasped as muscle and skin reformed over the mark, leaving only a white line surrounded by a subtle pinkish-red, as if the injury had happened weeks ago instead of minutes. He flexed his fingers in the water, then drew his arm out and let the droplets trickle off. "That is amazing," he said. "Thank the Power."

"I almost wish I'd been wounded so I do the same."

"Have a drink, anyway. It will do you good."

"I know." She knelt beside him and scooped up a mouthful in her hands. The water seemed to sparkle, even beneath the dull, overcast sky. She drank deeply and a cold shock of refreshment coursed down her back and through her limbs. She raised her head and gazed into the blue depths of the water. The intense kingfisher blue of the water danced before her, and the gemstones in the depths flashed. For a few heartbeats, the roar of the waterfall sounded lighter and almost musical. She stood up and flicked her hair behind her shoulders. *Wars really would be fought over this water. We're right to keep it secret.*

Farren stooped and tossed a stone into the pool, and she watched it plummet to the bottom. "I suppose you think I'm a coward for not going in that cave," he said sullenly.

She stared at the dancing water. "No." She twisted a lock of her hair around her finger and smiled at him. "You took a wound to your soul. If it hasn't healed enough yet, you shouldn't force yourself. You wouldn't be a coward if you avoided using your sword arm if it hadn't set fully after a break."

He tossed another stone into the pool. It sank and landed in the middle of the gemstones, making a dark spot in the middle of shimmering bottom. "Thank you."

"Do you want to talk about it?"

"No. I'd rather keep my mind on something else. Something in the present – but not that cave. It holds too many memories." He turned and looked back towards the bridge. "Why don't we see what spoils we can get from the bodies on the bridge?" he said. "We've got hardly any gear of our own and we ought to take the tack from the horses as well."

"Is that why you blasted that riderless horse after I'd killed the dragon?"

"Not exactly. I was aiming for the rider in front."

"If you hadn't told me that, I would have said it was a perfect shot." She ran her hand over his newly healed arm, tracing the pinkish line of the new scar. *If I hadn't seen the wound on him, I wouldn't know he'd been hurt.* "Let's go looting and pillaging."

The rain had passed and the sky had filled with soft grey clouds with dark underbellies that smudged down into sporadic showers. The wind was dragging one column of rain away downstream, leaving only the moisture flung from the waterfall to add more droplets to the rain-slick rocks. Princess looked up from the grass she was tearing at and snorted, ears pricked towards them. "Have a drink, my lady," Farren called. "You can use the stable as a cave if you don't like the rain."

They crossed the bridge to the dead Claws. Farren paused by the body of the dun stallion. "I'll go and get the saddle off that horse on the other side of the river and you can finish getting the one off this stallion here." He backhanded the saddle-skirts on the dead beast, then began to climb over it.

She followed him over the carcass in the middle of the bridge. A pair of crows flapped from the hills and perched on the chains holding the bridge, studying her with glittering eyes and shaking rain from their black feathers. She smiled at the carrion birds. *There'll be plenty for them and for their chicks, too.* Another pair of crows, the red bloodcrows, joined the pair of black ones, watching and waiting. She flexed a tense muscle in her shoulder and looked over the horse's body to the north. For a few moments, she stared at Moonlady Falls as it fell down to a foaming cauldron of water before dancing away as the Illin-Ast. Beyond the waterfall's mountain, she saw nothing but thick dark grey rainclouds. *Somewhere under that sky lies the island we're seeking.* She shrugged and bent to finish unbuckling the girths. The buckle beneath the dun horse's belly slipped open easily, letting the long band of the girth dangle into a gap between two planks. She wrestled and wrenched the saddle free from the dead stallion, the bridge bucking with her efforts. *This should fit Storm, by the looks of it, and the saddlebags are full.*

She carried the heavy saddle off the bridge and hauled it to a flat gravel bed just beyond the spray of the waterfall. After, unbuckling the pair of saddlebags, she shook them out one by one. "That's a good bit of loot," came Farren's voice over her shoulder. "What have we got?"

She picked up a large fold of grey woollen material. "Another blanket, for a start." The doubled layers of the of the material sprang back slightly as she squeezed it and she bent her head to rub the blanket it against her cheek. "And a new one, too, by the feel of it." The faint sour smell of damp wool rose from it and she breathed the scent in before shaking the blanket out then folding it ready to stow away. "What's in your bags?"

He knelt beside her and dumped a second saddle beside the first, complete with saddlebags, and they sorted through the bags and packages from the saddlebags. "A billycan, three cheeses, a bag of salt and some dried beef," he said, stacking the food into a pile. "That's a good find. I've been missing the taste of salt for days. What else?"

"A rope," she said, moving the coil of prickly brown hemp to one side. She picked up the tawny things that had lain beneath the rope and turned them over in her fingers. They felt hard and brittle, and hairs bristled along one side of them. "Rawhide strips for the dogs, I suppose." She tossed them aside. "We don't need those."

"Wouldn't you want to eat them if we were running short?" He sat back and looked at her, one arm draped over his knee which was bent into an archway over his other leg. His brown eyes flashed and the corners of his mouth twitched into a smile. "In wolf form, of course."

"I'll boil them and serve them up to you with the cheese if you tease me about that," she said, winking. "Let them lie and the carrion birds can have them. Taking a bit of horsemeat would be more appetising and we can both eat it. But let's have a look in the third bag from the stallion's saddle. This is like opening the prizes after the contest."

"Yes – and all this gear is even more valuable than gold and gems out here. Only the bacon and my dagger are any good to us now out of all the prizes." He patted the jewelled hilt then unlaced the strings of the next saddlebag. "Only a bottle of something, a horse brush and somebody's spare clothes." He shook out a pair of buckskin trews and a matching long-sleeved jerkin, followed by several pairs of greying undershorts. "They're too large for me and even larger for you. Unless you can adjust them with your needle and thread."

For the space of a heartbeat, a sharp pang of pity shot through her. *Someone sewed those for that dead man,* she thought. *Mother, sister, daughter, wife... or he did it himself.* She bit her lip. *But he would have killed us and taken our horses and gear if he could. He chose to hunt us and paid the price.* She flicked the hair back from her face with one hand and laughed, dispelling her brooding. "I don't think I've ever tried sewing in the saddle before but I can try. I hope you're not hoping for fine tailoring and embroidery."

He leaned over and hugged her roughly. "Fine ladies sew fine embroidery," he chuckled, unshaven cheeks rasping her face. "Does my lady wish for silk? There's some nice red cloth on their tabards?"

"And 'my lady' is what you call your horse." She twined her fingers through his hair and tugged at the chestnut strands lightly. "You're full of fun this morning."

He raised his head and looked into her eyes. "I'm alive, you're alive and the Claws aren't chasing us anymore. Isn't that enough to be happy about?"

"Thank the Power, yes!" She leaned forwards and kissed him hard on the mouth, ignoring the short, stabbing hairs around his lips. She drew away and turned her head to one side. "Keep the clothes. Too big or not, we'll probably need dry spares, even if we only get half the set each. And I will go and cut some more cloth and thread to sew with. I'm not going on a long journey without any clean underwear, and these Claws didn't think to make sure there were any women in this band to provide me with spares. Anyway, what's in the bottle?"

He uncorked the bottle and sniffed at the neck. "Spirits of some sort. I'd rather not drink it – too strong for me." He began tilting it to one side and a small trickle of amber liquid poured out.

"Don't waste it," she said, catching his hand and righting the bottle. The alcoholic fumes struck the back of her throat and made her eyes water. "We're not always going to have a healing spring handy and that stuff's good for washing cuts."

"Well, I'm certainly not planning to slash my arm open again," he laughed. "I think I've collected the scar to remember this journey by already."

She took the bottle from him and re-corked it. "It could also come in handy for coaxing a stubborn campfire." She placed the spirits on the stones with a soft clink.

"And people drink that stuff for fun? Give me a good glass of wine or cider any day." He shuddered, deliberately exaggerating it. "Let's see what else we've got."

The remaining three saddlebags yielded two more rather frayed blankets; a tinderbox; an assortment of coins from the Kingdom, Wayast and Elend; half a ham wrapped in cheesecloth; a tin of dry biscuits and another of tealeaves; a porcelain talisman with a scorpion on one side and a fourteen-point stag on the other; a whetstone and another set of clothes. Farren picked up the talisman and hurled it against the rocks, shattering the pottery disk. "Well, we've more or less got back what we've lost to the Claws, so we're quits."

"I think we're the ones better off. They've also lost a sorcerer with a dragon and a scrying mirror." She rolled the second set of clothes into a rough bundle and stuffed them back into the saddlebag she had pulled them out of. "Get whatever cloth you need and let's go. Unless you want to spend the night here."

He got to his feet and tugged her up after him. "Not in the least. I'd like to be well past Moonlady Falls by nightfall."

CHAPTER TWELVE

Azariel shuffled around on the unfamiliar saddle as they rode away from the river towards a saddle that separated the main range from mountain where Moonlady Falls cascaded down. Tussock lay ahead of them, sloping up out of the river valley for just under half a mile before beech forest spread down from the ridge to swallow it. A sweetish smell blew on the northerly wind from the forest, mixed with the scent of wet ground. She reached down to readjust the stirrup leathers again to a comfortable length and continued riding beside Farren uphill.

At the edge of the bush, where the first smaller beech trees were growing many paces apart outside the cover of the larger trees, Farren reined Princess in. "I was hoping to find a deer trail leading from the forest to the river somewhere here. Can you see anything?"

"I can shift shape and sniff something out if you want me to." Storm bend his head to tear at the tussocks as she halted him beside Princess.

"We'll have to make our own trail." He dismounted, then turned to tuck Princess's reins up into her bridle. "I'll go first and take the way of clearing out creepers and vines if I need to. You'll follow me without being led, won't you, my lady?" He patted the mare on the shoulder. "You'll have to lead Storm."

She dismounted and tugged Storm forward as they pushed between the trunks of the larger mountain beeches and into the forest itself. The gelding slanted his ears back but plodded forwards, his hooves stirring up the thick mat of leaf litter. The dim light of the bush surrounded them.

They made their way straight up the slope as best they could, weaving around the moss-covered trunks of the larger trees and places where dense tangles of ribbonwood barred the way. Farren pushed past a trailing creeper that dangled down from where it sprawled over branches, then stopped short as his cloak caught on it. He tugged his cloak, but the red wool had been trapped tightly by the tiny thorns on the creeper. He growled in disgust and plucked at the vine, carefully and slowly peeling it backwards from the cloak. "Treacherous little thing. It's barbed like blackberry but the thorns are so small I didn't see it until too late." He drew his sword and slashed at the vine.

"There can't be any deer or goats near here if that's growing thickly," she said, pausing while he finished freeing his cloak and sheathing his sword. Her calves burned from climbing the steep slope. "They'd eat anything of the bramble-kind." She unbuckled her cloak and rolled it up into a tight bundle, which she shoved roughly into one of the saddlebags. "We'd be better off without our cloaks for now. I'm certainly getting warm climbing this slope."

"Good idea." He removed his cloak and folded it neatly before stowing it. "I hope you're wrong about the goats and deer, though."

"I'll use my nose when we get to the ridge," she said. "If there aren't any bramble-eaters, there could well be other beasts we can hunt."

At the top of the ridge, the trees thinned out, leaving spaces where ferns clustered on the flatter ground. The branches forming the canopy slanted southeast as if a strong northwest wind was blowing, though only a light breeze stirred the forest and made the leaves whisper. Farren sheathed his sword and sat down on a moss-covered log. "Time for a halt and a rest," he said, wiping a sheen of sweat off his forehead with his arm.

She tucked Storm's reins up in his bridle and let him go. The black gelding turned towards the nearest clump of ferns and started tearing at them. She sat down beside Farren on the log, the wet moss dampening the seat of her trousers. She ran her gaze around the sparser trees growing at the ridge and noted a few shrubs where the tender spring leaves had been torn by something. She smiled and pointed to them. "The deer do come here," she said.

"Good. We can follow a deer trail down into the next valley. I'm getting tired of that snarevine. It grows everywhere." He rubbed his right arm, which bore a few fine scratches.

A high-pitched chirruping from a nearby branch caught her attention. She looked around as a fantail, broad tail spread wide, bobbed along a twig of the nearest beech tree, just above where Princess browsed on the ferns. It chirruped again and fluttered in a tight spiral, catching insects. More cheeps and twitters rang out and several more of the small birds appeared. One landed on the end of the log where they sat and stared at them, head cocked on one side. Slowly, Farren raised a hand to it. Another flurry of tiny wings and it swooped onto his finger. After perching for a few heartbeats, it danced away through the air to hunt tiny flies once more.

"Did you use your Gift on it?" she asked Farren, still watching the bevy of birds.

"Only slightly. They're not afraid of us and I think they like the way we disturb the leaves and stir up the insects." He drew a deep breath and let it out slowly, then stood up. "We'd better keep moving. This place is no good as a camp and we don't have any water for the horses."

"I'll lead the way this time – after I've shifted shape to smell out a good deer trail. Storm should follow you or you can lead him."

She stood up and walked several paces to the next tree, then shifted shape. The sounds of the bush intensified, the light breeze through the canopy sounding as loud to her wolf's ears as a gale to human hearing. The horses grinding their bits as they chewed ferns added a metallic note to the wet champing sound of them eating, and the thin hum of small insects mixed with the chirps of the fantails. Other sounds came from further in the forest: the calls of other birds and the occasional distant grunts of wild pigs. The scent of the forest sharpened from the general sweetish earthiness of the forest to a multitude of distinct smells, including the tang of sweat from Farren and the horses. She closed her eyes and concentrated on the scents, nostrils quivering as she sought the distinctive notes of deer. A faint trace, several days old, caught her attention and she swung towards it.

The scent led to a winding trail down through the forest that looked clear of snarevine and ferns. She headed down it, the steady trudging of Farren's boots and the horses' hooves behind her. Here and there, the leaf litter and mud was gouged with the prints of sharp hooves, some large and some small. In one place, the slope dropped away to form a sheer step. She paused and looked down to gauge the distance. Below her, the grey clay had been torn and trampled, and the scent of pig hung strongly in the air. *A boar's wallow. We had better take care that we don't stumble onto the boar itself unprepared.* She bounded down the two-foot drop, then scrambled clear to one side of the wallow as first Princess, then Storm leaped down to the lower part of the trail.

Farren stood on the brink, hands on hips. "I'm not a deer, horse or wolf but I can jump that," he said. He leaped for the moss on the edge of the wallow but one foot landed in the mud. He teetered on one leg, then fell onto his knees, coating his trousers with the grey clay.

She tried to laugh as he picked himself up and tried to wipe the mud off with a handful of leaves, the sound coming out of her wolf's throat as a whine. Her tail twitched to and fro, almost by itself. He glared at her. "At least I don't have to warn you off making any jokes about me acting like a pig in mud," he said ruefully. "I should put on those trews we found on the Claws. At least they're brown and won't show mud."

As soon as he had finished his rough attempt at cleaning off the mud, she continued leading the way down the slope. The rushing sound of water mingled with the hiss of the breeze in the branches, and the horses pushed forwards, drawing level with her. "Let them lead the way to the water, Stormwolf," he said. "They can smell it – and I suppose you can as well."

A stream ran through the bottom of the valley, winding through a steep-sided watercourse and leaping over a line of large boulders to fall bubbling into a deeper pool before sweeping eastwards. The mountain beech trees growing at the foot of the valley reached much higher than those at the ridge and formed vaults and arches covered by the canopy. Many kinds of moss grew thickly on the old fallen forest giants, and lichen and fungi grew up the southern sides of the trunks. Beneath the beeches, short ferns, bracken and other small shrubs grew. A dragonfly darted hither and thither above the stream, its wings glimmering in a finger of sunlight that reached through the branches. A low drone of bees filled the air, coming from a beech where the honeydew oozed from a thick black velvety coating over the trunk. The sweet scent of honeydew spread out throughout the valley, and a moonwattle bird carolled and belled somewhere high in the branches.

Farren halted on the side of the bank and prepared to either jump it or pick his way across on the waterweed-covered rocks. *At least if I fall in here, I'll wash off the mud from the last time I fell over.* From the corner of his eye, he caught a glimmer of silver light as Azariel shifted shape.

She stood up and flicked her hair back from her face. "Do you want to go further tonight? We need to let the horses drink at least."

He ran his gaze over the grove of taller trees. The light falling through the canopy had a golden tinge to it that made the greens of the moss almost glow. "It should do as a camp," he said. "I was hoping for shelter of some kind, but we can make one from all the dead branches and ferns." He strolled to the nearest fallen log and sat down on it, ignoring the dampness and sighing slightly as the muscles of his legs and back relaxed. "I hate to admit it but I'm exhausted. These woods are hard going, at least for human legs."

"The speedy healing and using a shield has probably drained you as well. You get to take first watch tonight. I'm not tired – or at least, I'm not as tired as you are." She leaned forwards and picked off a snarevine leaf that had caught on his shoulder. "Go and wash your trousers, if you like. I can take care of building a shelter and starting a fire."

"I'll do the cooking, though. I should be able to make some sort of stew with some of what we got from the Claws, if we add some young fern fronds. Although I can't promise that it will taste very good."

"Last time I was foraging in the woods, I had to eat skinny squirrels roasted on a stick. A stew of ferns, cheese, ham and ground hardtack sounds better than that." She smiled at him, then stooped to pick up a dead branch about six feet long. "Here's a good start to our shelter."

He waited until she had turned her back on him and walked several yards away to find more long branches, then changed his muddy uniform trousers for the buckskin trews they had salvaged. They fitted him well enough at the waist, although they sat lower, but they were slightly too long in the leg. He finished buttoning the fly and let his armour and tunic fall back down over them. Once dressed, he unsaddled the two horses and took his trousers to the stream to wash. The mud brushed away easily after he had moistened the leather lightly, but as he squeezed it gently, the water looked murky and dark. *They're dirtier than I realised. I suppose I have seated, ridden and fought in them for several days, and probably bled all over them as well.* He looked at the stream, then back at the trousers again. *I'd better not wash them thoroughly here and now. They'd get as stiff as wood drying too fast in front of the fire.*

He returned to where he had left the saddles and draped the damp leather trousers over a clump of ferns. Azariel had propped the end of one of the longer branches three against the trunk of a tree three feet up from the roots. She was placing other, shorter branches at right angles to the first, using the gnarls and spurs on the longer branch to hold them in place. After settling another in place, she looked up at him. "It will be a snug fit, but there'll be room for us to take turns curling up in there."

He smiled. "Would you like me to help build it?"

She shook her head. "But you can light a fire."

He cleared a space of damp bare ground in the moss and ringed it with damp stones from the stream. Storm wandered over and sniffed at the area, tore half-heartedly at the ferns then picked his way down the stream to where the bank was low enough for him to scramble down and drink. Farren gathered dried ferns and twigs as tinder, then thicker sticks and branches as fuel. By the time he had managed to build and kindle the fire, Azariel had finished building the shelter and was draping large fronds of tree-ferns over the top like thatch. He watched her wriggle inside the shelter, then coughed as the smoke of the campfire eddied and blew into his face.

Evening drew in as he set the rough stew to simmering in the looted billycan propped on a flatter rock at the side of the fire. The steadily cooling air rang with the shrilling of birds, all mingled together into a wall of sound that kept ringing until dark had fallen further. By the time they had finished eating the stew directly from the billycan once it had cooled enough, night had fallen completely, and the sounds of the forest changed to crickets, the occasional owl and the cries of other animals. Moths fluttered into the circle of light formed by the campfire, dancing crazily above and around the flames.

He settled down for the night well wrapped in blankets and cushioned by a pile of springy ribbonwood twigs and bracken. Azariel sat cross-legged beside the campfire, her needle flashing in the orange light as she sewed. He kept watching until his eyelids grew heavy and he drifted into sleep.

A terrified neigh jolted him awake, mixed with the thunder of hooves. He started up, knocking his head on the low sloping roof of the rough shelter. Outside, beside the campfire, Azariel stood with her back to him, her sword in her right hand and a burning branch in another. Beyond her, something dark and bulky moved just beyond the circle of light cast by the fire. Eyes glittered pale green, looking almost too small for the bulk. Azariel swept the burning branch through the air and the light fell on the hunched shoulders of a bear. "Farren, wake up!" she shouted. The horses neighed again, shrill but sounding further off.

He felt around for his bow and crawled out of the shelter. The bear lunged towards Azariel and reared up on its hind legs. It swiped at her with one massive paw, hitting the burning branch and sending it flying. It roared with pain and silver light flashed as Azariel shifted shape and darted into the darkness. Growling, it swung its head to and fro. Farren found the handle of his bow and reached down to his quiver for an arrow, his hands still clumsy with sleep and sudden waking. The bear's eyes looked into his and it reared up again. His mouth dried and his vision seemed to narrow to the massive claws at the end of each limb. *One blow from those would rip me in two. I can't miss this shot – but where's Azariel gone?*

The bear suddenly howled again and staggered forward. Azariel, in wolf form, had bitten it on the back leg just above the hock. It whirled around, surprisingly quick for its bulk, and roared again. The shewolf clung on, teeth locked firmly. Farren raised his bow and drew a deep breath to steady himself as he drew it. The bear abruptly stopped spinning one way as it strained to reach Azariel and began to turn the other way. It blundered into the campfire with another roar, then reared up again to swipe at the flames. The arrow leaped as Farren released the string, flying true into the bear's throat. It staggered forward, just missing the fire, though blood gushed from the wound onto the ring of hot stones around the fire, sizzling and smelling of charred meat as it burned. *That wasn't where I was aiming but it will be enough to kill.*

The bear fell forward, eyes glazing. Azariel released it and leaped clear, vanishing into the darkness again. The massive limbs jerked and kicked, then the bear lay still, blood still running from its severed throat. Farren's hands shook in the aftermath of the kill, and he lowered his bow. "Stormwolf?" he called. "Are you all right?"

The familiar silver light flashed from beside a bush. "Not a scratch," she replied. "I've tasted better things than a bear's backside, though. Can you build the fire up so I can find my way down to the stream to drink and remove the taste?"

"Of course." He knelt to put his bow down, then added several thin sticks into the fire, coaxing tall yellow flames into life. "What about the horses?"

"I think they're unharmed," she called from the stream, voice just audible above the chatter of the water. "They ran off as soon as the bear came, but you can probably call them back easily enough with your Gift. I'm not sure if the bear was coming for us or for the horses."

He glanced down at the carcass. One hind paw was still twitching. *Now we'll be eating it.* He set his bow down and looked down at the big carcass. *I'll have to gut it now to stop the meat spoiling.* Yawning, he built up the fire so that it blazed, then rummaged through the saddlebags to find the rope. As he fastened the rope around the hind paws of the bear, Azariel returned from the stream, her hair wet and glistening with water. She helped him haul the carcass away from the campsite and into a tree with the rope draped over a branch so that the head dangled an inch or so from the moss.

Together, they finished the bloody work of gutting the bear. Once the innards had been removed, both he and Azariel were bloody to the elbows. "Shall we skin it now?" he asked.

"We can leave that for the morning." She shook her hair back from her face. "At least we won't have to hunt for a while now. It's a pity it's springtime and it doesn't have much fat on it."

"It'll be good enough though. We can take the tender meat for the next two nights, then whatever else we can carry will have aged enough to not be tough. The crows will have to take the rest. I don't suppose it will take them long to smell it." He grimaced as the stench of fresh blood and entrails assaulted his nose again.

"I'll drag all this away so we don't smell it for the rest of the night," Azariel said. "It's not as bad to a wolf's nose as it is to a human's."

He wiped his dagger as clean as he could on the moss, then picked his way carefully down the rocks to the stream to wash. The water felt bitingly cold and raised the hairs on his arms. He splashed more over his arms to rinse them again, then washed his face thoroughly. Azariel, still in wolf form, bounded down beside him, paws scrabbling on the stones. She waded into the stream and almost sank her muzzle in the water as she drank. "I wouldn't want that taste in my mouth either," he chuckled, watching her.

She climbed out of the water, shook herself vigorously, then shifted shape. "I won't make the same mistake twice in one night, no matter how tired I am." She rubbed her eyes. "I think you slept for about three hours before the bear came. Can you take your turn now?"

"Of course, Stormwolf." He reached out and squeezed her hand, then stood back to let her find her way up the rocks to the campsite ahead of him.

***

Azariel hugged her cloak around her as the cold wind blew over the saddle between two jagged mountain peaks. Another night had passed since they had encountered the bear, and the dense bush had opened out to tussocks. A shower of rain had passed over them, leaving the long grasses beaded with water. She shivered as she scanned the terrain on the northern side of the ridge, screwing her eyes up against the wind. Storm plodded on steadily beneath her. *This is the second range we've had to find a way through. When will we reach the sea?* The wet wool of her cloak clung to her, and the hood smelt strongly of woodsmoke and horse sweat. *I haven't had a decent wash for days and this rain is making it hard for me to dry any underclothes I've managed to clean.*

She blinked and shook her head. *I can't start thinking like that or the discomfort will be all I see.* She slid her hands through her hair and shrugged her shoulders. *At least I can use that horse brush on my hair and my hair's not matted.* Storm paused to pluck a mouthful of tussock. *We can ride in this terrain and it's easier going than the forests, we can have hot bear stew tonight and at least I can sew more underwear from the cloth we salvaged.*

Again, she surveyed the land ahead. The land dropped away into more tussocky slopes and huge swathes of mountainthorn and bracken. Shadows from the clouds overhead crawled and scrambled over the slopes and vanished into a deep valley. She leaned towards Farren and nudged him. "See that?" she asked.

"What?" He turned and looked towards her. He was wearing the dead Claw's buckskin tunic under his armour, and the sleeves poked out from under the steel and hung over his hands.

"Do you think there'll be a river in that deep valley to the northeast?"

"I'd say so, Stormwolf." He pushed the hood of his cloak back from his face. "It looks like it runs out of the mountains, too. Let's get down there and follow it to the sea."

They rode down into the valley and found a broad river fringed with ferns and thin straggly bushes. The river flowed around large moss-covered boulders, alternating between rapids and smoother patches of deeper water. She stared at the river for a while. *Something's strange about the river.* Then she gasped. "Farren, that's flowing towards the north, not the south. We must be more than halfway through the mountains at last."

He smiled. "The mountains don't go on forever, even though it feels like it." He let Princess drop her head to tear at the ferns. A swallow swooped above one of the deeper pools near the eastern bank, catching the mayflies that danced above the water's surface. "All going well, we should reach the sea in a few more days."

***

On the morning of the fifth day since they had left Moonlady Falls, the spring sun shone warm and soothing onto their right shoulders. The slopes began to ease into gentle rolling downs and dunes, and Farren noticed the bush thinning out to a multitude of different grasses, flecked here and there with white wildflowers. Instead of hard mud and sticks grinding under Princess's hooves, he heard softer, more muffled hoofbeats and occasionally felt her slipping on loose sandy soil. A north wind was blowing, ruffling his hair. It was laden with a tang of salt and fish that he had once smelt in an Elendi trader's stall. *That must be the smell of the sea. We must be nearly at the coast.*

Princess scrambled up to the crest of a hill behind Storm's glossy black rump. "Time for a halt," Azariel said. He reined Princess in and looked ahead. The hill dropped down into a stretch of land undulating in hillocks of sand covered with green-grey grass. Beyond that lay a thin strip of ochre sand and a huge expanse of heaving green water flecked with white in places. "The sea!" he said softly. He ran his eyes from east to west, taking in the sheer distance that the water covered, spreading to the sky. "It's so big." Patterns of light and shade danced over the water, tinting it from deep jade to soft greys and hues that matched the cloud-streaked sky above. At the horizon, big billows of cloud smudged into the line of the water, looking for a moment like distant lands. *What lies on the other side of the sea? Is there even another side or does it go on for ever?* The sea-breeze tugged his cloak back from his shoulders, and Princess's mane whipped back over his hands. He closed his eyes and breathed the wild salty smell in.

"There it is!" Her voice rang with a triumphant note. He opened his eyes and sat up straighter in the saddle. She was pointing northwest over the sea and the wind was billowing her dark hair across her pale face.

"What?" he asked, guessing the answer.

"The island."

He followed the line of her finger and saw a green hill rising out from the sea a few miles distant from the coast. The colour looked smudged and dusty with haze, and the sunlight gleamed and danced on the waves. *Not quite how it looked in my dream – our dream – but recognisable.* His heart kicked at his chest and excitement quivered sharply in his stomach. "Come on!" he shouted, spurring Princess down the hill.

Princess's hooves beat a dull drumbeat on the sandy soil as she cantered downhill. He leaned backwards to keep his balance, then pitched forwards suddenly as they reached the bottom of the incline. The thunder of Storm's hooves rose behind him and soon the black gelding drew level with Princess. Storm galloped ahead and surged up the side of the first sandhill, sinking and slipping in the loose dirt. Then Farren was riding up the side of the dune himself. Sand blew back, stinging his eyes and cheeks. He passed his hand through his hair and felt grit in his scalp. He tried to scratch it out as Princess crested the dune but soon gave it up.

The mare paused at the top to graze a little on the coarse grass growing out from the sand. He looked ahead and saw the quiver and flick of the seawater between two dunes ahead of him. Above the hissing of the wind through the grass, he heard a roar like pine trees in a high wind. He tugged Princess's head up and nudged her down the other side of the dune.

He guided her between the pair of dunes in front of them. "This way's quicker!" he called to Azariel as he saw her beginning to urge Storm up a slope. She turned her horse towards him. The black gelding's chest and flanks was coated with a sheen of sweat marbled with white lather. "Good idea," she said as she trotted closer. "All those slopes and sand were hard going for him. Look at him; he's all drenched with sweat."

"Poor fellow," he said. "We'll find him some water soon."

They emerged from between the dunes and reached the thin strip of bare sand between the sea and the land. He reined Princess into a halt and looked up and down the beach. The waves reared up, and he watched them roaring down then retreating in a line of white foam across the water-darkened sand. Gulls rose screaming from the water, swooping and diving. "Well, here we are at the coast," he said. "Now what do we do?"

"Have a drink and a long rest somewhere," she replied. "The day's hardly begun, really. Look, there's the river again. I told you we'd find it after going around to avoid that bog." She pointed to a glittering path winding across the sand until it was swallowed up by the pounding wash. "That's the place for us."

"I'm not that surprised, Stormwolf," he said. "And I agreed with you about finding it again. It's hard to lose a river. Let's go over there. There's a tree for the horses to shade under, too."

By the river, he dismounted and took the tack off Princess. "Have a good drink, my lady," he said as he watched her gulping at the water a few paces upstream. "I could do with one myself." He unbuckled his cloak and folded it up before placing it near the upended saddle. *The sun is shining on us from two directions with that sand. It's like a mirror and this armour is roasting me.* He sat down under the tree and looked up at it. From a distance, it had looked like a pine, but close beside it, he noticed that instead of fine needles, this tree's leaves grew long and thick, like cats' tails and were covered with deep green scaly spikes. One jabbed into his hand as he nudged his quiver straight beside his leg.

"Why don't we go swimming?" said Azariel. "You go over there by those rocks and I'll go elsewhere. Once we've cooled off, we can plan how we can get over to the island."

"I'll drink first," he said. "Let's have the end of the food from out of the saddlebags, too."

Stooping over the river, he scooped some water up in his hands. He drank a little, then spat as the salt shock of brackish water flooded his mouth. "Better drink further upstream from the waves like the horses did," he said, mouth tasting sweet after the salt had gone. He walked away from the sea and bent over the river gain.

Azariel's shadow fell behind and across him and her boots scrunched in the sand. "I wonder how we are going to get over to where we want to go," she said.

He looked up at her. The sunlight was shining hazily through her hair. "Well, we flew in the first dream," he said.

"And in the second one, too. You remember how that one ended! But we can't fly, anyway. Unless I call one of the windspirits to help us again."

"I suppose we could." He paused with his hands full of water. "Northeaster – I don't know how easy it will be for two of us to ride a falcon, but I suppose we can if we have to, unless we wait for the wind to swing northwest."

He stood up and wiped the water from around his mouth. Bristle was starting to creep back onto his cheeks and rasped slightly against his hand. "Well, there's nothing obvious right now, so let's go swimming, like you said. Then we'll find out how we're supposed to get over to the island."

"Well, we could always camp here for weeks to fell trees and lug them down so we can build a raft or a boat or something of that kind."

"I think I'd prefer riding a falcon to riding a raft," he said hesitantly, heat rising in his cheeks.

"Why, beloved?" She stood with one hand on her hip, looking at him with her head tilted to one side. "It would make it easy coming and going."

The heat spread further up his face. "I haven't got much of a stomach for that," he mumbled, staring down at the sand by her boots. "Anna once took me out on a boat on Lake Tapatdehi when I was visiting her at her post down south. It got windy. First the motion gave me a headache and then it made me sick. And the waves here..." He gestured towards the sea. "I will if we have to, but I'd much prefer to ride a falcon or anything else. I'd even prefer swimming out there somehow while you took the gear on the raft."

"Oh." She touched him lightly on the arm. "I'm surprised, though. You're so good on a horse and a good swimmer."

"Swimming's different. So is riding a horse. Speaking of which..."

"Enjoy your swim by the rocks." She leaned over and kissed him on the cheek before turning on her heel and crunching away over the sand.

He walked down to a cluster of small shellfish-encrusted rocks by the water's edge. After glancing behind him to check if Azariel was looking the other way, he stripped off and waded into the sea. A wave curled around him, pushing him backwards. Another wave reared up and he dived through it, feeling it break into foam as he passed through. The cuts on his arm stung with the shock of the salt and he gasped.

He rose to the top and floated on his back, lips sore with salt, eyes stinging. With a toss of his head, he shook the water off his face and started to swim, rocking up and down with the swell of the waves. He paused and floated again, and let the waves nudge and tug him until he was lifted and heaved forwards with a rush of white foam that hurtled him towards the shore. His fingers bit into the sand as he jolted down onto it. He picked himself up from the sand as the brown and white water swirled away from him. *That was fun*, he thought. *I'll do that again.*

He waded back out into the surf until it rose to his thighs, then dived in. A few smaller waves crested then broke, barely enough to bob him up and down. He swam lazily towards the oncoming waves, foam tingling and bubbling over his bare skin. In the smooth gap between him and the larger swell, two triangular grey fins cut through the water. He froze. *That's a fish of some kind and it looks huge.* Memories of the Elendi trader's stall flashed into his mind, including the smoked side of a massive fish six feet long hanging to one side, and a jawbone set with teeth the size and shape of arrowheads. He felt for the bottom and retreated into the shallower water.

A slim grey shape leaped out of the water over the crest of a breaking wave then dived back below the surface. A second one followed it. For one heartbeat, he looked into a pair of sharp eyes set in a round, bulbous face with a long snout that seemed to be open in a grin before the beast vanished. The pair of fins swept in a tight circle, then the two grey figures hurdled over the crest of another wave. This time, one bobbed its head up and squeaked at him, almost birdlike. *Leapers in the water with the body of a fish and the face of a pig with a long muzzle. These must be those dolphin beasts that Elendi named his horse after.*

He waded back into waist-deep water. The second beast bobbed up beside the first and the pair of them chittered and squealed at each other. *They certainly aren't fish – they're breathing air like me.* The first one, which had a scar running across the prominent bulge of its forehead, lazily swam closer, coming within five paces of him, then swirled away, body undulating fluidly through the water before bobbing up and looking at him again. *They've never seen a human before.*

The scarred dolphin leaped completely out of the water, its body upright like a human's as it hung in the air. As it splashed down, the second leaped after it and bunted it with its long muzzle. A large wave heaved up behind them, and Farren drew a deep breath and dived through it as it broke, eyes closed. As the water swirled over and around him, something smooth but firm brushed against his leg. *Was that the dolphin?* He surfaced and shook the salty water off his face, treading water. Suddenly, the wet-leather texture pushed between his legs and lifted him from beneath, almost completely out of the water. A thrill like the shock of a wave pounded through him. He gasped then felt himself slipping off to one side. As he splashed through the surface, the grinning faces of the dolphins looked at him

He spat some of the salt out. "You're as friendly as tame beasts," he said to them. "Do you want to play with me?" He reached out one hand to them.

The scarred dolphin chittered back at him and surged forward and bunted its muzzle against his hand before diving between his legs again. This time, he tightened his grip around its belly as it swam under him and tossed him up. Powerful muscle moved beneath the thick, hairless skin. The second dolphin leaped over the top of him, and he dived off to one side. *It's almost like playing with horses.* He swam towards the first one and it darted in a tight circle around him before charging at him and knocking him off his feet with a blow that drove some of the breath out of him. *Definitely as strong as horses... Could we ride them like horses?*

Treading water again, he stretched out one hand and splashed his fingers on top of the water, training his mind on the scarred dolphin and reaching out towards it with his Gift. Invisible threads stretched out from him to it. He touched the mind of the first one, mentally running over the smooth, slippery texture that felt to his mind like the dolphin's skin did to his fingers. The dolphin swam closer to him and bobbed up to nuzzle at his cheek. The second one bumped against his leg as if jealous of the attention he was giving the scarred dolphin. *God Incarnate, these beasts are amazing. It won't take much to tame them.* His palm prickled and tingled with warmth.

For a few moments, he and the scarred dolphin looked into each other's eyes. He reached out both hands and placed them on the bulging forehead on either side of the scar. The dolphin chirped at him but held almost motionless, apart from the steady rhythm of its tail. His hands warmed, full of strong, gentle energy. Its mind felt warm, strong and receptive. He breathed slowly and deeply as every fibre of his arms relaxing. *Now to name it – him. I'm sure this is a male.* Again, he touched the dolphin's mind, probing more deeply. *I don't believe it – can I really touch it as deeply as I can Princess? They're even more intelligent than a dog.* A flurry of sensations met him, layered over and around the basic slippery texture: deep water that echoed, jagged rocks where danger lurked, luscious ribbons of seaweed promising abundance. "Your name is Captain," he said at last and felt something like an echo of response in the dolphin as a golden thread snapped into place between them. *"Aruso dea ker lypatho Minya. Ter assaw arkan van runach."*

He dropped his hands from the dolphin's head and reached for the curving triangle of its dorsal fin, then swung himself astride Captain's back. Captain squealed and surged over a wave and heading out to sea, body undulating beneath him like a horse, but smoother and more wavelike. He touched one side of Captain's thick neck and the beast turned away from the touch of his hand. He guided Captain in a half-circle, the other dolphin chasing after them, clicking and grunting as it leaped.

***

Azariel rose from the water by the stream, the retreating waves tugging at her.   She shook her head, sending sparkling droplets of water spinning off her hair.   She quickly glanced towards Farren's end of the beach. Storm was rolling in the sand, his legs flailing. *I wonder if Farren's ready for me to come over to him.* She dried herself with the rough wool of her cloak and pulled her clothes on. She stood up and threw her cloak around her shoulders. *I hope he's all right. I'd better check – but avoid walking around while he's standing there nude.*

She tucked her boots under her arm and walked barefoot across the wet gritty sand, then stopped, seeing Farren still in the water. Two dark shapes came out from the water near him. *What are they?* The strange beasts wove over and under the waves, then Farren mounted one of them. She took a step forward, amazed and curious. *It looks like a fish the size of a pony.* Then she stepped back again, biting her lower lip and feeling heat flood her cheeks. *I can watch from here. I don't need that close a look at him – not yet.* The grey animal round in a large circle while the other soared over and around them, tail flailing as if it were swimming through the air.

The beast and Farren finished their circle and Farren slid off into the water, sending up a shock of spray. The squeals and squeaks of the two beasts rang shrill but faint against the constant hissing roar of the waves.   Farren reappeared and shook his head, staring straight at her. He waved. "Throw me something to keep me decent," he called, voice blurred by the distance.

She found the pile of his clothes lying in the sand well away from the water, and rummaged through them to find his undershorts. *It feels so odd handling such private clothing, although I've seen them hanging to dry countless times. It's... intimate in a way.* She gazed back out to sea, where Farren was holding onto the dorsal fins of both creatures, a small bow wave whipping back over him. *I hope I can throw them far enough.* She wadded the white cotton up as tightly as she can, then walked to the water's edge and threw them as hard as she can. As soon as she saw them arching through the air, she turned her back on him and waited, watching the horses graze and squeezing a few beads of water out of her hair. The salt had dried to a crust on a few strands, leaving them stiff in places.

"Hey!" His shout rang out and she spun around without thinking, then bit her lip again. Farren had walked closer to the shore but had his back turned to her. The beasts were swimming around him and chittering, and one of them tossed a wet white object into the air. The other leaped out of the water and caught it neatly on the top of its long snout. *That's his underwear they're playing with!* He lunged towards them and tried to grab them as the creatures tossed the undershorts back and forth. Irrepressible laughter shook her as he continued trying to retrieve them, doubling her over until her stomach hurt and tears streamed from her eyes.

She sat up and wiped her eyes. He was wading to the shore, wearing the undershorts. "When you've finished having a good laugh at my expense, you can come out here as well."

She glanced behind him to the two grey creatures, which had bobbed up to watch. One glided closer to the shore behind Farren. "What are they?"

"I think they're dolphins," He turned and his voice became barely audible above the roar and hiss of the waves. "Come and meet your mount to the island."

The water churned around her legs as she waded towards him. "Do you think they're strong enough?"

"They certainly are." When the water reached to her thighs, he reached for her hand. "I'll introduce you to them." He tugged her forward into deeper water and the pair of dolphins swirled around the two of them. One nudged at Azariel's arm, then tossed the dangling strands of her hair to and fro with its long beak-like muzzle. "The one that's playing with your hair, the one with the scar on his face, his name's Captain. This one here," he said, caressing the fin of the other one, "is Coroastin."

She stroked Captain's sleek, slightly cool hide. *Coroastin means "swimmer" in the Old Tongue,* she thought as the dolphin nibbled at her opal ring. *A good name for a sea-creature, though maybe not original. But has anyone ever named and ridden dolphins before?* "Two males rather than a mated pair?" The second dolphin slithered the length of its body against her, blowing bubbles as it passed.

Coroastin dived between Azariel's legs and jerked her off her feet, making her gasp. Instinctively, her legs clamped around its side as it dived over a wave. She clung to it as it leaped and plunged, then whooped as the dolphin soared at least a foot above the water and landed with a sharp splash. Farren and Captain joined them, the two beasts racing side by side. Captain edged ahead and headed out to sea. As they hurtled over the peaks of waves about half a mile away from the shore, more dolphins joined them, squeaking and chittering as they almost danced around them. "We could almost get to the island now!" Farren called to her across the water.

With the other dolphins milling around them, they headed their mounts back to the shore and dismounted by the rocks. She followed him onto the shore, wringing salt water out of her cloak. "We'll get our gear and then we can go," he said. "Can you fetch it? I'm going to need to get properly dressed, as I'm not heading to an unknown and possibly dangerous island in just my undershorts."

"What about Storm and Princess?"

He stood still, holding the buckle of his cloak around his neck. The two horses were grazing on the coarse grass in the sand dunes, manes and tails streaming in the strong sea-wind. "They'll be all right here," he said after a while. "We haven't heard any wolves or seen signs of other large predators for a few days now. But we had better hide their gear somewhere while we're gone, and say goodbye to them, too."

"Assuming we're going to come back from the island in one piece." She shot a glance across the green water at the dark hill rising out of it.

"They'll look after themselves." He tugged at his betrothal earring and grinned. "Pity Storm's gelded. Otherwise they'd start their own herd if they do get left on their own."

"They'd have started their own herd already if that was the case, sharing a loose box and all." She wrung her cloak out one last time, twisting water out of it and making holes and curling watermarks in the sand. "Come on. We'll get back from this. There's every chance we can, with the Power watching over us."

She pulled her chainmail and boots on, and walked to where she had left the horses' gear. The sand clung grittily to her feet inside her socks. She stooped to pick up the bridles and heaved the two saddles one on top of the other on her forearm. Farren's whistle shrilled through the air behind her and Princess whinnied in answer. "Wait, Storm," she said, seeing the gelding beginning to trot towards him. She caught Storm by the mane and slung the saddles roughly over his back, stirrups clashing and jangling together as she tightened the girths of the one underneath. With a light slap on his muscular rump, she sent him cantering over the sand to where Farren was watching the dolphins frolic. She walked behind the horses carrying Farren's bow. "Where shall we put the gear?" she asked as she reached him.

He took the bow from her and ran his hand over the curved wood. "We'll have to move them well away from the water and somewhere under cover." Again his hand caressed the length of the bow. "I'll have to leave this behind, too," he said regretfully. "I'd get the string all wet and ruin it for anything. Pity – I might need it." He bent his head and looked at the bow again before scanning the beach. "Well, Stormwolf, you've had a wasted walk," he chuckled. "We're going to put these things under that tree where we drank. It's the only landmark I can think of so we can find the gear again."

She groaned and rolled her eyes. "You're taking one of the saddles," she said, tugging Princess's tack off Storm's back and handing it to him. "Let's go." She vaulted onto Storm and put heels to him. The big gelding snorted and thundered back towards the tall pine-like tree, ears pricked and neck arched.

She pulled the gear off Storm and unstrapped one of the saddlebags as Farren halted Princess in a swirl of golden sand. "We'll want to take those around our necks to keep them dry," he said. "We're going to be drenched through by the time we get to the other side."

"Better put our tinderboxes and cloaks in there, too." She opened the pouch beside her sword and fished the little tin box out. It jingled faintly as she stuffed it into one of the saddlebags, wrapping it up well inside her cloak. *I hope I've got enough cotton wadding for tinder in there still*, she thought. *It sounds like there's not much left.* She paused with one hand holding the leather straps for the bag open, then unbuckled her sword belt and slid it, complete with pouch, sword and dagger, into the saddlebag. The hilt jutted out from the opening, so she pulled the straps around it tugged them as tight as she could.

"Good idea." Farren's hands worked quickly, stripping the quiver off the belt before he stowed it neatly into the bag. His whole sword fitted inside the leather bag and the pack he slung across his shoulders looked neater and smoother than hers.

She eased the straps around her neck and pulled her hair out from between the leather and her armour. *How did he fit all that in there?* She watched him for a moment while he stroked and crooned to his mare before she turned to Storm and hugged the gelding's neck. "Goodbye for a while, old fellow," she whispered to the black horse. "I'll see you when we return with the Stone of Earth."

She felt his velvety nose nudge against her chest playfully as she released him. After giving the horse a last pat, she turned away from him. Silently, she slid her hand into Farren's and began walking down the beach towards the rocks. The saddlebag straps dug painfully into her shoulders. *I hope those horses stay safe enough here. God Incarnate, protect them!* One of the horses neighed behind them and she turned her head to see Storm bending to the stream for a drink. A twinge of sadness shot through her as she looked back across the water to the island standing tall and dusty black against the pale blue sky.

The dolphins bustled around them in the water by the rock, squealing and chittering. Wincing at the clamminess of wet leather wrapping her legs, she mounted Coroastin. The whole pod of dolphins swirled fluidly around and headed towards the hill in the shining water to the north, Captain leading the way with Farren on his back. Coroastin undulated gently beneath her and the waves slapped and crashed against her as she rose and fell with the movements of beast and water, sinking to where the water lapped at her breasts, then surging almost completely out. the other dolphins in the pod leaped and dived over, under and around them, coming close to nudge against her then swimming away again. Beads of water and foam leaped and flew with the sea breeze in her eyes and mouth, salt and stinging. Points of light danced off the water in diamonds and globes of silver. Ahead, the shape of the island grew larger and clearer.

The points of dancing light left the water as the dolphins swam into the shadow of the island. A haze still hung around the rounded peak in the centre of the island, but the rest looked green and smooth in places, and darker and tangled in others. A sweet scent of orchard blossoms drifted on the wind and mingled with the wild salt of the sea. Her heart kicked with excitement inside her. Soon, Coroastin's movements grew gentler as they approached the long curving line of the shore. White crests broke the glassy green of the water around her, then Coroastin let a wave carry them almost to the beach.

The sand met her feet and she slipped off the dolphin's slippery back. A breaker pushed her from behind and she stumbled. She regained her balance, bending and twisting the saddlebag off from around her neck as the waves retreated and dragged the sand away from under her feet. One of the dolphins whistled once, then they all swam away into the shining green water, leaving her and Farren on the shores of the island.

CHAPTER THIRTEEN

Farren threw his bag down onto the sand. "Well, we're here," he said, staring back at the mainland. A row of snow-covered peaks stretched almost from one edge of the horizon to the other. "What now, Stormwolf?"

"You tell me, Lieutenant Farren Blackarrow," she replied, tossing her bag down beside his. Even through the leather, the sword hilt gouged a hole in the sand as it landed. "Finding a way to get dry would be good. So would something to eat."

"A fire, then." He turned away from her towards the line of trees that marked the end of the beach. "At least there's going to be plenty of wood to scavenge over there."

"There's plenty lying on the beach, too," she said, scanning the shoreline. Piles of dried brown weed, twisted white wood and hundreds of shells stretched in a line along the length of the beach, cutting the strip of sand in half. Here and there, black and white birds pecked and pried at the heaps, while others squawked and swooped overhead. "Don't bother going to the woods." Her boots Water sloshed in her boots as she walked towards the nearest pile and she stopped to yank them off and empty them. The water poured out, scribbling curling lines in the sand as it drained away.

They dragged many loads of driftwood back to the place where they had come ashore and piled it into a huge heap. Sitting on the sand with small grey grains clinging to the damp leather of her clothes, she opened her saddlebag and felt inside it. Cool, dry wool met her fingers, along with the battered tin lid of her tinderbox. She pulled the tinderbox out and found half a handful of frayed cotton fluff inside. Taking the piece of flint from inside the box, she struck sparks from it using the blade of her dagger.

Eventually, the tinder ignited, and she blew and coaxed it into flame. The dry sticks crackled as the young fire engulfed them, and a mix of white smoke and steam rose into the air. Bubbles of water hissed at the ends of the larger logs, but soon they blackened and burned. She put the flint and the rest of the cotton back into the box and stuffed it back into the gearbag. "Come as close as you can and dry off," she said over her shoulder to Farren as she brushed the gritty wet sand off the knees of her soaked leather trousers. "I should have thought to stuff those spare clothes into the bags."

The fire burned for the rest of the afternoon and her leather clothing changed from cold, heavy and sodden to stiff and scratchy. She flexed and rubbed at the thighs of her trousers, but the leather stayed obstinately stiff. A thin coating of milky white formed over the black. *I wish I could take them off and give them a good beating until they're supple again! Farren must be suffering, too.* She shrugged and settled back into a comfortable position, head and arms resting on her bent knees as she breathed in the smells of salt and smoke.

The sun wheeled to the west and sank, golden as a new-minted coin and its rays dyeing the underside of the few clouds to rich yellows and oranges. Seabirds glided and spiralled on the winds, black against the sunset. The sun plunged into the sea, leaving a rich twilight above the darkening water. They ate the last of the food from the gearbags, rolled themselves up in blankets and went to sleep on opposite sides of the fire. The last thing Azariel saw before she closed her eyes was the red glow of embers swelling then dying with the night wind reflected in the metal of their drawn swords. Gradually, her breathing matched the steady rhythm of the sea's hiss and roar, and she slept.

Azariel woke the next morning to feel the sand beside her damp with dew. She stretched and sat up, shivering a little in the chill of the dawn air. Looking east, she saw the sun hanging low over the sea, a pale yellow globe shining through a pearly sky. The waves roared and sobbed lower on the beach. *That's strange,* she thought. *They're further away than they were last night.* She studied the line of wet sticks and seaweed that trailed a mark half-way up the narrow stretch of wet sand. *That's where the waves were yesterday. Is the ocean shrinking?* She watched the sea heave and pour itself onto the shore, her eyes travelling over the silver water to the faint, slightly curved line where sea met sky. *Maybe not. I think I remember something that a distant cousin told me about how the sea rises and falls. I thought he was making it up to impress us.*

She pushed herself to her feet, her trousers still scraping and rubbing against her calves. *Still not back to normal,* she thought as she worked the stiffened leather again. A light dusting of dried salt came off on her hand. *I hope that that leather will soften today with a bit of walking. I'll be rubbed raw by it if it doesn't.* She looked around the beach, then back to Farren beside the fire. He still lay asleep, blanket half covering his face. *I'll let him sleep a while longer. That gash on his arm still hasn't healed. I'll relight the fire and find something for breakfast.*

She found some wood high up the beach, damp but light enough to be fire-dry. A seagull squawked and scolded at her from a larger log of driftwood. She laid and lit the fire on the lumps of charcoal from the night before and watched the smoke curl up as she sheltered the young yellow flame from the gentle wind. The tang of the smoke tickled the back of her nose and made her eyes water. When the tongues of fire had licked across the wood and left it glowing red, she stoked the blaze up. *There,* she thought, looking down at it and then along the beach to a cluster of smooth grey rocks at the southeastern end of the island. *I should find something to eat by those rocks. Birds' eggs or even fish, maybe.*

The salt-stiffened leather of her trousers was chafing her calves and thighs badly by the time she returned to the fire carrying some gulls' eggs bundled up in her cloak. The briny smell of the sea mixed with the sweeter scents of the forest beyond the sand. Farren has woken and was bending over the fire with his back to her and doing something with the wood. "Good morning," she called.

He turned around to face her, dropping sticks from his hand. "Good morning to you, sweetheart," he said. "Where have you been?"

"Over to those rocks to find something to eat." She laid down her bundle and kissed him on the top of his head. "Only eggs, worse luck, but they should be tolerable once we've baked them in the embers."

After they had finished eating, she scooped up some wet sand to extinguish the fire. *There's not much chance of it spreading, but I don't want to start another bushfire. There'd be no escaping it on this island.* The pile of hot wood and stone hissed and steamed as she dropped the sand over it, smothering the flames. She shook her hands to clean them, but the grit clung to her fingers. A few grains worked under her rings and grated against her. She rubbed her hands on the hem of her cloak. Finished, she looked through the small curl of smoke rising from the damp, charred remains of the fire to where Farren stood studying at the trees and running one hand through his hair. "Stormwolf," he said. "Look closely at these trees. It's not a normal forest at all."

She wandered over to stand beside him and turned to look inland. Instead of seeing the random tangle of tree-trunks, brambles, bushes and shrubs she expected, she saw a thick wall of cypress trees, all growing closely together and neatly clipped to shape. Behind the tall hedge, the bright green leaves and purple-grey tips of birches stirred slightly with the breeze. "There's someone on the island," she said. "And probably not a friend, either, if they've got the Stone which should belong to the Kingdom. How are we going to get through there?"

"We'll have to work our way around the island to find a gap, if we can," he said. "We need to find a stream, and by the looks of that hill, there's bound to be one somewhere. And if there's one, it'll fall into the sea eventually. And we need a drink."

She stretched and shrugged her shoulders. "On the march, then."

Her head throbbed with thirst, her thighs stung with chafing from the leather, and her tongue felt dry by the time she saw the line of water snaking across the sand on the eastern shore of the island. She ran towards the little stream and eagerly scooped up the water, splashing and spilling it as she knelt down and drank. Gratefully, she dashed a handful of water over her head and shook her hair back. Droplets tickled and trickled down her face and neck. She looked along the line of the stream to where it came out of the trees. *Perhaps we can follow it under the hedge.* A patch of brown caught her eye and she stared at it. A low wooden gate stood under an archway cut neatly in the dense green branches of the cypress. She looked at it, then caught Farren's eye and nodded.

They walked to the gate and stood beside it, looking into the forest beyond. Cloud still blanketed the sky and moisture dripped from the young leaves to the forest floor. A grassy path led away from the gate a little way into the woods, then turned a corner out of sight. Farren put his hand on the gate, breaking a dewy cobweb. "Well, Stormwolf, in we go," he said. His right hand reached for her left as the gate creaked open.

The hinges slowly squealed as the gate swung shut behind them by itself. A ripple of cold spread down her spine and she glanced about through the densely packed trunks of the birches. Creaks and rustles stirred the branches, moving out from the gate into the depths of the wood. Far off, a pattering noise like the footsteps of mice rippled through the leaves. She clenched her fist, feeling the metal of her opal ring dig into the calluses on her palm. Overhead, the sun reached through a patch of thin cloud and glittered faintly on a cluster of dew-covered leaves, turning them to diamond. She smiled and tossed her hair back from her face. *Whatever's ahead, I'm ready.*

The path wound around many twists and turns through the white and grey-purple trunks of birches. Farren and Azariel rounded another corner and the trees changed abruptly from birches to trees laden with masses of lacy pink blossoms. She stepped onto the carpet of petals strewn across the path and breathed in the light scent of the flowers. "It's like the palace gardens," she murmured, looking up through the rosy clouds to the sky, now patched with blue among the grey.

To her left, she heard the tinkling of falling water. The path heeled around to the left, leading into a circular clearing filled with the white umbels and dark feathery leaves of hemlock. She pushed her way through the foliage, the liquid sound of water filling her ears. In the centre of the clearing stood a tall, slender ivy-wrapped column that sprayed glimmering drops of water into a wide basin from a spout at the top. "That's beautiful," she said. She stepped closer and saw that instead of growing naturally, the ivy was made of bronze, touched here and there by a greenish patina so it looked like true living ivy. *That is well worked. Who did that?*

Farren released her hand and strode forwards to kneel by the basin. "I'm glad we found this. I was in need of a drink," he said. He shuffled to one side slightly and reached down to pick up a knob of something white and tossing it aside. She glanced at it; it looked dull and porous like old bone or ivory. A sudden intake of breath hissed between her teeth as Farren bent over the fountain and scooped some of the rippling water up in his hands. *What died here? I hope it didn't die in the water – or of the water. Is the water safe? Is he safe?* A small white flower floated in his cupped hands. With a grimace, he tipped the flower back into the basin.

The hemlock bloom landed splashed down beside the artificial ivy. Beneath the jagged circle of ripples, the surface gaped open wide. A human-like figure broke from the deep valley in the water and rose in a wave of golden hair and pale gold-green skin. A second figure followed it and the two stood in the fountain, dripping beads of water from their long, bedraggled manes and down across their naked bodies, one male, the other female. Hard green eyes, which glittered like the water, glared at her and Farren. "Who are you?" said the male.

"You carry the marks, yet you do not have the aura of the master," said the female.

"The likes of you may not enter," said the male, speaking antiphonally.

"We will not let you pass."

"Others have come to the Island of Labyrinths."

"And they joined us beneath the foam and ripples of the fountain." The female shook her hair back, baring her breasts. "You will also join us."

Azariel backed away as Farren leaped to his feet and stumbled backwards, snapping stems of hemlock. A sharp smell of crushed greenery rose. She grabbed him by the shoulders and helped him roughly up. "You will let us pass," she replied.

Farren balled his hands into fists and the emerald ring on his right hand sparkled with green fire. "You can't stop us," he said.

We're sounding like those two now, speaking line by line like choirboys. She stifled a snicker as the fire pulsed in her veins. "In the name of God Incarnate, let us past."

The two figures staggered backwards as if struck. The male threw back his head, teeth bared in a ghastly grimace while the female screamed shrilly. The two toppled, entering the water without a splash, and disappeared. The water changed to a sickly green as if it had been standing stagnant and a stench of putrid kale rose from it. The fountain bubbled and churned for three or four heartbeats, then gradually began to run clear again, the clean water spreading bright fingers through the green.

She shook herself and relaxed her hands, feeling the tingling and prickling fire die away from her arms. A pang of hunger shot through her and her head spun for a moment. She drew a deep breath and released it slowly, dispelling the last traces of tension with the breath.

"Well, we got out of that one without a fight," Farren said. "Looks like I'm going to have to find somewhere else to have a drink."

"Let's get on before they decide they need to come back," she said. Her hand reached for his and found it before they walked on.

Farren edged ahead of her slightly, his hand still wrapped around hers. The sunlight danced in dappled shade on the close-clipped grass path, and the pink and white blossoms overhead trembled and hummed with thousands of bees. He relaxed his stride as the sound of the fountain faded away behind and to the left. The drone and whine of the bees became louder as the sun grew warmer. Ahead, the path narrowed and turned sharply to the right beneath the shadow of thick, gnarled silvery trunks.

Around the corner, the buzzing sounded almost as loud as a river. He stood aside to let her take the lead on the narrow path, his right shoulder pushing against one of the tree trunks. He strolled on and felt a sharp, burning itch high on his shoulder, between the blade and the spine. He shrugged and twisted, trying to scrape his chainmail across the spot. The itch grew from an irritation to pain. *The only problem with wearing chainmail is that you can't scratch an itch.* Still the point of pain burned and throbbed in his shoulder and a second was beginning at the nape of his neck at the right. He raised raked his fingernails at the itch, noticing Azariel clapping a hand to one thigh on the far side from him. His hand brushed something hot and a frantic, furious buzzing filled the air behind his head. He spun around, feeling the pain in his shoulder suddenly lessen.

Fifteen golden things the size of sparrows hovered and danced like burning insects in the air around them. One swooped down at him, buzzing shrilly and casting a haze of golden light around itself in the shadow. He noticed its vaguely human form and a long weapon like a spear in its hand before the thing settled on his right arm and jabbed him. The burning itch spread out from the point of its spear. He swatted at it with his left hand, and it leaped off him in a flurry of insect wings and more buzzing.

"Duck!" shouted Azariel. He dropped to one knee as a bolt of red light leaped from her hands. The fire-fays swerved out of the way of the beam, then converged on her. She beat at them with her arms, snarling.

"My turn now. Down!" He raised his hands and sent a stream of violet light at one of the fire-fays. Again, they darted away from the beam and the purple fire struck the tree trunks, blackening the bronzy-grey bark.

He batted and flailed at the fire-fays as he worked his way over to Azariel ten paces away. They darted swiftly, jabbing and stinging his hands, his back, his face and his legs. *And their spears are too small to be stopped by chainmail.* "Don't use fire anymore," he shouted over the shrill buzz. "We'll only set light to the forest and they're too fast."

"Do you think we can run fast enough to get away from them?" She shook her head vigorously as one jabbed her cheek, flicking the fire-fay off in a swirl of black hair.

"I doubt it." One particularly large fire-fay lanced the skin on the back of his hand and he beat backhanded at an overhanging branch to dislodge it. It flew clear as his knuckles cracked into the bark. It hovered in front of his face, the almost human features on its head taunting and teasing him. Then it swooped in and jabbed its burning spear into the tip of his nose. "Hellfire!" He clutched at it, and the tiny limbs slithered and rustled out between his fingers. Its wings buzzed through his hair as it flew up. He swatted at it as it left, his chest heaving. "I've got an idea," he said. "Wait until one jabs my right hand, then you grab it. Hold tight, and I'll deal with it."

He held out one arm, twitching back the metal links of the sleeves slightly. The skin on his arms looked reddened and swollen where the fire-fays had jabbed him, and the swellings itched. Another fire-fay landed on him, little lance quivering. He gritted his teeth as it raised another irritating blister. Azariel's gaze met his. She pounced, both hands closing around the small winged body.

The fire-fay writhed and struggled, squealing in a high, grating voice. "Hold it up away from your body," he said, feeling the clean, exhilarating heat of the Power prickle in his fingertips. The others swarmed around Azariel's head, suddenly glowing more brightly.

"Be quick," she said through gritted teeth. Her lips writhed back in a grimace. "It's burning me."

Two pulses of silver fire spurted from his rings and engulfed the fire-fay. A curling plume of smoke rose from her hands and fine, powdery ash fell onto the grass as the fire-fay crumbled. "That's one," he said, breathlessly. "Now for the rest. How are your hands?"

"Sore, but not burned. It felt like I was holding the end of a metal spoon that's been left in the soup too long." She looked down at her hands, then flailed at the descending fire-fays. "Your turn to catch one and I'll burn it away."

He grabbed at the next fire-fay that swooped in to jab her face. *Nobody does that to my Stormwolf!* It jerked and pulled at his hands like a hooked fish, squirming. Tiny sparks flew from it onto his hands like hot fat in a frying pan. He squeezed hard and felt something snap as he held it up. It shrieked and struggled more frantically. He turned his face away from the sparks as fire shot from Azariel's hands and turned the squealing fire-fay to ash.

Catching and burning the remaining fire-fays seemed to take hours, although the sun hardly moved. Finally, only one remained. It hovered in the branches of the trees, buzzing shrilly, then turned and vanished into the undergrowth. A faint murmur filled the air, the drone of busy bees in the blossoms.

Azariel leaned her head against the trunk of the cherry tree where the last fire-fay had vanished. Her salt-stiffened trousers gad rubbed her calves and thighs almost raw, and her feet ached. *I won't be surprised if I have blisters up and down my legs and feet at the end of all this. I've grown too used to riding.* She put the pads of her finger and thumb over her closed eyelids and rubbed before pinching the bridge of her nose in an attempt to banish the dizziness that whirled around her mind after the fire had faded from her hands. "On the march again, I suppose," she said. "I hope we come across a stream soon. I'm thirsty and those little pests took it out of me."

"I don't suppose you'd fancy going back to that fountain." His hand linked with hers as they started walking along the grassy path again. A faint sheen of sweat coated his forehead. "I wonder how long until we get out of here. This path must lead somewhere, and from the beach it didn't look as though the island was all trees. I've lost all sense of direction."

"It shouldn't be too much longer. We could climb a tree and see how much further – and where – the end of these trees is."

"Not until I've got over those fire-fays." He rubbed at his arm.

"Three more corners?" She shook her hair back from her face and clawed at one of the blisters left by the fire-fays on the back of her neck above the line of armour.

He nodded and they paced wearily on. The path wound right, right again, then left and out of the blossom trees into a riot of many-coloured azalea bushes. *Well, we've got somewhere.* The constant drone of the bees faded, leaving only the faint hiss of wind in the twiggy branches. *Now we're well away from where those fire-fays were, I'd like to rest my feet for a bit.* A cluster of cypress trees caught her eye. "Those trees look solid enough to lean against and to climb," she said, pointing. Looking more closely, she saw a dark wooden seat beneath the enmeshed boughs of the cypresses. A smile spread across her face as she studied at the high carved back and the tangled brambles coiling around the chair's arms and legs. "Look at that. Put there on purpose, though it doesn't look like anyone's been here for a while."

"And I don't really trust it." He let go of her hand and walked over to the seat. He prodded at the dark wood and kicked one of the legs. "Come and get me, if you're going to," he said to it.

"It's not doing anything. What harm can a chair do?" She swirled the skirt of her black cloak out of the way. "It's a bit small for two, but I don't mind sitting close to you."

She eased down into the chair, grateful to remove her weight from her feet. He pressed in close to her and she laid her head on his shoulder. The weight of his head nestled against hers and he pulled her closer. She closed her eyes and breathed in his sharp, sweet scent and felt his warmth against her. His chainmail dug into her chin and she shifted her head so that it rested fully on the shoulder of his cloak where his lieutenant's badge made a smooth, hard spot amidst the prickly rough wool under her cheek.

She heard a faint rustle and felt his head lift from hers. "Beloved?" she asked softly. She turned her face towards him and his lips pressed onto hers. Shifting her body, she glided her hand around his waist, feeling his taut muscles beneath the chainmail. He gripped her shoulder and held her tightly. She drew back her head and looked at him against the backdrop of the rustling creeper, savouring the sight of his deep brown eyes, his sharp nose and chin, the gently smiling line of his mouth. Her own lips parted in a smile and her pulse quickened. "You are irresistible," she murmured.

Something slid across her hair and a sharp pain stabbed into her scalp. She jerked back and tried to raise her hand to brush it off. Her wrist was held firmly by something. She looked down and saw a creeper wreathing around her right arm, coiling shoots around her. Farren's hold on her loosened as she withdrew her free arm from around him and groped at her right hip for her dagger. She plucked it loose from the sheath and started hacking at the thorny creeper.

She slashed her other arm free and stood up. The vines curled and twined up her legs and around her waist like snakes, rustling as leaves and thorns brushed across her clothing and armour. Spines dug into her and raked whitish lines across her trousers. She slashed and ripped at them, but they continued to grow, two tendrils curling around her where one had grown before. As she severed a tendril that reached for her arm, stinging red sap oozed onto her skin. To one side of her, Farren hacked with his dagger at the vines. Thorns raked over her bare forearms, her cheeks and her hands. She drew her sword, breaking part of the creeper as she unsheathed it. She slid the blade down her left leg between her trousers and the creeper, and sawed the coils apart. She kicked her leg back out of reach as a new tendril stretched for it, then freed her right leg.

She writhed backwards, shaking her head. The vine tore at her hair. She stepped away from the seat, free. Farren still wrestled with the twisting vine, left arm totally hidden behind a mass of tangled lime green. She dodged a reaching creeper and slashed through the vine that writhed and wreathed around his left arm, then pulled him clear of the leafy fingers that stretched around the back of the carved seat towards them. His chest heaved against her own as she held him and a trickle of blood trailed across his forehead. She raised a finger to brush the blood away and felt him pulling something from her hair. "It's still got hold of you," he said. "Let's get away from here."

With her arm still around his waist, they walked between the brilliantly coloured rows of azaleas once more. He reached for a bright red flower and snapped it free. "Here, Stormwolf," he said as he tucked it behind her ear. "Something to put in your hair that won't try to strangle you."

"Thank you," she whispered, leaning over to press a kiss onto his cheek.

The path broke out from the gaudy azalea bushes to a wide lawn, empty apart from a few trees studded about it and a small herd of white goats in the distance. She blinked in the sudden sunlight and looked around. Ahead of her stood the hill in the heart of the island, black against the blue sky and a dark mantle of mist around its head and shoulders. To her left lay a cluster of white marble buildings set out to form a square, each with many pillars framing tall arches.

Her eye flicked towards movement. A man was walking in the centre of the lawn beside the buildings. He wore robes of many shades of green, ranging from pine-dark to almost yellow, and his long grey hair was tied back in the fashion of the Wayasti men. He turned towards them, looking past them. Stamped on his face was an expression like that of a wounded warrior seeing the kill-stroke falling: eyes wide, lips thin and drawn back over his teeth. She squeezed Farren's hand and led the way forwards. The man raised his head to look at them and started, the terror widening his eyes and mouth further. Then the stark fear in his face vanished and a gleam came into his expression. "Whoever you are, greetings and welcome to the Island of Labyrinths. Are you *minyasti*, or are you sorcerers come to take my place?"

CHAPTER FOURTEEN

Farren dropped his hand to the hilt of his sword. *Fine words, but what sort of man lives ringed by a maze full of menaces?* His tongue ran around the inside of his lips and he felt the muscles down the back of his arms tense in readiness.

"We're *minyasti*," Azariel said, stepping forward. "But how did you know that we must be either one or the other?"

The robed man walked over to them, his bare feet making hardly any sound on the grass. Farren's eyes flicked up and down him. *He's unarmed, physically, it seems. Unless he's got hidden weapons like a Nightraven.* A small spark of silver and red flashed on the man's right hand. *And he's a sorcerer or* minyastin. His eyes met the hollow, worried gaze of the older man. *But would a minyastin know fear like that?*

"Only sorcerers or *minyasti* could come through the first maze safely," the other man said, lifting his ringed hand and gesturing behind them. "The path is filled with traps that allow only sorcerers to pass. But whichever you are, you are welcome. You'll be an easier death than what I expected."

The places itching on Farren's skin seemed to flare and he saw a bright tripartite leaf from the thorny creeper still hanging in Azariel's dark hair. *He did that to us?* A small coal of anger ignited in his chest and his hand tightened on his sword hilt. "You're a sorcerer then," he growled softly, slowly sliding the blade from the sheath.

Azariel's hand clamped over his wrist and squeezed hard, biting her nails into him. "Calm down," she whispered firmly, pushing his hand back. "Let him speak."

"You are angry, and I understand," the sorcerer said. "I am sorry. I never meant the maze and the island to become like this, but... well! It's a long story, but it's nearly ended for me." He looked down at the grass and the lines of fear deepened on his face again. "Have you come to kill me, *minyasti?*"

Farren glanced at Azariel and their eyes met. *He's a smooth talker, but can we trust him? We need Janna Greyhawk or Kiihaon here as truthreader.* "Only if we have to," he said aloud.

The sorcerer laughed and the lines of fear softened. "I doubt you will have to," he said. Then the sparkle of amusement vanished behind the anxiety like the sun hiding behind a cloud. "Unless ... never mind." He looked back up at them. "You both look weary after your journey through the maze. I am surprised that you got through the traps so easily."

"We met three," Azariel said. "The seat with the creeper, which nearly trapped us; the fire-fays, which have left us itchy; and the nymphs in the fountain, which left us alone."

"I am sorry," the man repeated. "But be thankful you missed some of the others. Come with me to where we can be seated and I will tell you my story and why it's nearly ended." A gleam entered his green eyes. "Perhaps you can help me when the time comes."

Farren pushed his sword back into its sheath and took Azariel's hand as they walked behind the old man. "Can we trust him?" he whispered to her.

"I'm not sure, yet," she answered, leaning towards him so that her hair brushed his face. "But we can't strike at him, an old man, unprovoked and unarmed, even if he is a sorcerer. I'd like to hear his story first. I don't sense danger from him. And even if he is, we should be a match for him. But there's something going on here, and I'd like to find out more."

He looked over at the old man, who padded over the grass, robes rustling and stirring as he walked with shoulders bowed. Farren flicked his eyes to and fro, scanning the wide lawn for any other living things apart from the goats. "Keep on your guard, Stormwolf. There is danger somewhere, even if it's not from him. I feel as if eyes are on me or as if something's waiting for us."

"On the top of the hill?" She turned and looked hard at him. "I can sense something there in the cloud and mist. Something like Crajaval."

He studied the centre of the island. The sky overhead was patched with blue and grey, but over the hill, it looked like it was filled with a thick black smoke that clung to the curves of the slopes. The wind stirred the haze and he caught a faint green light glinting amidst the darkness. *That looks like the mist that used to be around Moonlady Falls, except this is black, not white.* Memories roused in his mind and the back of his neck prickled. *Another of the Wayasti gods?*

He dropped his gaze down from the slopes to the old man once more and saw him seated on a stone bench beneath a magnificently shaped oak tree. The goats bleated to each other and one wandered out from behind the almost black trunk. "Be seated," the sorcerer said, gesturing to a marble bench nearby.

Farren brushed a light film of grey dust off the smooth surface of the marble. *I hope this one's safe.* He studied the swirling patterns as Azariel glided one hand over the stone. He collapsed onto the seat, crossing his legs to rest one ankle on his other knee. The stiff leather of his trousers chafed painfully at his thighs. *Good. I'll be glad to get off my feet for a little.* Azariel sat beside him, leaning forwards with her chin cupped in her hands. He slid his arm around her shoulder and ran his fingers gently through her hair. The leaf from the creeper fell loose and the breeze tumbled it away. The goat nearby sniffed at the leaf then ate it before meandering closer.

"Who are you?" Azariel asked. "Tell us what you want to say."

The old man rested both hands on the marble beside him and looked up at the still-bare branches of the oak. "My name is Kalmian Mazewright and for much of my life, I lived in Wayast, where I was born." His green eyes travelled down and met Farren's glance. "You are *minyasti*; you know of our gods and goddess."

"We do," he said. The marble suddenly reminded him of the floor of Crajaval's chamber when he had been her captive. His hand curled into a fist on the smooth surface. "Better than I'd like to, too."

The sorcerer's eyebrows raised. "So you have a story too? You can tell me yours later. But as for me, I had a quickened soul and a thirst to know things. I entered the College of Fire and trained there."

"You are a sorcerer, then." Azariel's shoulders tensed. "One of Izar Gardweil's people."

"Izar?" Kalmian's eyes flashed. "Is he head of the College now? I remember him. Bright enough lad but a real weakness for pretty women. Good luck to him – or maybe not, seeing as you're here." The lines on his forehead smoothed momentarily as he smiled. "But I had no wish to stay at the College. I have no taste for fighting, and my body and eyesight were little suited to a battlefield even then. But the hunger for knowledge was still hot in me, and I wanted to know more. I conversed with the gods and goddess, especially Majalis."

"Who's he?" Farren asked.

"Shayim's rival," Azariel cut in, turning her head towards him and pulling a tangle in her hair tight against his hand. "They're supposed to fight over Crajaval and take turns with her every year."

"Whore," he muttered under his breath.

Kalmian chuckled. "You are almost right. Majalis is the dark twin of bright Shayim the Horned. Year after year, he slays Shayim at the autumn equinox to become Crajaval's consort; year after year, he is slain in his turn by Shayim in the springtime. While he is waiting his time in the spring and summer, he is the Lord of the Dead who rules over the underworld. His season is the season of death, of endings and of darkness; Shayim's is that of light, fertility and the sun. Waxing year and waning year, stag and scorpion, they battle for the Moon Lady. For she is the lady of light as the moon waxes, then the dark lady as it wanes."

Farren smiled wryly and stared at the toe of his boots. A white bloom of salt marred the black leather. *The witch takes – took, or whatever it is – any man she wanted, not just those two. With a particular taste for redheads and* minyastini, *so I was fair game and lucky to escape.* He felt through Azariel's hair to the links of chainmail around her neck.

"Why did you seek him in particular?" Azariel asked. "I thought most in the Old Religion loved bright Shayim, not the Pale Man."

"The Lord of the Dead is also called the Lord of Secrets. As judge of the dead, he knows all hidden things, everything hidden in the dark. And that was all I desired. I served him and paid many prices for my knowledge. And he gave me a gift in return for my service. A stone – a green gem bound with silver that I could use to know the secrets of the future, of the land, of time. And I studied it and learned the power of earth. With it, I raised this island from the sea." He gestured around the green land and towards the black-capped hill. "I laid out the trees and rocks in the labyrinth paths to bring power and fertility on the land. I built the high place to set the stone in where I could gaze at the stars and into the Stone to read the future. I built my house, aligning it with the sun and the stars, and commanded hot springs to heat it. Everything I wished for, I had: books, musical instruments, gold, clothing, ornaments, fine food and horses. I've always been fond of horses."

"Wine, women and song, as the saying goes," Farren said breezily. *Careful. Don't let him fool you. Stay on your guard.*

"Not women." Kalmian shook his head. "I was pledged to Majalis, not Shayim, and Majalis is no lusty youth. His bond is with Crajaval alone. Like him, I never asked for women. No insult to you, lady, but women held no attractions for me and neither did men."

"No insult taken," she said. "But what changed? Why, if you don't mind me asking, were you looking so worried and so hopeful when you heard we were *minyasti* who weren't going to kill you immediately?"

"I will come to that last thing presently. All pleasure in this island is now gone. It is not my island; it belongs to Majalis. After I built the mazes, he filled them with pitfalls and traps to snare any who tried to enter without his permission – any except sorcerers. And I – I cannot leave. The traps keep me a prisoner here as much as they keep others out. He even demanded the blood of my horses: Daphne, Firefoot, Ebony and Nimbus. The beauty of the island I made became darkened. That wasn't the power I had hoped to harness when I built the labyrinths!" He struck the white marble slab with the flat of his hand. "And then I couldn't stop myself going to look in the stone, even when I had no wish to see more. He made me come and showed me more than I wanted to know about the Underworld. And then – two weeks ago – I saw my future. Tomorrow night, at midnight, I will die."

Farren stared keenly at the older man. *He's telling the truth. I'm certain of that now.* He let out a long, slow breath, becoming conscious that he had been breathing shallowly until then. *This man's unburdening himself. He trusts us. I think we can trust him.*

Kalmian got to his feet and paced around. "In the depths of the stone, I saw a woman, dark-haired and beautiful like you, lady. She came to the island in the springtime, like it is now. Then I saw my death. Majalis is to come and take me. I will pay the price of my knowledge with pain at that woman's hand, then go to the Underworld with him forever." He braced himself against the trunk of the oak behind him, clutching at the clefts in the bark with his fingertips. "When I saw you come here, lady, I felt the blow of the hammer fall. Tomorrow at midnight Majalis will come for me. But..." His glanced flicked from Farren to Azariel. "Something in the stone was wrong. The woman I saw lived after me in this palace and ruled it as mistress under Majalis. She was a sorceress. But you're a *minyaster*." His voice changed suddenly, becoming hungry and hopeful. "And you came through the mazes."

Azariel sat up straight, shaking the hair back from her face. "Then it was not me you saw. I've had your goddess trying to pull me into being a sorceress once. I won't bend. I wouldn't want to be mistress of this island. I'm a *minyaster* of the Kingdom and I don't want to leave it." Her hand reached for Farren's knee and her fingers kneaded at the stiff muscle behind it.

"You came through the mazes," repeated Kalmian. "Majalis could not keep you out, though he tried. You might be able to stop him when he comes for me. At the least, you'll be able to force him into killing me quickly rather than painfully and slowly. Can you, will you help me? Can you save me from the Lord of the Dead when he comes to claim me?"

Farren looked at Azariel and her sapphire eyes flashed fire. *No wonder he looks so haunted!* "We'll do what we can," he said aloud. *Although how we can keep Majalis taking him when he has a right to him, I don't know,* he thought grimly, trying not to let the thought show on his face. He studied his nails and rings. The emerald on his right had slipped to one side; he twisted it straight. *Unless the Power's brought us here to gain a new* minyastin *for the King of Heaven.* "It won't be the first time we've come up against your gods and goddess."

"At least it's not Crajaval this time," Azariel chuckled. "I don't think Majalis will be able to leave you staring like a stuck pig over his dazzling beauty and catch you like that. Or me, for that matter."

"Do you have to remind me of that, Stormwolf?" The chill prickled on the back of his neck. "It's not funny and – hellfire! You know that being her prisoner was no joke." Anger, fear, shame and misery churned inside him, and he bit his lip in an attempt to control the rising tide of emotion.

"Sorry, beloved." Her hand caressed his knee softly, tickling around the kneecap. "It's over now. I shouldn't have reminded you."

A smile washed over Kalmian's face. "Are you telling me that you've faced the Lady herself? And survived? And that you will help me? I can't thank you enough!" He spread out his hands. "The gods – well, no, not them. Luck has sent you here to me. What has brought you here over the water to me right when I need you most? But don't tell me now. I show you little courtesy, guests. I haven't even asked your names. You are weary, hungry and thirsty. Come to the house." He stood up and beckoned.

"I'm Farren Blackarrow," he said, getting to his feet. "And Azariel Stormwolf's my betrothed. We'll be glad of your hospitality. There's pretty slim pickings on the beach and even less in the maze."

***

Farren shook the water from his hair as he stepped out of the sunken bathtub in a green marble room within the many columned corridors of Kalmian's house. The veins on his hands and feet stood up with the heat of the water, and the air seemed bracing and cool on his naked body. *That's better*, he thought as he stretched his arms and legs, feeling the stiffness and weariness gone from them. *Hot springs – unlimited hot water. It beats having to heat bathwater over a fire in a cauldron like we have to in the Watchtower or using a furnace like the barracks.* He dried himself on a soft white towel and walked over to a closet in one corner of the bathroom. His feet left the slippery marble and sank into the thick pile of a carpet as he opened the door. The sweet scent of walnut leaves wafted out from the stacks of folded clothing and linen. *Good of Kalmian to lend his robes to total strangers so we can wash the salt from our leather clothes.* He glanced at his calf and saw it chafed and reddened by the rubbing of the stiffened leather. He touched it and flinched as the tender spot stung.

He took a white robe from the closet and shook the folds out, then slipped it over his head. *Robed like a priest or a Wayasti sorcerer, but at least I'm not bearded like an Elendi any more.* He passed a hand over his cheeks, feeling them smooth and sensitised to his touch. His skin felt slightly damp and it tingled. He murmured with satisfaction and pleasure. *It's good to feel clean again.* An embroidered belt in red and green fell out of the folds of the robe and he picked it up and fastened it around his waist. He turned to look in the vast mirror set in the door and critically eyed the loose robe as it draped from his broad shoulders down to his calves. *I'll do, but this looks odd.*

He walked out of the bath chamber to the columned cloister-walk that ran around a courtyard surrounded by the other rooms of the house. *These robes are strange to walk in,* he thought as the thin fabric billowed and rustled around his legs. Air wafted about his thighs uncomfortably. *I feel naked!* He looked around and saw Azariel seated alone beside a pool in the centre of the courtyard, trailing her white fingers in the water. "Your turn," he said. She looked up at him and smiled before she rose to her feet. Her glided trailed smoothly along his shoulders as she passed by him. Her footsteps tapped over the stone, echoing his as he walked over to the pool and sat on the raised rim beside it. Coloured fish darted in and out of the forest of pond weed under the water, light flashing from their gold, purple and red scales.

He watched the fish circle many times through their forest and around the sunken boulders before he heard soft footsteps behind him. He turned his head and saw her walking barefoot towards him. She wore a red robe, short sleeved and wide in the neck, and her damp hair was tumbled over her shoulders. A gold-embroidered belt sat just above her hips, joining with the skirts of the robe to accentuate the graceful sway of her walk. The crimson flower he had given her burned like a jewel against the lustrous blue-black folds. His heart leaped. *It's so long since I've seen her in any colour except her black uniform or the greys she wears on leave. She's...She's magnificent!*

Her robe rustled softly as she sat down beside him, the walnut-leaf scent spreading outwards. His gaze wandered over her, taking in the curves and lines suggested by the swathes of material. She leaned over towards the pond and he saw the embroidered collar fall a little to show the smooth white skin of her throat. His eyes travelled down, picking out the silver streak of the scar running down from her collarbone. Desire rose within him and he felt his pulse thump in his veins. *Get a grip on yourself, Blackarrow!* he told himself. He tore his eyes away from her neck to look at her face. "You look lovely," he said, trying to keep his voice steady.

"Thank you." She leaned over and kissed his mouth quickly, then drew back and winked at him.

Footsteps sounded from the cloister-walk and he hair brushed his cheek as she turned her head. "Here comes our host," she said.

Kalmian was walking towards them across the courtyard, carrying a tray with three horn beakers and a white pottery jug balanced on it. He set the tray down on the edge of the pool and poured a thin stream of what smelt like white wine from the jug into each beaker. "Now," he said, offering the tray of drinks to them, "tell me why you are here at such an opportune time."

Farren chose one of the beakers. *If this is poison after all and he's not to be trusted, King of Heaven protect us.* Tentatively, he sipped at the wine. It swirled over his tongue and palate with a sweet, sharp, fiery bite. *There's nothing wrong with that!* He drank again. "We've come hunting for the Stone of Earth. The Kingdom needs it. And the King of Heaven showed us it was here and sent us."

Kalmian's eyebrows arched. "Do you mean that stone Crajaval and Majalis gave me? I would have thought you Kingdom *minyasti* would want nothing to do with it." Kalmian glanced from Azariel to him and back again.

"It was the Kingdom's before it was Crajaval's," explained Azariel. "It's one of the lost Stones of Protection that kept our country safe. She stole it – or persuaded one of the guardians to steal it and betray the Kingdom. Now we've got to get them back. We've got one already." She paused to take a sip of the wine. "We won the Stone of Water off Crajaval. And now we need the Stone of Earth."

"Not for scrying," added Farren. "Is that what you've been using it for?" He gazed across the lawn. The goats were browsing from a row of willow trees three bowshots away.

"I have – or at least, Majalis has shown me things in it. It is a poor stone for scrying, wrapped with silver netting as it is, and has other uses. I prefer to use embers and ashes for scrying, but as I said, Majalis calls me to it and I'm forced to look." He shuddered. "Are you planning to take it away to the Kingdom? Take it – and welcome! I will be glad to be rid of it."

"Thank you," Azariel said. "Where is it?"

"On top of the hill in the centre of my greatest labyrinth," Kalmian replied. "And even I loathe travelling through that. It has many trails and paths and the whole maze is filled with horrors, darkness, terror and stench. If you want the Stone, you have to take it yourselves. I doubt I would be able to do anything against what's in there if I came without being summoned."

Azariel set her beaker down and stood up. "Terror and darkness won't hold me back," she said, tossing her hair back.

"We'll go in and we'll come out with it – now, even. Will it take long to travel the maze?"

Farren gazed up at the cloud-shrouded hill. "Do you really want to go right now, Stormwolf?" He got to his feet behind her and slid his arm around her waist with one hand. The taut softness of her body seemed almost bare beneath his touch without the usual armour, and intense longing filled him. "The day's more than half gone now, and I'd like to rest and take a decent meal before we set out. If that's all right with you, Kalmian."

"Tonight, then?" Her dark blue eyes flashed at him. "Why wait?"

"You don't want to rush into things too quickly this time." Farren let go of her waist and drained the end of the beaker. His head was beginning to spin slightly with the wine, so he gritted his teeth and tried to control it. *Why did I take strong drink on an empty stomach? I hate getting giddy!*

Kalmian shook his head. "You do not want to go in there at night. In the daytime, it is dark and has horrors enough, but at night… I would not do that. Stay here and sleep well. Share a meal with me. I have not had a visitor for at least ten years."

"We'll stay," she said. "And, Farren, you're right." She grinned at him and reached out one hand to squeeze his arm. "I'll be glad of any bed and good food after travelling, and this is more than anything I expected. the Stone – and anything that stands between us and it – should still be there tomorrow."

"You were easy to persuade this time, Stormwolf." He tugged at her hair and winked. "We'll take the time we need to get ready."

"Speaking of getting ready, if you are to be my guests, I must prepare the food." Kalmian put his beaker back on the tray, gathered the empty ones and stood up.

"We can help you," Her tone sounded light and courteous but a hard gleam flashed through her eyes, almost too quick to notice.

Clever, Stormwolf, Farren thought as her expression smoothed over. *If we help prepare the meal, he can't poison us. Am I being too suspicious or is this sorcerer truly willing to part with the Stone?*

"I will be glad of help," replied Kalmian. "I eat rather simply these days and I might easily prepare too much or too little for a vigorous young couple like you." He turned, the tray in his hands. "The kitchens are this way. Follow me."

The sorcerer led the way down a cloister-walk to a wide archway at the end, which led into the kitchens. A wide clerestory window ran along the length of three of the walls and the light fell onto the long pine bench in the centre of the room. A fireplace took up one half of the far wall, fitted with the stands for a spit and a pothook dangling above the dead ashes. On the other half of the wall beside the fireplace stood a conical oven made from brick with a hinged door and a narrow chimney. The other walls were lined with barrels, cupboards earthenware crocks standing on shelves, strings of onions and a collection of pots and pans. One of the cupboard doors stood slightly ajar, and as Farren passed it, a sharp smell of cheese wafted out. A small door led from one side of the kitchens into daylight. Kalmian paused beside it and turned to them. "I'll set the tray in the scullery and then I shall find what I can to offer you. It is a shame that Majalis demanded my black chickens last waning quarter moon, or I would have had eggs in plenty." He shook his head sadly and the haunted look hollowed his eyes again.

Farren leaned on the pine bench in the middle of the room until Kalmian returned. "Fresh bread, cheese, pickled vegetables and smoked fish will be the best I can offer, I think, and milk from my goats. And we will need to bake the bread."

"We can do that," Farren said.

"My thanks."

After finding a wooden bowl, flour, salt and a yeast culture, Farren set to work mixing and kneading while Kalmian lit the conical oven. The dough oozed through his fingers as he worked it. *I think I've put too much water in but now my hands are so covered with dough I'll spread it to everything I touch. At least it will taste reasonable.* He kept squeezing and kneading at it and eventually long stretchy strands formed in the mixture as it grew stiffer.

Azariel stood opposite him, carefully paring a red wax coating off a round of hard cheese. The slightly acidic smell made his mouth water. She glanced up at him and sliced deeper, cutting a thin slice off the cheese, winking at him. He held up his hands, the dough still clinging to his fingers. Smiling, she slipped the morsel of cheese into his mouth. His stomach clenched hungrily at the tangy saltiness. *I had better take the edge off my hunger. If this sorcerer does try to slip us something poisoned, it's going to be hard to avoid it.*

At last he patted the dough into a large ball and crumbled the last of the dough off his fingers. Kalmian set down several sealed crocks on the bench beside the cheese and the dough. "Come with me and I will show you where you can sleep tonight while the bread rises."

Farren fell into step with Azariel behind Kalmian, his hand reaching out to find hers. The older man led them out of the kitchen the way they had come, then into another of the cloisters ringing the central courtyard. A door in the middle of the cloister opened onto an iron stairway. Farren's bare feet slipped slightly on the cold bare metal, so he reached for the thin bannister, which sprouted curlicues that gave it a plant-like look. At the landing, woven carpets and cowhides, all in patterns of black and white, lay across the wooden floor. Two arched doorways with red curtains led off this corridor.

Kalmian pulled the left-hand curtain open and gestured inside. "Enter. This is where you can rest for the night."

Bright sunlight shone into the room through the glazed windows. Farren blinked. *I've seldom seen glass windows that size outside the king's palace.* A large bed stood in the centre of the room, piled with white sheepskins. Dust motes danced in the sunshine, rising as fresh air flowed into the room. Farren looked at the bed, then fidgeted uncomfortably with his betrothal earring, cheeks warming. *One bed but two of us. Does he expect us to... Of course he does; he's a sorcerer not a* minyastin. He stared out of the window at the green lawn and the bright azalea bushes ringing it, feeling helpless.

"Thank you," said Azariel. "It looks very comfortable but..." Her teeth raked her lower lip at one side. "I should have said. Farren and I, we're not yet married."

Kalmian's eyebrows arched. "Why is that a problem?"

"We don't sleep together," she replied, her voice expressionless and her face a mask. "Not yet. For *minyasti,* that's forbidden."

The sorcerer nodded slowly. "I understand you. Of course. I should have remembered." He stepped back over the threshold and let the curtain fall. "There is another chamber next door, so I can offer you my hospitality in separate rooms. Many years have passed since I hosted visitors from Elend, Wayast and Helmn who came by sea, but I have the space." He glanced at Farren. "Come with me, Farren Blackarrow. We can leave the lady this room."

Farren followed Kalmian behind the right-hand curtain into an almost identical room, except that black sheepskins were piled on the bed. A single fly buzzed against the glass in one corner of the window. Farren ran his hand over the sheepskins, feeling the soft staple of wool. Dust rose and stung his nose, making it twitch, and he stifled a sneeze.

"I shall have to fetch you linens for the beds," he said. "Then we must return to making dinner. I fear I am a poor host, as I have no servants."

"You were hardly expecting us." Farren rubbed his itching nose.

Kalmian led Farren and Azariel through the house, collecting bed linen as they went and taking it to the bedrooms, before moving on to the libraries filled with old books and workrooms that smelt slightly of sulphur and acid. When they returned downstairs and headed outside, the goats pressed around them, bleating softly. The buck, his long horns curling in a spiral, sniffed at Farren's robes and tried to nibble at the corner of them while the two does pushed against Kalmian. "Easy, my friends," the sorcerer said to the goats. "Am I late to milk you today?" He petted one of the does and looked back over his shoulder. "I will have to attend to that task before dinner, I am afraid. I would not want my four-legged friends to be forgotten, or at least by me." He sighed. "My hope is that Majalis has forgotten them and not demanded their lives, even if he has not forgotten about demanding mine."

Farren stroked the buck and scratched around the knobbly base of the curling horns. Yellow eyes with strange sideways pupils gazed at him keenly. "What are their names?"

"The buck is named Ash; the does are Birch and Poplar. Yes, my friends," he said as one of the does bleated loudly. "I will attend to you immediately."

"I can bake the bread easily enough," said Azariel. "I've used that sort of oven before. I can prepare the rest of dinner as well."

Farren brushed the white goat hairs off his hands. "And I can help you milk. My Gift is animal taming." *And I can watch to make sure that he won't poison the milk. However, the more I see of*

Kalmian, the more I trust him. King of Heaven, am I being fooled or are we right to trust him?

***

Azariel stared out of the window of her bedchamber at the army of stars overhead. The hill rose dark against the sky, the stars hazy beside it. *That's the mists,* she thought. A tiny glimmer of green came from the crest of the hill, barely discernible against the black. *And that's the Stone of Earth.*

She turned from the window and felt the legs of her leather clothes that lay draped over the windowsill, still damp from washing. She rolled a section of the leather between her hands. *It'll be soft again, that's good. I wouldn't want to walk another day with them chafing me.* She loosened her red robe and let it drop to the floor before turning back the thick eiderdown blanket and crisp sheets, and climbing into bed. *God Incarnate, help us do what we have to do tomorrow.* A sweet, dry, almost biscuit-like smell rose from the white cotton surrounding her. The candleflame flickered on the nightstand beside her and she blew it out.

She closed her eyes and began drifting to sleep. A gentle rustle outside in the corridor started her alert and her hands tightened into fists. "Stormwolf?" came Farren's voice softly.

"What is it?" She sat up, clutching the sheets around her. "Don't come in – I'm not decent."

"I'm going to keep watch outside for part of the night. If Kalmian's been trying to beguile us into trusting him, then he'll strike tonight."

"Make sure you get some sleep," she replied. "We've got another labyrinth to get through tomorrow."

"I'll wake you later. Sleep well, sweetheart. May the Power protect you." His chainmail clinked and his boots scraped on the wooden floor as he sat down.

May the Power both of us, tonight and tomorrow. She lay back down and rolled onto her side, one hand under her cheek, snuggling into the sheepskins beneath the by sheet. *All the same, I doubt we have anything to fear from Kalmian. I think he really does want to be free of Majalis and of the Stone.*

CHAPTER FIFTEEN

In the pale light of morning, Azariel met Farren and Kalmian outside the white villa. She stared up at the mist-covered hill. The wind blew strongly and the sky was covered in grey. The dark mist was billowing up and joining the tumbling, swirling clouds that fled across the sky. A drop of water fell onto her bare arm. "A rainy day," she said, catching the side of her cloak and wrapping it tightly around herself. "Let's get this over with." She flexed one leg. *Time for another long walk.* "Are you coming with us, Kalmian?" she said aloud.

The old man shook his head and shuddered. "No! I will not go in there unless he calls me. And even then, I only go because I have to. But not now – not in your company and not to take the Stone from him." He turned towards the hill. "I doubt he is there now. When he is, lightning crowns the hilltop. He will not come until he comes to take me at midnight tonight." He reached inside his robes and pulled out a folded piece of paper. "I have this for you, though. This is the map for the labyrinth – my original plan. Take it. You will need it."

"Hasn't Majalis changed your maze since then?" She briefly let go of one side of her cloak, then grabbed for it as the cold wind whipped it wide.

"He has not changed the paths. He cannot do that or anything else to the terrain unless a man – or a woman – wields the energy of the Stone of Earth. So they are unchanged. But what waits inside changes."

"Thanks," said Farren, taking the folded paper from him. "That'll save us losing time."

"I only hope we can read the map if it's as dark as it looks in there." She twisted a lock of her hair between her fingers and looked back up at the hill. "Should we take torches?"

"You'll need no torch to guide you in there, in spite of the dark," Kalmian said with a small smile. "There is a strange light in there. I cannot describe it, but you will understand once you are inside. It's one of my original parts of the labyrinth, although Majalis has turned it to his nature."

Farren tucked the folded piece of paper into his belt. "Let's go, Stormwolf," he said, holding out his hand. "Let's take the Stone."

She slid her hand into his and began the long, steady climb up the hill. Her boots slipped on the wet grass and once she stumbled, drenching her hands in rainwater. The sky darkened over the hillside, dim as twilight. "I almost expect to see the stars," she panted, legs aching from the steep climb.

"I can see where we're heading for," he said. "There's the hedge and the east-facing gap."

They worked their way up and around the hill to the tall hedge bordering the maze and reached a broad gap. The hedge blossomed with fresh green leaves and yellow-white flowers, but a sharp decaying stink rose from it. Above the top of the ten-foot hedge, a few straggly branches showed in the black mist. She drew a deep breath and gagged on the scent of decay emanating from within. The path inside the gap was paved with small white stones and bordered with bricks, but darkness swallowed it after a few paces. She took a second breath, trying not to gag again, and straightened her rings before clasping Farren's hand and walking in.

Mist swirled around them, dark like smoke and thick with the stench of death. She peered through the gloom and saw withered leaves hanging on the trees and scattered on the forest floor a few paces to the side. Then more darkness. The trees were covered with a pallid blight on their bark and the soil by the side of the path grew thick with moulds and odd-shaped purple fungi. *This is visible darkness I'm seeing by, not light.* Their feet on the stones sounded muffled and faint. Water slowly oozed off the leaves, dripping softly onto the path that lay in front of them, and onto another arm of the path that branched off to the left. "You've got the map, beloved," she said, voice sounding loud in the tomb-like stillness. "You lead."

"This way, then." He kept walking straight ahead, ignoring the left branch, the opening still behind them.

Darkness closed in around them, hiding the light from the entrance as the path twisted left at the end of the straight. Something hissed in the air, a voice like a whisper. A second voice answered it, fiercely, but still whispering too indistinctly for the words to be understood, like half-voices at the edge of dreams. The two voices argued frantically in whispers as Farren and Azariel followed the map around several hairpin bends and turns, never coming close enough for the words to be made out, never far enough to be out of earshot. One of the voices broke off in a scream that sent a shudder of ice down Azariel's spine, then silence fell. She raked her front teeth over her lip and tried to still the thundering of her heart.

Farren led her around another left-hand bend. More voices sounded from the trees, laughing this time and shouting words in a strange language. She pressed closer to Farren and his right hand reached for her left. His hand felt comfortingly warm and his ring even warmer against her skin.

She ducked beneath a branch as it brushed over her head, wet and clammy. Her hair felt damp and something sticky clung to it, smeared there by the branch. A voice began singing a high, eerie tune that sounded like a dirge. It ended abruptly with wailing and keening. "Keep watch behind as well as ahead, if you can, Stormwolf," Farren said as he crinkled the paper in his hands, studying the map. "We need to go zigzag along here until we get to the long stretch of hedge over to the right."

"Where?" She peered through the gloom. Another ghost-voice muttered to one side of the path. "I can't see anything more than five feet away."

A pale greenish face leered at her out of the mist, and ice seemed to wrap around her, leaving her gooseflesh. Farren's hand tightened around hers and she heard him hissing through his teeth. She forced herself to look at the face. It contorted into a mask of agony and moaned softly. Then it vanished, howling.

She turned to him. "Your face is white," she said, hearing her voice sounding a little shaky.

"I'm not surprised about that," he said. He let out a slow, whistling breath. "Let's press on. We turn left again here. At least a face can't do much more than frighten us."

She nodded. "If faces and voices are all Majalis is going to throw at us and we've got a map so we can't lose ourselves in this nightmare of a place, then this won't be too hard. It could be worse."

They walked on, following the path through a cluster of nightshade. More faces drifted in and out of the foetid mist and darkness, all moaning and all horribly distorted in exaggerated anguish. The keening, muttering and whispering continued in the background, none of them coming from the faces that floated past. She clenched her teeth tightly as a set of agonized eyes stared at her. *I'm going to ignore them,* she thought and looked down at her feet as Farren led the way: right, left, left and sharp right. *They're not real. Unless they are memories of... no! I won't let my imagination play with them.*

They walked along a long straight stretch, then swung right again. The voices and the wailing faded away. She raised her head and looked into the darkness. The mist still swirled in thick coils across the gravel path, but the faces had disappeared. "First attack passed," she said.

They zigzagged around several more twists. Suddenly, the grey gravel vanished and the path gave way to a chasm that sank beyond the reach of the not-light within the black mists. The tree trunks clustered thick and close on either side of the pit, gnarled and wry roots clutching at the dirt on both sides. "No way around here," she said. "Are you sure this is the right way?"

"Of course I am!" He thrust the map at her indignantly, his thumbnail biting into one spot. "We're here." The finger of his other hand jabbed at a curve in the path beside his thumb. "I can read a map, Stormwolf, especially when the path's marked out for us in red ink like this."

"So how do we, how does anyone get past here?" She rested one hand on her sword hilt idly.

"Kalmian comes past here whenever that Majalis calls him, so he must be able to get through. He did say it was in the centre of the map."

"Well, unless he flies over, there must be a way." She dropped to her hands and knees at the edge of the gap, wincing as some sticky substance on the stones clung to her fingers. "I'll look down here by the edge of the drop for some way over. You look by the trees."

She began at the corner of the drop, testing and prying with her fingertips along the dirt. Here and there pieces of soil crumbled and pattered down the edge of the chasm into silence.

Behind her, she heard footsteps and rustling as he explored the trees. "Ouch," he said.

She sat back on her heels and looked around at him. "What happened?"

"The trees – they're all covered with spikes. That's not the way over." He put the side of his finger to his mouth, then his face contorted and he spat. "They've got some foul stuff all over them too."

"Then there must be some way over near here." She turned back to the gap and continued groping along the edge. Her hands struck something solid and she tilted her head to inspect what she had found. Nothing met her eyes. She reached out again and pressed down. Something hard slid against her fingers, grained and splintery like wood. She tapped it twice and a firm *thunk – thunk* cut the air. Frowning, she ran her hands along the side of the solid mass. It felt twice as thick as her wrist and about a foot wide, appearing to stretch out over the deep gap in the path. "I've found it," she said. "An invisible bridge."

He squatted beside her and rested his arm lightly around her shoulders. "Sit astride it and shuffle our way across, I suppose," he said.

"I'll go first."

She flicked her cloak well back behind her and gingerly lowered herself astride the invisible plank. It felt as hard and solid as one of the wooden benches at the Watchtower and about as wide. Fumes rose from the black pit beneath her as she eased her legs either side of the narrow bridge, stinging the back of her throat and making her gag. A hissing and rustling emanated from the depths of darkness. A cold thrill raced down the length of her spine and she jerked her legs back up, bringing them onto the wood as something clashed together not far from where her feet had been dangling. Briefly, she caught a glimpse of scales and the slitted pupil of an eye before they vanished into the blackness. She bit her lip and nibbled at it nervously. *That will teach me to be so reckless.* "We have to walk over," she said, forcing her voice level. "It can't be that hard if Kalmian does it nearly every day."

She stood up, hearing her cloak rattle over the gravel on the path behind. *Don't look down,* she told herself. *It's no harder than walking along the benches back at home.* Tentatively, she took a step forward. The invisible plank held firm, without any of the wobbling she had half been expecting. *I'll pretend I'm walking along it like I would to dust down cobwebs, looking up.* Another step, keeping her eyes closed and feeling with her left foot for the next inch of plank. Her armour tightened around her chest as her breathing quickened. *Relax. If I don't rush, I'll be fine. Relax.* Ten more paces followed, then her boots crunched onto gravel again. She let her breath out and turned around. "Made it," she called.

"Right," Farren's voice replied. "I'm coming. Keep talking to me and stay by the edge so I can keep in a straight line. You're hard to see in the dark."

"Don't walk too quickly, will you?" she said, peering into the gloom. "Don't panic; I'm not fussing. I'm just making a noise like you told me to." She paused and cleared her throat. "Shall I tell you how good-looking you are? Or is there anything else you'd like me to talk about?" She broke off as he appeared over the abyss, seeming to float as he walked on air.

He winked at her and strode forwards, keeping his eyes fixed on her. A plume of black mist curled around him, briefly obscuring him. "Thanks," he said as he stepped off. He leaned down to kiss her on the mouth. "Perhaps I should have asked you to sing something instead and saved you from babbling."

"I'll remember that for the way back," she said.

"Oh, hellfire, yes!" He straightened up and ran one hand through his hair, raking part of it up. "We've got to get out as well as in. Damn! I was glad to have left those faces behind."

"Don't talk about them." She slipped her hand into his. Every ridge and callus on his palm felt familiar and comforting. "Where's your map, beloved? Not down the bottom of that hole, I hope."

"Of course not," he chuckled, crinkling the piece of paper. "Follow the path right, then zigzag away to the left. According to this, we'll be going along the outer wall of the maze for the last time before taking the inner twists. Look." He held out the map to her and pointed. "We've nearly made a complete circuit of the hill."

"I've lost all sense of direction," she replied. "Even the slope of the hill's getting confusing."

"In this dark, I'm not surprised. Let's keep going."

They rounded bend after bend and finally left the outer wall of the maze. Silence fell heavily, unbroken except for the constant dripping of water from the leaves around them. Azariel peered into the mist as far as she could and made out a faint sheen of light emanating from behind a thick tangle of trees, piercing the unlight of the mist. "Is that the way to go?" she asked, pointing.

"Yes," he replied, unfolding then folding the map again. "Can you see that light too? I thought it was only my eyesight playing tricks on me. I'll wager that's the next thing we're going to have to face. It can't be the Stone already; we've got two more major changes of direction to go yet."

"I never thought it was." She tossed her hair back from her face. "That light's white, not green."

The light increased as they walked on through the withered forest, a blur through the mist. As they approached, she saw a figure standing in the middle of the light, unfocussed and dim. They drew closer and the vague figure became a woman standing beneath a tree covered with red apples and white blossoms that glowed. The woman wore long flowing black robes and a matching cloak that draped in folds to her feet and onto the grass beside her. Her hair was braided into many plaits that framed her paper-pale face. *Like me, yet not like me,* Azariel thought. *It's like looking into a distorted mirror.* She ran her eyes over the woman again as she and Farren walked nearer to the tree. *Maybe I am looking into something like one and this is only an illusion.* "What are you seeing?" she asked Farren quietly.

"A woman with black hair and red lips like yours but much paler and her hair's plaited into lots of little tails like a show horse," he replied.

The woman looked at them and smiled, showing a mouth of perfect white teeth. A golden lozenge-shape glittered in the centre of her forehead in the glow of the blossoms. She beckoned to them and plucked an apple from the tree above her head. *Wolf-lady, come take it,* Azariel heard a voice ring in her head. The woman held out the fruit, light gleaming off its taut ruby skin and a sweet smell rising from it. *Aren't you tired? Aren't you hungry? Don't you want something that will strengthen you forever?*

"She must think we're stupid," Azariel said, squeezing Farren's hand. "Look – she's to one side of the path, so if all she does is thrust apples at us, we should be able to get past her without any bother."

"I'm keeping my rings at the ready." His hand tightened around hers. "I wish she'd stop saying things inside my head all the time, though."

She quickened her pace and felt him lengthen his stride to match hers as they crunched over the gravel past the other woman. The pale woman's face, exquisitely beautiful, looked winsomely at her and then at Farren, still offering the apple to them. *Take it, wolf-lady. Eat and see visions of past, present and future. Know everything you could ever want to know. Don't you want to? Just a little taste can do no harm.* "Oh, shut up!" Azariel said aloud. "Even a child of six would be wary of something that beautiful and enticing in a place like this."

"Guaranteed to turn you to stone or into a toad," Farren chuckled. "I wonder if she's one of Kalmian's original spells and things that he put here."

"I'm not so sure." The golden lozenge in the woman's forehead nagged and teased at her memory. "I don't think she's an illusion."

A shriek split the air behind them and Azariel whirled around to see the woman in black hurl the apple to the ground. A shower of sparks flew up as the apple struck the forest floor and a pall of thick, foul purple smoke billowed up to join the mist. The tree, the white light and the woman all vanished. Total darkness swirled over the path, hiding even the unlight of the mist. The smoke filled her lungs and she coughed and choked, eyes streaming and head dizzy.

Slowly the smoke cleared and the unlight illuminated the path again. They linked hands and walked on in silence for a while, throats too raw to speak. Right, left, right, right, along a straight stretch and through several zigzags, the path wound its way. "Thank the Power that smoke was all we had to deal with from her," Farren said at last. "But apart from that, why didn't you think she was one of Kalmian's conjurings?"

Azariel glanced backwards over her shoulder. "That mark in the middle of her forehead – the golden diamond. It's familiar. She's the woman Kalmian saw in his scrying mirror – the one who's going to kill him and take his place."

"But how did she get up that far into the island without Kalmian knowing?"

"She flew. She's a swan-woman. That mark of hers is a shapeshifter's mark."

"It's nothing like yours." Farren stopped and caught her by the shoulder, the map rustling as it pressed against her cloak. He studied her face; the curve of her red lips, the wide black pupils of her eyes almost covering the blue-grey in the strange light, and the thin dusting of hairs bridging her heavy brows that had escaped her tweezers. His hands rubbed over hers, feeling the long ring fingers that reached level with her middle finger. "Your eyebrows and hands. I thought those were the marks of a shapeshifter." He bent his head and kissed her mouth.

"Marks of a certain type of shapeshifter. My type." She grinned wryly. "Mine are the marks of a werewolf, as much as I hate that word. That woman had the marks of the swan-people."

"They're born with that huge golden mark?" He ran his fingers over and through hers again, feeling every familiar patch of rough and smooth in them.

"Oh, she's exaggerated hers. They all do, I think. What they're born with is just a small diamond-shaped mole. But that's how she got here and that's who's coming for poor Kalmian tonight."

"And that's who's also tramping around this labyrinth with us. We'd better keep our eyes open for her."

He unfolded the map and led her along the twisting gravel paths until the map showed a steep bend ahead that rose to another level of the hill, closer to the heart of the labyrinth. Hunger began to gnaw at his stomach and thirst rasped at the back of his throat. *I hope there's somewhere to sit down when we get to the end of the maze. At least we're over two-thirds of the way there now and all this twisting and turning means we get up the slopes easily.* He glanced down at the map for what seemed like the thousandth time, then folded it up again. *First left, second left, then straight past three right-hand turns* he told himself. *I should be able to remember that.*

A thicker patch of gravel crunched loudly under Farren's feet as they rounded the next bend. To the left, he heard something rustle, and he turned his head to peer through the unlight. *Was that the swan-woman?* He tightened his grip on Azariel's hand. A rhythmic padding sound came from somewhere behind them, then stopped. "Did you hear that?" he asked softly. "That sounded like footsteps."

"Yes," she breathed in reply. "We may see that sorceress again. I think she's following us."

He bent his head over the paper once more after passing the third right-hand turn, and they walked on through the mist and unlight. He heard their footsteps on the gravel path, but nothing else except for the continual drip, drip, drip of water falling from the trees. *It's beginning to remind me of the water in those caves Crajaval kept me in behind Moonlady Falls.* He shook his head clear from the memories that crawled and swarmed through his mind, leaving his breath shallow for a few heartbeats. Ahead of them, the path forked into three, all bending sharply to the right. "Which one?" asked Azariel?

"The middle one," he replied, quickly checking the paper in his hand. He took a few more paces forwards onto a slab of green stone where the trail split. A wall of orange-yellow flame sprang up across the middle path, flickering and licking at the mildewed undersides of the leaves overhead. He stopped, breath rapid and heartbeat pounding in his ears. "How are we going to get past that?" The flames crackled in answer. "I suppose we could try climbing over or around it."

"Not around – we don't want to lose the path." Azariel's hand glided along his arm. "Are the trees sound enough to climb over the fire? They don't look spiky like those ones by the invisible bridge."

He tucked the map into his belt pouch and inspected the tree near the wall of flame. The limbs grew stout and thick, jutting out of a bulge at the top of the trunk an arm's length above his head as if the tree had been polled, besides a few lower ones. He put one hand on the grimy bark and felt the lower branches. *Sound or rotten?* He wiped his palm free of the clingy, tacky mould and looked at the branches again. "They seem sound enough and we can use the lower ones as a ladder to the higher. Shall we try?" He placed both hands on the trunk and braced himself ready to start the climb. The hand he had first touched the tree with began to itch and prickle. He jerked it off the bark and rubbed it against his armour. The itching worsened and he looked at his hand in the dim unlight. "I don't think we'll be able to climb the trees," he said as he studied the reddened skin. "They're covered with irritant poison of some kind. Oh, hellfire, my other hand now!" He blew on them to try to cool the fierce burning and grimaced, stepping backwards.

"Watch out!" shouted Azariel. He checked himself and glanced behind him. The tongues of fire were dancing behind his shoulder. He snatched his cloak out of the reach of the flames. *That's odd,* he thought. *I never noticed the heat of the fire coming too close.* He turned to face the flames. The firelight burned brightly against the darkness, but no heat came from it. Cautiously, he stretched out an arm and held it near the flame for a heartbeat. The air quivered and he felt the hairs on his arms lifting with the currents. Then he plunged his hand into the fire. "What are you doing?" she demanded. "Are you mad?"

"It's not hot," he said. "It doesn't hurt at all. It's just there to frighten us." He stepped into the middle of the flames and watched them leap and play around him. *Like a fountain of light,* he thought, running his fingers through the tongues of fire, playing with them. He cupped his hands around one flame and watched the way the light danced and shimmered, picking out the calluses and tiny lines on his palm. He tossed the flame above his head and watched it fly upwards. "Come in," he laughed. "It's fun! Join me in the fire and enjoy it. It's the most pleasant light I've seen in this cursed place."

She slipped her hand into his and broke through the wall of fire to join him. Flames danced around her head in a halo and tendrils of light curled and wafted across her face. She raised her hand and brushed them aside. Several caught on her fingers and trailed behind them. Gracefully, she drew circles in the air with her hands in a dancer's moves, fire playing around them. "They're dancing with me," she said.

"Then dance with them," he replied. A memory of Azariel dancing Zenifi-style played in his memory. *That was the first night I kissed her.*

"Beat a rhythm for me." She clapped her hands lightly in a rolling rhythm. As he caught the timing, she tossed her hair back and raised her arms to dance, her hips rolling. Fire played along her arms and glinted off the links of her chainmail as she swayed and undulated, humming a dance tune. Her hands traced complex patterns in the air, the flames mirroring her moves. Finally, she swirled her hair in a full circle and threw her hands up triumphantly, scattering fire in a fountain around her.

"Beautiful." He smiled and circled his arms around her. Flames danced in front of his eyes as he leaned down and kissed her on the mouth. Smiling, he ran the side of his thumb gently along her lips as she drew back, fire playing around his hand and her lips. "I'd like to stay here and watch you for longer," he said. "Pity we've got to move on."

Her arm through his, they passed through the wall of heatless, crackling flames. His feet crunched on the gravel and the fire vanished, leaving only the unlight of the black mist. He waited as his eyes adjusted to the sudden darkness, then took the map out again.

They followed the map round many more corners and twists, doubling back as they rose up the slope of the hill. "We're nearly at the centre now," he said. "Only one more turn – to the right up here – and we'll have the Stone of Earth at last." He folded the map and tucked it into his belt again.

"I hope Kalmian's right about Majalis and company not being there."

"We'll soon find out," he replied. "Here's the turning."

They rounded the corner and he winced and blinked as bright light struck his eyes through the darkness. He raised his right hand to massage his eyelids with his fingertips before looking ahead. In the middle of the central circle stood a small pillar which held a globe of green light that drew the eyes irresistibly towards it. Mist swirled and billowed around the Stone. *Like the dream,* he thought. He stepped towards it but stopped as a low growl came from beside the pillar.

He looked down. Three pairs of red eyes met his gaze, blue fire flickering beneath them. A smell of burning wax wafted out. Instantly, his stomach doubled up in knots and the back of his neck prickled as if his hair was rising. Three large hellhounds, each shaped like wolfhounds the size of a pony, looked at him with open mouths, dripping flames from their red and white muzzles. He jerked back and gripped Azariel's arm. *Not them!* He shuddered as he looked at their teeth, imagining and remembering Crajaval's hellhounds closing around him, worrying him remorselessly all over his body. *King of Heaven, once was enough! Not again, not three of the large ones!*

"Courage, Farren," Azariel whispered in his ear as he stepped back towards him. She laid her hand on his arm. "This isn't like last time. You're at full strength now, not a beaten, weakened captive. Kill them!"

She felt his trembling calm down as she ran her hand up and down his arm. She pressed closer to him and stood on tiptoe to reach over his shoulder and press a kiss onto his cheek. He turned his head to her and kissed her on the mouth. Reluctantly, she drew her head away, spine prickling with awareness of the hellhounds beneath the pillar. He caught her eye and smiled as she heard the rasp of his sword from the sheath. She released him and drew out her own weapon, pressing her left side against his right.

The growls from the hellhounds grew louder as Farren and Azariel approached them. She stared into the eyes of the hound nearest her and its gaze narrowed as the lips writhed back from its fangs. Its long teeth glistened in the pale blue flame around its muzzle. *Its first move will be to leap and catch hold with forepaws and teeth, if I know anything of how a dog – or wolf – fights,* she thought. She braced herself, sword pointed forwards and ready.

It sprang at her, jaws wide. She staggered backwards as the impact of the leap took her full in the chest. Its weight pressed down onto the sword and she felt the blade slide home. the hellhound backed away, snarling and howling as blood welled from its belly. Then it reared again and lunged down at her in an avalanche of hair, flame, teeth and blood. From somewhere beside her came snarls and the scuffling sounds of Farren battling the other hounds. *Power protect him, facing two! I'm having enough trouble with one.* She tried to bring her sword up as the hellhound crashed down at her and felt it strike it in the chest again. Then the hilt of her sword was wrested out of her hand by the force of the beast. Jaws closed bruisingly onto her right shoulder, teeth crunching and clicking on the chainmail as the bite slid down. She drew her dagger then stifled a scream of pain as the beast's front teeth caught the skin on the back of her bare forearm and it shook its head, tearing her flesh open. Eyes streaming with pain, she drove the dagger into the part of the blur where its neck seemed to be. She stabbed again and again until the jaws slackened and the blue fire faded. It slumped down, twitching, releasing her as it died. Panting hard, she looked down at her mauled arm.

Another bubbling growl sounded beside her. She looked away from the bloody mess on her arm and spun around as the third hellhound launched itself at her, jaws flaming. Blood was spurting from a gash along its ribs, staining the white fur an odd black colour in the green light. She ducked and crawled beneath its leap and reached for her sword. The hilt met her hand and she snatched it up and stabbed upwards in one quick motion. The point caught the hellhound down the inside of the thigh, tearing a long gash down the length of the leg. Her arm ached and throbbed as she picked herself up from the gravelly ground. The beast whirled to face her and leaped again.

She lunged at it with her sword and heard the blade whistle through the empty air. *Missed!* She thrust the hilt of the sword into the hellhound's mouth as its jaws snapped down at her. Grabbing the thick hair and soft skin of its gullet, she held the hellhound away from her, ignoring the hard paws that beat and scrabbled at her. The quillons forced its mouth wide and hot breath mixed with the flame that dripped from it. It opened its jaws again and the sword fell clanging onto the stones below. The beast struggled to break loose, nearly jerking her from her feet, and it growled as it strained to reach her throat.

Her right arm shook with pain and the effort of holding the hellhound. She punched it with her left hand and her lapis lazuli ring scorched her fingers. Blue light blazed off the beast's white fur and the hellhound reeled backwards, burning and howling. She let it go and it crashed onto the stones.

She stood back from the dead hellhound, panting and heart thumping hard. Her arm felt wet, sticky and so painful no longer seemed part of her body. Slowly, the fire and heat from her rings died away. She dropped to her knees and picked up her sword, then cleaned and sheathed it, fingers feeling like lead. Her head slumped down as pain and exhaustion whirled inside it. Then gentle arms wrapped around her shoulders Farren's voice murmured in her ears. "Oh, Stormwolf, sweetheart, they hurt you." His hands glided down her arms and she flinched as his fingers passed over her torn skin, sending fresh waves of pain up.

She glanced down at her mauled arm, inspecting it in the green light of the Stone of Earth. "That cut will need stitching," she said, looking at one large flap of skin that was half torn off, exposing a deep gash.

His hands left her and he opened the pouch at his belt. "I think I've got enough thread left over after all that sewing you did while we were crossing the mountains. I hope it's clean enough."

"It'll do," she replied, clenching her teeth as she watched him threading a dark strand through the needle's eye. *This is going to hurt.* "Can you see clearly enough?"

"Turn round a little so the light falls on your arm more."

She shifted and brought her arm round so the green light fell fully on it. Gritting her teeth against the pain, she watched as he began to sew the torn flesh of her arm together neatly. "You're better with a needle and thread than I am," he said. "Perhaps you'd better do this."

"My right arm's hardly an embroidery screen. You're doing well enough." She laughed, then broke off with a whining gasp as the needle dug agonizingly into her again. "It almost hurts as badly as the original wounding."

Finally, to her relief, he bent his head and bit through the thread. A moan of relief escaped her mouth. "There," he said as he straightened up and coiled the end of the cotton around the needle. "How's that?"

She flexed her arm a few times and looked at the neat black line of stitching. "It hurts but I'll heal. I hope Kalmian has some ointments that we can put on it. Let's take the Stone and get out of here."

He pulled her up to her feet and walked with her to the pillar. "You take it this time," he said.

She reached out towards it. *Like the dream,* she thought as her hand formed a silhouette against the green light. The black mist swirled around the shining globe, slightly dimming the glow as it twisted into five tendrils like the clawed fingers of a dark hand. A ripple of cold went down her spine, then vanished as her fingertips brushed the silver network surrounding the Stone. She cupped her hands around it and felt the smooth, warm surface of the emerald-like jewel under the silver. It prickled and gave off tiny sparks and a thrill pulsed in her veins in answer. The hand of mist vanished.

"In the name of God Incarnate," she whispered. Ceremonially, she lifted the Stone high above her head and let the light glitter off her armour, Farren's sword and both their rings. Farren raised his sword in salute.

She lowered the Stone and carefully tucked it into her hood to let it nestle between her shoulderblades. "I don't care if it's raining; it's not going to fit into my belt-pouch with all the other stuff I've got in there." She winced as a movement made the pain of her wounded arm flare again. "I should have cleared it out before we set out. Let's go back." She slipped her hand into his and his fingers tightened around her as they walked out of the clearing.

They threaded their way back through the maze, past the wall of flame and on through the gloom. She listened carefully for the sound of footsteps or swan's wings, but heard nothing except the constant dripping of water from the leaves to the mould beneath. *We've passed the pit with the invisible bridge, so we must be nearly out by now. Only the faces left to pass.* She craned her neck to read the crumpled piece of paper in Farren's hand as he guided them around two, then four more corners. Ahead, clean grey outdoor light shone through the mist. "That's the gateway," she said, lengthening her pace. "You can put the map away; we don't need it now."

As they passed the second-last fork in the path, fire blazed in the middle of the white stones marking the track. It stretched in a bright ball outwards, flooding the dark trunks and mildewed leaves overhead with glare. In the centre of the fire stood the swan-sorceress, one hand on her hip and the other pointing a blood-red fingernail towards them. "You won't go any further, werewolf!" she spat. "This island will be mine, and only mine!"

"I don't want the island, sorceress," snarled Azariel. "In the name of the Power, let us pass."

The woman hissed and threw up her hands. Farren swiftly raised his armbands in front of him, ready to block lightning. The sorceress's robes and cloak swirled around her. As he watched, she transformed into a giant swan, its head as high as his own. It opened its beak and screamed at them, smoke and flame billowing up from its throat. A strong smell of over-ripe fruit wafted from its wings, heavy and nauseating. The witch-light faded to gloom once more.

In reflex, he reached for his sword and began to draw it. *Blackarrow, you fool, that's not the way to fight it!* he thought as he plunged the weapon back into its sheath. He leaped to his left as the blast of fire burned towards him through the darkness. He clenched his fists and aimed his rings outwards to strike. The stones glowed with pent-up energy: bright gleams of green and blue-black in the darkness. From the corner of his eye, he saw Azariel leap towards the swan then stop, standing between him and it.

Fire flared from the swan and Azariel's silhouetted stood sharp and black against the yellow blaze, her hair and cloak flying around her like stormclouds in the wind. She raised her left arm forwards in defence and the emeralds in her armband shone like green suns as they soaked up the energy. She struck at the swan, palms towards it. Lightning flew from her hands, silver and blue. The bird screamed at her as he strode to her side. His rings burned as he aimed at the swan and grey fire streamed out of them.

The swan flailed and threshed its wings before itself, striking down the flame. It stepped backwards and changed shape again, returning to a woman. She reached to her side and drew a dagger that blazed with fire. *Stormwolf, be careful!* The sorceress lunged at Azariel, stabbing at her arms and torso. He darted from side to side, seeking a place to leap in and blast the sorceress with lightning. Azariel's sword flashed from the sheath and met the fireblade of the other woman with a clash. Sparks flew into the air as the two blades hammered each other again and again.

He drew his own sword and slashed at the robed woman from the side. Her dagger clashed against his blade and the metal in his hand flared hot. His hold loosened on it in reflex, then he gritted his teeth and gripped it again, trying to ignore the scorching hilt in his palm. He slashed forwards and felt the tip of his sword catch the woman's arm. She screamed furiously and whirled away from Azariel towards him. He lifted his sword and blocked the blow of her dagger, but the woman's other hand struck towards him, long blood-red nails raking at his cheek. *Too close to strike with my sword,* he thought as he raised his right hand to wrest her fingers away from his face. Eyes clenched shut, he thrust her hand back. A savage blow bruised his ribs, hot and heavy. He staggered back, releasing her and opening his eyes. Blood dripped from her nails, both his and from the wound on her arm.

He ducked as she tried to scratch his face again. His hand darted to the dagger from behind the quiver on his left hip and struck up, gashing her arm once more. She swiftly stabbed at him and he parried across his body to meet her blow but could not catch her with the return stroke.

The sorceress lurched forwards with a choking cry. Behind her stood Azariel, eyes narrowed and smouldering, red lips writhed back to bare her teeth. The woman fell to the ground face first as Azariel tugged her blade from the woman's back. The metal was dark with blood. Her eyes met his, flashing with victory. She tossed her head, flicking her hair back from her face. Then her savage smile faded and her expression softened. "Are you all right?" she asked, placing her left hand lightly on his shoulder.

He sheathed both sword and dagger and raised one hand to touch his cheek. Stickiness met his fingers and pain spread out from them across his face. "I'll live," he responded, grimacing. "Thank you, though."

She glanced down at the fallen woman. "A shapeshifter," she said softly. "Dark hair, pale skin." A long breath hissed out of her as she stared down at her bloodstained hands. "If it wasn't for God Incarnate, that would be me lying there."

"If it wasn't for his help, we would have both been dead long ago. And we were fighting her two to one, so it was easy enough."

"That wasn't quite what I meant. I could have been her if I had spent more time with my uncles and been hauled off to Wayast the moment my Gift started showing. I'm glad I didn't."

"So am I." He wrapped his arm around her shoulder and pressed a kiss onto her cheek.

She bent to wipe her sword on the skirts of the dead woman before she sheathed it. "How badly torn is your face?"

"It could be worse. It's going to be painful shaving for the next few days, though." He laughed and reached for the paper tucked into his belt. "Now, let's leave this place."

They walked out of the labyrinth onto the wet hillside, his arm around her shoulders as they tramped back towards Kalmian's villa with the clean rain beating onto them, driven by the free wind.

CHAPTER SIXTEEN

Kalmian pushed back his chair after their evening meal in the dining hall of the villa. Rain and wind lashed the glass panes of the windows at one end of the hall and a large fire was burning on the hearth. "Well," the old man said, "the night is young but will not last forever. I hope you are ready. Majalis will come at midnight. How you plan to meet him? And what shall I do?"

Farren turned to look at Azariel and caught her eye. He nodded to her and took another sip of his beaker of wine. *Better that you tell him, arch* minyaster, he thought.

She cocked an eyebrow at him, then turned to Kalmian. "We can't fight Majalis as things are. It's useless as long as he has a lawful claim on you. We can't stop him taking what is his by right. We can try, but if he has a leash on your soul, he can still draw you. Trying to stop him would be like trying to dam a river in flood."

Kalmian rose to his feet, his chair squeaking on the stone floor. "So I am indeed caught in a trap of my own making." He began to pace around the room. "Is there no way? Can you, can I make him release his claim on me? I'll make any bargain to get free of him if that's what it takes."

"The only way to free yourself from him is to let someone else take your place," said Farren, fidgeting with his earring. "That will satisfy the Lord of the Dead: a life for a life."

Kalmian stopped pacing beside the table. "I have heard that before from the priestesses – the sorceresses, you would call them. A life for a life." He rested one hand on the table and gazed at the large rectangular window opposite him. "But Majalis will not take one of my goats this time. It's human blood he wants. One of you would have to go instead of me. I will not ask that of you. This is my problem."

Farren took another sip from his wineglass and leaned forwards with one elbow on the table. The cushion beneath him slid backwards and fell onto the floor with a soft puff and the hard edge of the seat dug into the back of his legs. "Not one of us, or even both of us, needs to take your place," he said slowly. "I doubt he'd take us. He's got no claim on our souls." He set his empty glass down. *I won't refill that just yet. It's good wine but this is not a night to get light-headed.* Another gust of wind drove rain against the glass window. *It's a cold wet night tonight,* he thought. *I'm glad we got out of the labyrinth when we did.*

"What do you mean? First you say Majalis will accept a life for a life, and then you say that he won't take one of you. Who's left? He won't accept the goats, I tell you. I've already tried to buy him off like that."

Azariel and smiled. She stood up and raised her gobbled where the light made it gleam. "How about the life of God Incarnate? Why not let him take your place?"

"What? How?" The furrows on Kalmian's face deepened. "That God of yours walked the earth years ago – how can he take my place now?"

"Sit down," Farren said. He reached across the table and cut himself a slice of bread. "We've got time enough to answer questions, if we can." He slathered the bread with butter and pickles, and nibbled at it.

The rain continued to beat at the windows as they talked on. One of the tallow candles alight on the table burned down to the holder and guttered out into a curl of oily smoke.

At last, Kalmian rose to his feet again. "Very well then. I accept the bargain and I'll be a sorcerer no more." He twisted the ring off his finger and tossed into the fire. The gold circle landed on the hot coals and blackened with smoke before beginning to melt. Then he stooped and added a few more pine logs onto the fire. They crackled and burst into a bright blaze. "I can think of more fuel for this fire. "I wrote books describing how I bargained with Majalis. I would rather not have those around for others to find and fall into the same trap I did. I'll burn them gladly." He gazed down at the fire, then turned and strode out of the hall into the dark corridor, robes rustling as he went.

Farren strolled over to the hearth. The gold had vanished and only the ruby lay on the embers, cracked and splintered by the heat. "We've got a new member of the guild now, arch *minyaster*," he said, twitching his cloak out of the way of the fire and leaning on the mantlepiece. *I'm glad I'm not wearing those robes of Kalmian's tonight. Cloaks are hard enough to keep clear of an open fire.* "If he'll come, shall we take him back home with us?"

She came to stand beside him. An unfamiliar scent clung to her hair, the sharp tang of thyme and lavender. "If he wants to. I'll ask him." She squeezed his hand and her sword brushed lightly against his. "He'll make a fine *minyastin*. Janna will enjoy the company of someone else his age – the oldest acolyte he's ever trained. Not that Kalmian will need much in the way of training."

"What's going to happen now?" he asked after a short silence. "Will Majalis come for him now?"

"Probably." She twisted a lock of hair between her fingers. "He won't know what's happened until Kalmian confronts him. He'll come. Those Wayasti gods won't let go of one of theirs without a fight if they're anything like Crajaval. She fought to keep you and she had no right to you at all."

"Do you have to keep reminding me of that?" He bent his head so that his cheek touched hers lightly. Her head turned and her lips pressed into his ravaged skin, sending out a wave of pain. "Careful; that still hurts."

"Sorry, on both counts. But as I was saying, we'll have a battle on our hands tonight. It'll be a nasty surprise for Majalis to find that Kalmian's left them for the King of Heaven, and another to find that we've got the Stone of Earth back. We'd better be ready."

"Where is the Stone?"

She patted her shoulder and tugged at the shield-shaped clasp of her cloak. "Still in the hood of my cloak."

A footstep and the bump of something heavy falling sounded outside the room. Kalmian's voice came from the corridor, growling in wordless irritation. He rounded the door with a small tower of thick leather-bound books. The old man peered around the pile. "Here they are," he said, letting the tomes thud and clatter onto the hearthstone. He clapped the dust off his hands. "There are other books in my library," he said slowly. "But I doubt I will need to burn them also; they will harm no-one."

"What's in them?" she asked.

"My studies of the natures of things – the properties of minerals of the earth and strange liquids. Should I burn them as well?" He drummed his fingers on the mantlepiece and stared down at the pile of books. "It has been my study for years. I would not see it wasted and it is knowledge anyone could find, if they had time enough."

"Anyone?" Farren ran one hand through his hair. "You mean someone who wasn't a sorcerer could work with it – that there are no spirit powers involved."

"None at all."

"I don't think you need to burn them, then." Azariel let Farren go and knelt beside the fallen books. "Will these burn easily?" she said to him.

Farren stooped, resting his hands on her shoulder, and looked down at them. "Parchment, paper and vellum. It will, but we'd better tear them up into pieces first." He dropped to his knees beside her and opened a volume. Red, black, blue and gold decorated the page in fine illustrations and capitals around curling writing in green ink. "That's beautiful writing," he said, hesitating with one corner between his finger and thumb. "Whose hand is that? I've never seen an alphabet like that one before."

"Mine," replied Kalmian. "I developed several alphabets for my studies; that one is my finest."

"It's a pity we have to destroy something so well-drawn." He tore the page out of the book, the threads binding the paper into place popping as the page pulled free. "Can you remember it? I'd like to learn that one – and any others you've made."

Kalmian smiled. "It's the script I like to use best. Are you a calligrapher too?"

Farren crumpled the sheet of parchment into a tight ball. "You'd better throw the first one in. They're your books, so you'd better start."

He handed the other man the ball of paper and watched as he flung it into the fire. The flames licked around the paper, blackening the edges and finally swallowing the ball into itself before spitting a shrivelled ruin through the grate into the ashes below. "We'll help you burn the rest," he said as he tore a second sheet from the book.

The fire was blazing greedily after two books had been fed in and it easily engulfed large portions of the books at once. Leaves of black ash danced in the currents of hot air above the blaze and raced up the chimney. Farren wrenched another section free and cast it into the fire. The flames roared, almost drowning the beating of the rain on the roof. A heavy, dull roar of thunder shook the windowpane. A shiver travelled down Farren's spine as if in answer and a cold weight of dread churned in his stomach. His eyes were drawn towards the window. Outside, the flanks of the hill were luridly lit by a circle of blue forked lightning bolts that hung in the clouds above the peak. More thunder snarled.

"He's here," Azariel said slowly. The firelight played on her skin as colour drained slightly from her cheeks and her lips slid back from her teeth. "Can you feel him too. We had better leave the fire and get ready."

"I can throw the books on to burn," said Kalmian. "You do what you need to."

Farren brushed a thin line of ash off his trousers and walked with her to the window, the air feeling chilly on his hands and face after the fierce heat of the fire. He leaned on the windowsill and looked out at the knives of cobalt lightning stabbing through the darkness around the hill. Rain streaked the glass and his breath misted it, blurring the blue light to a hazy smudge. *King of Heaven, help us fight,* he prayed softly, heart thudding quickly in his ears. Slowly, his rings began to heat, and energy pulsed in his veins.

A high, shrill shriek sounded from the hill, barely audible above the battering of the rain. "He's found the Stone gone and the hellhounds dead," she said behind him. He turned towards her and her eyes flashed. "Are you ready?"

His pulse surged and his palms began to prickle. "Yes."

In a sudden lull in the rain, music drifted down from the hill, eerie strains that sent a fresh shiver down his spine. "What was that?" he asked Kalmian.

"Majalis," the other man replied. "He has decided to come like that this time. I should have known." He shook his head sadly. "Well, at least he won't be able to take my soul. All he can do is kill me."

"What do you mean?" Farren yawned. "We're here to fight – we won't let him kill you if we can help it."

"You are growing sleepy," the other man said. "That is the way of his music. It causes everyone who hears it to fall deeply asleep – except me. I have seen a mouse fall asleep on the table with a crumb in its mouth when his music plays."

"We won't be sleeping," said Azariel, stretching. "We'll find some way to fight him."

"How?" A wave of heaviness crept into Farren's head as another strain of the slow, high melody played. "How do you fight music?"

She stood up and paced around the room, the lines of her shoulders tense, then stopped beside a shelf containing various silver ornaments: a harp, figurines of hunting hounds and a large ornamented bowl. "Fight fire with fire and steel with steel... and fight music with music, I suppose." She pointed towards the harp. "Is that tuned?"

Kalmian nodded. Farren leaned against the windowsill as she took the harp and sat down with it beside the fire. She ran her fingers over the strings once or twice, gently vibrating the long strands of metal, her eyes meeting his. He smiled at her and tried to shake the sleep out of his mind. Then she bent her head, hair covering her face in a dark waterfall as she began to play.

Her long white fingers picked out a few notes, the same tone repeated twice, then dropping and slowly working up in a chord. Farren pressed his head against the cool glass of the window and felt the heavy fog clear from him. The notes tumbled in arpeggios, shimmering sparks of sound. He smiled as he recognized the melody and began to tap the rhythm gently with his fingertips on the hilt of his sword.

She added her voice to the music, breathily singing a few wordless notes before releasing the words to the air. Her voice rose and fell, changing in timbre from warm, breathy and husky to high and clear. The firelight sparkled off the strings, bathing her hair and hands in light, glittering off the silver and gold candlesticks, and casting shadows across the hall. Kalmian's head began to nod and he let the book he held drop from his hands to the floor. Soon the old man lay curled like a cat on a thick sheepskin beside the fire, breathing deeply.

Azariel sang and played on, ignoring the soft, slow strains of the eerie music outside. She poured herself into the song, letting the fire that blazed in her veins out into her playing, letting each note burn against the music outside. The embers and flames in front of her blurred before her as she concentrated. A deep longing welled up inside herself, sharp and sweet enough to send the salt prickling in her eyes. The soft pads of her fingers ached from the hard strings, but she ignored the pain, playing on, singing strong and proud. She hit a wrong note and winced. *It's a pity I can't play more often. May the Power help me play strong enough to overcome that music outside.*

A flash and quiver of purplish-white lightning cracked overhead, closely followed by a deafening roar of thunder that nearly drowned out both musics. The wind shrieked outside and the eerie music rang shrill and clears in long, slow notes, more like a violin than a harp. She played louder, striking the strings like a weapon and almost feeling the fire burst from her fingers as the rippling melody of the harp cut through the other sounds. The two tunes warred with each other for several bars and she could hardly catch the sound of her own playing. Then she began to sing again, voice riding high and triumphant over the chaos.

Almost in answer to her song, the ground shook and every candlestick juddered and rocked, setting the shadows dancing wildly. Her rings flared with sudden heat and the prickling energy in her hands and arms doubled and redoubled so that her outstretched fingers quivered unsteadily. The fire sparked, sending one or two points of light onto the white marble at her feet and narrowly missing Kalmian. For a moment, the air carried the smell of smoke. She ended the song, closing the cadences with strong ringing notes, then set the harp down.

All the lamps in the hall went out, leaving the golden-yellow of the fire flashing off the harp and making it look as if it had been made of flame. Her rings glowed faintly, dark blue on her left and multicoloured on the right. She glanced to the window; Farren's rings gleamed green and greyish. She clenched her fists and crossed the room to stand beside him, blood coursing hot in her veins.

A blue fire flared in a circle in the middle of the hall on the floor between two tables. The wailing music and the thunder ceased abruptly, leaving only the drumming of the rain and the sound of her breath and blood. She ran her tongue around the inside of her lips and bared her teeth as she fixed her eyes on the blue circle. "Kalmian!" a cold bloodless voice commanded from the centre of the ring. "Kalmian, it is time."

The old man stirred in his sleep a little. In then centre of the ring, a nebulous shape began to form. "Kalmian!" the voice called again, louder this time, but still cold. A pair of pure white eyes without an iris appeared in the head of the shape as the cobalt flames crackled and leaped around the figure. She stood still as she watched it, pulse pumping loudly and rhythmically in her ears, mouth dry and all her body tense as a hound straining at the leash.

A roll of thunder crashed overhead. "Kalmian!" the voice screamed, and the nebulous figure took the form of a towering man shrouded head to foot in bone-white robes. Fire leaped from the circle and formed a blue flickering crown on his head beneath his hood, gleaming off his paper-white skin. A bitter camphor-like smell rose. The pale man turned his completely colourless eyes down to the figure sleeping by the fire, then his face twisted in fury.

Azariel swept her air and cloak back behind her shoulders and stepped forward, spine straight and stiff as a spearshaft. "Why do you call him, Pale Man, Lord of the Dead? What do you have to do with him?"

He spun around and faced her. One of his hands thrust suddenly towards her and white light seared through the darkness towards her. She dodged to the side and raised her right arm so that the diamonds and emeralds in her armband of protection blocked the bolt. The metal heated as the light struck, and the emeralds flared as they absorbed the energy. Farren's arm pressed on her back and waist from behind, steadying her gently.

"He is mine," the white man's thin voice hissed. "I gave him what he wanted; now he must pay the price. Who dares to take from me what is mine?"

"The One who bought him back," she answered, holding her voice steady. "Do you dare to challenge His emissaries?"

Majalis flung back his head and shrieked. She raised her hands from the guard and blocked her ears against the shrill cry. The circle of flame died away, leaving only the flickering crown on the man's head and the bitter smell. He fixed her with his glowing white eyes. "So that is how it stands," he hissed. "But I can take him anyway. I want him. You cannot stop me doing as I please. I am Majalis, the Scorpion, the Lord of the Dead. All people belong to me!"

"I don't." Farren strode beside her, hands balled into fists in front of his chest. "You can't take me; your Moon Lady Crajaval couldn't hold me. I belong to the Power."

"Then your Power had better help you now!"

Red lightning crackled from the hands of Majalis towards them. She leaped out of its path and answered with a bolt of magenta. "Perish, demon!" she shouted, the words feeling awkward and inadequate as they left her mouth. A muscle had cramped in her left arm and she pushed through the pain to throw her fire. On the other side of the hall, she saw a stream of black fire coursing towards Majalis. Her fire and Farren's wreathed and writhed around the white figure, and Majalis's pale face contorted.

"Vahrr shadarrasa dea!" Farren's voice thundered. Green fire leaped from his hands, adding to the blaze.

Majalis brushed the flames away and thrust his hand towards her, throwing steel-blue and gold flame at her face. She crossed her wrists and ducked behind them. The heavy silver bands flared, scattering the light the jewels could not absorb across the white marble ceiling. She let fire fly through and from her in answer, almost shaking with the rush and intensity of the energy within her. The white marble of the walls and roof flickered with multiple colours. She gritted her teeth, then rolled to one side out of the path of another bolt of lightning from Majalis. *God Incarnate, help us know how we can defeat this evil spirit, because he's strong.*

She threw purple fire at Majalis and it met an answering bolt of turquoise from Majalis in midstream. The two fires swirled into a fireball that spat rainbow shades that lit up the entire room almost as brightly as daylight. Dazzled, she darted behind a chair to one side, blinking and waiting for her vision to clear. Majalis spun as yellow fire from Farren took him full in the back. The pale man's blue crown of lightning flickered then vanished as he shrieked, the sound setting her teeth on edge.

She leaped to her feet, fresh energy coursing through her. Clenching her fists, she let a fierce stream of green and scarlet surge from her opal ring, followed by silver from her lapis lazuli. Her head whirled dizzily. *Much more going through me and I'll pass out. I had better be careful.* A black lightning bolt coursed towards her and she caught it on her left armband, biting back a cry as the metal scorched her.

Red and white fire flew from Farren's hand and swirled around Majalis, who beat it down to one side. *He's able to counter everything we throw at him. We're not doing much more than hurt him.* She drew a deep breath, keeping her hands steady, holding back the excess of power waiting to burn through her. Already her head was spinning and her arms felt weak and reluctant. She caught another bolt on her armbands and she staggered backwards with the impact. *That could have killed me and we can hardly touch him.* Desperately, she forced herself to stand straight and throw another lightning bolt at Majalis. It caught him on the arm and briefly set his robes alight but soon faded. *I'm going to have to give everything.*

She dropped her inner barriers. *Master, use me, even if it kills me, and let the others live.* Raising her fists with her rings pointing at Majalis, she let the storm of flame burn through and out of her. "In the name of God Incarnate and the Power, die!" she yelled, finishing with her wolf-howl battle cry. Wildfire crackled out of the stones in her rings in brilliant streams of green, violet and silver, tinged here and there with peacock blue. She swayed, thunder roaring in her ears, vision blurring to smears and white points of light. The energy crackling, pulsing and pounding through her kept her on her feet. Dimly, she felt Farren's arm around her waist again and saw black fire leaping from his other hand. The two fires caught Majalis squarely in the chest and face. Then darkness swamped her as the fire died, swirling through her head. Her legs buckled beneath her and she fell, senses overwhelmed.

Twin fires twined about Majalis. The tall figure stretched up into the air, elongating like something made of smoke and sparks blazing around him. "NO!" he screamed. "You may have banished me to the underworld, but you'll follow me! I'll take all three of you with me. May the Island of Labyrinths fall into the sea!" The figure twisted and writhed, then vanished in a plume of blue flame.

The earth juddered, shaking knives and plates off the table. A rumble deeper than thunder growled and roared, seeming to go on forever. Farren staggered, trying to keep his feet, then fell. A bowl of apples overturned on and several rolled over the edge of the table, hitting him. He raised his hands to cover his head. *If the roof falls in, we're finished. Master, not that!*

The tremor stopped. Farren picked himself up from the floor. His heart still hammered in his chest but his eyes had adjusted to the dull red light of the fire, which had burned low. "Stormwolf?" No answer came except the gentle crackle of the fire and the rain on the window. A candle fallen from one of the holders lay in a pool of wax near him, and he picked it up to light at the fire. The earthquake had scattered the embers into a flat bed and he blew on them to encourage a large enough flame to catch the candle's wick.

Once he had set the candle upright, he looked down at Azariel. She lay on her side, eyes closed and one arm extended. A green light shone from her hood. His stomach lurched as he saw red staining her face and arms until he smelt wine and noticed a matching stain on the tablecloth. He bent over her. "Azariel?" He gently stroked her face. "Are you all right, sweetheart?" She lay still, but her chest rose and fell. He ran his fingers down to the hollow under her jaw and tried to feel the blood beating in her throat, but the links of her chainmail blocked him. "Hellfire!" He seized her wrist and felt beside the prominent sinew. Tears of relief leaked from the corners of his eyes as he felt her strong, fast pulse. *She's opened herself up to too much fire and been overwhelmed.*

Another groaning, grinding shock sent the ground quivering. Green light flashed from the Stone of Earth. He looked up and saw a dark crack forming in the roof near the door. The white marble trembled, then collapsed in a chaos of rubble and dust, blocking the path to the hallway.

He ran his hands through his hair and looked about as he thought hard. *We've got to get out of here before it falls on our head. And I'm the only one conscious!* He strode over to the window, seizing a chair as he went. He raised the chair and smashed it through the window, screwing his eyes tightly closed as the pane gave way. He wrapped his arm in his cloak and battered the hole in the glass wider. Rain and wind lashed his face, stinging his cheeks as the pieces fell ringing to the stones outside. One or two splinters of glass bit through his cloak into his hand and arm. He ignored the scratches and continued to beat out the glass until only a few small jagged shards clung to the frame.

He turned back towards the hall. Kalmian stirred by the fire and got to his feet. "What happened?" the older man yawned. "How did the door collapse? Has Majalis come?"

"Yes," Farren said. "Yes and we overcame him. But he's commanded the island to break up and I think it's obeying."

"What happened to her?" Kalmian stood over Azariel and looked down at her as she lay supine. "Is she dead?"

Farren shook his head. "Overwhelmed. She let the full force of the Power flood her and it's done this to her. Doesn't that happen to you sorcerers as well? We've got to get out of here but the door's blocked."

"If the island is breaking up, we will have to leave it." Kalmian walked around her and began to pick his way past the fallen knives and forks to the gap in the window. "How did you get onto it?"

"We rode dolphins." Farren ran his hands through his hair again. "Oh, hellfire! How are we going to get off and take you with us? Those beasts will never be able to carry the three of us. And we've got no gear either."

"I like to fish from time to time; I have a boat," Kalmian replied. "But we will have to abandon your gear, unless..." He took hold of one corner of the tablecloth and yanked it hard, sending even more dishes and knives flying. Candles toppled to the floor, smoking and scattering drips of wax. "We shall take this and whatever we can lay hands on. You take the lady out and I will gather what I can." He grimaced and gave the tablecloth a final tug. "Even though this will mean leaving all my books behind. Damnation!"

Farren knelt beside Azariel. "Wake up, Stormwolf," he said, kneeling beside her. "The roof will fall in soon." *She's still out cold.*

He slid his arms beneath her shoulders and knees and lifted her gently. Her breath softly brushed his cheek as he bent to kiss her lips. "Wake up, sweetheart."

The ground shook again and he staggered, trying to keep his balance. His arms, already weakened by the battle, trembled beneath her weight. He carried her to the window he had broken, then kicked aside a few shards of glass before laying her down on the floor. The groan of masonry filled his ears as he fetched the rug that was lying by the fireplace. He draped it over the jagged line of glass at the bottom of the windowsill, covering the sharp points. Once he had smoothed it down, He bent to lift Azariel again and carefully balanced her on the narrow ledge of windowsill. Another tremor shook the earth and he heard a crash of something heavy falling at the far end of the hall. He clambered up onto the sill beside her, picked her up and leaped out into the rain.

He stumbled as he landed and her weight slipped slightly out of his grip. He clutched onto her, trying to steady himself and felt her weight shifting. Her eyes opened and she groaned. Rain was coursing down her cheeks and the wind tossed her hair across her face. She slipped her arms around his neck. "Where are we?" she said.

"Outside," he said. "The villa is collapsing." The ground shuddered again.

She slipped down out of his arms. "Thank you," she whispered. "Let's get further from the windows in case the building collapses outwards."

A crash of stone and glass from the darkness sent his heart into his throat. Kalmian appeared at the window and hurled out a large bundle wrapped in a white tablecloth. Then he climbed out after it, catching and tearing his robes as he leaped down and scooped up the bundle again.

"Which way to the outer labyrinth?" Farren called.

"This way. Take the bundle, lady." Kalmian looped his robes up, exposing his bare legs and strode away from the villa heading to the right. "Be careful," he called out. "The ground has split across the lawn. I am sorry for my goats. They do not deserve this."

Farren lurched forward and staggered after Kalmian as the ground heaved again. The wind was shrieking in his ears, but above the wind, he heard a low roar. He turned and saw first a pillar, then a wall of the villa crumble. Lightning flickered, showing cracks spreading like a black spiderweb across the plastered front. The façade wavered like a curtain then fell in a pile of rubble and masonry. Fire reached up to the night sky from one end of it, casting black shadows across the grass. Balancing carefully, he ran on. *It's like walking on a boat on the lake in a high wind.* A faint pang of nausea stirred in his stomach as the memory of riding in a boat returned. *Hellfire, what's it going to be like out at sea in a little fishing boat?*

The forest was roaring and crashing as he plunged into it. The groan and rumble of the crumbling hill and buildings was masked a little by the foliage once the shelter of the trees closed around him. The swift steady pace of Azariel's footsteps pounded as she ran like a shadow beside him with the bundle on her back.

He struggled on along the path through the trees, flailing branches lashing at his face and arms, and tearing at his cloak. He strained his eyes ahead through the darkness to make out Kalmian's path as he snaked ahead of him through the twisted paths of the labyrinth. The crash of falling trees and snapping branches filled the air around him, mixed with the deep rumble of the earthquake and the roar of the sea and storm. The earth buckled beneath him and a jagged black crack opened under his feet, tripping him. Kalmian seized his forearm and helped him to his feet as Azariel bounded over the crack and landed beside him. Another tremor juddered underfoot. A tree crashed to the ground behind them as they ran on. *How much further to the end of this maze?* The white bark of the birch trees loomed like ghosts around him, seeming to hem him in.

"Not far now," Kalmian said. "The boatshed's well above the beach with a slipway running down to the water."

Farren passed Azariel and ran around the next bend, feeling the earth shuddering under his feet. Salty spray showered into his face as he turned the corner, filling his mouth and stinging his eyes and wounds. He spat the water out and crashed into Azariel., then into a solid wall of planks. She barrelled into him and staggered in his arms for a few heartbeats, then they both regained their balance. "No need for the slipway," she said. "The sea has risen."

He leaned on the side of the hut to steady himself. "Where's the door?"

"Round the front," Kalmian said. "But these waves are too strong for me. One of you sturdy youngsters will have to open the door and bring the boat out."

Azariel thrust the soft heavy bundle at Farren and darted around the side of the hut. A few solid, steady thumps mixed with the crash and slap of the waves. She reappeared, towing a stout boat behind her, the oars waving like insect antennae above the rowlocks. "Throw the bundle in, then climb aboard," she shouted above the roar of the sea.

"How strongly can you row?" asked Kalmian, turning toward him. "I am used to it, but you look stronger and fitter than me."

He held out one arm and helped Kalmian scramble over the edge of the boat. "No," he said, stomach feeling cold and heavy. "I'm not much good in a boat." An embarrassed wave of heat flooded his face. "I get seasick. Badly."

"Kalmian and I will have to row," Azariel said, gripping the gunwale of the boat and steadying its mad rocking. "Get in."

He swung one leg over the side, soaking his trousers as he waded. The oars creaked behind him and the boat began swinging around. He clutched the prow and closed his eyes, salt stinging his scratches and the briny smell flooding his lungs. *I might be all right. I might be all right. I might not get sick.* The boat heaved and bucked like a wild horse and the pounding of the surf and the thunder of the earthquake began to die away.

Cautiously, he opened his eyes and looked around. A bolt of lightning smashed through the sky, shining off the foam and waves before darkness filled with wind and water covered the sea again. The prow of the boat dipped, then rose giddily. Nausea surged in his throat and he squeezed his eyes shut again.

Thunder mixed with the deeper roar of the splitting rocks of the island. A large wave rolled out from behind them, lifting the fishing boat high as it crested.

Azariel strained at her oar, her wounded arm throbbing with the sting of the salt and with exertion. "Keep her prow straight as it breaks!" urged Kalmian beside her. She trained her eyes on what she could see of the boat's end. The wave rolling out from the ruined island peaked and she braced herself. *Will this wave break like the ones near the shore? I never knew water could form a mountain like this!* Then the wave surged forward in a mass of spray, urging the boat forward as fast as a galloping horse. Kalmian lifted his oar from the water and she did the same. The boat plunged down into the trough as the tremor wave passed on beyond it. *Thank the Power! But I hope no more of those massive waves strike us.*

The rain and wind continued to lash them as the boat slowly made its way through the waves. The oars squeaked in the rowlocks and the wind whined.

On and on the boat pitched and bucked, and Farren continued to fight the sickness. His grasp tightened around the side of the boat as the wind whipped around him, pushing hard on his back and blowing spray around him. The oars creaked and Azariel said something indistinct to Kalmian, her voice sounding tired. Another bolt of lightning and another stomach-churning plunge and buck beneath him. *When will this end?*

The boat lurched and listed violently to one side before jerking upright again. The exertion of the battle against Majalis, the alarm and action of the earthquake and the constant struggle against nausea grew too much for him and his stomach heaved. Cringing with shame, he wiped his mouth with the back of his hand and curled up miserably on the hard boards, hugging his cloak around himself. He closed his eyes and tried to doze.

"More to the left if you can," Azariel called during a momentary lull in the noise. The slap of water on wood and the rushing of the wind swallowed Kalmian's reply. Farren felt the boat yaw to one side, pitching and rolling. Hastily, he heaved himself up and leaned over the side of the boat, vomiting again. *Hellfire, I wish I didn't get sick like this.*

After what seemed like an eternity of motion, noise and nausea, he heard the crunch of wood on sand beneath him. The hideous pitching and tossing had stopped and the crash of surf on shore surrounded him. The wind on his face felt cool and refreshing, and the nausea slid away from him, leaving him with an aching head. He scrambled out of the boat and trod gratefully on the firm gritty sand. Kalmian clambered out beside him, panting heavily as he fell onto his knees. A hole opened in the clouds, revealing a waning moon. Azariel was slumped over the oars, face hidden by her hair. "Are you all right?" he asked her.

She looked up at him, eyes ringed with black, and shook her head. *She's exhausted. It's a pity I couldn't have rowed instead of letting them do it all while I couldn't do anything except throw up.* He reached for her shoulders and heaved her up. "Come on," he said. "Let's get you out of there. We'll turn the boat upside down and the three of us should be able to shelter under it for the night." He lifted her out and carried her above the line of dark sand to where Kalmian was lying curled like a child, the bundle of tablecloth, tapestry and sheepskin beside and half under him.

He heaved the boat up the slope and overturned it above Azariel and Kalmian. It fitted snugly over them. After dropping to his hands and knees, he tunnelled under the rim and squeezed between the wooden bowl of the boat and the sand. Faint green light from the Stone of Earth filtered through the weave of Azariel's hood, illuminating the planks of the keel. Raindrops drummed lightly on the wood, a miniature orchestra of drummers. He tried to brush the wet grit off his hands, curled up between Azariel and Kalmian and slept.

He awoke hearing something sniffing and scraping at the sand outside. He stirred, each muscle in his body protesting and his stomach growling impatiently. Carefully, he wormed his head and shoulders out from under the boat, trying not to disturb the regular, even breathing of the other two sleepers. Strong, warm sunlight struck his eyes and he blinked as he eased his way out further, the wooden gunwale scraping over each link in his armour.

A chestnut horse was looking down at him, one hoof pawing at the sand. "Princess!" he laughed, recognizing the mare. He finished crawling out and sat up, his clothes feeling half stiff, half damp against him. "I'm back again, my lady." He wriggled fully out from under the boat and pressed his face against her smooth neck, enjoying the familiar horsy smell of her mane and her hot breath on his arms as she turned her head to whicker at him. "We've got it. We've got the Stone of Earth, my lady."

He stretched the cramped stiffness out of his arms, neck and legs, and gazed across the water. A dark shape still stood where the island had been, the hill flattened to a curve that barely swelled above the line of the waves. He smiled. *Maybe Kalmian's goats survived after all. It'll be the Island of Goats now instead of the Island of Labyrinths.* Princess rubbed her head against him, scratching her head on his armour. "I'd better light the fire and make the others some breakfast. We've got a long journey ahead of us on the road back home."

ABOUT THE AUTHOR

M.C. Foster spent a childhood reading Tolkien, mythology and folktales when she wasn't riding horses and climbing trees. She earned a B.A.(Hons) in Linguistics in 1996 from the University of Canterbury. She now lives in Southland, New Zealand with her husband, a rescue dog, several chickens and a cat who is a terror to the local mice. When she's not writing, she enjoys growing organic vegetables, trying out local walking tracks and doing things with yarn... discovering in the process that it is very difficult to prick one's finger on a spinning wheel.

www.ingramcontent.com/pod-product-compliance
Lightning Source LLC
Chambersburg PA
CBHW030103260626
47156CB00008B/2499